As the
Crow Flies

ROBIN LYTHGOE

ISBN: 1484077466
ISBN-13: 978-1484077467

First Print Edition

As the Crow Flies is a work of fiction. Any similarity between real
names, characters, places and events is purely coincidental.

Please visit the author's official website:
http://robinlythgoe.com

or follow Robin on Twitter:
http://twitter.com/robinlythgoe

For my dear Mom,
who introduced me
to the wonderful world
of words and books—
and encouraged me on my journey.
Miss you…

Acknowledgements

Special thanks to: Boyd, Kristie, Alan, Mickey,
Amy, Boyd J, and Tammy
for bravely daring to accept missions as first readers.

Contents

— 1 —
Flying Weather

I am called Crow, and I am a thief. The name and the profession go hand in hand and, like the bird, I am not at all opposed to appropriating what pleases me. I am good at it. Crows are smart and clever. Black of hair, dark of eye, and dusky of skin, I am as like that much-maligned bird as any man can be. My nimble fingers and quick mind have guaranteed me the most profitable jobs and a comfortable place in the annals of history.

I always work alone. Most of my life, in fact, has been spent alone, a situation I never felt inclined to alter until, in my thirty-first spring, I fell in love. Ah, Tarsha, my beautiful jewel…

It was for her sake that I perched on the ledge of a narrow window in Baron Metin Duzayan's residence more than three stories above the churning waters of the Zenn River.

The din of pursuit clattered down the hall behind me. Which way would the guardsmen most likely look for me? Down. Down was the easy way to go, the quick way, but any fool can leap to his death in a raging river, and I am no fool. With vengeful Winter tramping through the land, it would be bitterly cold, too. I would rather fly than take a wetting, so up it was.

From my pack I took rope and grapnel, and in a trice I made my way to the Baron's rooftop via an ornate corner finial. Fluted, ice-covered tiles made the roof a dangerous place and Winter, openly jeering, spat the first few droplets of a freezing rain in my face. Gaining a dubious perch, I loosed the grapnel and flipped it higher up the roof. Thank the god of ornate architecture, the hook caught on a fine-looking gargoyle straddling the upper peak. Scarcely I had pulled myself from view before I heard the shouts of the guardsmen. Baron Duzayan was the proud proprietor of many exquisite collectibles—one of which now resided comfortably in the belt at my waist—and employed guards touted as the best of the best. However, just because they were most likely to look down first didn't mean that they would altogether neglect to look up. I had only moments in which to disappear from this location, else suffer the consequences, a fate I had nimbly avoided thus far in my life.

I lay against the icy tiles, shivering, and looked around at my options. They were decidedly few: slide down the roof to the street, a drop of at least two stories, or continue along the peak. Having no particular desire for the probable death or crippling offered by the first choice, I naturally took the path of the second, all the while cursing the infernal, flea-bitten cat that had given me away attacking my ankles as I'd hidden behind a tapestry. I hate cats, and if not for that one, I would have decamped by way of the underground route that had been part of my original plan, and so been long gone by now.

Using the grapnel as an ice-hook, I pulled myself along the roof until I reached the end and another sturdy gargoyle protecting the eminent Baron from Evil. Darkness opened up below me. Baron Duzayan was a rich man, and could afford the narrow strip of garden that separated his building from that of his neighbor, but at the moment, I could find no appreciation for its doubtless beauty. The distance was only some twenty-five feet, and with my grapnel and rope I crossed it quickly and ran the length of the much nicer, flatter roof of the next house, and then the next. The sounds of pursuit faded behind me. I was going to make it! Praised be the god of quick thinking!

An alley appeared below me, but it was not so wide that I couldn't make the jump, and I took it with a quivering thrill in my heart. No wings, no strings, an unmeasured height—and the certain knowledge of the cobbled street below. That dizzying leap on the run was one of the few ways I could ever get close to flying.

I hit the parapet on my feet and leaned forward into a somersault that landed me on the roof proper. With a crow of delight in my throat, I skipped across the remaining space and vaulted down to the next level. The neighboring building was a burned-out shell, but along the edge of the river ran a high, narrow wall. Rather than going to the ground and stumbling through the ruins, I ran along the wall. Full of rain turning to hail, the wind at my back pushed me along. Still, if I missed my footing, it would be a nasty fall into the water. I made it without mishap, cornered, and ran a little further along the wall to where another roof hung low enough for me to scramble up. It was high time to cross the street and head for another neighborhood. Hooking my grapnel in the top of a chimney, I climbed up to the second story and made my way to the front of the house. Across the street stood another impressive mansion like the Baron's. It was three stories high, and much decorated with fancy frills, convenient balustrades, and more grimacing gargoyles. It was, in other words, a tiny castle begging to be scaled.

The wind coming from my right had gained in heartlessness. I shivered and flexed my stiffening fingers. Even the running I had done was not enough to keep me warm, and my flapping cloak did little to help. Tiny, frozen pellets stung my face and made my eyes water. It took a miserable four tries to hook the grapnel around my newest stone accomplice, and then I swung across the street and hauled myself up to the roof hand over hand. I slipped twice on a rope grown stiff and ungainly. Even so, I made it to the top without accident. The wind carried the noise of confusion and turmoil from the Baron's house. None of the guards had made it this far up the street yet. The best of the best had met their match. I grinned.

Turning to make my way down the ice-slick slope of the roof, something struck my shoulder. With a shout of surprise, I flung my arms out in a vain attempt to keep myself from falling down the incline. Swearing, I slipped and slithered across the tiles. There was nothing to grab onto, no purchase to be had. Gathering momentum, I skidded off the roof and into space. Was it luck or a curse that tangled my rope around my wrist? I only know I came to a swift and painful halt as my arm was nearly yanked from my shoulder.

The halt was temporary. I was, unfortunately, not *grasping* the rope, and I began the second stage of my descent with a shriek-inducing rope burn.

I am blessed with good fortune beyond measure. The god of chance set an opposing section of architecture beneath me to break my fall. It nearly broke both my legs, as well. I landed heavily and pitched headfirst into a wall. Dizzy and battered, I tried to blink the stars from my eyes. A few loose tiles smashed behind me, and someone opened a window and shouted.

If the shrieking and the tile flinging hadn't been enough to capture the attention of the guards, the shouting surely would. As if on cue, a handful of them spilled down the street on the run.

Pulling myself together, I scrambled up the valley to the lower ridge and slid down the other side. My head was still ringing, and my eyes refused to focus. My attacker, however, experienced no such problem, coming at me from behind and battering my head with hard, tiny fists. "Thief! Thief!" it squawked at the top of its lungs.

"What—?" Broad wings covered my face, blocking my view entirely while razor-like talons dug into my scalp. Predictably, I fell. This tumble was neither as graceful nor happy-ending as the last. I smacked into something—a chimney, perhaps. It caught at my shoulder and spun me around, hurtling me sideways across the roof. From there I banged into three more unidentifiable objects, which was probably a good thing, for it slowed my descent, however much blood the encounters drew. It was, therefore, no great agony to flounder over the edge and bash myself into a new pitch of the roof.

My body begged to lay there and gasp and moan for even a moment, but my assailant had other plans. Even had it not, I had to contend with the relentless slant of the roof. Still, the gods were obviously with me this night. I slid feet first into something solid and came to an abrupt halt. Surely something crunched. My knees were not going to stand up to much more torture.

I had no time to worry over my wounds, however. Tearing the creature off my face, I flung it away as hard and far as possible. It was a small, winged demon, of the sort occasionally enslaved for sundry menial tasks, such as guarding the valuables of the rich. I'd seen them a time or two, but only once had to deal with one. Disgusting creatures. Despite my muddled state, I found a few choice words to vent my irritation. Evidently the creature took offense at my verbal assault. It renewed the attack.

For all that it was a small thing, perhaps half again the size of the Baron's attack-cat, it packed an impressive wallop. It came for me, aiming at my head. The instant I put my arms up to defend my face, it dove directly into my stomach, howling fit to wake the dead. My breath deserted me. Gasping at the frigid night air, I tried to knock the thing away. My blows were weak and clumsy. Unaffected, the demon viciously bounced on my belly, swatting my fists away with its own cruelly clawed little hands.

Things were not going well. In desperation, I rolled away from it. However, I also rolled away from the chimney that had stopped my precipitous slide. Near death from lack of air, I finished my abrupt journey and plunged over the edge of the roof. One's life supposedly flashes before one's eyes in the moments before death, but I saw nothing at all. Not the building I fell from, nor even the ground below me. Perhaps I was concentrating too hard on trying to fill my lungs.

Surely the last bit of roof I had visited had been the one over the ground floor? Why, then, did landing come as such a shock? Did it, by chance, have something to do with the rosebush?

My leather jerkin was a blessed protection against the thorns, but it did not defend my carcass from the broken, jabbing canes. Neither did it cover my arms. A thousand tiny spears tore through my shirtsleeves and lanced my skin. Then, to add insult to injury, the demon landed squarely on my back. The fall seemed not to have slowed it at all, for it immediately began berating my shoulders with its fists. Still shrieking, of course.

Stunned, I lay there for a moment, accepting the abuse. It was, after all, the lesser of the evils besetting me. The first order of business was to retrieve my missing breath. The icy air tore at my lungs with a vengeance, but I sucked away like mad.

Ideally, I would have then leapt to my feet, thus freeing myself from the rosebush and dislodging my assailant at the same time. Unfortunately, it was all I could do to drag myself from the bramble and force myself into a more or less upright position, still encumbered with the wailing demon.

The first thing that came to mind was to smash it into the wall. Staggering, I backed as hard into the stone as I could manage without doing myself further injury. A strangled squeak preceded the creature's silence, and it fell to the ground when I stepped away from the wall. I gave a savage kick, sending it flying into a bit of shrubbery.

Now what? My breath was returning, but I'd lost my grapnel and rope. There would be no returning to the rooftops. Casting about, I found myself in a small, walled garden. I absently patted my waist, checking that the belt full of pockets in which I carried my tools—and the Baron's pretty bauble —was still in place. The sound of the guards' approach spurred me to inspiration.

Dashing across the yard to a door wasn't nearly as easy as it looked. Falling from a three-story building whilst being battered by a demon has an appalling effect on one's muscles as well as the steadiness of one's hands, and it took me an unconscionable amount of time to pick the lock and slip through into nearly complete darkness. I still had the foresight, however, to lock the door again behind me.

Trying to sort out the logical layout of the house, I made my way toward the front and succeeded in finding the main hall. The house was quite large and grand, with a vaulted and beamed ceiling soaring upwards. Four cunningly worked windows let in a faint gleam of light high overhead. Fine tapestries hung from the walls, thick carpets padded the floors, and artful niches displayed handsome statuary. What caught my eye—and 'tis a blessing indeed that I am well able to see in the dark—was a pair of massive chandeliers. I could use the one closest to the door. Finding the rope that raised and lowered the thing, I loosed it and hung on tight. The chandelier crashed to the floor, hauling me up into the rafters. Two hands wide and set apart by the height of a man, the beams made an ideal catwalk. I scampered (more or less) from one end of the room to the other and positioned myself next to a window. Yanking off my cloak, I wrapped it around my arm and smashed it through the glass. It produced a lovely, loud crash followed by a satisfactory shout from the guards. I trotted down the length of the beam and hid myself in the darkness of the shadows on the opposite side of the room.

I hadn't long to wait before the guard beat at the door and the astonished owner let them in. They came jangling through with their torches, finding both the fallen chandelier and the gaping window.

"He's gone out the front!" one of them shouted, and they all dashed toward the front door with the distressed master of the house tagging along behind in his night robe, wringing his hands and whimpering.

Returning to the window, I watched as the guards split into two groups and headed in opposite directions. For all their reputation as choice guardsmen, they were making this far too easy. I had to shake my head.

I padded quietly down to the front entrance. To their credit, one guard remained behind, quite cleverly concealing himself in the shadow created by a tall bookcase. It was my pleasure to relieve him from that duty with the handle of my knife bashed to the base of his skull. I caught him as he sank to the floor, and eased him down so as not to alarm the master, who had gone to his liquor cabinet to pour himself a drink with hands that shook enough to rattle his delicate glassware. In the light cast by the candlestick he'd set on top of the cabinet, I could admire the clarity of the pure, graceful crystal.

"Would you be so kind as to pour a drink for me, as well?" I asked politely, gliding up behind him. "Whatever you're having will be fine."

He whirled, his face paling. "What—?" He took one look at the knife I held in my hand—the blade a generous span of fine Taessarian steel—and his eyes rolled up into his head. I rescued the wineglass from his suddenly limp fingers as he measured his length on the exquisite parquet flooring.

"Tut, tut," I murmured. "Another poor fool who can't hold his liquor." I drank down the wonderfully bracing wine, fetched a pillow for the fellow's head, and started out. A small curio cabinet drew my attention, and I paused. Tiny ivory figurines crowded one shelf. Unless I was mistaken (and I knew I was not), they were Cataran. I counted the figures. Twenty-one. A complete set. I expressed my amazement and delight with a low whistle. A hundred years ago, Catara had been a premiere sculptor sought by the wealthiest and most discriminating of collectors. In his latter years, he had worked on commission alone, and this set—one of a dozen Emperor Gaziah had commissioned as special rewards after the Ten Years' War—was worth more gold pieces than I had time to contemplate. They made the transfer from the shelf to the pouch at my waist without a whimper.

Outside, the street was empty. Too empty.

Peering through the cracked door, I watched and waited for one of the guards to reveal himself. In my experience, patience is not a virtue to be taken lightly. However, the longer I waited, the more likely were the chances I would be espied by the Baron's returning lackeys and the more my abused body would proclaim its hurt. I most certainly did not want inactivity to stiffen my muscles. I chewed on my lip for a moment while my brain raced through the alternatives.

Behind me, the master of the house moaned. He did not, apparently, realize the true danger of his situation, else he would have remained unconscious a spell longer.

I went over to him, drawing my knife again from its sheath. I put on a show of examining its finely honed edge in the imperfect light of the candles. Even as he opened his eyes and let out another quivering moan an idea came to me. He was roughly my height and build except for an unfortunate tendency toward portliness around his middle. Hopefully his taste in clothing would run along the same lines as his taste in decor. If his robe and nightclothes were anything to go by, I was in luck. I couldn't wear my own torn and dirtied gear without attracting unwanted attention.

The moment he saw me standing above him his eyes journeyed to the back of his skull again. "Ah-ah, my dear sir," I scolded, going down on one knee to pat his cheek smartly. He blinked back at me, and his lower lip trembled. I stood up. "On your feet now. You have nothing at all to fear if you do as I request." He took my proffered hand and got up, shaking like a leaf in a gale.

"What—That is—Don't—"

"Not to worry," I assured him, offering a bright smile and patting him on the back companionably. "I need only for you to escort me quietly to your sleeping chamber. Do you think you can manage?"

He opened his mouth to speak, but instead nodded his head and said nothing at all.

"Very good." I gestured toward the stairs with the hand that still happened to be holding my knife. He blanched, picked up the candle, and mutely led the way.

"It's awfully quiet," I said, halfway up the stairs. "Is your entire staff on holiday?"

"N-no, they're in their quarters. Where I sent them when, er, when the Baron's men came."

He hadn't of course, but I suppose he couldn't have known I was watching. The absence of any sort of staff raised questions about his financial stability. Still, I kept an eye and an ear out for the possibility of the sudden appearance of a butler or maid. "Weren't you afraid?"

"Of c-course not."

I chuckled. "You're a terrible liar." Candlelight glimmered softly against the rich wood paneling, and I could make out portraits framed in gold hanging on the wall. We stopped in front of a closed door. A trickle of light seeped through the crack at the bottom. "Where is your wife?"

He gulped noisily. "In, er, Chatay. With her parents. Visiting."

I took his wrist and twisted it gently behind his back as I reached around him and pressed the tip of my knife against his neck. "Open the door and tell her to move slowly to the center of the room."

A tremulous little moan escaped from his throat. "D-don't hurt us, please!" he whined.

"Don't give me a reason to." He was disgustingly spineless. He possessed all the constitution of a bowl of gelatin. I put a little pressure on his crooked arm. "Your wife?"

"I c-can't—open—the door."

Ah, yes. Between us, we had all hands occupied. I pushed him aside and opened it myself with my knife hand. The blade banged noisily against the doorframe.

"Windel?" a woman's voice queried timorously. "Is that you, dear?"

We pushed into the room where a woman knelt on the bed. She covered her cheeks with both hands and gave a little scream, like a trapped mouse.

"Do as he says, Darling!" Windel gushed. "He's got a knife!"

Yes, I'm sure she missed that, poised as it was at her poor, sweet husband's throat. Glancing around the room, I guided Windel to a chair. "Darling," I said, addressing his wife, "fetch me a few of your pretty scarves."

She blushed. "Scarves?"

"Yes, that's what I said."

She scrambled off the bed, snatching up a robe as she went, and dashed toward a closed door. Opening it, she disappeared inside for a moment, then returned with a handful of the requested items. Shortly, Windel was snugly attached to his chair.

"Your turn, Darling." I pulled another chair over beside Windel's and gestured toward it. The woman meekly sat.

"Are you going to rob us?" she asked as I fastened one wrist to the arm of the chair.

"The thought has crossed my mind."

"Torture us?" she asked, a little breathless at this notion.

"Darling!" Windel protested.

"Would you like me to?" I inquired.

"Oh!" The color in her cheeks increased. "No, thank you!"

"Very well, then." I went first to the bedchamber door to close and lock it, then went to the door Darling had used. A peek inside revealed a decent-sized room filled nearly to overflowing with clothing and shoes. "Lovely," I smiled. I sorted through them until I found Windel's things, then picked out a pair of breeches, a shirt, and a coat.

"What do you think?" I asked, returning to my hosts and holding up the clothing for their inspection.

"That depends," Darling said. "What sort of look are you trying to achieve? Judging from your present attire, I would say you prefer a look of quiet strength and understated elegance." She tipped her head and examined me critically. "And perhaps just a touch of the unexpected."

"Darling!" Windel objected with a touch of outrage.

I beamed at Darling. "You are most perceptive, madam."

She fluttered her eyelashes and dimpled in a manner that was meant to be becoming, I'm sure. Her position and her sleep-tousled locks rather ruined the effect.

I popped back into the closet and came back with a new set of clothing. "How about this?"

"Oh, no," Darling shook her head. "Those trousers are strictly for morning. They're not at all appropriate for evening wear!"

Irritated, I tossed the clothes on the bed. "I don't have time to dawdle!"

"Well, I could help you," she offered.

"Darling!" This time Windel was really upset. "He's a criminal! He's broken into our home and tormented us! Gods alone know if he's robbed us yet, or what he'll do to us before he's through!"

"All the more reason to give him what aid we can. Don't you see, Windel? The better we cooperate with him, the better are our chances to come out of this unharmed!"

"She has a point, Windel."

"If you screamed, the servants would come to our aid," Windel reasoned.

"*Me?*" Darling squealed. "How did this suddenly become my responsibility? *You're* the one who brought him upstairs to our bedchamber!"

As they continued to wrangle in increasingly shrill voices, I loosed the lady's bonds. Taking her hand, I pulled her toward the closet. "Come along, Darling, let's go discuss the possibility of ravishment in privacy."

I somehow managed to escape unscathed; I don't know what *they* were worried about. I made my way through dark, snowy streets in a bitter wind, hugging myself tightly. I didn't see the Baron's men again. Their absence produced a repeated urge to rub the back of my neck.

When I arrived at Tarsha's apartments, I took up a post against the wall across the street, out of the wind. Then I waited. Anticipation made my heart race, and only the experience of years kept me in my place, making sure I hadn't been followed. Even out of the wind the night was cold, and my nose wore its own icicle in a matter of minutes. It didn't matter. In mere minutes I would behold the joy on Tarsha's perfectly sculpted face when I showed her the prize I'd won for her. I stayed until the soles of my boots had nearly frozen to the pavement and all of the cuts and bruises I'd acquired had set up a cacophony of complaint. Then I limped up the stairs.

I rapped out our coded knock and the door opened.

"Tarsha, my dove," I greeted, grinning. The warm air of her rooms embraced me, fragrant with the scent of her perfume.

"Crow." Her lovely eyes widened. "What's happened to you? You're a mess! Are you hurt?"

"Nothing your sweet kisses won't fix," I replied, reaching for her.

She laughed softly and touched her finger to my abused nose. "You're freezing, too."

"I am." I put my hands on her slim waist and tugged her closer. "Will you warm me?"

She spun nimbly away. "That depends on what you've brought me..." She gave me a coy look. The diaphanous fabric of her robe fluttered around her, barely enough to conceal. Her eyes were bright and expectant.

I followed her inside and took off the cloak and muffler I'd procured. "No small talk? No chit-chat?"

"Since when was that important?"

I contrived a pout. "I've been out for hours in the cold, risking life and limb for you. Weren't you the least concerned?"

She glided close and ran her fingers up my chest. "I was," she whispered in a husky voice. Her lips were warm as summer and sweeter than nectar. If there were ever an island upon which a man would be content to be marooned, it was the Island of Tarsha.

"Was?" I asked between kisses.

"Well," her arms crept up around my neck. "You're here now, safe and sound. What's to worry?"

"Indeed…" I slid my hands slowly down her back. Angling my head, I bent closer to taste the delicate skin of her throat. She made a small, adorable noise and buried her face in my shoulder. Her mouth was out of reach, but her hands remained busy.

"Where is it?" she asked.

"Where is what?" I wanted only to kiss her again.

"The Gandil. I know you have it." She backed away, looking at me seductively from behind the fall of her dark hair. "You mustn't tease…"

"Oh, mustn't I?" I laughed, catching her hand, refusing to let her escape. "That's hardly fair to say while you're carrying on so shamelessly."

The hint of a smile curved her lips. "That's different."

"How so?"

With her free hand she fanned out the fabric of her robe. "You've already seen what you want."

"True." I tugged her close and kissed her.

"Please?"

Still kissing her, I removed the jewel from my belt and held it high over her head. "Is this what you're looking for?"

She gave a little shriek and jumped to reach it. "You did get it!"

"Of course." I spun away, keeping the treasure out of her reach a moment longer. "Pretty spectacular for my final job, don't you think?"

"The bards will sing about it for decades. Let me see!"

"Ah-ah… I need another kiss first."

She laughed and paid her toll with an ardency that took my breath away. The pearl seemed made to fit her hand. Seeing her ooh and ah over its sky blue perfection made every bruise and scrape I'd collected worthwhile.

The Great Gandil, which had always sounded to me like the name of a hedgerow conjurer or a comedic play, was purported to have magical powers. Perhaps it did. Something transformed in my heart as I watched my love. I reached for her, brushing a tendril of hair behind her ear so that I might not miss one iota of her excitement.

An awful din on the door, accompanied by booming shouts, interrupted us. Tarsha pulled away from me even as the door burst open, a look of alarm on her face.

"Scream!" I ordered, pushing her backwards. Scarcely had I turned toward the intruders, my hand on the hilt of my knife, before a small brown shape attached itself to the top of my head and began screeching.

"Thief! Thief!" The demon. "Robber! Pirate! Brigand!" It had a voice like an un-oiled hinge, only worse, and a grip that belied its size.

I shouted and struggled to pull it off before it raked my face with its claws. Hands grabbed me and dragged me to the floor, pinning me down like a prize hide. I could neither move, nor see. Nor could I do anything to resist as my person was searched rather more thoroughly than civility required.

"Here it is," someone said.

The pearl? How had it got into my pocket?

"And these." A small, clinking sound came to my ears.

"Get it off."

The demon was removed from my face. Half a dozen athletic and dangerously scarred men looked down on me. There wasn't a friendly face among them.

One man, still standing, gently tossed the Baron's pearl up in the air and caught it. "You're a thief," he stated. He had a remarkable way of making the word sound like something dredged up from the bottom of a latrine.

"I'm not," I protested.

"Ah, and a liar, too." I don't know how he managed such a sublime aim with so many men holding me down, but the toe of his boot connected solidly with my ribs.

"You're wrong," I grunted.

"You saying you don't know anything about this?" He held up the stone between two fingers.

"It's mine."

"And the demon?"

"I don't know anything about the wretched thing. Ungh—" His foot smashed into my side again.

"And these?" He produced two pieces from the Cataran set.

"Mine," I choked.

"Wrong answer." He kicked me again. "Get him up."

They did, easily. "Let me go," I said. "You have—"

This time it was a fist in my belly. I would have crumpled, *wanted* to—but the soldiers held me upright.

"Don't!"

From the corner of my eye, I caught sight of Tarsha, arms wrapped tightly around her middle, and lips compressed into a hard, tight line. She looked irritated. I could hardly blame her; the interruption made me quite cross, too. I had, after all, a retirement to celebrate and a lovely woman to accompany me.

The man who had spoken—I assumed he was their captain—gave her a stiff nod. "We'll get him out of your way. Thank you, ma'am."

I feared they would take her prisoner, too, but it was me they dragged willy-nilly out the door and down the stairs without the benefit of my cloak or the use of my own feet. Out in the snowy street, the captain faced me again.

"You sure you don't want to tell the truth about your little collection?"

"I told you the truth."

"Liar."

"Thug."

His smile was not a comforting sight. "Do you know what liars and thieves are good for, fool?"

I smiled back. "Inventing admirable tales and redistributing wealth?"

One corner of his mouth twitched. "For an educated man, you don't seem very smart."

"I've done pretty well so far."

"Until now."

"I think I can manage."

He shook his head and folded his bulging arms across his chest. "Why don't you boys teach him a lesson?"

— 2 —
Tails Of The Crypt

I gradually became aware of something hard striking me again and again. The motion rocked my body. Just as I realized it was the butt of a spear jabbing my ribs, consciousness of pain rolled over me like a wave. My belly twisted itself into a knot, churned once, and heaved. I was vaguely aware of someone nearby swearing.

I ignored it and slowly rolled onto my back. It took a moment for my eyes to focus on the glaring face above me. "Tanris," I croaked. The name was as sour as the spittle on my lips.

"Aye, little bird," he answered. "In a cage where you belong at last. How does it feel?"

I closed my eyes. He was too ugly to look at in my current condition— or any other condition, come to think of it. "Feel?" I asked, running the thing that passed for a tongue around the inside of my mouth. "Reminds me of the morning I woke up in bed with your sister."

"You're such a donkey, Crow."

The butt of his spear slammed into my ribs, forcing me to agree with his analysis. Only a donkey would request a willing antagonist to continue a beating, and Tanris treasured his personal grudge against me. His lengthy dislike for me hinged entirely on flimsy things like circumstantial evidence and professional jealousy. It was an astounding thing, really, for he had no hard evidence that I had ever caused him any harm or affliction. I had never touched his sister; didn't even know he had one, for that matter. If she looked anything like him, I'd prefer to keep it that way. No, Tarsha filled my dreams, and the temptation to ask after her hovered on my lips, but I dared not let him know how I cared for her, or she might end up in a cage of her own.

"You have no idea of the pleasure it brings me to see you in a cage, and to know that I am responsible for it."

I cracked one eye open. "On the contrary." A cough helped to clear my throat, but lanced my side in agony. I stifled a groan with clenched teeth. "You've worked very hard for a long time to get me here. Congratulations."

He snorted. "Congratulations? Is your brain completely addled?"

"It might be." My arms were stiff and heavy, but I managed to lift one hand enough to gingerly examine my face and head. "How do I look?"

He snorted again, his disbelief quite clear. "You look like you've been royally beaten and tossed into gaol."

"Ah, Tanris, you have such an awe-inspiring sense of imagination." I turned my head cautiously, trying to make out surroundings mostly shrouded in darkness with one eye swollen almost completely shut. As he had stated, I was indeed in gaol. I shoved down my alarm. *One thing at a time,* I told myself. "Is there a wall close?"

"No. Only bars." His voice held an irritating hint of glee.

I hitched myself close to them and, with a tremendous effort, sat myself up. "Got a drink?"

He handed me a flask, then stood back to watch with his arms crossed over his chest. "Aren't you the least bit curious to know what's going to become of you?"

I frowned as I caught sight of a cat winding around his ankles. The light was poor and I was not any sort of expert on cats, but was that the same mangy creature that had earlier attacked me? It couldn't be…

"Not yet." I raised the flask to my lips and drank deeply of the stale water it held. I would have expected him to carry something with a bit more kick to it, but it was certainly better than nothing, and I took my time about it, pausing to explore a split lip with my tongue before I took another swallow. "Now then, what's to become of me, oh Clever One?"

He didn't answer right away, and when I looked up at him his face was creased with an appearance of intense consideration accompanied by an emotion I could not identify. For some reason it made me uneasy. "Well?"

He shrugged and looked away. "You're to wait." He made a gesture toward a shadowed doorway outside the cage and two men appeared.

"Wait?"

"That's right. Not here, though. You're to be moved to better quarters."

"What? No bars?"

He smiled with great satisfaction. "Nope. No bars."

The two men came into the cage and hauled me unceremoniously to my feet. My knees buckled. They caught me before I fell and dragged my arms up across their broad shoulders. They were so tall that my toes barely scraped the ground as they carted me off down a dim corridor. My head swam with pain and my vision blurred. What felt like eternity could have been no more than minutes, and then they deposited my carcass on the floor. While I blinked stupidly up at Tanris, one of them held me down with a foot on my chest while the other removed my boots and my belt.

"Slop bucket in the corner," he said, pointing. "Meal in the morning. I wouldn't waste it, as it will be the only one you get for the day. If you get chilly, there's a blanket at the foot of the bed." He grinned and bowed extravagantly. "Enjoy your stay."

The door thudded closed behind him, immediately immersing me in darkness so black that not even my excellent eyesight could penetrate it. Panic grabbed me by the gut and yanked me into motion. "Tanris!" I yelled, scrambling for the door. The thud of a bolt sliding into place answered me. "Tanris! Don't do this!" Another bolt slammed. I pounded the thick wood with my fist. *Tanris!* The third bolt gave a scream of delight as it locked. Muted laughter came from the corridor, then nothing.

I banged on the door with both fists, then put my sore hands to better use searching for a handle. Again, nothing. The walls and ceiling closed in on me, and I sank to the floor, pressing my back against the door. My breath was loud and harsh in my ears. In and out, in and out. Like a bellows. Stars danced in front of my eyes, and my lips and fingers tingled strangely. Had Tanris poisoned me?

Reason battled with Panic, slowly gaining a small advantage. Tanris had already got what he wanted. Me. In a cell. He had no need of poison. His pleasure depended on putting me in a cage forever, not by killing me quickly. I concentrated on breathing slowly and carefully. I had to think.

How had I fallen into his hands? He was always moving from job to job on the enforcement side of the law—Who was he working for now? How badly did this new employer want to hurt me?

To my relief, the stars and the tingling faded. It still felt like the ceiling was hovering just above my head, but when I stretched out a hand I could feel nothing anywhere around me except the door and the floor, which were right where any reasonable person would expect them.

I had to get out of there. Knowing Tanris, there would be no hidden escape routes, but I had to look. I searched the walls and the floor, running my fingers over every square inch. I pushed and pulled at every protuberance. I knocked, listening for a hollow sound to indicate hope.

My knee knocked over the slop bucket. The clash and clatter of it sent my heart leaping into my throat. With a shout, I scooted backward, smack into the opposite wall, slamming into it so hard that I bounced off it and onto my face. In a flash I was seeing stars and experiencing numb lips again. I struggled to breathe, gasping air desperately. My cheeks tingled, then my forehead. My hands and feet followed suit. Reason fled and Panic stood towering over me, arms akimbo, shouting with laughter. It was the last thing I saw.

:-:

When I regained consciousness, I opened my eyes. For a moment I feared I was blind, and my heart skipped a beat. Then I remembered where I was, and my heart banged so hard against my ribs it nearly escaped. I was trapped. Caught. Imprisoned. Jailed. Worse, I was entombed. The thought of being confined was more than merely loathsome; I couldn't abide small, dark spaces. Shut away in this crypt, I was going to die. I would soon exhaust what air I had left, and my life would end. Crow would never fly again. Never know the warmth of the sun on his face. Never see the clear blue sky. Never kiss lovely Tarsha…

"Tanris!" I shouted, over and over, until I could hardly even croak. "Let me out of here! *Let me out!*" I found the door and beat at it until the warmth of blood trickled down my wrists. Then I sank into a useless heap on the cold stone floor and wept hysterically.

My tears eventually subsided and I laid there listening to the weight of the darkness. Only my hitching breaths disturbed the absolute silence. After a time I ventured to explore the space around me again. My outstretched hand found the corner of the blanket. I dragged myself to the pile of straw that made up the bed. It smelled clean, so I crawled onto it, drawing the blanket up over me and covering my head. A ridiculous thing to do, perhaps, childish even, but it worked to hold the enveloping stone away.

I would be all right. I had to believe that. Giving in to hysteria was stupid and useless, neither of which were characteristics I cared to employ.

Tanris had said I was to wait. I could do that. I was good at waiting. I was a waiting professional. What made me nervous was wondering about the amount of time involved in the endeavor. Hours? That was manageable. Days? That was iffy. Weeks? How long did it take for one to go insane, locked in a small, dark tomb?

I shivered. This line of thought did nothing at all to help. Very well. What was I waiting for? I had a hard time believing anything could be more torturous than my current condition. Anything seemed preferable. If I could be free to enjoy the sunlight again, I wouldn't even argue with the customary chopping off of a thief's hand. And if my prosecutor hated me so much as to desire to take my life, why I would go as meekly as a lamb to the block. But I would not—*could* not—endure the rest of my life shut up in the dark!

And just like that, I was on the verge of panic again.

Was I actively pushing myself toward the brink, or had insanity got its claws into me so soon? I sat up and pulled the blanket around my shoulders tightly, then peered into the darkness in an attempt to discern the slightest shading that might indicate a shadow, and thus some minuscule source of light. I held my hand up in front of my face. I brought it closer and closer, until I touched my nose. I still couldn't see it.

Laying back down, I yanked the blanket back up over my head. This enclosure I could control. "Get a hold of yourself, Crow," I muttered. "Now then, who is making you wait?"

I went over a list of possibilities, checking them off one by one. I had made enemies, to be sure, but for all I wracked my memory for a name, I could think of no one whose pride, honor, or livelihood I had damaged to such a drastic point. I gave up, and as soon as I did, an unbidden memory suddenly surfaced: I remembered, as a tot, hiding in an empty box in a warehouse. Through the slats I had witnessed a fight, the blood and brutality of which had both fascinated and horrified me. I had stayed in my hiding place long after the combatants had left or been dragged away. I remembered rocking. I rocked and rocked until I fell asleep.

Shouts filled the air. A body crashed into the box, crunching the wood and shoving the box backward, hard. More shouting. A man approaching, his face a mask of rage. Suddenly a blade protruded from his throat. Blood gushed in an arc toward me, pulsing. I screamed—

—and sat up. Covered in a cold sweat, my breathing was fast and hard. A scraping sound and a bang made me jump.

"Who's there?" I asked. My voice quavered. No one answered. I waited, fighting down blind, nauseating fear. Pulling my blanket into a wad and holding it close to my chest, I found a wall and crawled cautiously around my little cell until I came to the door.

"Tanris?" I held my breath, waiting for his mocking voice. After a time, I moved a little farther along, exploring the worn-smooth wood, searching for the opposite edge. My knee bumped something, and I heard the same scraping sound as before. Calming my racing heart, I felt around on the floor. I found the tin plate the same time my nose caught the odor of food. Food!

My belly, ignored and unimportant until now, set up a sudden chorus of growls. The tin was filled with bland-tasting gruel. With no spoon, I had to scrape it into my mouth with my fingers, licking every morsel from its surface, and then licking my fingers clean.

Breakfast was the only thing of note to happen. That day passed frighteningly like the first and then the next. On the fourth day I was diverted by a skittering, scratchy noise, which I chose to ignore in spite of visions of snakes, bugs, and other ne'er-do-well denizens of the dark lurking at the edges of my imagination. I was not going to invite trouble—I hung on by a thin rope, filling the time by reconstructing my life in detail, pretending I was writing an autobiography. I had made it to the year after I turned thirteen. I remember little of my earliest childhood, but life with my adoptive "family" had been anything but dull. They were thieves, and even now I am not entirely certain of their true relationships with each other. They were a colorful, wild lot who lived fast, hard lives. They told half a dozen stories about how they had come to possess me, and each held just enough truth to make it believable until the next tale.

One of the older men in the Family had ensured that I had a rudimentary understanding of reading and writing, simply because it helped him to pass the time, but it didn't take me very long to decide I wanted more.

My last year with the Family had been spent with my uncle Crush, living from moment to moment in the chaos of the city of Meluna. I have no idea what his true name was, if he even had one. I remember very clearly though, my last sight of him as the City Watch took him away. We had pulled a heist that was meant to be quietly spectacular. Instead, all the Hells broke loose just as we were taking our leave.

Crush and I led the guard on a merry chase all through the entire western quarter. In an alley near the wharves they nearly had us trapped. Crush must have thought so. He shoved his sack full of booty into my hands and shouted, "I have the little devil! Here's the bloody thief!"

I will never for a moment forget the shock and dismay of his betrayal. It was like acid poured on my heart. But the gods were with me even then: I swung the sack at his head as hard as I could, knocking him right over—a feat that must have astonished him as much as it did me. As he lay on the ground, dazed, I stuffed the sack into his shirtfront, then yanked the grate off the sewage drain running under the boardwalk and slithered inside. Thank the gods, I hadn't reached my adulthood yet, else I never would have fit. While there was plenty of room to either side, I had not so much as a hair's width to spare from top to bottom. I fitted the grate back into place just in time, and lay still, watching with my head twisted at a cruel angle as the guard pounded into the alley and found Crush with the stolen goods and no scapegoat in sight. And it is said there is honor among thieves...

Not long after I left good old Uncle Crush to the tender mercies of the City Watch, I took myself north up the coast and hired out to a tavern keeper who owned an establishment in one of Marketh's better districts. In return for sweeping floors, toting coal and water, and helping out in the devilishly hot (but always well-stocked) kitchens, he refined my reading and writing skills and went on to teach me how to do sums. Yes, I know you're thinking that a consummate thief such as myself never worked at an honest job in all his life. I will refrain from pointing out that being a good thief takes skill, practice, and actual labor. My continued education included holding down numerous positions of employment not listed as unlawful occupations in the magistrate's wordy tomes. I learned to adapt to any situation. I learned the habits of certain classes of people in order to take advantage of their patterns of predictability. And to supplement those forms of education—and to attain a higher style of living—I helped myself to books and scrolls and maps and accounts of every kind. I have an extensive library, and it amuses me to envision the astonishment of my suppliers when they discovered those works missing. Some of the pieces are quite valuable as well as educational, and while most of them are kept in my country house where I retreat when things get altogether too warm in

Marketh, some of them adorn bookshelves in my apartments in the city.

For all my reminiscing, the scraping noise still didn't go away. It bit my leg sharply. Shouting in horror and surprise, I took up one of the empty breakfast tins and beat the area all around me. Whatever it was escaped, only to return later. After several such confidence-devouring attacks, I achieved success. My tin didn't clang raucously as it made contact with the floor, but made a solid thump against *some*thing. I whacked it several more times for good measure, then dared a cautious exploration.

It was a rat.

I sat back and rubbed my hands roughly over my head several times. A rat! The filthy rodents were bad enough on their own, but in the dark?

My tenuous grip on reality slipped several notches. I got up to pace. If I held my arm up I could touch the low ceiling, which helped to keep it from closing in on my head. From end to end the cell measured exactly five paces, and I kept my other arm out in front of me to be sure I didn't run into the wall. Back and forth I went, praying aloud in desperation to gods that had deserted me for the first time in my life.

At last my words no longer made sense, even to me. I stopped. "You're ranting, Crow," I said. "Buck up. Just wait. That's all, just wait." I swallowed my anxiety. "The rats? Why, just think of them as sport. It'll keep you on your toes."

Six tins and nine rats later the door opened. Light from a torch blinded me, and I covered my eyes with my hands.

"What? Still here, little bird?" Tanris's voice was unmistakable. "I thought you'd have flown the coop by now!" he laughed at me. I lunged toward the sound of him, but I was weak from abuse and lack of decent nourishment and he held me off easily, laughing the louder for my efforts. "I see you've been keeping busy."

"Of course," I spat, pulling away from him and reaching for the safety of a wall. "My days are simply filled to overflowing with things to do and places to go."

"I was talking about the rats, boyo. I'm surprised you aren't eating them yet. Lots of the customers do, you know."

"I find them a little under-seasoned."

"Well, I'll leave them here for you. Let them ripen a little longer. Maybe then they'll be more to your liking."

"Your generosity is overwhelming."

"So glad you noticed."

Still blind as a bat, I listened to the thumping of the bucket and the rattle of my tins. "How much longer am I to wait?" I asked, adopting an air of nonchalance.

"Until you're ready."

"And who gets to decide that?"

"Me, of course."

I folded my arms across my chest and leaned against my security wall. "Would you mind leaving one of those tins?"

"'Fraid not," he chuckled. "You only get one week's worth before we collect them. Besides, we want to give the rats a sporting chance."

"In that case, I'll try to leave the ones you're related to alone."

"Always the wit, Crow. Always the wit."

The door thumped closed behind him and I closed my eyes against the despair of those three bolts sliding into place.

— 3 —
Of Frying Pans And Fires

Food didn't come on tins after that. A loaf of bread was stuffed through the slot in the bottom of the door, and the rats were just as likely to find it as I. I took to sleeping right in front of the door so I would know the moment it arrived. Of course, I was reduced to pounding the mucky rats with my hands. One good thump usually sufficed, but I can't begin to tell you the number of times I missed and smashed my fist against the hard stone floor.

I lost all track of time. I fretted about Tarsha. Did she try to visit? Had Tanris found some reason to arrest her? Was she safe? I spent uncounted hours thinking about her. My autobiography dwindled into confusion and at one point I found myself holding one of the dead rats as I petted it and talked to it. Horrified, I tossed the thing away, shouting and carrying on like a madman.

And finally, the gods returned.

Tanris came again with his eyeball-searing, soul-warming torch. "Are you ready yet?" he asked.

"Am I ready?" It masqueraded as an innocent question, but it set off something within me. The Something came out in a tide of hysteria. "Am I ready?" I screeched. "I'm moldering away in this hellish excuse for a tomb! My beard is completely grown in. My hair and my armpits are infested with fleas. I talk to *rats*, for the love of the gods!"

Somehow I found his shirtfront and wrapped both hands in the fabric. "What's worse," I whispered, "is that the rats are answering."

"Are they, now?"

"Tanris, I'm going to… I'm going to…" I didn't know what I was going to do. I sank to the floor and wept uncontrollably.

"Well, well, well… Lookee here. The invincible Crow crying like a baby."

It was true, I could not deny it, but having my old archenemy watching me come apart at the seams irked unbearably. It was enough to give me the wherewithal to pull myself together somewhat. The tears stopped and I wiped my face on the hem of my filthy shirt, unwilling to let him witness my embarrassment any further.

"That's all?" Tanris asked, disappointed.

He wanted pitiful? I could give him pitiful. "I can't let them see me," I confessed.

"Who?"

I gestured surreptitiously toward the corner with my head. "*Them.* They see everything. They hear everything. If I let them know I'm weak—" I shuddered fearfully.

"What will they do?"

"No, no. I won't say out loud." I shook my head vigorously. "No, no, no…" I let my voice sink into a whisper and started rocking again. "*Garley's gone to Hamden town,*" I sang, still whispering. "*Garley's gone away. Garley's goin' to make his fame, Or so they say…*"

Tanris squatted down in front of me and took my chin in his hand, looking intently into my eyes. My gaze darted to the corner and back, and I licked my lips, twice.

"You want out of here, little bird?"

"Out?" I licked my lips again. Then I leaned closer to whisper in his ear. "They don't let *any*body out. Except in pieces."

He drew back and frowned at me. "I know a way."

I hunched closer. "How?"

"It's a secret. From them." He nodded at the pile of rats in the corner. "But it'll cost you."

"Cost me what? I'll give you anything—my shirt—" I started pulling it off. It would be lovely if some of the fleas took up new residence on him.

He stopped me with a grimace and a rough hand on my arm. "No, no, not that."

I sat back on my haunches to rock again. "Not fair. You're needling me…"

He shook his head. "There's a job that needs a professional touch."

"A job? For you?" My posterior hit the floor with a thump and I started laughing. I laughed so hard tears came to my eyes. I was still laughing when the torchlight disappeared and the door thudded shut. Then the tears became sobs.

"Idiot!" I shouted at the darkness. "Stupid, brainless, addleheaded *idiot*! What have you done?"

It is no small wonder that the gods deserted me. They had handed me my life on a silver platter; I could not have been more unappreciative had I launched it back at their heads like a weapon. I began to wonder how many other times in the recent past I had inadvertently insulted them.

I humbled myself, prostrated myself on the floor, and begged their indulgence, forgiveness, and unequaled charity. The list of gods was a long one, and I feared lest I should forget any of them. Not one, but two sly, bold rats interrupted my anxiety. It took all of my faculties to defeat them. I tossed them into the growing pile.

"Loathsome creatures," I grumbled. "Why can't you have the good sense to leave me be? Surely you cannot think that I will meekly sit by and allow you to steal my food, shred my clothing, and snack on my person? Ha! I assassinate every one of you, and still you drive me to distraction lying there in the corner, rotting. You rot. The slops rot. I rot. Could anything smell worse than the lot of us locked up in this room together?"

In the middle of my tirade the door opened again.

"The Master will see you now," Tanris announced without preamble in a voice seething with contempt.

"Whose master?"

"Yours, if you know what's good for you."

A light blossomed at the end of the proverbial tunnel. I heaved a sigh of relief. The gods had forgiven me. Who was I to argue over their methods?

My escort consisted of no fewer than four guards—and the now-familiar feline. Likely, the wretched animal worked for Tanris. Our path kept us below street level. Nary a single window marked the walls until we had nearly reached our destination. The hallways we traversed were well lit, austere, and scrupulously clean. We marched up and down stairs, wound through this corridor and that hall, and made more turns than my addled head could keep up with. Frequently, my companions were called upon to support me. It was a long trip and I was weaker than I cared to admit.

Much to my surprise—and then my discomfiture—I was taken to a large, ornately tiled room. Sunlight, beautiful sunlight, streamed in through high windows, and for a moment I was carried away in an ecstasy of rapture. Collections of towering greenery arranged in tasteful groups adorned each corner. A huge, footed bath gave off clouds of enveloping steam, which would have been infinitely appealing under other circumstances. Before I had a chance to further examine my lavish surroundings, I was summarily stripped of my clothing and physically deposited into the water. All four guards stationed themselves, box-like, around me. A servant hovering nearby produced a long-handled brush. Wordlessly, he approached and began vigorously scouring my hide.

"Hey!" I knocked the brush away. He came at me again. "I am not so incapacitated that I cannot bathe myself!" As soon as the brush came within my reach I grabbed it.

"Let go!" he said, yanking hard.

"You!" I hauled on my end.

A quick-thinking guard saved the servant from a dunking, and the flat of Tanris's blade smacked my hand.

"Ouch!" I let go of the brush. "That hurt!" My next words were lost in a gurgle of water as Tanris grabbed the hair on the top of my head and pushed me under. He kept me there until I was certain I would soon have a face-to-face interview with every god I had ever neglected. When he was satisfied with my saturation level, he dragged me to the surface and leaned his face close to mine.

"I am *not* in the mood for your foolish antics today. Unless you have gills as well as feathers, you had best behave."

"I'll behave!" I said, choking and spewing bath water. "But I can wash myself!"

Under I went. At times like these I fear I have a secret attraction to torture. Someone grabbed my flailing arms and legs, and the servant applied his brush with renewed energy, scrubbing away grime and whatever might remain of the scabs I bore from my beatings. I must confess that he possessed a sure, swift hand, for he finished before the world had gone completely dark around me. It was a feat I shall appreciate to the end of my days.

Tanris hauled me back into the realm of breathability. Unaffected by my coughing and sputtering, he continued lifting me, still holding me by my hair, until I dangled at the vertical and my feet found purchase on solid ground.

The trusty servant, apparently not satisfied with the rosy color of my hide, buffed me with a towel coarse enough to have passed for sandpaper. My howling notwithstanding, I was then thrust into silk stockings and a pair of emerald green breeches, then roughly escorted to a stool.

The servant produced a razor and applied himself to stropping the blade. Just how much of me was that edge going to remove? A hot towel was wrapped around my face and two guards held onto my arms. Tanris kept his hold on my hair.

"Mmmmh!" I shouted, completely muffled.

Tanris loosened the towel. "What?"

"Shave?"

"Yep."

"Let me? Please?"

"Nope." He let go of my hair long enough to drag a small table next to me. He had the guard stretch my arm across it, then Tanris himself leaned on my elbow, holding it down while he held his sword poised above. "You sit still for this, and you can keep your hand."

"You're all heart."

He lifted the blade menacingly. "Shut up."

To my vast relief, the servant was much gentler with blade than he had been with brush. My face was efficiently bared of its overgrowth, and then my hair was trimmed, oiled, and combed. The oiling I could have done without. The strongly perfumed smell of it brought more tears to my eyes.

They garnished me with a white, lace-frothed shirt; a purple vest heavily embroidered with thread of gold; a crimson cut-away coat with deeply slashed sleeves and silver buttons the size of saucers; a pair of well-made leather shoes with ridiculously pointed toes and finally, a tiny blue hat with an overgrown peacock feather jutting out the side.

"This is ridiculous," I said, examining myself in a full-length mirror. I could only imagine what my sweet Tarsha would say if she saw me like this. She'd hide the laughter behind one hand, but her eyes would give her away.

"You don't appreciate the master's generosity?" Tanris fingered the hilt of his sword hopefully.

"His generosity, yes. His taste?" I snorted and waved one hand at the reflection. "I feel like a clown. Still…" I couldn't help but consider the price the overly ornate clothing would fetch. "Do I get to keep them?"

Tanris wore an expression of disgust well and often. "I imagine that will depend on whether you choose to accept your new task."

"Which is?"

"You'll find out soon enough."

Tanris and the four overwhelming guards herded me out of the bathing room and back into the hall for another trek through a labyrinth of halls.

"Which do you enjoy most, Tanris?" I asked, eyeing the contents of a half-moon table appraisingly as we passed. "The look of surprise on your victim's faces, or the power you wield by withholding information?"

He glared at me, but didn't answer.

We stopped next in a kitchen area suitable for a sizable kingdom. The wafting odors of fine, hot food floated enticingly down the corridor. I inhaled appreciatively. Without even trying, I could make out the presence of roasted lamb, sweet rolls, apple pie and fresh lemons. My belly rumbled loudly and eagerly.

Tanris took me to a small, scarred table in a corner and pushed me into a chair. A servant slapped a bowl down in front of me, and I stared at it in a quandary of disappointment. It held a hunk of ordinary bread—buttered nicely, to be sure—and a goopy mess that might have been stew at some point in its existence. Cutting words sprang to my tongue, but I forestalled them by stuffing the bread in my mouth. I was not going to let my spontaneous wit deprive me of much-needed nourishment.

Tanris gave a curt nod and watched impatiently as I wolfed down my first hot meal in weeks. Although it did not live up to the advertising of the aromas filling the room, it was edible, and it served to fill a gnawingly empty place in my belly.

"Where to now?" I asked, licking my lips and standing.

"Now that you're clean and fed, the Master will see you."

"I don't suppose there's any way I could persuade you to reveal his identity?"

"No." He strode away at a speed that required me to jog to catch up.

"I've never actually met any of the Magistrates," I confessed. Except for some minor brushes with the law in my youth, I had thus far eluded capture. "I understand some of them are quite cruel."

Tanris forbore to reply and we continued along, this time above street level. Many windows decorated these halls, and I made a point of passing as close to them as was reasonable, soaking up the light of the sun. The windows wore dressings of the finest fabrics, and the walls bore a variety of highly artistic, painted coverings decked out in expensive frames. Sconces of solid brass decorated the wall, and imported urns held beautiful, lush greenery. The rugs—well, suffice it to say that it seemed sinful to walk on them. Everywhere there was beauty beyond imagining. It felt almost homey. In fact, I felt distinctly as though I had been here before. The servants we passed were garbed in saffron-hued uniforms of one sort or another. I was certain I'd seen them before, but Emperor Gaziah's colors—and therefore the colors worn by the guards and the magistrates and their sundry officers—were sapphire blue. It stood to reason, then, that this was not the Hall of Justice. Perhaps, then, the private dwelling of one of those distinguished officers of the law. Shrugging off my uneasiness, I passed off my inability to associate the uniforms with any particular house as a result of my confinement.

:-:

My audience was with none other than the illustrious Baron Metin Duzayan—the man from whom I had stolen the Great Gandil. Duzayan was no magistrate, so what did he want with me?

"Baron," I greeted, bowing deeply and respectfully as I covertly canvassed the tastefully appointed room. It was evidently Duzayan's personal study. One other door offered egress and, unless I missed my well-trained guess, it would lead to a receiving parlor where some poor fool admitted or denied entrance.

A plain-looking man of average height and build, Duzayan dressed in subtly exquisite robes. He stood before a globe carved entirely out of ivory and inlaid with precious jewels, one finger tapping the surface. He examined me cursorily, as though he was dealing with an insignificant underling. "You know me?"

"I try to make it a point to know all my marks."

Tanris gave a hiss of outrage at my temerity, but the Baron smiled in genuine amusement. Something in his demeanor shifted slightly. "You're not afraid."

I shrugged. "I have little left to fear."

"Not even death?" he asked, coming closer.

I moved away from him, toward the desk standing between the door and the window. Its surface was inlaid with a border in a geometric pattern of mother-of-pearl. I ran my finger over the design appreciatively, then sighed. This beauty would never fit into my pocket. "Not particularly," I answered. A carved ivory dolphin sat on the far corner, and I went to examine it. "I have been at death's threshold too many times for it to impress me any more."

The baron followed me slowly as I made my way around the room. A collection of exquisite glass figurines caught my eye.

"No misgivings about what might lie beyond?"

"None." My imagination supplied me with a vision of the stacks and stacks of gold coins that the things in this room would fetch. The baron made no bones about being a very, very rich man. On the wall above hung a painting of a raging sea. "Allabet?" I asked, surmising the name of the artist.

"Yes." The baron joined me in examining it. "Some say that it depicts one of the Four Hells."

"Some say that sometimes a storm is just a storm."

He chuckled. "I take it the Hells don't frighten you either."

"Oh, no. I've visited them a number of times."

"And if you had your druthers, which one would you choose: endless darkness, or burning light?"

He'd left out two of the Hells, but his tone of voice suggested the latter would be every bit as horrible as the former. He certainly didn't waste any time getting to business. I quelled a rush of apprehension and moved over to look out the window. We were close to the room from which I had made my original escape. Three stories down, something in the quality of light at this time of year made the water look incredibly cold. "Well, let's see: pain or pain…" I mused, adopting an air of carelessness.

The baron glided up behind me and adopted an uncomfortably close position. His breath brushed my ear as he whispered. "Do you need help choosing?"

"I've already seen what darkness has to offer. What is included in the light option? Do you offer previews?"

"Not usually, but this instance is exceptional."

I wanted to look at his face, to see what he was thinking—but he had me neatly pinned against the window. Escaping would only indicate weakness on my part. I turned anyway, but held my place. Our noses nearly touched, and he didn't back away. Bully. I arranged my lips in a small, appreciative smile and looked him straight in the eye, trying to ignore the way he made me feel like a bird in the grip of a hungry cat.

I let my gaze wander slowly over every feature of his face. Then I lifted the silver pendant hanging against his chest and rubbed it thoughtfully. Did my casual demeanor slip? A cunningly worked puzzle created of interlocking silver triangles, an icon of wizardry. When I land in a dung heap, I like to make sure it's a big one. I was going to have to tread very carefully. It would have been helpful if I hadn't still been scraping together wandering pieces of my mind. I crooked a brow at him. "Is there a penalty to be paid for this information?"

"No penalty," he said, his voice soft as warm silk. "You will choose between the unbearable and the impossible. The rest of your life hangs in the balance. I think it only fair that you be fully informed of all the inherent risks."

My pulse pounded in my ears and, considering his proximity, I wondered if he could hear it as well. I pretended he couldn't. It was unbelievable that my investigations had not revealed Duzayan's dealings with magic. I had been so thorough! Anything less was to put life and limb in peril. What price was he going to extract from me for my audacity? I continued to hold his gaze, and the moment stretched out between us, very thin and very taut.

"You are kind," I managed last, "to allow me the opportunity to make an intelligent decision." I was amazed at the calmness of my voice but his smile made my belly clench.

"I don't honestly care what means you use to make your choice: intelligence, emotion, the flip of a coin..." His breath smelled like mint leaves. "But I am somewhat—" he paused dramatically, "curious. What force will motivate the indomitable Crow? Does his conscience have a voice beyond indulgent self-interest? What of self-sacrifice?"

I didn't appreciate either his smooth insults, or his reference to selfishness, but at the same time, my curiosity was piqued. "We wouldn't want such burning questions to go unanswered, now would we?" I couldn't think clearly with him literally breathing in my face. Impulsively, I licked the tip of my finger and wiped away an imagined blotch on the baron's chin. It had the desired effect: he backed away as if he'd been stung.

I shrugged. "Smudge," I said by way of explanation. Free at last, I sauntered back to the desk, dropped into the chair, and propped my elegantly clad feet on top. The elongated toes blocked my view of Duzayan, and I had to twitch them a little out of the way.

Tanris, nearly forgotten in the corner by the door, nearly choked on his indignation. His hand went to his sword hilt, but the baron held up one hand to forestall such foolishness and came to perch on the desk's corner. The one farthest from me, thank the god of small favors.

"Do you place little value on your life, Crow? Or do you not believe I'm serious?" he asked.

I picked up the golden seal he used to imprint the wax on his correspondence and turned it over and over in my hand, just to give me something busy to do. "I know you're serious. I also realize that my life doesn't seem to be my own any longer."

He smiled that wicked, shiver-inducing little smile. "No, it's mine now."

"What do I have to do to gain it back?"

"A job. One particularly suited to your talents."

"My lord baron!" Tanris stepped forward, a look of outrage on his face. "That is not what we agreed to! He was to advise only!"

Ah, the seeds of dissent! I looked curiously from one to the other. Duzayan merely lifted a hand as though to wave off a buzzing fly.

"The game has changed, Captain," he said. "We'll discuss it in a moment."

Stiff and angry, Tanris held his peace. It was the only sensible thing a common man could do against a wizard, particularly without reinforcements.

Duzayan continued to look at me expectantly.

"You want me to steal something?" There had to be more to it than that, there must be a catch. I frowned, remembering how he'd said that I must choose between the unbearable and the impossible. "Something from another wizard?" That would be a hazardous undertaking. Smart people don't trifle with wizards. To the mere earth-bound, non-magical mind, a wizard is illogical. They don't play by the same rules. They're unpredictable, contradictory, and unreasonable.

"No." He shook his head. "No, of course not. What kind of challenge would that be for a thief of your stature and renown?"

As if I would submit to being buttered up by a wizard. And a mocking wizard at that...

"I have something more ambitious in mind. I want you to steal a dragon's egg."

I nearly laughed out loud, but that routine had already proven too treacherous for my liking—with this crowd anyway. I restricted myself to a wide grin. "Dragons? Are you joking? There are no such things as dragons, except between the pages of children's books and in old wives' tales!"

"The learned know that all myths and folk tales have a basis in reality, my skeptical young friend."

I chose to ignore his reference to my youth. He was a wizard—for all I knew he'd been alive practically forever, though if that was true one might expect him to have more common sense. "Prove it."

Tanris made another strangled noise, and I glanced his way. His face was strangely contorted and had taken on a peculiar hue.

"Are you well?" I asked him. "Do you need a physician?"

"I—This—You cannot be serious, my lord!"

Duzayan waved him silent, which was just as well. The poor soul had completely lost the connection between his mouth and his brain.

Leaning toward me, the baron went on. "Here lies one of the beauties in our relationship: I don't have to prove anything to you. You will do as I say or—" He shrugged expressively and smiled. "The choice is yours."

"Not much of a choice," I grumbled. "Besides impossible, what other restrictions will you affix to this little engagement?"

"Don't you trust me?"

"I don't trust anyone. I don't trust sneaks, extortionists, or bullies. And I especially don't trust wizards."

Tanris risked dying of apoplexy.

Duzayan merely nodded. "Probably a wise course of action in your line of work."

"Tell me the rules by which I am to play," I said, dropping my feet to the floor and leaning my folded arms on the desktop.

"Of course. Can I pour you a glass of wine?"

I shrugged.

The baron went to a sideboard and picked up two of the silver-chased wineglasses there. With the other hand he lifted a crystal decanter. "White?"

I could easily have gotten into one of those interminable self-debates about the tricks wizards play. Did he offer the white because it was poisoned? Or did he offer it knowing that I'd know it was poisoned and thus choose the red? And if he knew that I knew the red was poisoned, then clearly I'd need to choose the white. "Red, please."

He inclined his head gracefully and brought the glasses and decanter over to the desk. Setting them out, he poured the startlingly crimson liquid as he talked. Naturally, I watched. Closely. "I have only two stipulations. First," he held up one finger, "you have four months in which to place the egg in my hands. Second, you will be working with a partner of my choosing."

"I work alone, as I'm sure you know."

"Have you a preference as to which glass you'd like to drink from?"

He'd performed the operation in front of me specifically—but did he plan to ease my natural mistrust or increase it? He had made every movement slowly and purposefully, and I had noticed nothing untoward. Such limited information by which to make a hasty judgement. My head began to ache. I supposed that if he planned on killing me outright the deed would have already been accomplished. I shrugged again.

He slid one of the glasses across the desktop. "This time you will have a partner or you will have that dark little room. You don't think I trust you, do you?"

I didn't like it. Still, being forced to accept a partner beat the alternative. I sipped my drink. It was delicious, very smooth, and assuredly costly. "How much input will this partner have?"

"Consider yourselves equals."

I smiled and shook my head. "No one is my equal."

"As a thief, no, I'll give you that." He sighed and looked off into space. "We went to a great deal of trouble to arrange this meeting."

"Why didn't you just ask?"

He chuckled. "Would that have made you any more amenable to going off on such a preposterous quest?"

Preposterous, indeed. How was I to find a nonexistent dragon egg and bring it back in four months? "Probably not, but you may have been able to persuade me, for the right price." I took another wary drink from the wineglass. Just because a wizard didn't place much value on my life didn't mean I felt the same way.

"And trust that you would keep your end of the bargain? I think not."

I slouched down in the chair and tipped myself over to one elbow. "Doubtless you have a plan for assuring that I do keep my end of the bargain?"

"You agree to accept the task, then?"

"I'm suspending a decision until I hear all the details."

He chuckled. "You almost make me wish that our business could have been taken on under different circumstances. You are possessed of an acerbic wit I find amusing. Few men are so at ease in my company."

"I can't begin to imagine why not." I took another drink. I should exercise more caution, but it had been a long time since I'd had a glass of wine, and the presence of a wizard guaranteed trouble. "What insurance do you intend to use?"

"Nothing complicated—just the poison in your wine."

As I should have expected. Still, my stomach flip-flopped and the hand in my lap convulsed into a fist. I pursed my lips and nodded, struggling to maintain a calm façade. "You put the poison in the glass before I came in."

"Even so," he nodded.

"You realize I'm not going to finish it."

"I did take that possibility into account, yes."

"How does it work?"

He settled back onto the corner of the desk and rubbed his hands together. "Actually, I've concocted my own unique recipe."

Could my heart sink any further? Unless he told me what he'd used, identifying a combination of obscure ingredients would be nearly impossible. Talk about your needle in a haystack. "Who's the partner to be?" I asked, as if the information he'd just delivered was of no import at all.

If he was disappointed to be robbed of gloating rights, he didn't show it. "Tanris."

I shot out of the chair with a yell. At the same moment, Tanris bellowed his dismay and moved swiftly toward us.

"Master, no!" he shouted. "I can't work with him! How can you ask it of me? You know what I think of him! You *know!*"

"And will he not still be in your custody?"

"Yes, but—"

Duzayan raised a warning brow, and Tanris immediately fell silent, the horror upon his face unmistakable. "Who better to see that he behaves himself?"

"I do not need a nursemaid!" I growled.

"No doubt. In case the two of you haven't concluded the obvious yet, this little exercise is crucial to me and to numerous others as well. You can hardly blame me for setting up a few safeguards." He strode to the shelf-lined wall and opened a small cask. Withdrawing a nicely sized purse, he tossed it on the desk in front of me. It made an enticing sound. "Buy whatever supplies you need with this. You may work out the details however you please. If I may make a suggestion, I would advise that Tanris take charge of travel arrangements and whatever defensive measures might be needed. Crow will be responsible for acquiring the egg." He might have *said* it was a suggestion, but it had the definite sound of an order.

"And if we happen to disagree on any of the particulars?"

"I don't care. Draw straws." He took a parchment from the shelf and handed it to Tanris. "This is a map to Hasiq jum'a Sahefal, where you will find the dragon. Memorize it and burn it."

"What's to keep us from killing each other?" Tanris growled. His hand tightened around the hilt of his knife, which was hardly a reassuring thing to see in my new partner.

"Self-preservation." The baron sighed in exasperation and massaged one temple. Rather suddenly, he'd lost his appetite for baiting his victims. "You, Tanris, can't steal the egg. And you, Crow, have no experience traveling in the wilds." He strode to the door. "Come with me, both of you."

— 4 —
Whatever Shall We Do?

Duzayan beckoned the waiting guards, and as we went past they fell in behind us. Down the corridor a little, he stopped in front of another door and rapped out a pattern. Just before he opened the door fully, he turned to us. "I should warn you before you go in. If either of you attempt anything heroic, the consequences will be, well… fatal." He pushed the door open and stepped back.

Tanris and I both had a clear view of the room's occupants. Bathed in the light that flooded the high windows stood two women. Their clothing was dirty and torn, and bruises marred their faces. They wore heavy chains. A pair of guards held each in position, knives poised at the women's throats.

Shock turned my blood to ice. At that moment I hated Baron Duzayan more than I had ever hated anyone in my entire life. "Tarsha." My voice came out strange and harsh, as though it belonged to someone else. My chest hurt with a sharpness of pain I never knew existed, and confusion threatened to overwhelm me. I did not expect her here.

Both of the women burst into tears. Beside me Tanris moaned and took two impulsive steps forward, dragging me out of my stupor. The guards' knives twitched in their hands.

"No!" I shouted, grabbing him by the arm. "No."

He stopped, reaching out to the other woman, his face etched with hopeless pain. "Aehana!" he whispered. "What have I done? I'm sorry. I'm so sorry."

"What has he done to you?" I asked them sharply. "Are you badly hurt?"

"Oh, Crow!" Tarsha wept. I had never beheld her so pale, or in such common clothing, either. The rags insulted her grace, though at least they covered her decently. "I—we're fine. But I'm so frightened! What's going to happen to me?"

"Baron?" I grated, clenching both my teeth and my fists. Tanris had the misfortune of having his arm still grasped in one of them.

"They'll be fine, providing you both behave." Supremely calm, untouched by the flaring emotions around him, Duzayan brushed invisible dust from one sleeve. "I even promise I'll have them cleaned up and put in comfortable rooms until your return."

Anger shook me to the core. I whirled to face him. "What good are your promises?"

He held his hands out in a placating manner. "Truly, I have no desire to harm them. They may even prove to be entertaining as well as decorative. At the moment they are but insurance of your cooperation. Deliver the article we've discussed within the allotted time, and they'll be returned to you."

I didn't like it. What kind of man fought his battles using women as a shield? "I don't trust you."

"And why should you?"

"Why are you doing this?"

He tipped his head to one side and regarded me intently. "Balance," he said at last. "Guards! Show them out."

Abruptly, and with little care for our persons, the guards yanked us out into the corridor and the door shut behind us. The women screamed, their voices desperate.

"No! Wait!" I shouted. "We are not through here, Baron!" Shouting and protesting all the way, we were shoved brusquely to the main entrance and thrust out into the street. The great doors slammed and the bar behind them banged into place. Tanris whirled about and launched himself in a frenzy of rage at the doors, but they remained firmly closed.

The struggle through the halls had taken their toll on me. Leaning against one of the columns flanking the portals, I watched for several moments. "This isn't going to help, Tanris."

He whirled on me. "What are we going to do?" he shouted.

"I suppose we could kill him." Little details stood in the way of this, namely the locked door and an army of guards.

He started to say something, then snapped his mouth shut. His shoulders slumped and his features drooped. "What are we going to do?" he repeated.

"Who is she?" I asked.

"My wife."

Tanris was married? The notion struck me as absurd, but I refrained from commenting. Instead, I sighed and took off the stupid little hat to run my hand roughly over my well-oiled head. My knees wobbled, and my head swam. "We'll come up with something. In the meantime, I need to sit down somewhere. I've had far more excitement this afternoon than I can handle."

"Curse that!" he shouted, abruptly angry again. "We can't just leave them there! You got in before—you can do it again."

There was such insistent hope in his eyes that I was reluctant to say anything. "Tanris, in case you're forgetting, I was allowed in. And when I came out I was carrying a tiny pearl. I went over the rooftops and was nearly killed in the process. Even supposing I could get past the baron's guards and the gods alone know what magical protections he's put up, into just which pockets do you think I could stuff two full-grown women?"

He looked at me for the longest time before turning to stare for a while longer at the baron's residence. "We can't leave them there."

"You said that." I turned and walked down the street.

"Do you have a plan?" he asked, trotting up beside me.

His assumption that I could come up with an immediate and infallible solution should have been gratifying, but I found myself irritated. "Yes. The first thing I'm going to do is find something to eat. I'm going to wash. I'm going to rest. And I'm going to get rid of this ridiculous costume."

"That's it? That's your plan?"

"So far." Catching sight of a hackney down the street, I whistled and waved. "Would you care to accompany me, or would you rather meet somewhere later?" The carriage pulled up in front of us and I opened the door.

"Crow…"

I had never seen Tanris look so powerless, so lost, in all the years I had known him. To find that the man who had hounded and plagued me to distraction actually had a heart and could be vulnerable was—I don't know what, but it bothered me. This wasn't a side of him I wanted to see. "We'll figure something out, Tanris."

He nodded dumbly, blankly.

"You can find me later at the Loaf and Jug on Elm Street." I climbed inside. He just nodded again and watched the vehicle move away down the street, wearing the look of the most woebegone hound in the world.

I paid for the ride out of the baron's purse and settled myself at a table near the window in one of my favorite eating establishments—not the place I'd mentioned to Tanris, for I didn't want to deal with him just yet if he should decide to follow me. Although I had eaten just a short while ago, I was still ravenous. I'd had too little to go on and too much adrenaline raging to find satisfaction with one little bowl of stew. When I had finished two plates of roast beef and potatoes, half a loaf of bread, a full quarter of an apple pie, and a pitcher of ale, I sat back and watched the traffic outside the window for a while.

Here was my sunlight. No more stone walls closing in on me. No more invisible rats scurrying across the floor or chewing on my hide. No more vain wishing for the slightest glimmer of light. The world was mine again, yet I was still not free. The baron had known his business when he had taken Tarsha. If it had been anyone else, I would have walked away without a backward glance. I wasn't certain which made me the most angry: the fact that I had allowed myself to fall in love, or the fact that such a weakness could be used against me. They say love is blind, but apparently it is blinding as well. I had no idea how Tanris managed to dupe the pair of us, but I would pry the story out of him. Catching me was such a momentous occasion in his life—temporary as it may be—that I suspected he would rub my nose in it at every opportunity.

Captured, blackmailed, poisoned...

My hand trembled. The terror of poison in my system engendered a fear that made my blood run hot and cold in turns. At best, I could expect it to cripple me, and then I would be no good to Tarsha at all. Could an apothecary tell me what toxins might have been used? Suggest something to counter it? I'd had dealings with a few, but having my own life on the line inspired a rare kind of pickiness. Him first, then.

I took a deep swig of ale and banged the empty tankard down hard on the table. However this situation had come about, it was not to be tolerated. I would free Tarsha, find the blasted antidote, and then I would deal with the baron, wizard or no.

The Loaf and Jug was as crowded and smoke-filled as usual. I had chosen it for its standing as a sort of halfway house. The only stipulation for mixing class or moral station was to leave your troubles at the door. It was a rule strictly enforced by the owners—two brothers of enormous proportions and little fear.

I made my way through the throng, exchanging greetings and insults with those I recognized and picking the pockets of those I didn't. I could justify the activity as re-establishing my routine, but the truth was that the game amused me. The real challenge was in lifting something of value from one person and planting it on someone else. I paused for a moment, squinting through the smoke in search of my new partner. A disgruntled growl came from behind me.

"Where's my purse? Someone's stolen my purse! And what in tarnation is this? Where did these come from?"

"Hey! That's mine!"

"How did you get my flask?"

I turned to watch, feigning innocent interest as a small group near the bar began to sort things out with increasing outrage and a tendency toward shoving and punching. Within a few moments the brothers were compelled to sally forth from behind their station at the bar, shouting and swinging small clubs. They efficiently cleared the room, and I caught sight of Tanris sitting in a dark corner. Three bottles were carefully arranged on the table, and he held a fourth, studying it with the careful consideration only a drunk can manage.

It infuriated me that he was deliberately poisoning himself while I would do anything to be rid of my own. The apothecary had a long list of possible combinations of herbs that might induce the results Duzayan had described, but the baron's declaration that he'd concocted his own recipe complicated the issue. I was probably dying already, and I'd been too addled to ask for the blasted draught before we got ourselves escorted out the door and dropped on the street.

"I went to see the baron," I said, sliding onto the bench across from Tanris. Knocking on the baron's door and requesting an interview had failed, which meant I would have to find another way in. "He is not receiving visitors."

"Thash a shuprise. Ha!"

"I have a plan." I plucked the bottle from his grasp. The first step was accomplishing Tanris's sobriety. I tipped the bottle up and took a pull.

"A plan?" He looked at me blankly.

"For storming the baron's citadel." I drank again, then set the bottle down clumsily. It tipped, overbalanced, and rolled off. With a satisfactory *clink!* the contents spilled all over the floor. Alas, there went his ready supply.

"Hey," he said without much enthusiasm. "My wine."

"Sorry. I'll get you another, but first answer me a question." Tanris had been working with the baron for some time and I wondered how well he knew his master. "How well do you know the layout of the mansion?"

"What masshon?"

"The baron's."

"The baron?" He shook his head slowly from side to side. "Don't like him mush. He's a sheet—a lorry shackin'—" He trailed off in confusion, then tried again, peering sadly through bloodshot eyes. "He's a two-fayshed son of a—of a cow."

This wasn't going to be as easy as I hoped. "Indeed. Why don't we go take a look?" I suggested, making a sudden decision.

"Look a' th' baron?"

"I want to show you someplace." It wasn't a place he would thank me for, but Tanris himself had made a detour necessary.

"Wha' plashe? Th' baron's? I know where tha' is," he said with a somber nod. "Ish very big. He hash a lotta money."

"That he does. We'll look into redistributing some of it later. Come along, now." Tanris was not a particularly small fellow, and it took considerable heaving and grunting, and the assistance of one of the invincible brothers, to get him out of the tavern and across the street to a hostel chosen purely for the sake of convenience.

Praise the gods of the afflicted, a room was available on the ground floor. Tanris was past caring about the casual bumps and bruises acquired getting him through doors and into bed, but even in his cups he had a fairly decent singing voice. And lungs, too. I have no doubt whatsoever that they heard him all the way to the emperor's palace halfway across the city. I tucked him into bed, pocketed the wizard's map, and gave him a pat on his shaven head. He promised to lock me up and throw away the key, and I went on my way. There was, after all, work to be done.

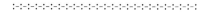

Marketh, the seat of Emperor Gaziah's considerable domain, is a dazzling metropolis of diverse cultures, ethnicities, commerce, and opportunity. Touted as the city that never sleeps, it is a fact of nature that people *do* sleep, and the dealer I'd chosen was not at all happy about me waking him in the wee hours of the morning to do business, in his esteemed and unhappy opinion, better done in daylight hours. A substantial portion of Baron Duzayan's purse convinced him otherwise—a portion the wizard was going to replenish, whether he knew it or not. I would simply have made my way inside the dealer's establishment and helped myself, but in some instances such boldness is too detrimental to be of value. Take, for instance, the acquiring of a dangerous and unpredictable bird of prey. And appropriate feathers.

Two blocks away, I stuffed my pale, fluffy, far-too-expensive owl into a sack I'd brought along for the purpose. While it weighed not much more than an average chicken, I am no falconer and I had no patience for putting up with its wing constantly smacking me in the face as it rode along on my uplifted and already aching arm. Nor was I particularly fond of the idea of having my skin pierced through by talons that could be put to excellent use on weapons. Perhaps someone had already thought of that business opportunity; I would have to look into it. Of course the owl grossly objected to confinement in a sack and fought for freedom every step of the way. After several blocks and vainly repeated assurances on my part that I would soon relieve it of its misery, I'd had enough. Not only did the thing's squawking annoy the spit out of me, but with that kind of noise the Baron's Best would hear me coming for blocks and blocks. Adamanta Dust was potent, rare, costly, and not a drug to use casually. It was a product of the seed capsules of the lovely and frail adamanta flower from across the Rahiya Strait, a flower that grows wild in small, isolated places and refuses domestication, which is something of a vexation for dealers in arcane medicaments and poisons. A breath of it will cause unconsciousness; more than that can induce a comatose state or, if one is using it even more generously, death—though there are other, less expensive means of murder. I didn't want to murder the bird, no matter my extreme dislike, but trying to administer just one very tiny dose nearly changed my mind. The bird finally fell silent. I had to stop twice to make sure I hadn't inadvertently killed it.

My earlier study of the baron's residence, together with the investigating I had originally done prior to purloining the Great Gandil, provided me with the knowledge that Duzayan's magical protections were confined to the upper levels, and the best-of-the-best guards did a smashing job of securing the ground floor. Long past midnight, normal people—with the exception of the guards—were fast asleep and consequently out of my way.

Getting to the baron's rooftop was a tricky endeavor made more challenging by the icy grip of deep winter, but it was not impossible, even with my sack wriggling and complaining. I picked out a window on the third floor—and hopefully out of the immediate reach of the guards—set my hook, and carefully made my way down. Clever and skillful as I am, I had chosen the leeward side of the mansion to make my entrance. While the wind whistled merrily and quite noisily between the buildings, I took a moment to reclaim my hook and rope, then warmed my fingers a bit, rubbing my hands together briskly. I also waited to discover whether such close proximity to a window had set off any magical alarms. When nothing untoward happened after several moments, I loosed my bagged bird from where it hung on my belt.

I had not anticipated the difficulty of removing the bird's hood and jesses with fingers stiff from the cold in spite of my attempts to warm them. My fumbling revived the owl, which attempted to peck me. Fortunately, he'd not fully regained consciousness. "One more minute," I grumbled, and stuffed it back in the bag. "Uncooperative ingrate. Do you not listen to me? You are to be a hero, saving countless lives. Well… Two or three, at least, and mine in particular. You could have made this a great deal easier on yourself, you know."

Fortunately, the bird did not answer or I cannot say what I might have done. The bag hooted and grumbled in obvious displeasure. Calmly, I stashed the leather hood and straps safely in the pouch I wore at my waist and withdrew a small bag full of feathers I'd obtained at the mews. Taking a fistful of them, I bashed the window. The glass made a satisfying jangle as it crashed inward.

*

— 5 —
Bearding The Lion

Quick as a wink, I reached in and unlatched the catch, heaved up the sash, and upended the wobbly owl onto the floor amidst the ruin of glass. I shoved the glove and the sack into my pouch and slipped into the room. I had to work swiftly, and I had to make sure I avoided the glass, lest I inadvertently create a trail—or slice my boot (and possibly my foot) to unpleasant ribbons. Quickly lowering the sash again, I stepped carefully around the glassy area and retired from the room before the herds of the Baron's Best arrived.

Thank the gods of floor-coverings, thick carpets served to cushion my footsteps as I ran down the hall. I needed a suitable hiding place. A quick peek into the first door revealed what I already knew: this floor was relegated to sleeping quarters. Very grand sleeping quarters, but Duzayan was a rich man and could afford to devote space the size of a decent cottage to rooms whose occupants would spend most of their time with their eyes closed. There was, alas, no place to hide.

The second and third doors offered the same lack of sanctuary, along with the knowledge that Duzayan didn't entertain a lot of guests. All three were quite empty but for their furniture, which was probably good news for the maids, as cleaning an unoccupied room was surely easier than cleaning up after careless visitors who assumed they could make messes because someone else would tidy them up.

Victory was mine behind the fourth door, and none too soon. The rich carpeting and tapestries Baron Duzayan preferred did nothing to conceal the clatter and thunder of the arriving guards. Speedy as they were, I could only surmise that there was some sort of guard station on each floor, and it had been my supreme good fortune to pick the hall furthest from them when I arrived. I flung open the trunk at the foot of the bed, only to find it filled with linens. Linens! Did the staff not have a better, more central place to store such things? Surely the baron could have converted one of his monstrous—and very empty—bedrooms into a linen closet!

A quick glance around revealed the shadowy bulk of a wardrobe on the other side of a canopied bed. That was far too obvious, but the bed had possibilities. I transferred the contents of the trunk to the bed, stuffing them between mattresses, then giving a quick brush to the bedclothes—velvet, of course, and I wished briefly for a light so I could discern the color, but I had no time to dawdle. Drawing a deep breath, into the trunk I went.

Now, one might recall at this point that I am somewhat averse to dark, cramped quarters. Trust me, I did not forget. A person in my line of work is, however, ofttimes required to avail himself of whatever concealment is handy, and that includes trunks, closets, crates, sewers, privies—though privies are a last resort, as the stench they impart has a particular quality impossible to miss—baskets, barrels, cisterns, and the like. A professional of my caliber can usually avoid such confines by careful planning beforehand. Notwithstanding, it is always wise to be prepared.

From the pouch at my waist, I withdrew a length of wire to wrap tightly around the prongs of the catch so it would not become locked. I closed the lid all but an inch or two, and waited for the guards to arrive. At least the smell of cedar was comfortingly rich and aromatic. There was considerably more shouting and banging down the hall than I might have expected from the Baron's Best, and it took a few moments for me to realize that the owl was living up to the heroic potential I had envisioned. The strangely high-pitched cries were not the shrieks of operatic guards, but the outraged squawking of a trapped owl. My lovely, expensive trapped owl…

I left the lid of the trunk somewhat ajar so that I could listen. I do not know by what means the bird was subdued, but it didn't take terribly long for the shouting to die down to purposeful conversational tones, and the Best set out to make a cursory inspection of the rest of the floor, as I had known they must. Truthfully, were I the one answering to the wizard, I would have made a very, very thorough inspection. When the bedroom door opened, I quickly, quietly closed the lid of the trunk and put my weight on the wire I'd twisted around my gloved hand.

Sure enough, one of the guards had the intelligence to attempt to look into the trunk. My weight held the lid down and he, most naturally and just as I had anticipated, assumed it was locked. The doors of the wardrobe banged, knees thumped into the pile of the carpet as someone looked beneath the bed.

They took their sweet time.

The scraping and bumping as they searched the room reminded me of the noise of rats sneaking closer to crawl into my clothes. Cold sweat dampened my skin. Teeth clenched, I hung onto the wire and breathed in the scent of cold, damp stone.

No! No, it was rich, warm cedar. My breath came faster and my nose tingled. I forced myself to concentrate on the noises outside, and when it finally grew quiet I made myself stay put for a little longer—until the air in the closed chest became uncomfortably stifled and I had to open it or pass out.

My hands shook so badly I could hardly unwind the wire. I wanted nothing more than to gasp in great lungfuls of breath, but common sense demanded I be as silent and as unobtrusive as possible. Once I had regained my aplomb, I had but to exercise my incredible patience for a bit longer while the residual hue and cry of an owl crashing through a window settled down.

Morning dawned much too early, and although I had made good use of my time and searched a great deal of the baron's immense home, I did not find the women. The ways to the subterranean levels were carefully guarded, and if I was to do any searching there I would need some clever distractions and time I feared I didn't have. Duzayan struck me as a man who would keep his newly leashed pet on a very short tether. If he said that I had four months, then it was four months to the day, and no time for bad weather or unforeseen circumstances taken into account. But I have always been blessed by inordinate good luck and I could devote one day, and one day only, to my endeavor while I puzzled through my dilemma. It pained me to think what might become of my beautiful Tarsha if I did not find her. What had the nefarious wizard already done to her in the time since my capture?

As the palace came alive, I made my way to the wing devoted to cooking and cleaning and other such menial chores. A darkened alcove above a stair landing more than comfortably held an ancient suit of armor and myself. I'd run into a spider's web whilst climbing up into the space, and in spite of having wiped my face and neck several times I felt like it still clung to me. Worse, the funny little tickling sensation it produced migrated beneath my shirt until I wondered if an entire colony of spiders lived in the armor and I, having just invaded their space, was being invaded myself. I have dealt with spiders and webs before. I do not like them, but as spiders are considerably smaller than I, and quite susceptible to being flattened, they do not much trouble me. I could not see any spiders, and the occasional irresistible urge to slap the tickle on my neck or face produced no oozing little bodies. I even got up twice to look about and finally concluded I was imagining things, but more and more I felt the urge to leave.

A good twenty minutes of lurking finally produced a servant about my height and weight. Soundlessly, I slipped out behind him and glided up close. One hand grabbed the handle of the bucket he carried while the other took the mop and brought the handle up to whack sharply across the lad's skull. He was sturdier than he looked. He stumbled sideways, but did not fall, and I had to thump him again. I supported him as he slid to the floor. Much to my consternation, he was still conscious, looking at me vaguely through glassy eyes. The mop handle came down a third time, and his eyes rolled back into his head at last.

I concealed the mop and bucket in my nook, then dragged the servant after. I froze—albeit briefly—as a pair of maids took to the stairs. My weakened condition made getting up into the alcove with the servant an extremely difficult business, and all praise to the gods of chattering women, they did not spy us up above them as they passed. Up the stairs and to the left was a convenient storage room for clerks and such. Holding the servant tightly 'round the chest, I hitched him up a bit and searched for the ledge with my foot, then down onto the stairs proper. I had scarce begun my journey upward before hushed chattering assaulted my ears once again. Did the maids not know that they were supposed to be working, not lollygagging up and down the stairwell?

Back into the alcove I dragged the servant, hugging him close and hoping the maids were too busy with each other to notice me. The steady rising of the sun was making my hiding place less and less "hidey" by the moment, and I was more than ready to leave the invisible spiders behind. Our ascent brought us into contact with the suit of armor and I froze again, waiting for the thing to go crashing and banging right into the path of the maids. Perhaps they would run away shrieking and I would be blessed with a moment in which to recover the situation before the Baron's Best were once again underfoot.

To my vast delight and relief, some of the deities were watching out for me again. When I had a moment I would ardently thank the gods of armor, armorers, thieves, good intentions, and as many others as might qualify for the occasion. Perhaps the armor was fixed solidly into place, which would explain how the thing stayed together at all, it was so old. In that case I should thank the gods of good sense who'd inspired the decorator to take such precautions. At any rate, the armor did not so much as budge, so I squeezed my eyes shut and waited. It is a well-known fact that some people can sense when others are looking at them, and I had no desire to test the theory on the maids.

"His name is Remzi," one of the girls insisted.

"No, I'm sure it's Ramazan," the other argued.

"We shall have to eavesdrop and find out," the first declared in a loud whisper.

"Does it really matter?" the second giggled. "He's soooo handsome!"

Their entire conversation was in whispers, but I suppose that, given the earliness of the hour, it was only prudent. Lords, ladies, and assorted nobility would take a dim view of any noise that might wake them from their precious slumber.

"And did you see the tall blond with the scar on his face?"

"He frightens me! Even so, I'm glad the baron has finally hired some replacements."

Replacements? I strained to hear them as they continued their passage down the stairs.

"What a terrible thing to have lost…"

Their whispering voices dwindled away as the conversation got interesting. What had the baron lost? People, obviously, but why? How? And to who? I would likely never know, but my perpetual curiosity was piqued—and doomed to disappointment, for I had not only an unconscious servant in my arms, but ladies to rescue, a potion to find, and a mythical dragon's egg I must attempt to steal. Even supposing dragons really did still exist, all the stories portrayed them as gigantic, magical creatures with really big teeth. Ending my life as a snack did not come high on my list of glorious ways to die.

Hitching up the servant again, I eased out of my little nook. The armor stayed cooperatively in place, the servant remained unconscious, and we made it to the landing without incident. Three steps up toward my goal, and the sound of voices came to me again; male, this time, and coming down the stairs. I scurried back to my concealment—with the servant—and prayed fervently that we would continue to remain unseen, for I had not just picked a stairwell reasonably convenient to the staff area, but a major highway. At least the men talked loudly, so I had a little more warning.

Once again squeezed into the cramped space behind the armor, I held my breath and closed my eyes. Some bit of decorative masonry dug at my shoulder, and I shifted in irritation. This was getting quite ridiculous. Already plagued by passersby, I had no desire to be stabbed by chunks of rock, no matter how lovely and—

Hold just a moment, what was that? My keen ears brought to me the faintest grating noise, and a whiff of air that was different than the rest. Musty, like… a library. Crates full of parchment exuded a similar smell.

Carefully, I turned my head. The crack opening up in the stonework just behind my left shoulder was as black as—well, black. A secret passage. That was interesting, though a wizard could certainly be expected to have secret passages. The question was whether it could be lit and whether the door would lock behind me and leave me trapped. Having already escaped attention thrice, the odds of remaining unseen decreased by leaps and bounds. On the other hand, if the hidden door squeaked or groaned or otherwise gave me away—admittedly unlikely, since a noisy door does not remain a secret for long—I would be caught. However, if the door was a secret, the men coming down the stairs just now were unlikely to know how to open it, and thus the baron would need to be summoned. And if they did, well… I needed to talk to Baron Duzayan anyway.

Giving the masonry a cautious shove, I dragged the servant into the area beyond, and pushed the door with my foot until it was nearly closed, but not quite. A passageway of perhaps six feet opened up into a large area. Glowing warmly, an assortment of glass-corked bottles hung at intervals along the shelf-lined walls. Another sat on the desk, and a pair hung on an iron candelabra. Witchlights!

I had seen these before, and very handy they were, too. And rare, though you wouldn't guess it by the number of them adorning the chamber. I should have one, perhaps even two or three. Easing my servant to the floor, I went to study one of the lights more closely. The bottles were rather too bulky to go lugging about in my waist pouch. I needed something smaller. Glancing about, I spied ink bottles lined up in a little tray on a desk. How terribly convenient. I pulled the cork out of one and was immediately treated to a most obnoxious stench. Maybe they weren't ink bottles after all. A little more rummaging about uncovered a wooden box full of empty glass jars similar in size to the ink bottles— useful things for storing eyeballs and elixirs and other wizardly knickknacks. I made quick use of them. Prying the glass stopper from one of the witchlight bottles, I poured some of the contents into each of three of the empty jars, careful that they didn't escape and go flitting about the room.

Now, witchlights, in case you are unfamiliar with them, rather resemble fireflies, except that—well, no they don't, except for the bit about flickering and flying about. Insubstantial blobs of light no bigger than a thimble, they will burn your skin if you touch them. That, and when left to flit about in the air they tend to disintegrate after a week or two, leaving behind a sad little wisp of ash. Harvested somewhere in the northern regions, the difficulty in finding and catching them makes them rare and, as you can imagine, quite expensive.

With three tiny witchlights in my pouch, I had myself a leisurely look about the room. Along one side stood a work table. All sorts of curious paraphernalia littered its top—decanters and crucibles, pestle and mortar, candles, bones, feathers, jars of nasty things labeled with meticulously written tags. The descriptions meant little or nothing to me. Some of them were written in a language I didn't recognize, and none of them said "Crow's Antidote," more's the pity. A curiously worked knife garnered my acquisitive attention but remained untouched. Who knew what spells a wizard might have wrapped around it? I searched with great dedication through the jumble of goods, but if the antidote to my poison was there, it didn't volunteer itself. Any number of the vials and bottles I sniffed at might have held it, and me none the wiser—a depressing fact, indeed.

The books and scrolls lining the shelves were old, and many of them written in foreign languages which, considering Marketh's reputation as a crossroads of the world, was not entirely unexpected. It was impressive, though, that Baron Duzayan could read so many diverse tongues. Those whose languages I recognized seemed to be about magic (shocking, I know), science, and history.

They served me no purpose and, quickly bored, I sat down at the desk and picked up a sheaf of papers weighted down with an ordinary-looking rock. I did not believe the disguise for even a moment, but it didn't erupt with dire magical spells, and when I turned it about, it continued with its impressive disguise of ordinariness. The letters appeared to be fairly trivial correspondence and hardly worthy of being kept hidden away, but... looking more closely, I discovered that several came from a place called Hasiq something-or-other. The name sounded familiar. Taking out the map the baron had given us, I spread it out on the desk to have a look. Sure enough, that was the name of the wretched little village where he'd said the egg would be found.

My curiosity was aroused all over again. Stashing the map away, I looked more closely at the missives, which were from a certain Magister Ammeluanakar. What a horrible name. The poor fellow. The term "magister" generally referred to the senior member or leader of certain orders, and so I could assume the man with the awful name was just such a one. A quick glance through the sheaf of letters revealed a few reports about the baron's recent activities, mostly of a militant nature—not that such a thing was wrong or even particularly unusual, but as I was eventually going to destroy the baron, the information might come in handy.

With a groan that startled me right up out of the chair, the servant reminded me of his presence and my duty. The unremarkable rock worked well to shut him up again, and I suffered a passing moment of sympathy for the headache he was going to be nursing. It is a tragic thing to be an unwitting victim of circumstance, and the poor fellow would likely never know the part he played in the epic events of the day—nay, in my life!

Undressing an unconscious man is not easy, but I accomplished the task with minimum fuss, and donned his servant-for-the-House-of-Duzayan garb. He wore shoes and not boots, and though I was loathe to trade those, I must, or be unmasked right away. I bound the useful bits of the uncommonly interesting correspondence around one calf beneath the covering of my new pants. The servant was also safely secured; I didn't need him announcing my presence to all and sundry.

It was time to get back to work.

Applying my considerable talent and experience, I went through the room with an eye toward redistributing the baron's wealth into my own pockets. Well, not pockets, precisely, because that would be dangerous and foolhardy. Into my pouch went a purse full of gold coin that came from an embarrassingly large collection, several of the gems I found hidden away in a dusty disemboweled book, and a tiny ivory figurine of exquisite craftsmanship. While there were several other things I might find a market for, I restrained myself lest they were ensorcelled.

The door opened easily, and I spent a moment with my eye to the crack, waiting for the next flock of servants migrating through the stairwell. Now and again I had to wipe from my face cobwebs that I could not see and which should not have been there at all on account of my having passed this way just moments ago. The traffic had died down to nonexistence, but whilst waiting to ascertain that fact, I had some time to consider the situation. Perhaps, just perhaps, it might be to my benefit to keep my knowledge of the secret room to myself—and that meant I couldn't leave my servant there, no matter how amusing I found the notion.

— 6 —
Fitting And Sowing

I did not relish lugging the fellow about, but there was no help for it. Closing my eyes and bowing my head, I murmured supplications to several appropriate gods, checked the stairwell again, then collected the unfortunate lackey. Thankfully, he was no strapping guard. After wriggling him out the door and past the armor, I tried to get him up over my shoulders, but nearly succeeded in toppling us both down the stairs. Grabbing his wrists, I dragged him thumping up the stairs and around the corner to the closet I had earlier espied. It was so full there was scarcely room for the servant, even with his legs propped up on one of the lower shelves. The simple latch took only a moment's work to jam without making the damage look deliberate—a moment in which another servant came tromping up the stairs, humming noisily to himself. I was forced to stand on the unconscious fellow and hold the door closed until the passerby was gone, and it seemed a small eternity until I could dash back to the alcove to claim the rest of my disguise.

Armed with mop and bucket, pouch tucked under one elbow, I began the next stage of my home invasion, which included lifting every small item of decent value that I could find—still searching for my stolen woman. It wasn't as though I was greedy—not about women, anyway. I had avoided women for a long time; they were such a tedious, carping lot, but this particular one was different, and I was not going to let the stinking baron have her, nor think he could get away with such woman-stealing behavior unscathed.

When my pouch had become quite heavy, I found myself another bag and some linens, then made my way to the top floor of the mansion. With my mop and bucket and a cowed expression—and the proper clothing, of course—I had considerable freedom, though not without cost. The bucket was cursedly heavy and I got scolded several times for missing spots and doing shoddy work. Rolling up the baron's unwieldy, expensive carpets in order to do the alleged mopping was a royal pain in the backside, too. I did a slapdash job at each task, for which my taskmasters lamented and threatened to fire me, but with the baron desperate to fill the ranks, they could not expect better. It would take time to find decent replacements for those who had been lost.

There it was again, that hint of tragedy and countless deaths. I took advantage of my temporary position as a menial to make a few inquiries, and discovered that a good number of servants had accompanied the baron on a recent (and apparently long) trip, during which the traveling household had been attacked and all the poor servants killed. It was lucky indeed that the baron and a handful of soldiers had escaped.

Ha. I found it disheartening to discover that I had come so very close to never knowing his annoying lordship. A two inch correction of trajectory by some imaginary archer might have relieved me of much hardship.

A good portion of the fourth floor was given over to living space for the staff, and those rooms were cramped and suffered from low ceilings. I also discovered that the windows were nailed shut, which must have made for horrendous conditions in the heat of summer. It was another exercise in my substantial patience to pry the nails out of one of the windows without making noise and thus drawing untoward attention. Thankfully, with the sun well up the rest of the staff was busy working to make the baron's residence exude cleanliness, efficiency, and—in the kitchens—delectable aromas.

My newly acquired assets were transferred from my pouch to the bag I'd picked up, and I carefully wrapped each item in lengths torn from a purloined sheet in order to protect them. Broken goods were useless goods. The nails from the window, too, went into the bag, as I could not hammer them back into the wood, nor leave them lying about for someone to discover. Humming to myself, I tied the bag tightly closed and lobbed it far out onto the neighboring rooftop. I have a remarkable aim, and the bag tumbled down the slope to rest neatly against a chimney for me to retrieve at a later time—providing that none of the items within were protected by shrieking, bothersome demons. I watched for a little while, and when none appeared I smiled in satisfaction, then made my way out of the room.

As it happened, the shrieking, bothersome mistress of housekeeping accosted me. Viciously. Making my way back down the long, narrow corridor, I turned the corner and nearly ran the woman right over.

"What are you doing up here, boy?" she demanded, propping her fists on her bony hips and glaring at me as though I'd somehow just muddied the entire length of the hall.

I darted her a look. Had she really just called me "boy"? Quickly, I lowered my head in an appropriately submissive gesture. "N-nothing, mistress."

"Nothing? Who gave you permission to do nothing? You don't get paid to do nothing!" She boxed my ears soundly, and I blinked in surprise. The ringing saved me from most of the scolding she delivered, but I made out something about my wages being docked and how I should be more appreciative of my employment. Countless numbers in the streets would gladly trade me places and would doubtless do a better job than I. Then she grabbed at the tool pouch tucked under my arm.

"What is this? Are you thieving? They'll cut your hand off if you're thieving, boy. What is your name? I'll report you myself, I will!"

"No!" My elbow clamped the pouch tightly to my side, and for a moment we engaged in a brief bout of tug-of-war.

"Give it over, you oaf!" she said, and clapped me upside the head again.

"I cannot, mistress!" I wailed, the tenor of my voice aided by an extreme sense of indignation. Such were the eccentricities of disguise. One had to roll with the punches, so to speak, and improvise a great deal. "I am supposed to deliver it to Andari House on Sycamore Street in Copely End. Personally."

"Personally?" The housekeeper glared at me, suspicion in her steely eyes. "Who gave you such orders?"

"I-I don't know his name, mistress." I didn't know the name of every guest, of course, but during the course of the day I'd recognized some of them as gracious donators to my upkeep over the years. "He is a short man with a fringe of white hair and a bald spot. And, um... a wart on his chin." I pointed to the appropriate position on my own much handsomer jaw.

That bit of description worked better than I had hoped it might. The housekeeper's mouth struggled to contain a sneer. "Oh, *him*. I might have known." She recovered her aggression swiftly. "Then why are you up here rather than on your way, boy?"

Why indeed? "I came to get my cloak."

She walloped me again. "There are cloaks by the servant's entrance for such things, you fool. Now be off with you before I take that mop handle to your thick head!"

"Yes, mistress!" I fled down the hall as fast as I could whilst still toting the pouch, my mop, and the mostly-full bucket.

Once clear of the housekeeping harridan, I made my way to the opposite side of the building. The windows there were nailed shut, too, and I spent precious time prying the nails out of another sash. Apparently the baron's magical defenses didn't extend this far, or he need not have wasted his time with anything so mundane as nails. Or maybe he'd tired of would-be escapees from his generous employ setting off his alarms. By way of reassurance, my earlier breaking and exiting had not raised a hue and cry, so I had no qualms about repeating the performance. I sailed my pouch with its precious tools and sundry other items out onto the rooftop next door, handily landing it against another convenient chimney.

From there I descended to the third floor and made my way to one of the bedrooms I knew was in use. I knocked boldly, and when no one answered, I slipped inside. Going directly to the wardrobe, I rifled through the contents until I had assembled myself a new outfit, exchanging the servant garb for a white silk shirt, a finely worked navy tunic, fawn-colored trousers, and a pair of exquisite knee-high boots. They were a little big for me, but nothing an extra pair of stockings didn't fix. They worked, too, to hide the parchments strapped to my leg, which I'd somehow neglected to add to the collection of wealth in the bag now resting on the roof of the adjacent mansion. I blamed it on the harridan housekeeper.

I stashed the bucket and mop inside the wardrobe. Aside from the practical consideration of making it less obvious to anyone casually looking through the rooms, I treasured the imagined expression on the face of the room's wealthy tenant.

Availing myself of a lovely leather belt and sword, I stepped out of the room and nearly got myself run over as a detail of guards clattered past. "Whatever is that about?" I inquired of another of the hall's occupants, a man well into his senior years. The two of us stared curiously after the soldiers.

"I've no idea," he confessed, "but it's the second group in the last ten minutes. Did you not hear the first?"

"Indeed," I lied. I must have yet been on my way downstairs and managed to avoid the others, thanks be to the gods of evasion. "Do you suppose we're under some sort of attack?"

The old man turned to blink at me in dismay. "Goodness, I hope not. Perhaps we should consider... leaving. Just until the mischief-makers are rounded up, you know."

One could only imagine the sort of intrigue that had him wanting to make a dash for it at the first sign of trouble in the residence of his host. "Oh, I'm sure the baron and his men will have things sorted out in no time. He is a very competent man, and his guards are famous all up and down the country for their stellar efficiency."

"Well..." He took off his spectacles and polished them absently on one sleeve of his robe. Ettarian damask, unless I missed my very well educated guess, and worth a considerable amount of coin. The rings on his fingers boasted modest but handsome gems—amethyst, ruby, pearl, and—quite rare in this part of the world—lazurite. The gold-and-pearl pendant he wore around his neck would fetch a pretty penny, too, and make an attractive addition to any collection. Especially mine.

I crossed the hall to stand next to him and peered after the disappeared guards. "I did hear tell of an attack upon Baron Mosson. Quite tragic. An entire troop of mercenaries launched an assault upon his home—right in broad daylight, mind!" The city of Marketh is littered with countless numbers of alleged nobility, and suffers a particular glut of barons—perhaps because they're noble without being *too* noble, and can get away with their alleged nobility without anyone looking closely. I picked one of them out of thin air. I'd heard something about Mosson not too long ago, though the exact nature of it escaped me at the moment. The man had the worst luck, and it was entirely possible to believe nearly any story about him.

"I had not heard!" the old man gasped.

"Oh, yes," I nodded. "The whole thing—well, after the assault itself—was kept very hush-hush, but apparently two of Mosson's cousins and several of his guests were murdered in cold blood. One of his daughters was kidnapped, as well."

"Oh, dear, dear…" he murmured, twisting his hands at his waist. "How terrible. How *terrible…*"

"It is. I don't know whether the daughter was ever recovered. Her father must be distraught."

There followed a small, uncomfortable silence. "Perhaps I should go. I'm sure my wife would not be opposed to an early return from my travels."

"Do you travel often?"

"Yes," he nodded. "Oh, yes. Business and all."

"Your wife must miss you awfully."

"She has never truly been fond of all the trips I must take."

I patted the old fellow on the back, loosed the catch on the chain that held his marvelous pendant, and smiled at him brilliantly. "There you go, then. Go home and see your lovely wife, and I shall make your excuses to the baron myself."

"You would do that?" he asked, blinking at me owlishly. He had forgotten to put his spectacles back on.

"It would be my pleasure." Smoothly pocketing the pendant, I offered him my hand. "Stenlis Throckbottom," I announced, attaching myself to a wealthy and numerous family of merchants.

"Of the Marimore Throckbottoms?" he asked. He had an admirable grip.

"The very same! Do you know us?"

"Who does not?" he smiled. "I am Tarold Rebster. You must give Denil my greetings. Are you one of his sons?"

"Nephew," I laughed.

"Oh, I do apologize."

"Not to worry," I patted his gnarled hand. "There are so many of us that even we have trouble keeping track."

"Yes, well." He nodded. Twice. "I had best tend to my packing."

"Shall I find someone to help you with your things?" I inquired solicitously.

"That would be most helpful. You are a dear boy."

It had been some time since I'd been a boy, but I supposed it was all a matter of perspective. Lord Rebster and the housekeeping harridan both had several decades on me. "It is my pleasure." And so we said our goodbyes and thank-yous and well-wishes for the future, and I went to snag someone to go help Rebster hurry home before he missed his pendant.

In spite of the dismaying crowd gathered downstairs in the hall that housed Duzayan's business office, I had no trouble insinuating myself into his private domain. Easing through the assembly, I availed myself of several particularly captivating bits of jewelry and a tiny knife with a gem-encrusted hilt. A clerkly-looking man guarded the door, peering anxiously down the hall with the rest of the sheep—er… guests and associates of the baron. I bumped into him rather hard, which dislodged him from his post, and turned to scowl at a large man in a crimson coat.

"Some people," I muttered under my breath, then turned to the startled clerk. "So sorry, I didn't mean to run into you. What's going on, do you know?"

"I—really can't say," the clerk murmured, looking suspiciously at the red-coated fellow.

"We're not under attack, are we?" I asked in a voice that wasn't quite quiet. It had the desired effect of startling nearby gawkers, and the information quickly spread through the crowd.

"Oh. Oh, no!" the clerk exclaimed. "No, not at all."

"Under attack?" someone inquired. "Are we?"

"What's happened?"

"Is there fighting? I'm sure I heard fighting…"

"Entirely possible," I put in, adopting an anxious look. "It wouldn't be the first such thing. Did you hear about Mosson?"

"Mosson!" someone exclaimed, and just like that, rumor and speculation came to my rescue. The gods truly do watch out for me. While the clerk frantically tried to calm people, I slipped into the baron's office and closed the door.

Taking in a deep breath, I puffed out my cheeks and let out a noisy sigh as I glanced about the inner sanctum. Or maybe it would be more correctly labeled as his "outer sanctum," as the hidden room was much more "inner" than this. While I had admired the room and its contents on my previous visit, circumstances had altered my perspective. More bookshelves decorated the space as well as a desk fronted by two exquisitely crafted chairs of the Kegharti Dynasty, a sideboard with several expensively crafted wine decanters, the globe I had previously noted, and many other valuable items that simply begged adoration and relocation.

Unfortunately, I had no feasible way of transporting them, so I settled for helping myself to some of the wine, drinking straight out of the decanter rather than risking further poisoning from the goblets set on an engraved tray nearby. Who knew what preparations a wizard made for unwanted guests and enemies? I dragged the globe over to the desk to examine at my leisure. It was a beautiful thing, cleverly pieced together with seams too well joined to discern. Perfect scrimshaw delineated all the countries of the known world, outlined mountain ranges and described bodies of water. Brown dye worked into the scores defined the delicate grooves. Tiny, flawless gems marked the seats of power. It was perfect, it was unique, and I wanted it.

As wondrous as the thing was, it couldn't occupy my attention forever, and I eventually went to fetch a book from the baron's well-stocked shelves. Seated in his chair, which was delightfully carved with all manner of birds and would have looked quite impressive in my own study, I propped my feet up on the desk and settled to reading *"The Compleat Adventures of Iastysuir Knirinarn, King of Namende"*—wherever Namende was. I couldn't find it on the globe, and thankfully didn't have to pronounce the count's name aloud. In any case, the book held my rapt attention for three entire chapters and part of a fourth before the door to the office opened.

I marked my place with one finger and looked up to give Duzayan a winning smile. "Busy day?" I asked.

A muscle in his cheek twitched as he closed the door behind him. "I might have known you had something to do with it."

"I can't imagine why. I'm supposed to be long gone."

"And yet, here you are." The decanter I'd set near to me on the desk received a considering look, then he went to the sideboard to pour himself a drink. He had no qualms about using the goblets.

"Where are they?" I asked, referring to the ladies I had spent so much time and effort looking for.

"Not here," the baron returned, and whatever seething thoughts he'd been entertaining disappeared behind a knowing smile. "As I'm sure you're well aware by now. And your misplaced heroic delay could prove to be— shall we say "painful"?"

I should like to have leaped up and beat him about the head with one or two of his perfect decanters. As it was, a knot clogged my throat. What if Duzayan punished Tarsha for what I'd done? Suddenly, the jewelry secreted about my person seemed foolhardy in the extreme. Still, giving him the slightest inkling what I might think or feel would be poor strategy on my part. I lifted the decanter and took a swig of wine too exceptional to treat so casually. Setting it down, I reached for a daintily carved reed pen. Only someone as rich as Duzayan would spend his coin decorating something so disposable. I turned it around in my fingers, then tapped it with apparent absence on the edge of the desk. "Neglecting this little visit would have proved more so."

"Oh?"

I nodded. "You gave us money and a map, but no antidote for your clever little poison."

He appeared pleased. "You do not disappoint me." Going to a cabinet behind his desk, he removed a small vial. How utterly vexing to discover it was so close. "I am glad sentiment hasn't clouded your good sense."

Remaining on the opposite side of the desk, he set the container down and slid it across to me.

I held it up to the light. A silver-colored cylinder, it was decorated with miniature leaves around both top and bottom. The cap, which screwed on, provided a loop through which to pass a chain or cord. "How does the poison work?"

"Very simple really. With the aid of a small spell, it will remain in your system until your scheduled return. Two tiny drops of the antidote per day will keep the poison from growing and spreading throughout your body. There is, by the by, enough of the antidote to last four months exactly. When it is gone and there is nothing to retard the growth of the toxin, it will spread quickly. You will be nauseous at first. The nausea will become progressively worse and more painful. Then your muscles will begin to disintegrate. Your death will be fairly slow and wildly excruciating." He smiled, delighting in his sense of theatrics and horror. He was exceedingly enamored of himself.

"So it has been growing all through the day."

"Indeed."

"And what if I had not come back for the potion?"

"I would have been grossly disillusioned, and you would die."

"And you would have had to engage the services of someone else, thus wasting a valuable commodity. And here I thought you were efficient. Smart, even." Uncapping the vial, I took a sniff. It smelled strangely like mushrooms. Dubiously, I tipped it up to allow one drop to roll out onto my fingertip. It looked like muddy water and tasted horrendously bitter.

The baron watched with patent amusement. No doubt he'd planned the flavor carefully. "If you were too stupid to request the antidote—or even the nature of the poison—you are too stupid to be in my employ."

Capping the vial and tucking it away, I snorted a small, indelicate laugh, though I felt not even one iota of humor. "A test, then."

Duzayan shrugged, and I closed the distance between us, hiding my horror in a careful examination of the wizard's elegant clothing. I rested one finger on a lacquered and gold button, automatically calculating its worth. It would feed me—comfortably—for at least a week, and seven more of them paraded down the front of his velvet tunic. "Very nice," I murmured.

He moved around the desk and took his seat, his expression ever-so-faintly smug. "You really should be going," he reminded gently, setting his elbows on the desk top and steepling his fingers.

I nodded, wondering if he could read or sense in any way the sheer hatred directed his way. If not for Tarsha and the need for the cure for the poison, I would dearly love to see him burst into flames on the spot. "Supposing I actually return with this mythical dragon's egg, do you plan to cure me or kill me?"

One elegant brow lifted as he considered, then he shrugged. "That rather depends on you. Your talents have a great deal of potential."

I couldn't help but bristle at the insult. I would not stand for it. Except... I didn't have much choice. "You are offering me a partnership?"

He laughed. "Careful, Crow. You fly a very fine line."

"I don't work for anyone," I pointed out, bridling my indignation.

"On the contrary, you work for the highest bidder."

"As an independent contractor, not a common laborer."

"You would do well working for me," the baron said, a musing look on his features.

"Or, on the other hand, you would do well working for me."

He waved a dismissive hand. "You couldn't afford me."

"No?"

"If you had that kind of coin, you wouldn't need to be... contracting."

I offered him my best, most charming smile. "On the contrary," I mimicked. "I have been doing this for a long time. If the highest bidders are paying me, I won't be running out of coin soon. And if I am collecting for them, why not for myself as well?"

Duzayan's eyes narrowed, and a sliver of fear stabbed through me. Foolish Crow, taunting a wizard.

"And what items of mine have you collected whilst scampering about beneath the very noses of my guards?"

I held out my hands. "I haven't got one single item from your truly magnificent collection of rare and precious things, although," I pointed to the globe near his chair, "I would really like to have that." I did not lie. My new collection resided safely on a neighboring rooftop, not on my person.

"Empty your pockets," he said.

I made a show of rolling my eyes, and upon the desk I set an emerald ring and two small but precious bracelets. Then I turned my pockets inside out to show there was nothing more.

He looked at the jewelry for a long moment. "Do you know who these belong to?"

"Not a clue."

"I think you should leave before you get into any more trouble."

"I don't suppose you'll tell me the components of the poison in return for those?" I asked, nodding at the jewelry.

"In return for those, no. In return for the egg, possibly."

"Ah." I wondered if my smile was as faint and lackluster as I imagined. "And Tarsha?"

"Bring the egg," he shrugged carelessly and took a sip of his wine.

"You are not very easy to bargain with."

"I don't have to be."

"True enough," I sighed, and turned to go. My hand was on the door latch when Duzayan spoke again.

"One more thing," he said, and got to his feet to return to the small cabinet from which he'd retrieved the antidote. He held out a small, black leather bag.

I looked at it suspiciously. "What is this?"

"Consider it a gift."

"Ah, yes, because you are so kind and generous, gifting me with beatings, prisons, poison, kidnapping, insults…"

Duzayan chuckled and tossed the bag at me, and I caught it automatically. "I have not yet decided if you are brave, brash, or something else altogether, but I find your attitude… refreshing."

"Then you should more seriously consider increasing the possibility of exchanging witty badinage in the future." Loosing the ties, I peered inside the bag. Inside was a plain white ball about the size of a walnut.

"It is a Beisyth Web," he explained. "You may have need of it in the future."

A web. Right. He acted as though I should recognize the significance. I hadn't the least notion, except to hazard a guess that it was enchanted.

"Though I hope you don't need it, it may save your life."

Another stupid piece of wizard tripe accompanied by more wizardly evasion. Perhaps I could get a decent price for it on the streets. "Very well." I tucked it into my tunic. "Pardon me for not promising to return it as soon as possible. Circumstances, you know."

"I have confidence in your abilities, even if you don't." He waved a hand and returned to his place behind the desk.

"My abilities are not in question." How *did* one steal something from a dragon? "Your sanity is."

"We shall see. Be good now, and be quick, Crow."

Be good. Ha. I could be very, very good. He would regret the day he ever crossed my path. The door banged shut sharply behind me.

A wizard was not to be trusted. Was I poisoned or not? I knew only one way to find out. I would simply not take the draught. And in the meantime, it would do me well to pay my favorite apothecary another visit.

— 7 —
When It Rains, It Pours

"Wake up." The shake I gave Tanris's shoulder was none too gentle. I still could not decide why I bothered. In the employ of various city and regional governments, he had hunted me for years, chasing me up one side of the empire and down the other. And the first thing he'd done in our so-called partnership was to collapse like a piece of parchment in the rain. I had the coin and the map, did I truly need him?

When he did naught but groan, I slapped his beard-fuzzed cheeks. "Tanris. I am leaving."

He pried open red-rimmed eyes and stared at me as if I had sprouted an extra head. "I thought you left me," he croaked with an exhalation of dragon breath.

I withdrew to safety. "What, without saying goodbye? I have better manners than that. I'm leaving now, though, so goodbye." In spite of the fact that he'd always been a thorn in my side, I had always respected him. He was doggedly determined and fairly clever; all in all, a decent opponent. The disappearance of his few endearing qualities put a damper on my opinion. As I turned away from him, my foot knocked into something, producing a gentle clunk. Going down on one knee, I fetched not one, but a threesome of bottles from beneath the bed. They were ample reason for him to sleep all the way through a night, an entire day, and then another night. I straightened and *thonked* him smartly on the head with one, though not hard enough to knock him unconscious or break the bottle, however tempting.

He sat up abruptly, clutching his abused noggin. "*Ow!* What was that for?"

"For your wife, and because I've been wanting to do it for years." I tossed the bottle onto the bed next to him and went to collect my gear, such as it was. Rather than attempting a probably dangerous shopping trip in the middle of the night in the city that never slept, I'd opted for a good meal and some well-deserved sleep of my own. In a more perfect world, I would have had a week or so to recover from the indignities heaped upon me whilst tucked away in Duzayan's dungeons. Thus far, I had enjoyed exactly one full night's sleep since my release.

"Where are you going?"

"If you recall," I said with as much sarcasm as I could muster, and it was a wagonload, "we have been volunteered to become the stuff of legend. In order to do this, we are supposed to hunt down a mythical dragon for its mythical egg to give to a mystical—and clearly deranged—wizard. And after we have accomplished this wonderful quest, he is going to kill us."

"Kill us? Why would he do that?"

Such a fantastically idiotic question was worth the minimal effort it took me to cross the small space again to flick my finger sharply against the side of Tanris's head. "Will you pretend for just a moment that you are intelligent?" I snapped. "Try to put the clues together, my dim-witted friend."

He frowned and rubbed his head again. "Stop yelling."

Snorting, I held up one finger. "Duzayan is a wizard. Did you know that?"

His mouth worked for a moment or two, then he finally nodded his head. "Yes, I knew."

"Let me guess—he swore you to secrecy."

Another nod. "People don't much like wizards. He couldn't let his talent become well-known."

I snorted again. "Safer for him, of course, and easier to dupe unsuspecting fools like you." Finger number two lifted. "He's kidnapped your wife and my lover, threatened them both with death or worse, poisoned me, and asked us to steal something he deems highly valuable." It occurred to me suddenly that Duzayan must be afraid of me, though not Tanris. Why else would he poison just the one of us? Or perhaps Tanris wasn't really marrid and the kidnapping of his alleged wife had been an elaborate ruse to buy sympathy for my new "partner." Safest to keep such observations to myself. "After going to such lengths to acquire this incredibly valuable *egg*, by what logic would he leave the witnesses alive? We might steal the egg back. We might blackmail him. We might start some vicious rumors that would upset his careful plans or reveal his filthy *secret*."

Tanris's already pale face blanched further. "We must turn him in to the authorities."

"Oh, yes, brilliant idea. That will, of course, assure the safety of the women," I went on in an acid tone. "And Duzayan will happily hand over the antidote, which is good because I am extremely enamored of breathing."

"Then what are we going to do?" he asked like the sodden lump that he was.

He disgusted me. "I advise you avoid getting drunk when things get difficult. It severely hampers your already limited thinking ability. In the meantime, we are going to leave this unsavory hovel in favor of—Where do you live?"

Picking up the bottle, he held it with both hands against his chest, his expression utterly doleful. "Yesterday, I was Captain of the Guard and living at House Duzayan."

I might have expected as much. "Day before yesterday, but never mind. We're not staying here. Put your boots on." I swung my new knapsack, sweetly heavy with yesterday's booty, over my shoulder and headed for the door. Tanris stomped his feet into his boots, grabbed his coat, and stumbled after me. I was certainly not going to take my arch-enemy to my own quarters, but there were plenty of other places where we could put up, and I had the wherewithal to pay our way. "I need you to draw a map of the underground portions of the baron's citadel—everything you know. Closets, sewers, passages to other parts of the city, secret doors. Everything."

"What for?"

"So we can look for Tarsha and—What's your wife's name?"

"Aehana. He won't have kept them there."

"As ex-Captain of the Best of the Best, do you have any idea where, then?" His former position ought to give us some kind of advantage. One could only imagine the knowledge entrusted to the leader of a guard force. When and why had Tanris shifted from the government and into the private sector?

Outside, the wind was bitterly cold. I turned away from its bite and headed down the street toward a more savory area in search of transportation.

Tanris waved his hand in a wild gesture. "They could be anywhere, Crow! In the city. Out of the city. Across the gods-forsaken ocean, for all we know!"

I leveled a warning finger at him. "Pull yourself together, man! Now is not a good time for you to go from "thorn in the side" to "pain in the rump." You can help me, or I can leave you so fast your fuzzy little head will spin."

Grim-faced, he shoved his hands in his pockets and stalked along beside me. "You wouldn't dare."

"Try me."

"You need my help traveling through the wilderness."

"I'm not going through the wilderness." I lifted my hand to shield my eyes from the wind, then whistled for the first hackney I saw.

"Of course we are. We must, Crow. The mythical egg, remember? The women? Your life?"

As the carriage pulled up, I gave the driver directions, then swung inside, well-pleased to escape the wind. Tanris was right behind me. "*Mythical* being the key word, here, Oh Wise One. We have better things to do with our time than going traipsing off across the empire on a wild-goose chase that will take us away from both the women and the antidote."

Tanris put his hands back in his pockets and glared out the window while the carriage rocked along.

"What if it's not an actual dragon's egg?" he asked after a long moment of sullen silence. "What if it's a figure of speech or a—a similar description for something else entirely? Say, an item that looks like an egg, or the answer to a riddle?"

That was the Tanris I had come to know and appreciate over the years of our association, a man like myself, quick-witted and not confined to the obvious. He had come up with the perfect answer to our utterly impossible question, and at that moment I cheerfully hated him.

"I'm not going to argue about it any more, Tanris." Draining my tankard of ale, I thumped it down on the battered table of the dull little public house in which we found ourselves and folded my arms, distinctly tired of the badgering that had lasted all the way through our meal. "I'm *not* trekking off across the country on a wild goose chase."

We had originally set out to rent a room from which we could work to free the women. Tanris—as I well knew but had not experienced in such close quarters—was a dog with a bone. The quicker Tarsha and Aehana were freed, the happier I would be. And now, several hours later, we had neither room nor women. Instead, we had spent the better part of the morning contending the best course of action.

"You're not being reasonable."

"So you have said. Repeatedly."

"Well, it's true." Tanris leaned back in his seat, copying my posture. A hard-looking man with a shaven head, his nose appeared to have been broken on several occasions. The glower he gave me might have intimidated a lesser man. "And if you're going to complain about repetition," he sniped, "I swear if I hear the phrase 'wild goose chase' one more time, I will stuff your tankard down your scrawny throat."

"Then you agree, it would be best if we cease and desist this line of conversation."

He drew a deep breath and let it out very slowly. One could almost see his temper rising. "Let me break this down into something more simple for you."

"Not another word." I glowered and narrowed my eyes dangerously, but that did not dissuade him from proceeding.

"If we stay here in the city, we *might* recover the women. Your apothecary *might* duplicate the potion which *might* extend your life. If we go after the egg, then we have a tangible item to use in exchange."

"And I am still dead." More glowering on my part.

"You might like it."

"I might take you with me."

Tanris shrugged and gave me a cheeky smile. "Taking on a dragon, we'd be heroes."

"Martyrs. What fun is fame if we're not alive to enjoy our celebrity?" I asked.

"Is it going to be fun dying anyway, taking Aehana and Tarsha with you, and knowing you could have bought their freedom with one little dragon's egg?"

My chest tightened, and the stuffy air of the public house suddenly seemed fresh and clean. I would do anything to save Tarsha, and although overcome for a moment by the thought of actually exchanging my own life for hers, I kept the emotion from my companion. "Fine," I said, contriving an off-hand manner. "How long is it going to take us to get to the dragon's dire lair?"

Years of interrogating suspects and prisoners had inured Tanris to surprise—most surprise, anyway. One perhaps ought not count the emotional shock of seeing his wife weeping at knife point. My sudden capitulation only made him look at my eyes intently, first one, and then the other. Then he reached into his jerkin and promptly ruined my theory about his resilience. His eyes widened in horror.

"It's gone," he said in a strangled voice.

"What's gone?"

"The map. I had it right here! I put it *right here* just after Duzayan gave it to me!"

Priceless panic filled his rough features, sorely tempting me to let it turn his scanty hair gray. The trauma, however, might very well lead to another round of drinking and moaning about how he'd let his wife down and was a miserable failure. May all the gods protect me. "This map?" I asked, producing the folded parchment from my pouch.

"You stole it!"

I snorted. "I did no such thing. It is ours, and I took it for safekeeping while you were so soused you couldn't even stand up."

"I wasn't that badly off." He frowned again, as if getting drunk was my fault.

"If you weren't, you'd never have let me get away with it. Besides, better me than some common thief."

"You are a—"

"Ah-ah…" I waggled a cautionary finger, my voice soft. "Do not insult me, friend Tanris."

His mouth curled in a most-unattractive sneer. "But it's all right for you to insult me?"

I considered briefly. "In a word, yes." With baited breath I waited for his witty rejoinder.

Instead, he reached for the map. "You're insufferable, Crow."

"Isn't that what inspires you to devote so much time to trying to catch me and lock me away forever?"

He did not answer, but unfolded the parchment and smoothed it carefully, his brows furrowing as he studied it. While he worked out the details of distance and time, I pulled out the little white ball Duzayan had given me, turning it over in my fingers. It looked like a ball of thread that had been painted. The paint did not entirely cover the minuscule, hair-like ridges that went round and round the thing. When I squeezed it, it gave just a little under the pressure, but otherwise remained unfathomable.

Rolling it in one hand, I looked about the room, idly considering which patrons might unknowingly contribute funds to our upcoming journey. This particular tavern—dull, as I have already pointed out—didn't exactly cater to people with heavy purses, although, to be sure, there were always those like myself who had funds they didn't flaunt. Those sorts presented a more challenging target. Modest in dress and manner, they invariably concealed their ready money in places other than the obvious coin purse.

A few tables over there were a pair of rough-looking fellows in homespun. Common laborers, likely. Further on was a man in fox fur and brilliant green velvet. Both the color and the glimmering collection of rings on his fingers were gaudy and tasteless. He talked loudly and made free with the serving maid when she came to refill his tankard, as though he had unquestionable authority to do such a thing. Now and then I could catch a whiff of the heavy scent he wore, even at this distance, and cast him as a vulgar social climber with more money than taste or sense. He might have contributed a healthy amount to the Journey Fund but for the threesome of men sitting across the table from him. The trio were outfitted in leather and steel and hard features. Mercenaries, the lot of them, and too much trouble for me to want to bother with.

Past them I beheld a modestly gowned but very well-lubricated young woman with attractive features, a pretty blush, and a pair of young men with obviously lecherous intentions. They looked to be merchants—or perhaps the sons of merchants—and therefore somewhat promising, at least for what I was contemplating, if not in the matter of the lady's doomed virtue.

"Do you ride?" Tanris asked, interrupting my scheming.

"Ride what?" The following silence from my dour and moody companion could only be described as pregnant. I turned a distracted look on him to find him regarding me with patent disgust.

He smiled faintly and without the slightest trace of humor. "I'd say that four months is a fair estimate of the trip there and back. Optimistic, even."

That was not news I wanted to hear, though hardly unexpected. I could not even begin to comprehend what a two-month-long ride in the deep of winter would be like, never mind the obvious lack of civilization we would have to look forward to. Dragons, after all, don't take up residence in elegant apartments in the upper districts of cultured cities like Marketh. Collectors of falsely named dragon's eggs, however, ought to have better sense. At least we could enjoy Spring on the return trip—flowers budding, birds singing, poison creeping inexorably through one's system, and all of that.

As I contemplated the heartbreaking turn my life had taken, another group of thirsty patrons made their way inside. Victims of recent precipitation, they crowded near the large fireplace, immediately inflicting the rest of us with the odor of warm, wet wool. One of the newcomers pushed a wide-brimmed hat off his head, revealing a shock of red hair and a scarred, hawkish face. Raza Qimeh! Him, I did *not* need to see.

"We should be going," I said, getting to my feet. I needed a hat like Raza's. Why didn't I have one? It would surely be handy now, but I would have to make do with my cloak. And Tanris.

"Now?"

"You did say four months was a generous estimate. You're not going to argue about it now, are you?" I speared him with a reproachful look.

"No, but—"

"Fine, then let's be on our way." I did not give him opportunity to quarrel, but wound my way between the tables and toward the door, scooting around behind Raza and his lackeys, and manufacturing a struggle with my cloak in order to obscure my face as I slipped past them.

"Crow…"

I could happily have crammed a loaf of bread down Tanris's throat at that moment, but I pretended not to hear him as I sauntered out the door. Running would draw attention I didn't want—not that the use of my name hadn't. I would have to have a word with Tanris about flinging it around so freely. Later.

"Did he say *Crow?*" someone asked behind me. I left the door open, ostensibly for my companion to follow, and pulled up the hood of my cloak. Outside, a dreadful deluge filled the gutters and drains, running in rivers down the cobbled street. Wind drove icy sheets of water straight at me, prompting an instinct to turn my back and protect myself. Instead, I clutched my cloak around me, ducked my head, and hurried straight into the storm.

"Crow!" Wind and rain muffled Tanris's voice.

As soon as he came abreast of me, I grabbed his arm and steered him across the street. "You said we need horses, no?" I had to shout over the ruckus of the storm as half-frozen raindrops the size of hen's eggs beat the living daylights out of rooftops, overhangs, the street, and us. "I know a very fine horse trader over in Harley Court. It's not far!"

"It'll wait until the storm lets up!" he shouted back, and tried to pull his arm free.

I was having none of that, and dragged him into an alley. An interception by Raza and Company would only delay our departure. That, and they might try to break me into little pieces. Some people held grudges for inordinately long periods of time. Some years previously, before branching out into his "protection" services, he and I had been competitors, or at least he liked to believe so. The truth was that my talent exceeded his, a fact irrefutably proven when we both took jobs—from different clients, mind you—to liberate the same item. I got to the scene just barely ahead of Raza, skipped away with the precious jewelry, and left him to be arrested by the City Watch. He was not well pleased by that, though while he'd been caught trespassing fair and square, they couldn't prove that he'd stolen the jewelry, and naturally I was long gone. Things were complicated further by my involvement with a woman, but truly, I had no idea at the time that Raza had his lumpy little heart set on her! Is it any surprise that she didn't share that tidbit of information with me? She was a woman, after all. And Raza, well... we never had the kind of relationship that allowed for discussion of romantic involvements.

The very narrowness of the alley gave us some protection from the rain, and I hustled Tanris along. We still got incredibly drenched. "How many horses are we going to need?" I asked him. "Do you know where we can purchase a wagon?"

"A wagon?" He yanked at his arm again and I let him go, taking the moment while he was being all indignant to cast a quick glance over my shoulder. The rain ruined visibility in the darkened alley, but I saw a movement against the dull light of the further end.

"We can't take a wagon, you flappin' fool," Tanris went on. "The place we're going is supposed to have dragons. Dragons don't need roads, wagons do. No wagons."

"Surely there's a road."

"If you'd like to call it that, feel free."

"You've been there before?" I prodded curiously.

"There? No, but places like it, yes."

"Then you can't know for sure that there's no road."

I did not intend for him to stop to glare at me, but that is exactly what he did. "No," he ground out, "I don't know for sure that there's no road to that particular little village, but I do have some map reading skills, and I do know the country we have to travel through."

"Excellent!" I beamed at him, took him by an elbow and got us moving along. We popped out the other end of the alley and I took a left, pulling my cloak up around me as I headed into the wind again. Soaked through, at least the cloak kept the sleet from perforating my skin which, all in all, I found better than the alternative. "Have you done much traveling in the wilds?" I inquired, more to keep him engaged than because I cared particularly.

"I was a scout in the army."

"Really?"

"No, I just made that up to entertain you," Tanris snapped.

His unexpected touchiness about that aspect of his life intrigued me. The future offered plenty of opportunity for ferreting out such secrets, though I could hardly imagine the two of us cozying up by the campfire, sharing the stories of our lives.

"What's the name of this horse seller?" he asked.

"Fyrka Valiscu, do you know him?"

"Never heard of him. Have you robbed him?"

"Men are hanged for stealing horses, Tanris, don't you know?"

"Men are hanged for stealing other property too, but that's never stopped you. In here," he announced and shoved me unceremoniously through a bright red door and into the din of a crowded tavern. I squawked in surprise, but a fist wound in the back of my cloak kept me from stumbling.

"We already had our midday meal," I protested, and turned right back toward the exit, yanking my cloak about me. His hands on my shoulders stopped me.

"I'm not going back out in that, so save your breath." Looking past me, he gave a solid push and pointed. "There's some room over there by the wall."

"How comfy." I had little choice but to follow him through the mass of stinking, steaming bodies, and soon we were the proud tenants of a narrow space against the wall. Surely everyone on this block and the next had sought refuge in this particular—and particularly second-rate—tavern. A pair of windows flanked the door, obscured by the press of bodies. "How are you going to be able to tell when the rain's let up?"

"Soon as folks by the door start heading back out."

Wasn't he clever? And what were the chances that no one else would be heading in? The ever-watchful gods must have their little jokes. Wise to their ways, I kept one eye on the front door and one on the door that led to the kitchen, and a very good thing I did, too. It *had* been Raza behind us in the alley, and his timing was impeccable. As he and two of his men came in from the street, Yahzir—his trusty second, and a man of rather extreme notions, notably in the matters of persuasion—appeared from the back way with two friends.

"We should go now," I told Tanris.

"Not until the rain lets up," he repeated, and muttered something most uncomplimentary about the gods and my heritage.

I would be offended later, although Tanris's pigheadedness begged argument. I refused to give in or call unwanted attention to us—or worse, to me. So I did the only thing I could. "Fine," I said. "Then let's get something hot to drink."

"Let's not."

"Aren't you cold?"

Tanris rolled his eyes, heaved a sigh, and waded toward the counter. Strategically, I kept him between myself and Yahzir, and my head down in the hopes Raza would overlook me—with the help of the fickle gods. I couldn't keep it down all the way, of course, as there were personal belongings amongst the crowd to rearrange. First and foremost, I regained possession of the map, clutching at Tanris and swearing as I ostensibly tripped. And just like that, the map went from inside his jerkin to a cozy place down my shirt, right next to my skin.

"Watch yourself," he complained, and steadied me.

"I have no problem doing that," I informed him with some asperity. "It's the big feet belonging to other people that sometimes trouble me."

A nip here and a tuck there, and soon the fabric of mayhem was sewn. The disquiet of confusion erupted around us as people discovered the redistribution of their effects. What I really needed was something gaudy and obvious. I left off my reorganization for a moment, both to throw off suspicion as Tanris and I moved through the crowd and to look for a suitable mark.

"What will you have?" Tanris asked, actually making it right up to the bar.

"A mug of kaffa would be lovely, but unlikely in a place like this." Impossible to get drunk on the "wine of the bean," as it were, and this did not appear to be a house that would cater to such diversity. "Mulled wine? Ale? I'm not picky."

"Ha."

While Tanris tended to the business of giving his coin away, I checked the progress of Raza and Yahzir, who had sensibly chosen not to give their prey an obvious advantage by limiting their combined search to one side of the room. *Now* would have been an opportune time for one of the gods of extravagant belongings to put in an appearance. I calmly helped myself to a hammer suspended from the tool belt of a carpenter. I felt briefly sorry for him having to do that kind of menial labor in weather such as this, but it was just as well that he did and that it was storming, else he would not have sought shelter and would not have stood so conveniently close to me, happily swigging his bracing ale before heading back out into the tempest to earn a living for himself and his bevy of children.

He must have felt the weight lift from his belt, for he started to turn toward me. "Think we'll be so lucky as to find a table?" I asked Tanris in a loud voice and, turning around as though to look for one, I smoothly lobbed the hammer right at the lovely russet waves crowning Raza's head.

— 8 —
Head To Toe

Who expects to have a hammer thrown at them in the middle of a crowded tavern? Certainly not Raza, and he had barely time enough to turn his head to avoid getting bashed in the eye. He bellowed. I would have, too, quite frankly. I was quite pleased, however, when every eye in the room turned toward the noise he made, including those of the poor carpenter who looked quite capable of taking care of himself in a brawl, or perhaps even starting one. Even Tanris turned to see what was going on, a tankard in either hand.

Accepting mine, I sniffed and sighed. Just ale. Ah, well. I took a swallow, edged behind Tanris, and watched for our cue to leave. Not unexpectedly, Raza put up quite a commotion. The man had the constitution of an ox, for while the blow certainly staggered him, it didn't knock him out—or even down. Blood ran down his forehead, and his face turned an uncomplimentary shade of red that clashed brutally with his hair. "Who did that?" he asked, retrieving the hammer with a growl. Waving the erstwhile missile in the air, he glowered in our direction, but the burly carpenter stood handily between us.

"Hey!" he hollered. "That's my hammer!"

I perhaps should have advised him that it might be wise to keep quiet on that little detail, but I didn't. Raza pointed, and all five of his men converged on the unlucky devil. Well... maybe not too unlucky. He had friends, and they were only too happy to doff their coats, push up their sleeves, and show Raza what friends were for. It might have made an interesting fight to watch, but this was just the diversion we needed.

"You know this fellow?" I asked Tanris, all innocence.

"Looks familiar, but I'm going to say no, not well enough for this sort of thing." He drew back a step or two, a sour expression on his features.

I ducked an elbow drawn back to deliver a punch, sidestepped, and took another swallow of my ale—which wasn't as bad as I'd feared. "What do you say we get out of here before the City Watch gets involved?"

A woman next to him—nearly as broad as she was tall—hurled a tankard into the brawl, spraying half a dozen fighters with her brew.

"We're witnesses," Tanris pointed out, raising his voice over the din.

May the gods of patience preserve me. "To what? I didn't see how it started, did you?"

"No, I just heard Red hollering." He waved in Raza's direction with his tankard, then tipped it up for a drink. "But I know some of those who didn't do it."

Raza, in the meantime, used the hammer to good effect, which only reinforced my determination that we get away as quickly as possible. The carpenter, too, was making some decent headway in his attempt to reclaim his weapon. Tool, I mean. Yahzir hadn't made it to Raza's side before he and his companions became embroiled in an offshoot of the general melee, which put him firmly between us and the back way out.

One last quaff of ale, then I abandoned the tankard on the counter and tugged at Tanris's sleeve. "I'm leaving," I said, leaning close to his ear to holler at him. "You stay if you want, and talk to the Watch."

"You can't go," he hollered back, his frown full of fierce moral rectitude.

I smiled and patted his arm. "The City Watch might want to talk with me for a little more time than I can dedicate just now, if you know what I mean." My words had the desired effect, and Tanris's eyes widened. His mouth opened as though to voice further argument, but then he nodded. Together, we made our way around the room's outside edge and to the door. Once there—and it took no little work dodging fists, flying chairs, projectile tankards and so forth—I paused to look back at Raza. He and his men were firmly embroiled in a fantastic battle unlikely to release them soon. Maybe the City Watch would further detain him. It made me smile to picture him tucked away in some dank, moldy little cell.

Outside, the rain continued to pound mercilessly at the world. "Hey, look, the storm has let up!" I smiled with false cheer, hooked one arm around Tanris's neck, and thumped his chest with the other hand—and so the map was returned to his keeping again, and him none the wiser.

He shoved me off and glared as he pulled up his hood. It hardly mattered; we hadn't dried out in the least from our last foray. "Where's that flappin' wonderful horse seller of yours?" he growled.

"Are you sure you don't want to find someplace else to wait out the weather?" I asked solicitously. The rain plastered my hair to my face and ran down my neck underneath my shirt, but I pulled up my hood anyway.

"We're already wet; let's just do this," he grumbled and turned to head up the street, entirely missing my triumphant smile.

The purchasing of horses, saddles, bridles, saddle packs, supplies to put in those packs, and all the various and sundry items required for a lengthy trip into the wilds was not only horrendously boring, but time-consuming. Tanris's patience stretched thin with my many questions but, boring or not, I refused to risk being stuck somewhere outside the realms of civilization with no guide and no clue about what I was doing—not that several hours spent going from shop to shop provided a reliable education. Tanris was only too happy to inform me that the rain and sleet of the coast was usually snow in the mountains. Thank the gods of adventurers, we were not actually going into the mountains themselves, though he assured me the elevation was plenty high enough for frozen white stuff. I cannot begin to tell you how many times I wondered what was so significant about this "egg" that it couldn't have waited for decent weather.

My traveling companion cheered me endlessly with the promise of dry, crisp flatbread; dry, chewy jerky; dry, but not moldy (because it was too cold) cheese, and a generous supply of kaffa, but no honey to sweeten it. Before he could depress me utterly I left him to go get my own gear. Some of my tools had been lost in the escapade prefacing my stay in the baron's dungeons, requiring me to spend time and coin replacing them. I also disposed of most of the goods I'd lifted from Duzayan's residence. The wilderness held a dearth of people who could appreciate such fine collectibles, much less own coin enough to purchase them from me. I bought a waxed leather tube a little longer than my forearm in which to keep the baron's illicit letters, then made my way to the apothecary's shop.

The news was not good. He needed more time to attempt to deconstruct the potion, and more of the potion itself to use as a comparison. His advice? Take the antidote and pray to the gods. For his continued study, I surrendered enough blood to make me giddy.

In a daze, I left the shop. I walked for a while, going whichever way my feet took me and the crowd pushed me.

I sat in one of the gardens at the edge of the market.

I walked again, unable to sit still.

Utter despair alternated with hope until I came to the conclusion that despair offered me nothing at all, while hope could at least provide opportunities for my future. The gods, after all, loved me and I did not believe they would desert me now. Somehow, I would survive. On a sudden whim, I bought myself a hat. Wide-brimmed like Raza's, it boasted a low, flat crown and a beautiful white feather curling over one side. It cheered me somewhat and it would perhaps distract Tanris from interrogating me too closely.

I had scarcely stepped out into the street with my handsome new acquisition when I was abruptly and rudely accosted. Two hulking pieces of manhood caught me by either arm, and I nearly lost both my hat and the burlap sack of supplies I carried. Lifting me right off my feet didn't trouble either of them, and while they whisked me off down the street, I took a moment to recover my breath, my composure—more or less—and to study their identities. "Do I know the two of you?" I inquired politely while they plowed through puddles I would have chosen to go around. The first splash caught me rather by surprise, but I had the forethought to lift my feet for the second. No sense getting wetter when there was an alternative.

"Raza wants to have a chat with you," the bruiser on my right informed me.

"Jolly for him. Would you be so good as to put me down? I think I remember how to walk."

"We'll help."

"You're too kind. Really." I looked from one to the other, but they showed no sign of responding to gentle persuasion and we were making good speed down the street in a direction I had no desire to go. So I held on tight to my belongings and stuck my foot between the legs of the less chatty fellow on the left. He went down in a heap, and I went with him, rolling half onto him. The other man swore and scrambled, trying not to fall, too. I helped him out as best I could by swinging my sack at his head. There were a pair of grappling hooks in there, a climbing rope, metal cleats, and other sorts of paraphernalia a thief might find handy on the job. It knocked him backside over teakettle, which was rather satisfying and alarming at the same time.

Both my delight and my worry at the damage a hook might have caused were arrested by an arm around my throat. I do not know what the fellow could have been thinking. I had just flattened his companion, and I still had the bag in my hand. The obvious course of action was to clobber him, too.

"Help!" I choked, on the off-chance any helpful passersby might step forward. "Thief!" There was no need for anyone to know I was probably more guilty than my assailants. Since the hold on my throat didn't slack at all, I clonked him again. He made an awful noise, but he let me go, and I clambered to my feet. The first villain was out cold, but the second one moaned hideously and clutched his bleeding head.

I looked around. An elderly couple held onto each other and stared uncertainly at the scene; a pale-faced delivery boy stood there gawking; and a pair of shabby, middle-aged workmen stopped. None of them said anything as I retrieved my hat and banged it on my leg to shake off the moisture. The beautiful feather was irreparably damaged and dirty. Reluctantly, I tossed it on the ground as the elderly couple turned and hurried away.

"You—you all right, mister?" the boy managed. At least he pretended to care that I might have received some injury in the scuffle with a pair of men twice my size. Speaking of which, the conscious one was making an effort to get to his feet, and the look in his eyes promised exquisite pain should he manage to get his soggy hands on me.

"I might have *died*, attacked like that," I muttered in a voice loud enough for the others to hear. "Bloody thugs. Think they can get away with attacking a helpless man on the street. In broad daylight, mind you!"

The boy looked nervously at my assailants, then up and down the street. "Want I should run and get the Watch?" he asked, brave soul.

Rather than answer him, I shook my bag at the brute currently glaring at me. "You better stay right there, mister!" I advised him in a blustering voice. If I should ever be forced to make a change of career, I could do admirably as an actor. Of course, he was having none of it, growling fiercely as he staggered upright. Blood ran down the side of his face, his eyes fairly glowed with rage, and he looked quite awful. I took several strategic steps backward. "I mean it!"

"I'm gonna hurt you, little man," he snarled. Pulling himself together, he lumbered toward me.

"Run, mister, run!" the boy advised with fervor, and wasted no time taking his own advice. Up the street he scampered, ducking down an alley and disappearing from view.

The workmen, only slightly less speedy, turned their apathetic noses away from the scene and beat a retreat, leaving me alone with one possible corpse and a fairly lively and vengeful bully.

I settled my new hat firmly on my head. It was wet, but then I was too, so it hardly made a difference. Only a few short minutes in my possession, and already it was achieving character. "You'll have to catch me first," I pointed out. "And while I realize you just barely did that, the chances of repeating the feat are now drastically reduced." I quick-stepped backwards down the street while the clod lurched toward me with grim, purposeful determination. It didn't faze him in the least that he was walking oddly.

"Come here," he ordered, and I paused long enough to stare at him in astonishment.

"Yes, of course I am going to fling myself right into your arms so that you can beat me to a pulp," I shot back, my voice dripping with sarcasm. "I have, in fact, been dreaming of this moment my entire life."

He grinned at me, and I wish he hadn't. I must have knocked him soundly in the mouth, for his smile was a gory shade of crimson. I took three steps back for every one of his forward. "Do I *look* like an idiot?" I inquired.

"Matter of fact, you do."

Rude, just plain rude. I chose to ignore the insult; he was likely suffering the ill effects of a concussion. "You really should go find yourself a healer or a surgeon." I gestured toward his face. "You're bleeding."

The grin turned to a ghastly sneer, and I decided that it was an auspicious time to vacate the area entirely. "Well, it's been nice chatting with you. Give Raza my best, and good luck with—that." I waved at his face again. He growled and lunged. I spun around and ran. I was faster than he.

— 9 —
Unavoidable Detour

"Tanris, what are you doing?" Of all the things I might have expected to find Tanris doing, I would not have guessed to find him sitting atop the baker's roof.

"What does it look like?" Nails he clenched between his teeth mangled his words. Balanced carefully, he wriggled a roof tile straight, set one of the nails, and lightly tapped it into place.

"Roof repairs?" I ventured.

"There, see? That wasn't so hard."

"Why?"

He looked at me critically. "It leaks."

A fantastic aroma wafted all up and down the street. What is there that is so utterly appealing about the smell of baking bread that even a man with a full belly will pause in whatever he is doing to appreciate the scent for as long as possible? "Yes, well, let the baker tend to that himself, or hire a roofer."

"The baker is not a he."

Ah, so. And Tanris a married man…

He shifted a bit to continue his work. "Besides, I had nothing better to do while I was waiting for you." He implied that I'd been gone forever, deliberately dragging my feet.

I debated telling him about Raza and Friends. "I'm here now. Let's go."

"When I'm finished here, Crow." He set another tile into place.

I couldn't resist a look up and down the street, half expecting the appearance of hulking brutes with swords. "How long will you be? Have we got everything? Are the horses loaded?"

"It'll take as long as it takes." He paused to lean an elbow on one knee and look at me for the better part of a minute. "Do you see those animals tied up to the rail, there? Kind of big beasts with long legs, long tails and manes? A mane is the hair that grows along their necks."

Funny. Two of them wore riding saddles and bulging saddle bags. The other two—Well, I would have to assume that the oiled canvas bulges with legs were the pack horses.

"Those are the horses we bought a few hours ago. You might want to get to know them, just so you recognize them next time you see them."

Was that sarcasm? I peered up at Tanris in the growing gloom of evening. Rain-threatening evening, no less. "They're horses. Brown horses. All brown horses look the same." I could swear I heard him snort, then he turned back to his work. "Which one am I to ride?" I asked.

"The one with the white socks in front and the snip on her nose."

"Snip?" I could figure out the socks perfectly well, but there were two with white marks on their feet. I deduced that I wouldn't be riding the pack animal, and went to look at the other, which wore a patch of white on its muzzle, lopsided and ridiculous-looking. I looked at the other mount, a much prettier animal to my way of thinking. "What do you say we trade?" I called to Tanris.

"No." And a very firm *no* at that.

I shrugged. There were more important things to argue about than which horse I was going to ride to make my escape from the city, and I'd choose my battles. So I wound my bag up tightly and fastened it atop of the pile of other things behind the saddle. "Are you ready now?"

"No."

"Daylight is fading, and we need to make the most of it." I examined our surroundings before I went back into the street where I could look up at him again.

"We've got the horses and the supplies. I trust you've got what you need. I'm helping out with this roof. Then we're going to find food and lodging, get a good night's rest, and be on our way in the morning."

Utterly logical planning except for the tiny detail about Raza Qimeh and the small army he employed. "Fine. Then let's go look for someplace to stay. It's not exactly warm out here, you know." I pulled my wet cloak about me more closely—as though that was going to help at all—and hunched my shoulders. Now that I was no longer fighting or running I was beginning to shiver.

"Do you always whine like this?" he asked to the accompaniment of another scrape and some more banging. As if he had any room to ask such a question.

"Not if I'm warm and dry and well fed."

He snorted again, but didn't say anything, and I bounced to keep myself warm while I looked up and down the street, just waiting for my nemesis to appear. After an age, or maybe only a quarter of an hour, Tanris finished and made his way down the ladder. I would have gone inside to get some of that bread that so tantalized my taste buds, but someone had to keep watch. I waited another age while he put the ladder and tools away and went inside to talk to the proprietor. Bless the gods of the unjustly persecuted, he brought a bag of bread out with him and handed me a thick, hot roll. I nearly sobbed in relief. Without a word, he untied three of the horses and mounted up, leaving me to follow suit, and we were on our way.

We got an entire four blocks on the path to food, heat, and a warm bed before someone slipped out of an alley to trail along behind us. Another block, and two more joined the first. I scratched my cheek and turned forward again, saddle leather creaking underneath me. "Tanris, don't look now, but we're being followed."

Commendably, he didn't whirl around to see if I was telling the truth. "How do you know?"

"There are three men behind us. Well, technically, it's two men and a woman. And they're on horses."

"What do they want you for?"

"Me?" I stared at him in astonishment. "What makes you think it's me they want?"

Tanris shrugged. "I don't know, your criminal tendencies maybe?"

"Look, there's another one," I said as we passed a cross street. Where were all the regular people that usually filled these streets? Just because it was dark outside and freezing to boot…

"Four now? And probably more circling around to get ahead of us."

"There's a cheering thought."

"Well, it's what I would do."

"Have done."

"Yes. Do you want to talk to them?"

"Not particularly. You?"

"Not really. Turn here." He turned down a street that lay in the opposite direction from the one the fourth man had come down, crowding my horse to do it. It responded placidly enough, in spite of the way I clutched the reins in surprise. The pack horses followed along without any protest, and I looked back over my shoulder. Tanris led us back around toward the baker, started off in another direction, then abruptly stopped.

Three men stood directly in our path. One of them slapped a cudgel against his palm. Another casually inspected the sharpness of his blade, and the third propped a nasty-looking mace against his shoulder. Behind us the other four closed in speedily. "I don't think they want to talk," I pointed out.

"Doesn't look that way," Tanris agreed, securing the lead ropes of the packhorses to his saddle. "I'll take the two on the right, you take the one on the left."

"Fine by me." The less fighting I had to do, the better I liked it. I pushed my hat down securely on my head, then untied my lethal bag of hooks and cleats. My knives would do me no good in this case. Tanris, on the other hand, had a most impressive sword, and he slid it out of its sheath with a theatrical hiss.

"We get through here," he said, "head down to the riverside. If we can't lose them at the docks—"

"Maybe we can take passage on one of the boats." It was a reasonable plan, and plenty of people frequented the docks, day and night.

"Hopefully, we don't have to do anything that extreme."

"What, and blowing through a trio of lethally armed men isn't extreme?"

Tanris pulled a face as he looked at the other four coming up behind us. "Less than it will be in a minute."

"Let's do this, then," I agreed, putting more confidence in my voice than I felt. Give me a castle to break into, rooftops to fly across. I was much more at ease with those than with hand-to-hand battle. Tanris took me at my word. The flat of his sword struck my mount's hindquarters, and we were off like a bolt shot out of a crossbow. I heard another smack and a high-pitched whinny, but I was too busy trying to stay in the saddle and bring my inelegant weapon to bear to worry about what else was going on. The fellow with the cudgel had been designated as mine, but I made every effort to steer my frightened horse around him.

His grin was knowing, his stance ready. I spared the briefest of glances toward the other two, but they ignored me. I yanked the reins hard to one side and my trajectory abruptly changed. The cudgel-bearer was no longer, waiting to knock me clean out of the saddle; he was directly in my path. To leap backward would send him crashing into the swordsman, so naturally, he threw himself forward. Unfortunately, that took him out of harm's way from my savage sack, but it didn't keep him from getting knocked sprawling by my horse as we thundered past. And, since I had the sack in my hand, I struck out at the swordsman. The solid thunk of contact reassured me that I hadn't missed. I didn't wait to discover the results. My horse carried me through and we thundered down the street. A terrible racket came from behind me—screaming and banging and more screaming and hoofbeats on cobblestones. It was enough to wake the dead, or at least the City Watch, and in this case that might actually be a good thing, but one can never be certain. They might take it into their minds to arrest Tanris and myself, though we were clearly the victims. The best thing to do was to run. Fast.

As we got closer, the noise of the docks grew, voices and sounds carried to us on a wind that grew even colder by the water. By the time we hit the street that ran parallel to the water, the horses were at a flat-out run. We skidded and careened on the icy cobblestones as we came around a corner. Dock workers and sailors scattered, yelling and swearing at us. I'm not sure what my horse crashed into, but my leg smashed against something brutally hard. Excruciating pain shot up my shin and stabbed my knee, but there was no time to stop and look, never mind tending to an injury. I saved screaming for later and gripped the saddle in a desperate attempt not to fall.

Tanris somehow kept the pack horses on their feet, and after a few moments' confusion all four animals bunched together and trotted smartly down the street, white showing in their eyes and ears working madly. We plunged headfirst into the constant busyness of the docks and Tanris handed me one of the packhorse leads.

"Tie it to your saddle—tightly, Crow!—and fall back a bit. Follow me. Keep up. Do you hear me?"

"I hear you just fine," I glared, though my throbbing leg offered him some fierce competition. I even knew what he was about: four horses traveling together were easier to spot than two separate pairs. I secured the rope and waved him ahead, then twisted about as best I could to gauge the progress of Raza's men. Unfortunately, we hadn't lost them in the brief conflict and the mad dash. Five of them spread out across the wide street, moving together as they searched for us, pushing roughly through the crowd. I took off my hat and jammed it into the cords holding gear to my saddle, then glanced around for a likely-looking fellow wearing a coat. Three subjects and a generous amount of coin later, the cloak Raza's men were looking for walked away on someone else. My new coat was just as damp as my erstwhile cloak, and smelled like fish. I kept a sharp eye on Tanris during the exchange, and when he turned down a street ahead, I marked it and went past, taking the one that came after.

Tanris waited for me on the corner. Only one block away from the docks, it was unmistakably quieter. He gave me a sour smile and nodded at my change of attire. "I thought I'd lost you. Good idea."

Of course it was a good idea. It was logical. If someone you didn't want to find you was looking for you wearing a green cloak, you switched it for a brown coat.

"Let's not wait for them to find us again." I nudged my horse into motion, teeth clenched against the pain in my leg. Tanris fell in beside me, and we took a twisting, zigzagging course through the lower districts that edged the river, then headed into the merchant's quarter and through an area of residences scattered with small shops, livery stables, and a few parks. It all looked very domestic and tranquil, but we looked often over our shoulders. The rain, bless the gods of weather, became our ally. Heavy clouds blocked the light of moon and stars, and the steady drizzle obscured vision.

Twice more that night we narrowly avoided Raza's men. Once just before we left the river district, and once again when the convoluted path we took managed to bring us up behind them. We were passing through an area thick with warehouses and distinctly thin on people when I caught sight of them. On such a night the group looked out of place, and there was absolutely no mistaking that fellow with the cudgel. I reached for Tanris's sleeve, but he was out of reach. "Ssst…"

His mount stopped abruptly, and his pack horse a heartbeat later. I gestured to a space between the buildings and we eased into it, careful of the noise of the horses' hooves on the street. The footing there turned abruptly to thick, oozing mud, which quieted steps but made the horses uneasy. Tanris silently soothed his mount, rubbing its neck and then doing the same to the pack animal. I followed suit on the off chance that he knew what he was doing. If petting the great beasts would save me from unwelcome attention, I'd get down right then and there and break out a brush or two, mud or no mud.

We waited until the others passed from view, then a little longer. Moving at a slow, mostly quiet walk, we went in the opposite direction, keeping close to the buildings as much for their deeper shadows as for some protection from the rain.

It was not a night for talking. Danger and weather assured that, and we spent an interminable time slogging through the unrelenting deluge. When Tanris finally spoke it startled me. "Your friends have seen us with the pack animals, and they seem clever enough to figure out that we're leaving town. The city's too big for them to put a watcher on every road out, but that won't keep them from asking questions and figuring out which way we've gone. Especially if they want you bad enough."

"You're determined they're after me, aren't you?" I asked, irritated by his unjust speculation.

He shrugged eloquently.

"I assume you have a plan?" I inquired, rather than pursuing the topic of his irreproachable virtue. He was right, of course, about what Raza's men would do, and I knew from personal experience that they would follow the trail until there was no trail to follow. The best and most thorough way to throw them off the track would be to take to the river.

"Leave the city on the east side, ride south and come in again to the west. Find passage upriver to, say... Fesefi, where we can cut across country. Maybe get a day or two travel time back."

It was somewhat disconcerting to have Tanris following my line of thought so closely. Sometimes a crow's path isn't perfectly straight. "Best not to stop anywhere before then," I agreed, and rubbed my aching leg. Dismounting when the time finally came would likely land me in a graceless, moaning heap, but I was so tired and cold right now I just didn't care. All I wanted was to be still and warm and dry.

None of those things happened with particular speed. It took nearly forever to cross the city, another eternity to ride around the southeast edge, cross the river to further throw off the hounds, and then we made our slow way up the river itself in search of passage, stopping and starting until all six of us—men and horses—were ready to drop from fatigue. I was too numb for relief when the captain of *The Nightingale* agreed to take our horses on board, and I hadn't the energy to protest when Tanris haggled the price down. He had no idea how unlikely it was that we would run out of coin, and it was probably best to let him remain in ignorance.

As predicted, my dismount was less than elegant. A death grip on the saddle held me upright, but only just. A pair of deck hands came to lead the packhorses aboard, and I just stayed still, clutching leather and waiting for the fire in my leg to die down to a bearable flicker.

"You all right?" Tanris asked, bringing his horse near to mine to give me a critical inspection.

I nodded. "Fine."

"Don't lie. What happened?" His voice was unexpectedly curt. In the dull light of another rainy day, he looked gray and tired. He needed a shave.

"Horse banged my leg into something. I'll live."

He studied me for the space of several breaths, then wiped the back of his hand across his mouth. "Can you walk?"

I didn't have the slightest desire to experiment, but there was something about his grim expression that said I needed to. The sudden awareness of what a broken leg would mean filled me with frigid apprehension. I forced myself upright and, teeth clenched, I took one small step, putting my weight on the injured leg. It gave beneath me with another stab of pain that forced a gasp out of me. Tanris's hand around my upper arm kept me from collapsing, and I clutched at the leather gear he wore, finding a handhold in the buckles.

"You, there!" he called out over my bowed head. "Come get this man below decks, and send someone to help me with the horses! Do you have a healer on board?"

I have no memory of how I made it down the companionway and into a narrow berth in a crowded, dark little cabin, but it was a relief to lie down —clear until someone peeled off my boot. I let out a strangled scream and lurched upward to beat my assailant off, only to bash my head into the bunk above me. My attacker had no trouble at all pushing me back down onto the bed. I heard something about "headache" and "less troublesome that way," but my ears rang too loudly to make out the rest.

"Here, take this," someone said. "Hold it on your head."

"What is it?" I asked, words slurring.

"Ice."

"Ice?"

"From the river." There was only ice on the river in the coldest years. Sometimes chunks floated downstream, but it had never frozen over. Not here on the coast.

"Here, what's that on his hand? Blood? Sir, did you get hurt anywhere else? Sir?"

A gentle shaking made me pry my eyes open, and I looked at the hand that was being wiped with a clean, damp cloth. I did not want damp, I only wanted to be dry. It struck me that I was going to have to take off my wet clothes. "No... No, it was just the leg. Tanris? I grabbed Tanris."

"Sir?"

"What?"

"No, the other sir."

I was too confused to do more than stare at the two blurry figures crammed into the room with me. Even that was too much. I closed my eyes and left them to do what they pleased.

Tanris didn't let me sleep right away. The cruel swine shook me awake—most violently—and made me strip off my wet clothes, claiming he didn't want me to catch my death. It was a miracle several times over that I hadn't already. In just one night I'd escaped from Raza's lackeys six or seven times, spent countless hours soaking wet and playing keep-away in the rain, then knocked myself on the noggin so hard I'd probably be dented. To his credit, however, Tanris had managed to conjure up a mug of hot soup, and he made me drink all of it.

My leg, in spite of its loud protestations to the contrary, was not broken. Black and blue from the ankle to above the knee, it hurt something fierce, but the gods had protected me yet again. Best to stay off of it and let it mend, the healer said, and I agreed wholeheartedly. Unfortunately, our schedule didn't allow for weeks of lazy recuperating.

Tanris had been lucky. A vicious slash across his side—imperfectly deflected by his leather armor—might easily have been a fatal stab to the belly. The swordsman he had so fearlessly taken on had been a bit more of a challenge than either of his other comrades. Tanris remained reticent on the subject, though I couldn't imagine why. Most warriors enjoy bragging about their skills, at least enough to gain the respect they believe they deserve, whether merited or not. Tanris was not like them, and it made me curious.

We spent most of the first day sleeping, and why not? *The Nightingale* offered little in the way of entertainment, and it was too cold to spend much time on deck. Between naps, I daydreamed about Tarsha. Thinking about how I'd been forced to leave her was unproductive, so I fantasized about the little white-washed house I would buy her in the islands, the garden we'd grow, the sailing we'd do, and the children we'd have. A boy and a girl. Tarsha would dance only for me, and I could safely and comfortably retire. Ah, what a dream…

Nausea made my convalescence uncomfortable. I thought it a result of pain, or perhaps the herbal tea the healer gave me, but it worsened by leaps and bounds. Even more alarming was the advent of cramps. Duzayan's words rang in my ears and much against my will, I had to face the fact that he had not deceived me on this particular count. Tanris, thankfully, left me alone to rest, only checking in on me now and then. I was able to conceal my sickness, though he did once lay a hand on my forehead to see if I had a fever. He announced that I was clammy and my color was poor, and promptly went to fetch the healer. I took the opportunity to dose myself with the bitter antidote. Not long after, I began to recover. The healer, none the wiser, gave me another unpleasant brew to down, hoping to fight infection.

When I ventured from my berth the next noon, the first mate entertained me with lessons about the current and then educated me about proper caulking techniques, which was nearly too exciting for words. After dinner I cheerfully fleeced him and two of the other crew members in a game of cards. Lucky for them, Tanris came along and stared at me for an unforgivably long time, or they might have lost even more. It was not that I didn't think I could cheat while he was watching, but he made my opponents nervous. We played a few more hands in which I let them win back a little coin and confidence. "You're welcome to join us," I invited Tanris, but he declined, saying he didn't play.

"Do you want me to teach you?" I asked, idly shuffling the cards as my last opponent drifted away.

"I don't play," he said again.

"Because…?" Sitting at the narrow trestle table in the galley, I laid out an arrangement of the single-player game, Blind Path.

"Because I dislike what men become when they get greedy."

I don't know why he looked at me so pointedly. "And what about passing the time? How do you do that?"

"I keep myself busy."

He was so marvelously stoic and focused. I could understand how he might make a first-rate soldier. "And if the busy work runs out?" I asked, counting and turning cards, moving them from one column to another. He didn't say anything, and when I finally looked up I found him watching me rather than the cards, as most men might have done. His face was still and silent, revealing nothing of what he was thinking.

"We'll be another three days on the river," he said at last.

"Yes, I've been to Fesefi before." I went back to playing my game and attempted to ignore the way he stared at me.

"Do not steal from the crew, Crow."

One brow lifted, but I did not look up at him. Three cards I counted out, then slowly played each in its proper place. "Do you think me a fool?"

"A fool, no; a risk-taker, aye."

"Some risks, yes. I find it invigorating, but I haven't stayed alive this long by choosing them carelessly. And you needn't speak as though taking chances is immoral. You take them as well. Everyone does."

"Not everyone does it so he can lord it over other men." His voice was mild, but carried a tone of censure.

"You have no idea why I take chances, Tanris. Maybe I don't think what I do is chancy at all."

He made a small sound of dismissal in his throat, then straightened from his lean against the wall. "Maybe I know you better than you do," he said.

He could not possibly know me better than I did myself, but his words had me thinking for a long time after he'd gone. I played several more rounds of Blind Path, but it did little to distract me. Being a thief wasn't just a choice, it was a vocation. It was a talent. For centuries, the priests had been drumming into the heads of their followers the admonition—nay, the divine law—that to waste a talent was to affront the gods. Each of us, with our diverse gifts, was a part of the greater balance. Without people like me, people like Tanris would be out of work.

— 10 —
Tall Tales

The next days were every bit as tedious as the first which, all things considered, was probably an advantage. Pain and immobility are surprisingly exhausting. I slept a lot, took my foul-tasting medicine every morning, played cards with the crew members, swindled the same—modestly—and learned from another passenger more than I ever wanted to know about whaling off the chilly coast of Uburrh and the multitudinous uses of the parts of said whales.

I also discovered what occupied Tanris in his free time. The ship's captain wouldn't allow him to help out with the crew's duties, so he checked and polished the horses' tack, checked and polished his weapons—a fairly large collection—mended his mangled armor, and sorted through our supplies, reorganizing and redistributing them—a pointless exercise, seeing as how we'd just purchased new gear and Tanris had expertly loaded the pack saddles the first time. When he had done all that could conceivably be done, he read.

Frankly, I wouldn't have taken Tanris for a scholarly man, but I discovered him in the cabin we shared. He'd taken the musty, straw-filled mattress from one of the unused upper bunks and used it as a cushion against the small table attached to the wall between the two sets. Our collection of horse blankets covered him where he curled up in his cozy little nest, reading.

"What is that?" I asked, squinting and twisting my head to get a look at the title as I sat on my own bunk, mindful now of the low clearance.

"A book," he said without looking up.

"So I see. What book?"

He read for another moment or two before peering at me over the top. *"Tales of the Amber City.* You've heard of it?"

"The Amber City? Yes. I had no idea you were interested in fables and children's tales." I winced as I adjusted my leg more comfortably. What I wouldn't give to soak in a hot bath for an hour or so.

Tanris watched my struggles without volunteering to help. "I had no idea you were so well-traveled."

"I've been a great many places, I'll have you know." I pulled the blanket up around me, but it left my feet exposed.

"So you've been there."

"The Amber City? Of course not. It doesn't exist, except in the minds of dreamers and desperate academicians attempting to anchor their flagrant flights of fancy in their own selfish interpretations of reality." Gathering the blanket up again, I held onto the edge and tossed the bulk of it foot-ward, then smiled at my success.

"If you've never been there, how can you say with absolute certainty that it does not exist?"

I wriggled myself into a semi-comfortable position and tucked the poor excuse for a pillow beneath my head. The berths aboard a boat built for river transport are not exactly spacious. Narrow boxes nailed to the wall, they could use considerably more cushioning. Luckily, they didn't have lids. "I have been to one of the places it was reputedly located, and it was certainly not there. Scholars, historians, and explorers have been trying to prove its existence for years, and they have come up with nothing more than vague interpretations and conjectures."

Tanris lowered his book to study me thoughtfully. "So… In a couple hundred years when some scholar comes across an obscure reference to an allegedly notorious criminal going by the ambiguous name of "Crow," and there is no obviously marked grave site, memorial, or structure to commemorate his life—will he not have existed?"

Try as I might, I could fabricate no logical argument. "Can we not make it a well-told legend rather than an obscure reference?" Something dug at my hip where it pressed against the board. Recalling the hard, knobby ball Duzayan had given me, I took it out of my pocket, turning it over my fingers. I'd meant to sell the thing in Marketh, but Raza had upset my plans. At least I could be happy it didn't weigh much and didn't take up a lot of space.

He gave me a sour look. "You'll have to work much harder on your reputation. Perhaps you can write a book." He looked back at his own. "You should probably start now."

"Now? Why now?" I squirmed into a slightly better position. Tanris, in his cramped corner, somehow managed to look comfortable.

He turned a page. "If you don't die from poisoning within the next few months—or from any of the other hazards we're likely to encounter on our journey—I suppose you might write your stirring autobiography from a gaol cell."

I gave him a narrow-eyed look. "I have no intention of going to gaol."

"Mmm. And I have no intention of letting you go free."

He certainly had a way of putting a damper on a conversation. "Do you imagine you can catch me again?" I asked. "It took you years to do it the first time. Maybe the next time will take even longer."

"In case you hadn't noticed, you are not exactly free."

"You can see things however you like." Pocketing the Web, I turned away from him, signaling an end to the conversation. That I would rather die than go to gaol seemed a foolhardy thing to claim, so I kept my mouth shut. There was a very real probability that I *would* die. If the baron's poison didn't kill me, the baron would put every effort into doing the job himself, I was certain.

Eyes narrowed, I considered my companion in a new light. What if Duzayan was paying Tanris to assassinate me? The plan was beautiful in its simplicity: as Duzayan's sworn man, he would accompany me and "guard" me until I had the dragon's egg. The fake kidnapping of his wife, if it was indeed his wife at all, had been arranged merely to get me to lower my defenses by promoting sympathy for him. And then, when I least expected it, *ssrriikk!* One of Tanris's blades would bring an untidy end to my too-short life.

That certainly put things in a new perspective, and it wasn't a pretty one. I could always part ways with Tanris in Fesefi, but he knew where we were going and could probably get there faster, even if I regained possession of the map, which I didn't foresee as a difficulty. Our destination—a place with the ridiculously lengthy name of Hasiq jum'a Sahefal—was little more than a village, and avoiding him there might pose problems. I did have to wonder that such a remote and inaccessible site was so craftily constructed or guarded that Duzayan needed a thief of my caliber to infiltrate it.

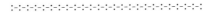

"What are those?"

I blinked eyes bleary from reading manuscripts in the paltry light of a single, swinging lantern. "Letters."

Tanris's jaw worked. Evidently he didn't much like his own sarcasm exercised on him. "Whose?"

I toyed with the notion of stringing him along a little further. "You didn't happen to bring me some tea or kaffa, did you?" I asked.

To my surprise, he held up a mug. He didn't hand it to me right away, and I thought for a moment he meant to keep it for himself and have his own little joke, but after a lingering hesitation I could not possibly miss, he crossed the small space of the cabin and handed the drink over. "More of the healing stuff."

"Ah, yes, knitting bone and sinew for optimal health." I set my reading materials aside and swung my legs over the side of the box. Er... bed. The effort wrung a grimace from me. I missed the luxurious convention of a table and chair. And plenty of light. "Thank you."

"The letters?" he pressed, foregoing any comfortable small talk.

"Mmm. Communications between his supreme ugliness, Baron Duzayan, and friends."

"Are they supposed to help us find the egg?" Perching on the edge of the bed beside me, he picked up one of the papers.

"Hopefully." I drank my tea while he read. Someone had added an extra dollop of honey, which made the tea nearly palatable.

"Duzayan didn't give these to you, did he?" he asked suspiciously.

"Not that he's aware. Shall I give them back?"

He glared.

"It's an interesting assortment. Some are between him and a certain army captain concerning the rerouting of supplies and troops."

"He's not attached to the imperial army."

"A few hundred gold pieces are involved. I've heard gold can sometimes be used to purchase loyalty."

"Yours?"

"Maybe." I flashed him an artificial smile, and he glared harder. "Another of the baron's engaging friends controls a small fleet of ships based on Reandi Island. Should we be surprised that he's consorting with pirates?"

"I knew that."

I rolled my eyes. Of course he did, he worked for the toad-sucking louse. "You can skip those intriguing chapters then and go ahead to the highly suspect missives between him and two lords sitting on the emperor's High Council. In the margin of one is a list of names, all crossed out. You might recognize them. A few of them belong to noble houses. There's also an intriguing discourse written by one Magister Ammel-something of the Temple of Nadimesh about moon phases, rare ingredients and a library. Why, when there are so many beautiful combinations of letters, do so many people choose to give their children unpronounceable names?"

"Is that why you opted for Crow?"

"Beautiful, don't you think? Simple and evocative."

"If you like noisy, thieving birds."

"Clever and charming."

"Right. You know, I've just figured out the connection. Crows steal things. You steal things. You fly the notorious straight course—from treasure to treasure." He flipped through some of the other letters. "Is there anything in here about the egg?"

"I don't know if I should tell you if you're going to be rude."

"How would you like to be stuffed in a barrel to be transported to Hasiq?" he inquired conversationally.

"Since you put it that way, I haven't come across anything about the egg, but I haven't finished reading yet. When I was in Marketh I heard a story about a lot of Duzayan's men being killed recently. What do you know about that?"

"He was ambushed."

"Unsuccessfully, alas. Do tell?"

"He was moving to take over another barony, only his ally in the coup switched sides. Duzayan lost. Got an arrow in the shoulder for his troubles."

I couldn't believe how close my fantasy with the imaginary archer had been. "Were you there?"

"No." If he frowned any more intensely, his brow was going to end up on his boots. "You can decipher this?" he asked, holding up one of the letters from the magister.

"Some, but it doesn't make sense."

"Maybe it's in code."

I sipped my tea. "Yes, if I was a cleric I'd certainly code all my letters."

"You would if the two of you were plotting something illegal."

"Priest robes do make a pretty good disguise," I mused. "Incredibly, hardly anyone ever suspects them of wrongdoing."

He flipped a page. "That's one of the most obvious tricks in the book."

"Really? Because I got away from you twice that way. Once in Halim City in the Gilahabai, and—"

"You did not."

"Did so."

He finished reading the page before he responded. "You're unbelievably childish."

"You're a sore loser."

He peered at me over the edge of his paper. "Remind me again which of us was the victor in our last encounter?"

"Hmpf," I replied elegantly.

Trying to put together the pieces of Duzayan's activities, I found myself irritatingly restless, and before long I abandoned the cabin. I took my blanket topside, wrapped up in it, and made myself comfortable on the poop deck. From there I could watch the shores creep past and mull over the fact that a man could probably walk faster than the ship moved. How this route might gain us time eluded me, though the comfort of a deck easily beat sitting in a saddle. I had spent most of my life on the central coast side of the Bahsyr Empire, where the land was more densely populated than the interior and therefore more lucrative for a man in my line of work. I'd crossed the Rahiya Strait any number of occasions, but again, I tended to spend more time in the big cities than I did the smaller villages and hamlets. The latter served well when I needed to lie low for a while, but rarely provided much opportunity for profitable work.

I knew enough about the geography of the Empire to know that the relatively warm coastal lowlands stretched toward the interior before rising abruptly into the mostly uninhabited Kerdann Moors. A few large cities dotted the trade routes, and my work occasionally took me to them but, for the most part, vast tracts of wilderness filled the area. The Aiobi Plains took up the south, along with miles and miles of farmland. Farmers make terrible suppliers, and they rarely know how to cook more than the simplest of meals. Beyond the Moors are the Darya Mountains —craggy, rocky country plagued by snow, wild animals, and tribes of bandits. A constant source of trouble for the peaceful citizens of the empire, their incursions require regular and extensive patrols by the Imperial Army. I was more than happy to listen to stories about the Daryas and leave them entirely off my travel itinerary. The coastal lowlands, called the Gilahabai Strip, were much more hospitable, which is one of the reasons I seldom left them.

Beautiful as the passing view was, it could not keep me entertained indefinitely, and I must have dozed off—a feat aided by the unexpected appearance of the sun and its warming rays. The sky had been overcast all morning, so no one expected the break to last, but by the middle of the afternoon the sun had burned the clouds away and left me basking in its sweet warmth. The shouts of the steersman woke me, giving orders to lay on the oars as we came into the docks at Fesefi, a sizable town bustling with the activity of fishermen and merchants, farmers and vintners. The fertile river valley produced grapes and tart Taharri plums for wine. The latter was something of a luxury item, the serving of which was a symbol not only of one's social status but the depth of one's pocket. Many of the nobility and well-to-do owned country homes here, where they retired when the hustle and bustle of Marketh became too overwhelming, or when the political climate—which was constantly shifting—became a little too hot for them. It was a good place to collect items from private collections, although one must expect those collections to be most carefully guarded.

The animals were the first to be unloaded, so we had not long to wait before we were on our way. The open market abutted the noisy, smelly dock area, and Tanris stopped to procure us a dozen ridged, jade green winter squash.

"I have a stop to make before we leave town," I told him, watching a pair of boys running in and out of the stalls. Likely, their pockets would be full of illicit goods by the time they reached the far side. I had half a mind to follow their example.

"Where?"

"The Sularem Temple." While he stared at me with an unreadable expression, apparently the most common one he wore, I made my way through the market booths where herbs and incense were sold. An oblique glance over my shoulder revealed Tanris trailing after me. I made my purchases and he said nothing until we had mounted and set off through Fesefi's streets.

"You are serious," he said, and it was not a question.

I saw no reason to reply, and with the ease of familiarity, I made my way through the narrow, winding streets to the temple. Circular in configuration, thirty-two intricately carved columns surrounded the edifice, supporting an ornate cupola. A matching ring of columnar evergreens stood sentinel around the building. The Sularem Temple, like many throughout the empire, housed a collection of small shrines to the Greater Gods. There are those who complain that it is a commercialization of religion, but it is convenient, especially for those who travel often.

Leaving my horse tied to a railing outside the evergreen fence, I paid a handful of copper *sentini* to one of the elaborately uniformed temple guards to keep thieves from making off with either the horse or my belongings. Tanris paused to speak to the man. I limped up the gravel path and climbed the stairs, then stopped to remove my boots and leave them in the shelved vestibule. One did not wear coverings on their feet or their head in the temple of the gods, whether it accommodated multiple shrines or the more traditional single variety.

Tanris waited at the doorway as I made my way around the building, visiting each niche and leaving the appropriate coin or herbal offering upon the altars. Barefoot and bareheaded, I knelt and prayed at every one of them, offering my profound gratitude for the protection, guidance, comfort, and assistance they had provided me, and begged their continued indulgence in the future, particularly in the matter of dealing with the wizard, and the safety of my beloved. I had a feeling I was going to need all the help I could get.

"Crow!" Tanris called out, impatient before I'd gotten halfway.

"Ssshh!" I hushed him and continued my obeisances. I lingered longest at the altar of the god of merchants and thieves, and left the best of the items taken from Duzayan—the ivory figurine. Last, but not least, I made my way to the simple round altar at the center of the temple. A deep, hollow bowl received the offerings to gods other than those with dedicated shrines. The clink of my coins made Tanris growl and mutter, but I ignored him and devoted the next several minutes to thanking all the other gods who might play a part in my continued safety and well-being.

"Are you quite finished?" Tanris asked when at last I got to my feet and bowed my way backwards toward the door.

"I believe I am, yes."

He clouted the side of my head roughly. "How much of our coin did you give away? Half? More? Where are we going to get more? And don't tell me that you'll steal it, because there isn't anyone to steal from where we're going even if you did think I was going to let you get away with it. Have you any idea where that coin goes, you dolt? It purchases pretty uniforms and fine houses for Temple Custodians who lounge on their feather beds and drink fine wines while they laugh at the bird-brains who pay them exorbitant *sacrifices* to do nothing more than guard their horses and sweep the bleedin' stairs!"

I rubbed my head and glared at him with furrowed brow. "You are free to believe whatever you like, but do not hit me again."

"Or what?" He gesticulated wildly.

"Just don't." I sat on one of the benches that faced the shelves and pulled on my boots.

"Oh, now I'm scared." He sounded more sarcastic than frightened. "Don't throw our money away on nonexistent gods and I won't have to hit you."

Getting to my feet, I straightened my coat and ran a hand over my head. Then I gave him a thin, humorless smile. "Have you ever seen a god?" I asked.

He glowered at me ferociously.

"If you've never seen one, how can you say with absolute certainty that they do not exist?"

He pointed at me in a threatening manner, and it wasn't the pointing itself that unsettled me as much as the absolutely furious look in his eyes. I preferred the indecipherable one. Even so, I was not going to let him bully me. I did not back down, I did not give a single inch. Finally, he swatted at the air in front of my face and stomped out and down the stairs. I sighed in relief, bowed again toward the interior of the temple, and followed him out into the sun.

Predictably muddy, innumerable carts and wagons churned Fesefi's northern road to ooze underfoot. Forced to a sedate walk, it didn't take a mind-reader to discern Tanris's growing frustration. I let him take the lead without argument, for I had no great desire to have his angry gaze burning holes in the back of my head and I doubted that my hat would do much in the way of diverting his glare. The vagaries of flight had robbed the thing of its fashionable mien, and I mourned the loss of its beautiful, jaunty feather. I'd forgotten about it while aboard *The Nightingale*, but in my defense, I'd been somewhat preoccupied by pain and the distraction of conning the crew. The captain, bless him, refunded most of our passage, though he hadn't known at the time. It is one of the sad circumstances of my life that I rarely get to admire the astonished faces of those whose lives —and pockets—I've touched.

Having got such a late start in the day on our journey by land, we planned to ride north until we came to Batifa village. I looked forward to a good meal and a real bed, and determined to enjoy them thoroughly, as it would probably be the last for months—a thought I found utterly depressing. I cheered myself by chatting with travelers on the road, several times earning searing glares from Tanris. I could not imagine what had put him in such a sour mood. We had plenty of supplies, coin for more, and good traveling weather, despite the awful state of the road itself, and riding for hours on end put him out not at all. Still, his mood soured further when we were twice called upon to help free mired carts.

I didn't take pleasure in the chore, either. It was hard, filthy work made more difficult by my game leg—and with no reward but having done the deed. I couldn't even appropriate any items from the carts. Well, I could, but while the horses might appreciate the load of hay carried by the first, I couldn't carry the stuff off in sufficiently useful quantities. The contents of the second were much more appealing. It was a shipment of Taharri Red, the wine of aspiring godlings. I could hardly fit the barrels in my pockets, and watched with deep regret as the cart trundled away down the road to Fesefi.

Tanris heard my heavy sigh and gave me another sour look. "It is a good thing they didn't offer to pay us with one of those jars they had up front."

My heart sagged. "They had jars?"

Tanris grunted in the affirmative. "The big, two-handled kind."

"And they didn't even offer us one?" I turned around to catch a last glimpse and consider how I might obtain one, but the wagon had already disappeared around a tree-shrouded corner. It wasn't far; I could run to catch it if not for the way my leg pained me after all my efforts. I would not have helped at all after the first occasion with the hay wagon, but Tanris had little sympathy for me and several sharp knives, the hilts of which he'd fingered meaningfully when I had begun to decline.

"Perhaps they're worth more than a half hour's labor."

His voice held a distinctly cutting edge that I didn't like at all. "But was our help worth *not* being stuck in the road indefinitely?"

A few vehement kicks against a large rock on the side of the road dislodged most of the dirt from his boots, then he headed for his horse. "'Indefinitely' being until the next travelers come along."

"That could be tomorrow." I followed his example. One kick with my game leg, though, convinced me not to work too hard at the task. I would just have to be muddy. The promise of a bath in Batifa grew more appealing by the minute.

"Or it could be right now."

I hated when he was right. A small, lightweight cart came into view at that same corner around which my Taharri Red had disappeared. The farmers driving it even passed a leather flask back and forth between them. "Do we have any wine?" I asked, limping to my horse and pulling myself up into the saddle while Tanris efficiently got the pack horses under way.

"We have kaffa."

Odious man. How could one travel without wine? Clearly, I should have stayed with him and helped with the supplies. Just because he was going to kill me once I got the dragon's egg, he didn't need to torture me beforehand.

As twilight settled around us, the traffic thinned even further. Most of it was local, and nearly everyone was inside their snug homes at this time of the day, enjoying hearty meals, the aromas of which wafted cruelly from the cottages and domiciles we passed. Knots of houses huddled together on the edges of farms. We could make out the lights of bigger manors further off the main road, some of which I'd had the opportunity to visit myself. The further we rode, the more spaced out the homes became. Occasional stands of trees broke up the monotony of farmland, and now and then we clattered over bridges that crossed the dozens of meandering streams that gave the Fesefi area its lushness and wonderful fruit for wine. The bridges were somewhat long and quite high, arching over stretches of water that could become torrential in the spring. The horses did not like them, and tossed their heads in melodramatic outrage as we trotted across, hoofbeats thundering loudly.

Darker and darker it grew, and the going became even slower. I wondered if we would have to stop and ask for lodging at one of the many farmhouses along the way or, better yet, one of the more stately mansions. The latter offered more luxuries than the former. The day's pleasant temperatures dropped speedily which, while it had me shivering in my saddle, also made the mud much firmer and easier for the horses to traverse. Just as I was about to propose to Tanris that we look for a place to put up, the moon began to edge up over the horizon. Tanris picked up the pace and it felt like we were making good time. I didn't ask. I still wanted to curl up someplace warm and go to sleep, but as moody as my companion had been throughout the day, I could manage to wait a little bit longer.

— 11 —
Shining Champions

The scents of food cooking still tormented me, and then came a more acrid odor. "Someone ruined their dinner royally," I commented, imagining the blackened remains of the unfortunate pot.

"That's no dinner," Tanris murmured. We rode along for a few more minutes before he slowed his mount and pointed ahead. "Look."

I peered past him into the scene of black and—blacker.

"House burned down," he said, and the horses twitched their ears and fidgeted a bit. "Looks recent. Maybe a week or so ago."

"Smells recent," I agreed. As we plodded past, I looked at the remains: a pair of chimneys, parts of walls, lumps of deeper blackness within the shadows I could not identify. Perhaps the remains of furniture. The edge of the road bore a pale splotch. The splotch made noise. Tanris pulled his horse up and slid from the saddle. "What is that?" I asked. "What are you doing?"

The noise revealed itself as the pitiful mewing of a cat. Another *cat...*

"Oh, no." I shook my head, invisible in the dark. "Leave it alone, Tanris."

"C'mere, cat," he said instead, in a voice more gentle and sweet than the caress of a new spring sun. It was a shock. In my wildest dreams, I could not have imagined him so tender, and for the space of several heartbeats I just stared. "Come here, little one," he murmured. "Was this your house? Where did your people go? They just leave you behind?"

It was revolting.

The cat didn't appear to think so. Delicately, it stepped over the sodden grass, sniffed a little, then crawled up onto his leg. Tanris, in an expert movement even I had to admire, tucked the thing into the crook of his arm and straightened. He petted and cooed, and even from fifteen feet away I could hear the thing purring.

"There's a good baby," he said softly, one broad hand enveloping its head and massaging its ears. I fully expected it to scratch and bite and wildly claw its way to freedom—which would have been amusing to watch, especially if it included Tanris yelling and swearing—but it simply climbed into his coat. Tanris helped, unfastening the top few buttons so the useless creature could curl in and get comfortable.

The thought of having a cat so close to my face made my nose itch, and I scratched reflexively. "What are you doing?" I asked again as he made his way back to his horse.

"Going to Batifa," he replied, and saddle leather creaked as he pulled himself up.

"You can't bring that," I objected.

"Why not?"

I searched for a logical answer. "It belongs to whoever used to live here."

"Whoever used to live here hasn't bothered to come back for it." He helped the cat get comfortable. It was still purring. Then he gathered up the reins and urged his horse forward.

"Cats make me sneeze," I tried.

The pack horses fell into step behind him as the lead rope drew taut. "Then stay away from it."

"Tanris, we can't feed a cat. What's it going to eat?"

He looked back at me over his shoulder, and it was probably just as well I couldn't make out his expression in the dark. He just kept riding.

A sleepy little town, Batifa possessed a grand total of four streets arranged around a picturesque green, and by the time we arrived the waxing half moon had risen to a height sufficient to illuminate the scene nicely, silvering the landscape and throwing shadows into sharp relief. The Belching Bull sat directly across the square from a huge barn or grange. A small temple occupied the middle of the northern side, and opposite that stood a fine house that could only belong to the mayor. Typically quaint houses and shops filled the remaining spaces.

The proprietor of the Belching Bull was not altogether keen about being awakened in the middle of the night. Decent folks apparently arranged their travel schedules more considerately. After an extra pair of silver coins crossed his palm, he allowed as how the rainy weather this time of year made the roads miserable, and he pointed out that we were lucky to have had such a singularly lovely day, and how fortunate none of the bridges had washed out yet.

"He has a cat," I pointed out. Tanris gave me a freezing look—much different than the searing ones he'd given me earlier for talking to strangers —and the innkeeper shrugged and passed over the key to our room. A room, mind you, that we were going to have to share, as the inn was full up. He apparently did a brisk business here.

"Just keep it away from my big gray tom," he warned. "Old Moggy will tear it to pieces." He opened a door at the back and hollered for someone to come tend to our horses.

I looked around hopefully for Old Moggy, but he didn't show himself. Maybe in the morning I could arrange a meeting over a nice dish of cream or something. Tanris jostled my elbow, and I swear he knew the scene in my mind exactly. I gave him a look of sleepy surprise.

"If you've got any leftovers from dinner, good sir, we'd be mighty grateful," Tanris said in a voice much kinder than the freezing look he'd given me.

"Aye, I'll bring a couple plates up for you, and I've likely got some warm water left, too."

Not exactly the hearty dinner and hot bath I'd envisioned, but I was too tired to put any energy into indignation. I hobbled after Tanris as he mounted the stairs. Several hours riding and pushing two wagons out of the mud had certainly had a detrimental affect on my healing leg, and I barely managed to take the steps one at a time. My unfortunate acquaintance with the saddle had only just begun, and already I feared being bowlegged for the rest of my life. One thing I knew for certain: there would be no wagon pushing or pulling on the morrow, no matter how my companion threatened.

Tanris turned the key in the lock and we peered inside, only to discover that our single room had a single bed.

"I am not sleeping with you," I said.

"Suit yourself," came his response. He grabbed a sorry-looking pillow off the bed and tossed it onto the braided rug covering the floor. "Better go out and get one of the horse blankets. Feels chilly."

"Surely you jest."

He dropped his saddlebags on the floor and sat on the bed to pull off his boots and gear without replying. The cat, evicted from its cozy nest in Tanris's coat, jumped down and began a curious exploration of the room.

"I'm wounded."

"So am I."

It took a moment to recall the gash he'd taken across his belly. It must not have been very deep, else he'd have declined the unnecessary labor on the road. "But I can hardly walk."

"So what are you doing standing there?"

Thinking about holding a pillow over your face? Thinking about locking your cat in a cupboard? I did not like animals. Having to deal with the horse was imposition enough. Cats—and dogs and pet birds, not to mention noxious demons—had an annoying habit of appearing at exactly the wrong moment. They gave away the presence of the most clever, soundless of thieves. I knew. I had experience. Grumbling to myself, I limped to the room's single chair and sat down to take off my own gear. All the while, I silently and vigorously practiced telling him to go put a hot poker up his nose—in four different languages.

While we waited, I took out the vial with the potion for my usual dose. I tried to check the level, but it was utterly impossible to see inside, no matter which way I tipped it or held it to the light. Disgruntled, I swallowed the requisite two drops. I just knew Duzayan had made it hideously bitter on purpose, the wretch.

A gentle tapping on the door a few moments later announced the innkeeper with a tray full of food, which was wonderful, and a bucket of steaming water, which was less so. Bad enough I had to share a room, but the bed and the bath as well? Staring at them with lips pursed, I wondered where my scathing humor had gone, for now would be an excellent time to wield it. Obviously, I was tired.

And wounded.

And don't forget the cat.

The food tasted delicious, but it was a toss-up whether the credit belonged to my starvation or the talent of the innkeeper's wife. It pained me to watch Tanris feed the cat some of the perfectly tender roast and gravy. I would have happily eaten it myself if he wasn't particularly hungry. We solved the problem of who got the warm water first by using it at the same time—an event I would never repeat, even if it meant bathing in cold water.

"The cat stays *off* the bed," I warned Tanris as we settled ourselves on either side of the mattress. He didn't even bother to look at me.

The cat, of course, did not stay off the bed. In fact, it liked my side better and particularly enjoyed delicately stabbing me with its needle sharp claws as it kneaded my leg or my chest, purring so loudly it was a wonder the innkeeper didn't come banging on our door. I lost track of how many times I pushed it off. The last time was more energetic than the others, provoking an odd-sounding grunt from the creature.

His back to me, Tanris didn't move, but he did speak. "You hurt the cat, I hurt you."

"So how long have you been married?" I don't know what prompted the question besides utter boredom. I was glad for my hat, for the rain had begun again and the brim kept the constant, relentless drizzle off my face and the water from leaking down the back of my neck—a small boon considering my overall sogginess. While clever Tanris had provided oilskin capes for us, they could only do so much.

I was beginning to think Tanris had either dozed off or died when he finally spoke. "Two years tomorrow."

"Ah, well, happy anniversary."

He slanted me one of those consummate sideways looks proclaiming my idiocy, and that if it wouldn't hold us up further he'd reach across the way and knock me right out of the saddle. He had yet to do any such thing, but the promise was frequently displayed in his expression. I pretended not to notice and looked about at the scenery with artificial interest. It was the same drab, gray, wet, muddy, cold, utterly miserable scenery I'd been looking at for the last weeks, and I'd run out of synonyms to describe it adequately.

Batifa lay behind us, and I had decided I loathed camping. If the stars still existed, I did not know it. Only the fact that I'd viewed the stars and the moon in my previous life supported the assumption of their continued existence. We had no light to speak of, except my little witchlights, and as far as Tanris knew I only had one. I'd brought it out so he could see to light a fire one night. How he'd found dry wood I had no idea. He'd stared at the witchlight for several long, silent moments, and when I'd asked him if there was a problem, he'd simply bent himself to the task of striking the fire. It was the only fire we'd had, and I found myself missing it now. Passionately.

"River ahead," Tanris announced.

"How can you tell?" It would not surprise me at all to discover the entire world had turned into a gigantic swamp and I recalled the southern strait with a sudden wave of nostalgia. It would be lovely and dry and warm this time of year. There was something to be said for the desert in winter.

"Listen. There's a rumble in the air. In the ground."

I listened, but all I heard was rain, rain, and more rain. "How far?" I inquired, adroitly sidestepping my ignorance.

"A few minutes. Just over the rise," he pointed.

What rise? I peered into the misty, uniform grayness and couldn't tell. On my own, I might come to a cliff and not known until I fell off—which very nearly happened. It took perhaps ten minutes to top the rise, and the road curved abruptly to run along the edge of the world. I pulled my horse up a careful distance away and attempted to peer into the bottomless chasm, which turned out to be only about thirty or forty feet deep and filled with a river, a startlingly cold mist, and an abundance of fog.

"Don't get too close to the edge," Tanris warned kindly, but unnecessarily. "Wet as it is, the ground might crumble out from under you. Wouldn't want that."

"No, indeed we wouldn't." I backed my mount away and scratched my bristly cheek, recalling the layout of the map and mentally placing us on it. I could imagine us as a little ink-splotch on the squiggly line indicating the road from Batifa northward. A second squiggly line running parallel to the road was the River Le'ah, which joined the greater Zenn and subsequently flowed through Marketh and into the sea. In spite of riding forever, the ink-splotch hadn't gone terribly far. The distance we'd traveled was hardly a drop in the bucket compared to how far we still needed to go. I laughed softly at my own warped sense of humor. Of course I was thinking in terms of water and buckets. Was there a dry place left in the world? Oh, yes, I reminded myself, the desert across the straits.

The road stayed far too close to the ledge for my comfort, and it had washed away in two places. Unperturbed, Tanris merely guided the horses around each jagged gash. I looked into them both as we passed and couldn't help but imagine some further piece of road giving way and dumping us into the river. Even after we reached the bottom, the river continued to roar loudly between the walls it had carved out of the earth. Here was no gentle riverbank, but a steeply cut passage in which the water battered fiercely at its rocky confines as it hurled itself toward the sea. I studied the gorge curiously as we rode along.

"Hold up," Tanris ordered, reaching for my reins and jolting me out of my reverie. His voice was unexpectedly terse, his frowning gaze fixed on some indefinable point ahead of us. I stretched my senses and immediately made out thumping and grunting, then a distinct scream. Tanris hauled the cat out from its cozy nest inside his coat front—quite unceremoniously—and dropped it on the ground. It made a hideous noise and sped off into the fog. Goodbye, kitty. Untying the pack horses' ropes, he handed them to me. "Stay here."

Of course I was going to stay there, safely hiding in the rain and fog right in the middle of a road that anyone at all might come riding up or down while he, an expert warrior, went off to deal with—No, I don't think so. Giving a quick look around, I espied a pile of head-high boulders some short distance down the slope. I pulled the packhorses behind them and tied the long leather reins to a boulder, which gave them no room at all in which to maneuver but was certainly better than having them wander off or run away. Yanking off my gloves and tucking them into my belt, my half-frozen fingers worked at unknotting the ropes holding my gear so I could remove one of the grappling hooks. Yelling joined the thumping and screaming, and I scrambled back into the saddle and kicked my mount into a run.

It was a surreal thing to go galloping off into the thick fog having no idea what awaited me. Fear and excitement pumped through my blood in equal measures. We slowed to take a turn and started to slide down an unexpectedly steep incline. I pulled the horse up completely, and while it stood there, straight-legged and shaking its head, I swiftly surveyed the scene below. I picked Tanris out easily. He'd shed his waterproof cloak somewhere along the way and stood in his stirrups, heroically swinging his sword at a pair of men armed with long clubs. Bodies lay on the ground, and another huddled near the wheel of a wagon that had apparently become stuck. A horse sprawled lifelessly in the traces.

More alarming was the sight of another figure running up on Tanris from behind, and that one had an axe. "Tanris! Look out!" I hollered at him, and kneed my horse forward onto a little outcropping of rock. Tanris twisted and brought his sword around in a deadly arc, and I swung my hook, letting it fly straight toward one of the other attackers. The rope burned as it slid through my hand. I was a good shot, and it nailed the man right in the head, knocking him over sideways. Immediately, I gave the rope a tug and a flip, and the hook sailed back my way, clattering against the rocky wall. I reeled it in as the figure by the wheel—female by the look of it—struggled with another man. In a trice, the man knocked her down and dragged her toward the other side of the wagon and a measure of safety.

My horse danced and fidgeted beneath me, and I couldn't help a snarl of irritation. "Be still!" I ordered it, and realized that in throwing the hook, I'd been pulling rather wildly on the reins. What did fighters on horseback usually do in such situations? I only had so many hands. I gave a sharp, authoritative tug, then let them fall. Likely, I was asking to be promptly tossed from our rocky perch, but I hadn't time to dwell on that. I launched my hook again. It sailed true, but the girl's assailant jerked to one side. The hook skimmed the side of his face and banged over his shoulder. He started to turn around. Gritting my teeth and bracing for what I knew was coming, I pulled as hard as I could.

He screamed, spun around completely, and flailed wildly to the ground with two of the hook's claws anchored in his neck and shoulder. The girl fell, tangled in his legs. She didn't stay there long. Her face a desperate blotch of white, she grabbed a rock and proceeded to batter her attacker. It was more gruesome a spectacle than I wanted to watch.

Tanris, in the meantime, had dispatched the fellow with the axe as well as one of those with the clubs. He was on foot—a move I'd missed—and now had a knife as well as his sword. "Do you surrender?" he bellowed at his remaining opponent.

"Oh, please," I said, astounded that he'd show such clemency to a bloodthirsty highwayman who had not only attacked a wagon out in the middle of nowhere, but clearly had a hand in killing or maiming some of the occupants. I rather doubt they had a shopping excursion in mind for the girl, either. "Just run him through and be done with it."

He ignored me, of course, even when the fool bandit launched into a new attack. Swiftly, smoothly, Tanris parried the swinging cudgel with his sword, twisting it about in a remarkable fashion to pin it against the earth and bring its wielder to his knees. He clubbed the back of the fellow's head with the hilt of his knife. Just like that. It was rather beautiful to watch, however impractical the result.

Chest heaving, Tanris turned to glare at me. "Didn't I tell you to stay with the horses?"

"Oh, you did. And you're welcome. So happy to save your life."

"Where are they?"

"The horses? I left them tied up." I pointed back the way I'd come.

"Go get them."

I made a face at him. "Yes, *sir!*" Giving the hook's rope a flip, I turned my horse around and went to fetch the pack animals, which were right where I'd left them. I returned to find Tanris standing in the road with the girl clinging to his neck, sobbing her eyes out while he awkwardly patted her back.

"Crow, can you—?" He gestured at her behind her back.

I waved a dismissive hand and eased myself out of the saddle to the ground, which was fairly gravelly here and didn't immediately sink me up to my ankles in mud. "You look like you're doing fine," I said cheerfully, and went to rescue my hook from the mutilated corpse. I shouldn't have looked at it too closely. I had to step away from the scene of the crime to spew my midday meal behind another convenient rock. There was plenty of water available to wash my face and rinse my mouth; I had only to tip my head up to the sky.

"So, what's the story?" I asked when I could manage a casual tone.

"I don't know. All she's done is cry."

It was rather satisfying to see Tanris look so helpless and uncomfortable. I left him that way to go check the other bodies. It was fairly easy to tell who was who; the owners of the wagon wore simple farmer's homespun, and the bandits had various bits and pieces of armor and weaponry about them. Both of the farmers were dead, and when I looked in the back of the wagon I found a third body, but this one, an elderly woman, looked to have been dead for some time, and there wasn't a mark on her. Some foodstuffs occupied the space along with a pair of shovels.

"On the way to bury this one, I suppose," I said to Tanris, and the girl clung to him even more tightly, her body shaking with great, hiccuping sobs.

"Go tie him up," he said, pointing to the fellow he'd knocked out.

"Can't I just—" Well, clouting him over the head had lost some of its appeal after witnessing what the girl had done to her attacker.

"No."

So I tied him up. I'm not exactly sure how it came about, but shortly after that I found myself helping Tanris dig a grave some little way off the road. The rocky soil made for ridiculously back-breaking labor, and after I'd worked up a sweat discernible even beyond my already-drenched state I leaned on my shovel and looked pointedly at Tanris until he straightened. "This is a waste of time."

"It is not a waste of time to give folks a decent burial."

"Do you think they're actually going to care?"

"I wouldn't expect you, of all people, to speak so blasphemously."

I rolled my eyes. "Tanris, they're dead. I, on the other hand, am merely dying. I would like to avoid that outcome. And surely you don't want our years-long story to end with me simply keeling over in the middle of nowhere. Where's the satisfaction in that?"

Jaw knotting, he looked at me, then over at the girl hunched underneath a boulder for shelter. "Will you help me cover them with rocks?"

Rocks I could do. We ended up having to put the bodies in two separate piles when the girl had produced further tears over the idea of the attackers sharing the same ground as her erstwhile companions. Then Tanris volunteered me to say a few words over the graves of her kin. I briefly contemplated adding him to the stack. Then I held my much-abused hat in my hands and bowed my head. I had never been to an actual funeral before, and had no idea what the proper prayers were. That, and I was in a bit of a hurry to carry on with our journey.

"Hail, oh gods of Life, of Death, of Passage, of Sorrow and Joy!" I named off several I thought might be appropriate. "Make known the path to the afterlife to these poor men whose lives have ended so unexpectedly. May they continue in peace." I lifted my head to find Tanris glaring at me, but when didn't he? I looked down at the ground. "May they enter on the shining way to their paradise and not become lost. Give comfort to their kin. And so may it be."

The girl choked pitifully and promptly burst into tears again.

— 12 —
Socializing In The Wilds

She wouldn't talk to us, this girl whose life we'd saved and whose relatives we'd buried. Not a single word could we pry from her lips. We couldn't just leave her—well, I would have been willing, but Tanris would have none of it. With its broken axel the wagon was useless. Neither would he let us just leave the thing and be on our way. No, we had to cut the dead horse free and use our own to haul the corpse off the road, and I refused to give a *horse* a proper burial and got clouted upside the head for inquiring whether we might make use of some fresh meat. It seemed a hideous waste to leave it behind for wild dogs to feast on when we had been restricted to damp flatbread and leathery jerky for weeks.

After we dealt with the horse, I had to help him chop the wagon into pieces and move it out of the way of the next traveler. There was no getting out of that, though I tried. Not only did we have our own hatchet, but the dead men left us a lovely, well-sharpened axe. At least Tanris had the good sense to lash some of the broken planks to the pack horses so we could later use them in a fire, providing we could get one lit. Of the bandit's horses, we found only the muddied ground they left behind. Tanris suspected that whoever had been given the duty of watching them had run away, which left us wondering if he was long gone, or if he was following us with the intention of freeing his crony, then murdering and robbing us.

Hours later, when the perpetually gray sky had dimmed nearly to charcoal, we were on our way again. And where did the girl ride? With me, of course. "You can take her or the cat," Tanris said. Too hastily, I'd accepted the burden of the girl. It didn't come to me until quite some time later that if I'd taken the cat, I could have figured out a way to accidentally-on-purpose lose it forever. I had forgotten the cursed thing until it had wandered up to me as we prepared to leave and wound itself around my ankles. Tanris had scooped it up and tucked it back into his coat, heedless of its soggy, stinky condition.

And what, you may ask, became of the unconscious bandit? Why, we'd brought him along, too. We couldn't kill him, and we couldn't leave him tied up by the remains of the ruined wagon, though I couldn't even begin to understand why. No, we had to take him with us to the next village to turn him over to the proper authorities. One rescued cat, one rescued girl, one rescued bandit. We were turning into a blasted circus.

Revived from his stupor, the bandit got to walk. We were quite the merry little band slogging along through the wet and dark, and I had very little to say to Tanris, very little at all. The bandit, on the other hand, was a fairly chatty fellow. He was called Kem Bohadri and, having come across the wagon during their travels, he and his fellows had meant only to rob it and be on their way, so he knew nothing about the girl. Not her name, nor from where she'd come. And she still wasn't talking.

Since Tanris had the pack horses to tend to, it fell to me to deal with the girl and the prisoner, the latter of which had his hands tied behind his back and a rope around his neck and fastened to my saddle. I told him a little about what life was like in the city, and then got him talking about the area through which we traveled. The weather, he said, was quite warm, the consequence of which was considerable rain rather than the snow which usually fell at this time of year. The precipitation had flooded out the bridge at the village of Uzuun that we needed to cross if we were going north, he said, and the one further upriver as well, but he knew a way through the Snags.

I did not know whether to laugh or cry.

"What do you think?" I asked Tanris later, when we had set up camp in a stand of trees. A tarpaulin helped protect us from the weather. After leading us a considerable distance from the road, Tanris allowed a fire on the grounds that the trees hid the light, and the branches and rain dispersed the smoke well enough.

"I do not trust him, do you?" he murmured, his voice for my ears only.

I snorted.

He took out the map and the two of us pored over it, but it was too simple to give us the information we needed. A straight path from here to there, it left no room for catastrophic contingencies.

Kem sat across the fire and a little apart from us, barely under the edge of our makeshift roof and securely fastened to a tree lest he get ambitious ideas about escaping. I didn't care if he escaped. I cared about whether he'd bash my head in as part of the plan. He lowered his eyes when I looked his way. Hunched over, firelight flickered on his face, making the shallows and creases deep and forbidding. With mouth down-turned, I watched the nameless girl as she crouched close to the flames next to Tanris, rocking back and forth. She was thin, her features too sharp, and her tear-swollen face spoiled by smudges and shadows. After a moment or two of their scintillating company, I worked the waxed leather tube out of my pack to remove Duzayan's letters. Rolled as they were, the sides curled stubbornly. I'd perused them several times before, and the curl only got worse.

Tanris tucked the near-useless map away and took some of the missives from me, tipping them toward the light. "He knows the area. We can bring him with us and see if what he says is true," he suggested. "If it is, perhaps he can guide us."

"Or perhaps murder us in our sleep. Maybe we could cross the river another way."

"With the horses?"

"I don't know, Tanris. I just see us losing more and more time."

He glanced up at me, his face hidden in shadows. "We will get through in time."

"How?"

"There is a way," Kem said.

How had he heard us? It made the hairs on the back of my neck stand up. I did not even realize that I'd reached for my knife until Tanris put his hand on my arm.

"How?" he echoed.

Kem licked his lips and looked from one of us to the other. "There's a way, but I'll only take you in exchange for my freedom."

"How do we know we can believe you?" Tanris asked.

"How do I know you'll keep your word?" he countered.

Tanris let out a long, careful breath. "Tell us about this way of yours, then we'll decide if it earns your release."

Kem was unlikely to get a better offer, and he knew it. "Here," he said, looking at us both then turning to point with his chin into the darkness, "is where the Snags jut down out of the mountains—the Daryas, yes?—into the midlands. The river Le'ah comes through them, hard and fast. It cuts through the Snags in the Funnel, which runs miles to the south." He bent his head back the way we'd come. "There's a bridge to the north at the town of Uzuun, where the river is wide and runs fairly shallow through the valley, but the rains washed trees from the banks and took out the bridge."

"So you said earlier. Go on."

Kem nodded. "The Le'ah flows through the mountains in a steep, narrow gorge. A waterfall brings it into the valley at the north end, at Uzuun, and the only other bridge is further upriver through sharp, rocky country. The crossing is treacherous. The road is often flooded, and the bridge is small and shaky. Difficult to take horses across it. No wagons go there."

"I sense a *but*," I put in, eyes narrowing. What was he getting at, and what was it going to cost us?

"Above the falls there is another road. It goes west for a little, then down."

"Down where?"

"To the Ghost Walk."

"Which is…?"

"A passage under the river." Kem watched us, waiting.

"*Under* the river? Through a cave?" Sudden horrible memories of Duzayan's dungeon, and rats, and every other dark, narrow place I'd ever been in overtook me.

"Wide enough for the horses?" Tanris asked.

"Yes, barely. You cannot ride, though, the roof is too low. Almost too low for the animals in some places."

"How long will it take to go through?"

"Three days maybe, if all goes well."

Three days? In a skinny little cave? "Is there another bridge?" I interrupted.

"No other." Kem's dark eyes were serious in the small light of the flames.

"How far back to another crossing? South."

Kem pursed his lips, then shrugged. "About a week."

"Maybe we can build another bridge." The looks the pair of them gave me made me doubt my own sanity. "Not a real one, just a temporary one. We have ropes. We can ferry our supplies across."

"And the horses?"

"If we have a rope from one side to the other, we can ferry them, too."

"Over a gorge?" Tanris shook his head. "They're too heavy, even if we had the proper equipment."

I rubbed my cheeks and eyes with both hands, then pressed them in fists over my mouth. I could not go into a cave. Not one as narrow as Kem described. I trembled just thinking about it.

"How long to go up around the second bridge to this other way you know?" Tanris asked Kem.

"All the way?" He shrugged again and hitched closer to the fire. It wasn't very big or very warm. "Two weeks, if the weather is good. Maybe twice that in this rain, and you still need to come down the other side."

"A *month?*" I protested incredulously.

"Easily."

I stared at him for a long time. Abruptly, I pushed myself to my feet and walked away from the camp and into the rain again.

"Crow." I hadn't gotten far before Tanris caught my shoulder and pulled me to a stop. "Don't go walking out here in the dark. You could fall and break a leg, or get lost."

"What difference does it make?" I asked bitterly. A misting rain fell, and of course I'd forgotten my hat. I licked moisture from my mouth and did not look at him.

"It is the difference between Tarsha and Aehana living and dying."

The accusation that Tanris only lived to betray us hovered on my lips, but I did not speak it, and I couldn't think of anything else to say that would cut him deep enough.

"Look at it this way—at least you'll be out of the rain for a few days."

I grunted. I had no words at all. None.

"You won't be alone."

No, I would be stuck with one man who would probably rob me given the slightest chance—not that I could blame him—and another who wanted to kill me, but not yet. No, he would do his utmost to keep me alive until I had the jewel, or egg, or whatever it was. I sucked in a breath and let it out in a harsh exhalation, then nodded.

Tanris nodded, too. "We're going to have to stand guard. We don't want our guide escaping, or his friend coming back to surprise us."

"May he look up at the sky for too long and drown," I muttered, and Tanris surprised me with a laugh.

:-:

Kem's friend did not come until the second night. The rain had stopped the evening before, but the woods dripped and dripped. Even without leaves to hold the water, the trees leaked like over-saturated sponges. I had grown accustomed to the abstract melody during the long hours while the others slept, and the wet, shuffling sound that crept into my awareness was not the same.

The shelter Tanris had chosen for us was a good one, thank the gods of outdoor skills. The sparse and sometimes sudden little hills that dotted the moors had disappeared behind us about the same time we'd come across the attack. The road had become steep and ragged, with frequent signs that it had been widened to accommodate wagons. As usual, Tanris had led us off the road and out of sight of other travelers. Rounding a towering outcropping we discovered a wide, grassy area backed by leaning rock on one side and a sheer gorge on the other. A pile of rubble tucked against the larger rock protected us from the wind and allowed us to have a fire again, which was pure luxury. Trees came right down to the flat area on one side and covered the hill across the gorge, which gave the intruder the cover he'd needed to creep up on us. He did not, however, expect me to be perched above the camp on a small ledge.

I'd been toying with the Beisyth Web, and I slipped it into my pocket to creep down from my hiding place, footsteps silent on the stone. I kept my gaze on him, feeling with my hands the way I'd previously marked. The pattern of crevices and protrusions on the face of the rock was not as regular as those found on buildings in the city, but I had spent my entire life climbing, and I knew exactly where to go and what I would do. I could not kill him outright. I am a thief, not a murderer, even if I do entertain wild fantasies of spectacular executions now and then. I could not just capture him, either, for Tanris would simply tie him up and tote him along to hand over to the nearest authorities, and he would eat our food, slow us down, and annoy the spit out of me. Hands icy, I eyed the space between him and the gorge at his back.

And then the cat, which had apparently been out hunting or whatever it is that stray cats do in the middle of the night, strolled into camp. It hopped delicately into view and picked its way across a little ridge of stone.

I froze.

All unsuspecting, the intruder straightened and eased forward toward where Kem lay bound and sleeping. The cat—a ridiculously friendly thing —strolled right up to him and between his legs. It was a wonder to watch the abrupt jerk upright, the funny little dance of shock that took him backward several steps, and then the pinwheeling of arms as he strove to keep his balance. The cat leaped nimbly out of the way. The intruder, unable to recover, let out a strangled croak and then disappeared over the edge of the gorge.

Tanris, who probably slept with one eye open, came abruptly upright, sword in hand. Then he relaxed. "Come here, you," he murmured, and of course the cat went right to him, purring like an avalanche. Murderous creature.

I walked over to the edge of the cliff to look down, but the body was lost in its dark depth.

"Crow, what are you doing?"

"Relieving myself before I go to sleep. It's your turn to take the watch." The gods really did love me.

It took another day and a half to come to the little mountain village of Uzuun, and the higher we climbed, the colder it became. We spent the night on the fringes of the snow line, and all the next day the stuff grew steadily deeper, though the road and a few patches of ground here and there remained mostly clear. The frozen ground made easier going for the horses, but made little difference to me: I rode and walked and ate terrible bread and jerky, then rode and walked some more.

I admit the area possessed a certain rough and terrible beauty, and I had never seen so many evergreen trees in one place, but the air grew progressively thinner and I was not much enamored of spending day after day toiling ever upwards into less air and more snow.

We did a great deal of walking. Tanris would not let us ride for the entire way for fear of damaging the horses. We kept up with them easily enough, and moving warmed us. Besides, he generously pointed out, my injured leg needed the exercise. My leg—and my body—got more exercise on that single trip than it had in my entire life, and I had always prided myself on being fit and trim. Mostly, I was just sore and tired all the time. If Tanris suffered the same, he did not confess it. The girl, I noted, got to ride more than any of us, though Kem rode not at all, and had his bound hands attached to one of the horses into the bargain. He did not complain. He seemed to be a man who got things done without much fuss, simply because they needed doing.

We saw nothing of his erstwhile companions, though that did not stop us from keeping a sharp eye out for them nor posting a guard when we stopped for the night. In spite of his loquaciousness, he declined to tell us if any of his fellows remained alive and how many they might be. To my disappointment, Tanris didn't force the information from him.

The sun dipped below the horizon as we struggled up a particularly steep bit of road and finally found ourselves on the southern edge of the Sammaron Valley. The town of Uzuun occupied the opposite end, and it was the strangest place I'd ever seen. Many of the houses were built directly into the looming granite cliff. The valley spread out before it, wider than it was deep, and covered with a blanket of pristine snow. The criss-cross hatching of fences defined farms and pasturage dotted occasionally with animals. The river cut almost straight down the middle of the idyllic scene, fat and looking deceptively slow. The sun's farewell rays turned the snow and the drops of water that hung over the river into glittering gold. The sight impressed even me. I caught my breath as much for the last leg of our climb as for the marvel that lay before me. When I turned to look behind me, all the world stretched out at my feet in a glorious tumble of shapes and exquisitely muted colors. The view extended for hundreds of miles, though the falling darkness and the mist that clung to the world obscured its furthest edges. I had sworn off the moors and the elevation, but I considered bringing Tarsha to see this beautiful, wondrous view.

"Worth the climb, isn't it?" Tanris asked softly, almost reverently, from beside me.

"It is," I had to admit, "though I don't think I'd want to do it again."

"No?" He smiled a little. "Do you not feel a sense of triumph? You have come a long, hard way."

"Ask me again when we get to the highest point of this little journey."

On the outskirts of the village a gang of curious, noisy children and several farmers and herdsmen greeted us. The men carried tools they wouldn't likely use that time of year—shovels and hoes as well as a few staffs, even a pair of axes. Friendly, but wary, they wanted to know our names and where we were headed. And most keenly, they wanted to know why we had a rope-bound prisoner with us. Even as Tanris explained how Kem attacked the family of the girl with us and he intended to deliver him to the authorities, someone recognized him.

"I've seen him b'fore. Runs with Kiral's band."

"Buncha no-goods. Stole some of my sheep."

"Took grain right out of my barn," someone else said.

This turn of events prompted a flicker of alarm. If all these people wanted to claim Kem Bohadri so they could exact their justice, where would we find a guide? Kem, in the meantime, edged over behind me as best he could, tied to the horse still.

"Here, now, what's this?" A dark-haired man with a vigorously receding hairline and a fairly decent paunch stepped brusquely through the gathering crowd, and Tanris had to explain all over again. As it turned out, the man was the mayor of Uzuun, and quite adept at getting things done. "We can take that one off your hands," he said, nodding understanding.

"Actually, sir, that won't be necessary."

I tried not to appear too interested in what Tanris had to say, and busied myself assessing the crowd to see how well they could support the next leg of our journey. Most of them wore simple but well-made clothes and hardly any jewelry at all, and primitive at that—wooden beads and discs and an occasional metal or stone item. Prospects for lining my pockets or contributing to my comfort were dim.

"Kiral Stone," Tanris went on, and wasn't it a marvelous thing that I'd been chatting up our prisoner? "and his men are wanted for numerous attacks and robberies, and there's a good-sized bounty on them. We ran into them several days back." The way he propped his hands on his hips, right next to his sword and the axe he'd inherited, emphasized that he could and would use them. Everyone backed up a little, pretending nonchalance.

"You're a bounty hunter?" the mayor asked.

"That's right." And if he hadn't been five minutes ago, he was now. Can you even imagine Tanris lying? I wondered how he'd collect the bounty—and where—and still manage to give Kem his freedom.

The mayor's gaze shifted to me and my obvious lack of weaponry. "And that one?"

Tanris smiled thinly and not altogether pleasantly. "That's my other job."

"Oh?" The mayor's curiosity was certainly piqued, and I could have happily kicked Tanris in the shin. The last thing a thief wants is unnecessary attention.

"Paid protection," I offered smoothly. "And a good thing, too. Criminals these days are getting more and more bold, as you can see!" I waved a hand at Kem, and he just pursed his lips and wisely kept his mouth shut.

"I see. Where are you headed?"

"Baichu," I said, naming the capitol of Chatahai Province on the far side of the Daryas. Tanris narrowed his eyes, but I ignored him.

"You chose a poor time of year for the journey," the mayor responded, cool and assessing. No dummy, he.

I shrugged and grimaced. "My uncle chose a poor time to pass from this world." I wondered if there was ever an opportune time to die, not that I actually had any uncles to concern me.

The mayor gave a slow, sympathetic nod. "That is unfortunate news. You have my condolences."

I gave him a brief, wry smile. "I never cared for him, but my mother is all alone in the world now, and I must fly to her."

"Ah, mothers, yes. The sweetest of gems." He stepped forward to clap my shoulder companionably and, just like that, he took us under his ample wing. He escorted us through the town, ordered care for our horses, put our prisoner under guard, and explained how Uzuun didn't have a formal gaol or sheriff, but managed things quite nicely anyway. Not unsurprisingly, Tanris elected to attend to our bags himself.

There was no inn, for the village saw too few travelers to make it worthwhile, but the mayor had a grand house that was half in and half out of the cliff and boasted plenty of extra rooms for guests. I luxuriated in the first hot bath I'd had in over a month. I shaved! Delighted to have someone to feed and stories to listen to, the mayor's wife plied us with hot pumpkin soup, loaves of mouth-watering bread oozing creamy butter, roasted venison and potatoes, and some local vegetable unfamiliar to me. It tasted mellow and sweet, and I had three helpings, which made the mayor's youngest daughter, a girl about nine summers, giggle until she nearly fell off her chair. Then, for dessert, Mistress Mayor produced a rich, moist spice cake drizzled with honey. Who could have known that such a remote little village could boast such an extraordinary cook?

The mayor basked in pride, and after the children went to bed he fetched a bottle of well-aged brandy to share with us in exchange for news from the coast and a story or two. I was glad to oblige him, though the news was old and relatively mundane. I had no restriction on the stories though, and several times made Tanris cough in his snifter while the mayor and his wife howled with laughter.

And then, much to my joy, when the meal and the fine drink had come to an end, there was the bed. Such a deep, soft mattress! A fire—in a real fireplace, right in my room!—was warm and crackly. Best of all, I need not wake up to the cat licking my nose, Tanris's snorting snores, or water dripping on me.

It was paradise.

At least until Tanris roused me at the crack of dawn, insisting that we needed to get an early start. Logic agreed with him, but oh! that bed was soft and I hated to leave it. Still, Mistress Mayor filled us with scrambled eggs, hot cakes smothered in boysenberry syrup, and rashers of mouth-watering bacon—which very nicely banished the taste of the morning's dose of bitter antidote. Then she gave us a basket with a few loaves of bread, fresh cheese, an entire leftover chicken from the previous day's cooking and—be still my heart!—the remains of the spice cake, which she had noted I loved particularly well. Tanris modestly protested her generosity. I, on the other hand, thanked her profusely, and she blushed prettily when I kissed her plump cheeks.

Her daughters giggled.

Tanris just looked sour.

After all that, we replenished our supplies and I made sure to purchase a bottle of kemesh—that excellent beverage made from fermented honey and plums, the flavor of which delights the tongue and offers as well a cure from headaches to rashes and everything between.

We also foisted off the still-silent girl. What would eventually become of her I did not know, and I didn't particularly care. She had done nothing to endear herself to me. The folks of Uzuun seemed a friendly enough people, and if they couldn't find a way to return her to her kin, they would find her a place to stay and work to do. With the parcels of real, edible, enjoyable food tucked away, I even forgave them for having nothing at all worth stealing.

Another day and a half of travel, and I revised my opinion somewhat. I wished we had stolen—or even bought—some lanterns. And I wished I could put Kem Bohadri in a little, tiny box and toss him down the mountain.

To use the word "passage" to describe the narrow black crevice before us would have been generous in the extreme. To get the horses inside we were going to have to unload them, and they were going to have to duck their heads—no easy feat. Reassuring me the cavern got wider a few feet inside did not help, but the horses were happy in their ignorance.

"Are you really afraid of the dark?" Tanris asked as we removed our gear from the pack saddles and reorganized it to carry some of it ourselves. Now and then he looked back the way we had come and around the edges of the hollow in which we worked, still watching for Kem's missing companions. I didn't tell him about the fellow in the gorge, and Kem didn't tell us if there might be any others. Even if he did, one could expect him to lie.

"No, I am not afraid of the dark," I said shortly.

"You're afraid of caves?" Tanris set his ugly cat atop a rock, where it promptly settled down to clean itself. Licking the dirt off one's body, never mind ingesting body hair along with it, was a disgusting habit.

"What could I possibly have to fear from caves?" I prevaricated.

"Small, tight places. Billions of tons of rock pressing down on you. Some people don't like that."

I suppressed a shiver. "Even if that were true, it's only three days."

"If nothing happens," Kem put in, working on another unsuspecting victim—er, horse.

"What's going to happen? Isn't it stable?" I asked, busy hands stilling suddenly. "Are you saying there could be a cave-in or something? Isn't this thing shored up? No supporting beams or anything?"

Kem kept right on with his task and pointed to Tanris. "Make sure those top packs come off easy. We'll need to carry them ourselves to get the horses through some places."

"Has anyone ever considered enlarging this byway?" Were they even listening to me?

"Do you remember its name?" Kem asked, threading a strap through a buckle and pulling tight.

"The Ghost Walk," Tanris said.

"Yes."

"Which means what, exactly?" I asked. "It's haunted?"

"Yes."

I stopped again to stare at him, then at Tanris, then back. "You believe in ghosts?"

"Yes." Not the slightest trace of humor showed in the man's face. If anything, he looked a little strained.

"And you?" I turned to Tanris, who set about resolutely reorganizing our supplies and tightening things down. He could make a career out of reorganizing.

"I've never seen a ghost, so I can't say with absolute certainty that they don't exist." There we were, back to that argument again.

"I have seen them," Kem said soberly. "You will see them."

"Joys," I muttered under my breath, and for a moment or two I stared at the evil black crevice and considered what I knew of fictitious ghosts. They were disembodied spirits. Phantoms. What could a phantom do to me? Nothing. The thought cheered me somewhat.

"How'd this place get its name?" Tanris asked.

Oh, good, a story to feed my insecurities.

"A long time ago, before there was even an empire, the ancestors of my people lived in these mountains. They lived much as the people of Uzuun live—simple lives, raising horses and sheep, trading with travelers, farming." He tugged another strap tight and the horse shifted, reaching down to nibble at the winter grass at Kem's feet. "They lived in tribes then, and guarded their territories with great determination. As the tribes grew, it was necessary to expand territories. In one particularly fierce war the Mazhar Tribe suffered great losses at the hands of the Nahzym. Men, women, and children were forced to flee their homes, and the Nahzym chased them for many days. They chased them into the crevice, where the Mazhar hoped to escape out the other side and block the way and thus get away from their enemies, but the Nahzym had come before them."

"If the Nahzym blocked the openings, who reopened them?"

"They did not."

"Then what happened?"

"They burned them," Kem said tersely. "They filled the passage with oil and burned them. And when the Mazhar tried to flee to safety, Nahzym archers picked them off."

Sometimes having a vivid imagination was not such a good thing. I could picture all too well the smoke billowing from the opening, people on fire trying to run away, only to be shot down. My stomach churned.

"You all right, Crow?" Tanris asked, looking me over critically.

I swallowed the bile in my throat and straightened. "That is a horrible story, but it was hundreds of years ago. People do terrible things to each other all the time. What difference does it make now, besides turning peoples' stomachs?"

"You will see." Without another word Kem led the horse closer to the opening.

"Not afraid of ghosts, are you?" Tanris asked, and I didn't much like the mocking gleam in his eyes.

"No, but you should be, because if I die of Baron Duzayan's poisoning, I'll come back to haunt you both. Regularly and noisily." I dragged my horse over with the others, then went back for the pack Tanris had made for me. I would not miss the snow that clung to it in icy patches. Flicking it off, I hefted the thing to my shoulder.

Kem disappeared inside the crevice, then reappeared again a moment later holding a meager half-dozen torches.

"Are there more of those?"

"No, no more." He handed two to each of us. "We will burn only one at a time, and only when it is necessary."

"Darkness requires torches." They would each burn for a couple hours, and six of them would get us halfway through one day. "Are there others stashed along the way?"

"It wouldn't do any good if there were," he replied cryptically. "Take this."

I recognized the remains of one of Tanris's shirts as he handed me a piece, then proceeded to cover the horses' eyes as Kem instructed. As I tied one onto my mount, I considered blindfolding myself. I refused to ask how the three of us would manage four horses. No doubt Tanris would sort it out.

"Kem will take the lead with my horse," Tanris advised me, reading my mind. "You'll follow him, and I'll bring up the rear."

"Who's going to slit his throat if he betrays us?"

"That would be you. Unless you want to switch places?"

I found neither position particularly appealing. In front, I'd bear the brunt of whatever catastrophe Kem might have in store for us. In the back —What could happen to me in the back? I did not even want to consider. I have far too vivid an imagination. "I'll take the middle."

He made an amused snorting noise. "Don't get too close, or you might get yourself kicked," he warned.

Or stabbed or led into a pit or… "Yes, Father. Shall we go now?"

"Can you think of any reason we shouldn't?"

Yes, several, but the alternatives were just as abhorrent. "How about if we eat first?"

I was stalling, but he considered my request seriously, then nodded. "That's probably a good idea. Kem?"

"I'd like that." He gave us a strained smile, and I could tell he was in no particular hurry to enter the crevice, either. It should have made me feel better, but it made me feel worse. After all, he knew what to expect.

Just ghosts. Ghosts aren't real, and even if they are, they can't hurt you, I said to myself several times. We sat down on the rocks scattered near the opening and enjoyed the tasty meal the mayor's wife had provided. I took my time and made Tanris and Kem wait for me. By then, even Kem was peering at me dubiously. The cat even gave me critical looks, the tail wrapped around its feet twitching with unveiled impatience.

— 13 —
Fascination Cast A Spell

We shouldered our packs, Kem lit his torch and then he led the way inside, bringing Tanris's horse behind him. The horse balked and protested, whickering a soft sort of terror that made gooseflesh creep over my skin. Tanris put a hand to its rump and helped push him along, talking quietly the while. The broad backside disappeared suddenly, and then it was my turn. Settling my hat firmly on my head and bracing myself with a last lungful of fresh, icy air, I stepped inside.

Darkness wrapped around me like a wooly blanket and the bulk of the horse blocked the faint glow of Kem's light ahead. The air of damp and of earth I expected, yet it didn't seem as cold as the slope of the mountain. "Careful, it's tight at first," Kem said, his voice oddly disembodied.

Pulling my horse through immediately occupied my attention for the first several feet, so narrow the saddle scraped against the walls. She—I had learned her gender during the course of our tedious journey—braced her legs and refused to budge. Tanris said something about moving out of the way, and there came a sharp *whack!* that startled us both several feet into the passage. I danced backward to keep out from under the mare's hooves and had to lean into the poor creature to get her to stop. She stood still, shivering and twitching.

I stood still, shivering and twitching.

"Crow, you must come."

Right. Instinctively, I looked at the ground behind me so I could lead the horse, for all the good it did. I had to grope my way carefully. One hand on the bridle and the other on the wall, I pulled the mare gently ahead. "Come on, Horse, let's go."

She came along in spite of her reluctance, trusting me. Noise filled the entrance as Tanris brought one of the packhorses in behind him. Kem kept moving. He reassured me that the passage grew a little wider about twenty feet inside, and to my relief he spoke the truth, though I knew the more generous space would not last. We waited while Tanris went out again to get the other horse.

"All right," he called softly. "All set."

He blocked whatever daylight might linger behind him in the cave's entrance. Torchlight reflected off the cat's eyes where it crouched atop one of the packs. I shifted my cold hand on the bridle and patted the horse's nose.

"We're ready," I lied to Kem, in case he hadn't heard, and the torch abruptly winked out. "Kem?"

"I'm here."

I could hear him working to light a spark with flint and striker. "What happened?"

Tension marked his voice when he finally answered. "The torch went out." A soft scrape announced him stowing the useless torch.

Another pause. "It just... went out," I echoed doubtfully. Torches do not simply extinguish themselves.

"Probably the wind," came Tanris's reasonable voice from the back.

I felt no wind. I did feel a prickling up my neck, however. The torch flared to life and I let out the breath I'd held. I could not see Kem's face to judge his expression, and when I looked behind I could make out precious little of Tanris.

"Are there any other openings?" he asked, lifting his voice for Kem's benefit.

"No, nothing but a few false passages, and they are short." He set off, and the horse clopped along behind him.

"Guess we can't get lost then," he laughed, but Kem didn't laugh back.

As we walked along the hideously narrow cave, the horses eventually settled down. At least it wasn't raining, and as we walked we actually got warm enough to take off our coats. I kept reassuring myself by thinking about how the passage was not a box, or a city drain, or a gaol cell. Deliberately, I refused to consider the mountain of rock between me and the sky. Mostly. Still, I kept lifting my hand to check the ceiling, and it was far too close, though every once in a while I had to stretch to touch the coarse stone. Then I'd encounter a cobweb and worry about spiders. The idea of spiders in a cave alarmed me much more than spiders in Duzayan's stairway. Several times, I felt one tickling the back of my neck, but when I reached up to smack it or brush it off, I found nothing, but then I started to wonder about rats. Did rats live in mountain caves? I thought not. It would be embarrassing to start talking to the rats again at this point—but I could talk to my companions, so I did.

The conversation I tried to strike up with Kem quickly faltered. He'd assumed a taciturn and moody silence I found not at all encouraging. Tanris at least made an effort, but then that conversation dragged, too. We had to speak with the bulk of a horse between us, and the ringing of hooves on the stone drowned out our words, and the various indiscretions of the rich and famous of the empire apparently bored him. I turned to musing—silently—about the various ways I could ruin Duzayan's life when I returned to the city. I had discarded two variations that included setting him up with women of ill repute, one that framed him for murder—only I didn't want to have to provide a body—and was working on the possibility of treason when I became aware of a gently hummed melody. The tune was familiar, but I couldn't place it.

"What is that song, Tanris?" I asked as it came to an end.

"What song?"

"The one you were just singing."

"I wasn't singing anything."

"Fine, the one Kem was singing."

Kem said nothing for three or four paces. "I wasn't singing, either."

"Don't be ridiculous. *One* of you was singing."

"Not me, and I didn't hear anything," Tanris said, and from up front Kem agreed with him.

The only sound now was the clop of horse's hooves and the heavy breathing of the one right behind me. "That's not funny, you two. Who was it?"

"I told you there were ghosts. Just keep walking."

As if I'd stop right there. Trapped between the horses, I couldn't even turn around and run back the way we'd come, which I found suddenly and keenly unsettling. I definitely should have taken the position in the back. "All right, I'll sing." See how the ghosts liked that! I chose not to copy the melody I'd heard, and commenced on a long and fairly gruesome ballad involving a knight dying in a war, his true love, and a flock of ravens. I possess a respectable singing voice, but the acoustics in the passage left much to be desired.

"How spritely and cheering," Tanris remarked drily when I had finished.

"If you don't like it, you could always sing something yourself." Had I ever heard Tanris sing? I thought not.

"Or you could choose something more... uplifting."

"Why don't you stop criticizing everything I do?"

"Why don't you stop being such a selfish, conceited weasel?"

"*Me?*" I turned around, face to face with the horse, and shouted back at Tanris. "Why you arrogant, self-absorbed, sanctimonious *twit!*"

"Twit? Is that the best you can do?" he laughed.

"You must not argue," came Kem's firm voice. "It is them."

"Don't interrupt me in mid—"

"Them who?"

Tanris's voice overrode mine, and I wanted to push his pompous nose right through the back of his head. *"Augh!"* The space between my horse and the wall was not big enough for me to push through, no matter how I tried, and my aggressive behavior displeased the mare. She backed up, taking me with her but getting me no closer to my goal.

"Crow, what are you doing?"

"Coming after you!" I shot back, getting nowhere at all. With any luck the horses would trample him.

The already paltry light flared, wavered, and then went out altogether, leaving us in a darkness so deep, so heavy that I couldn't move.

The cat mewed piteously, sending shivers down my back.

"The torch has gone out again," Kem said calmly.

"Then light a new one!"

"We need to make them last, and we need to remain calm." That was easy for him to say. He hadn't been insulted past the point of endurance. "Everything is greater in here," he went on, apparently reading my mind— which did nothing at all to calm my apprehension. "They feed on it. On you."

"They?" Tanris asked. "The people that died here?"

"Yes, the Ancestors."

"That's just great," I muttered, and petted Horse's neck a little desperately. After a moment, I pushed myself free of the jam I'd got myself into between her and the wall. "What else do they do?"

"It is different for everyone. It is best if we remain calm and focused, and move as quickly as we can. We save the torches for when the way becomes difficult."

Kem had some things to learn about lifting morale. "If that's the case," I challenged, adapting an air of bravado, "what are we waiting for?"

It was impossible to measure time in that abysmal blackness, and impossible to move very quickly. Not only did the passage twist and turn mercilessly, but the ceiling sometimes dipped down so low we had to take gear off the horses, move the stuff ahead, then go back for the animals. One at a time. The pitch of the floor changed constantly, tending mostly downward. Even blindfolded, the horses had a strong aversion to such close quarters. I empathized with them, especially after banging my head innumerable times, but I quickly grew impatient with their lack of cooperation. At one point, we had to stop entirely while Tanris went back for the rearmost horse when the wretched thing refused to be coaxed along with its mate. This endeavor entailed forward movement until we found a space suitably wide enough to allow Tanris to squeeze past the slightly more cooperative pack horse.

I suggested he leave the stubborn animal. Tanris argued against the waste, prepared for a fight. After reluctant consideration, I decided he had the right of it. Nowhere in this gods-forsaken hole could we beg, borrow, or steal another horse or the supplies it carried, and we were going to need them once we got out.

I sat on the floor with my back propped against the wall. How long since I'd taken a dose of the antidote? I'd had enough practice that I could perform the procedure with my eyes closed. Why *was* I closing my eyes? I couldn't see anything one way or the other. I pried one open and then the other to test the theory. I tried opening and closing them together, then paused. "Kem, does quartz run through these walls?"

"I have seen some, yes."

I leaned across the passage to trace the faintly gleaming lines in front of me. "Does it usually glow?"

A pause. "No."

I scooted closer—not that it aided my vision at all—and studied the odd markings. "These are far too uniform to be quartz. It looks like writing or symbols of some sort, but it glows."

"Perhaps it is magic."

Always reassuring. Magic—and mages—were nothing but trouble. A look over my shoulder revealed the same indistinct markings on the other wall. I looked up at the ceiling again, and although dimmer there, I could still make out the marks. "They go all the way around the passage except for the floor, and I think they used to go there, too."

"Sometimes the Ancestors make us see things. They are not real."

"Look at this. Can you see them?"

The rustle of clothing betrayed his movement. "No," he said, peering between the horse's legs.

"I can *feel* them, Kem. Scratches—carving—in the wall." Shallow and slight, my sensitive fingertips could still make them out. I'd spent years seeking out secret panels and closures, lifting purses and jewelry from uncounted marks, and I could tell a copper sentin from a gold dural without looking. A glance up and down the passage revealed no other such symbols, but I got to my feet and went to my horse, only a few steps away, to peer into the darkness beyond her. When I looked back, the marks had disappeared.

My heart turned in my chest. I had been so sure!

"Do you have a sweetheart?" Kem asked, and I knew he was trying to distract me, trying to keep me calm.

"Yes." I dragged my hand along the wall as I retraced my short path.

"Tell me about her."

"Her name is Tarsha. She's a dancer that I met in—" I blinked. The marks had reappeared. I took a step back, and they disappeared. A step forward, and they were visible. Another step forward, and they were gone again. "You have to stand directly in front of these to see them. Come look at this."

Clothing rustling as he got to his feet, then eased past his horse. "Where?"

"Right here," I pointed.

He inched along until he bumped into me. "What is this?" he whispered, and his questing hand blocked out some of the symbols as he explored the cuts in the wall.

"You've never seen these before?"

"No."

"Never heard of them?"

"No."

"You have been through here before, haven't you?" I asked dubiously.

He made a soft, huffing noise through his nose. "Several times. What do you think it is?"

"Magic?" I echoed drily.

"But what for?"

"You know as well as I do." Clearly he knew nothing at all. I dragged my fingers up overhead, exploring the regular markings in the irregular texture of the wall and discovering a pattern to them, a sort of rhythm.

"Crow?"

As I rubbed the marks they transformed into things of beauty. The glow intensified, becoming a clean, bright white, while the writing itself shifted to a lovely emerald. Then they moved, flowing into each other and then lifting completely off the wall. What a strange kind of illusion! Astonished, fascinated, I rubbed more quickly, wiping away centuries of dust and grime.

"Crow, stop! Something is happening!"

As if in a dream, I turned my head, and even without the benefit of a torch I could clearly discern Kem's face, his eyes filled with fright. The symbols drifted between us, a lovely liquid script that became more and more distinct as it gently swirled off the wall and wound around my outstretched arm.

"Look at that, will you?" I murmured, watching in wonder.

"*Crow!*" Kem grabbed hold of my tunic and pulled hard. I staggered backward, but the symbols came too. With a frightened noise, he let go and backed into the horse. The creature whinnied and danced down the passage several paces, shaking its blindfolded head. My own horse reacted by backing up and bumping into the pack horse. Her movement barely registered. The glowing symbols settled on my tunic, clung to my pants and my boots, attached themselves to my bare hands.

"Kem?" My voice quavered. I shook my arms but I couldn't get rid of the things.

He edged closer, but when he tried to brush at the symbols, his hand went right through them. There was nothing he could do but watch in horror as the figures seeped through cloth and leather. Fainter and fainter they became, until at last they found my skin.

They burned with an icy heat that frayed nerve endings and sent panic pounding through my veins. Pinpricks of light pierced my clothes and radiated outward so brightly I had to close my eyes. It did not banish the light. It filled me. Sounds rushed through me, leaving me gasping. And then the images came, hundreds of them, one on top of the other, faster and faster until I could not tell one from another. Faces. Symbols. Buildings. Places. *Weather*, gods save me...

But the gods weren't there at all.

:-:

"Why is he glowing? What happened?"

"I don't know! I don't know!"

Terror brushed prickling fingers across my cheeks.

"Is he breathing?"

No answer.

"Did you even check?"

"No." The voice came from further away than the first. How could I hear distance? "It could be dangerous. You shouldn't—"

Warmth touched my neck.

"Crow, can you hear me?"

The question carried fear and something else. Concern. From Tanris?

"What are we going to do?"

"Get me a water flask and some of the blankets."

"We can't stay here. We don't even know if he—"

"I'm not going to leave him behind."

The firmness of those words astonished me. I felt them as though they had physical substance, and the sensation was altogether different from the terror. It was reassuring. My head and shoulders were lifted, then moisture touched my lips. I drank greedily, suddenly aware of a terrible thirst.

"Easy, easy now..."

"We should go."

"We will, in a little while. Let him rest a bit, and then we'll figure out what we should do."

The fear rose again. "We must keep moving!"

"We have to rest at some point, it might as well be now. Whatever attacked has him, not us. It left you alone."

"And when it's done with him?"

"Sit down and shut up."

:-:

"Someone is coming." The awareness, the words, came out of my mouth of their own volition, the voice that spoke them hoarse and rasping. I had no idea how I knew, but the impression was as certain as the rock beneath me.

"Crow?"

I pushed myself upright and looked around, frowning. "Who else would I be?"

"I don't know." Sitting cross-legged next to me, worry and fatigue etched Tanris's face. The cat curled up beside him, watching me with diabolical eyes. "I don't know much about magic. Something took you over. Do you remember?"

Oh, boy, did I remember, and remembering sparked a throbbing headache. "I'd rather not. I need a drink." Tanris passed me a water bottle. Not really what I'd had in mind, but better than nothing. I was so terribly thirsty! Then the awareness pressed on me again. "I'm serious, Tanris. Someone is coming."

He looked at me skeptically. "How can you tell?"

I just shook my head.

"All right, which way?"

I pointed back the way we'd come, and he looked over his shoulder as though he could see anything lying beyond the pool of light in which we sat. I blinked. He'd borrowed one of my witchlights. I'd forgotten all about them and could have kicked myself. He held the thing in his lap, and it gave off a fragile, comforting glow. "How long have I been out?"

"I don't know. We burned through one of the torches, and Kem was getting a little anxious." Behind Tanris, the other man watched us warily. No, he watched *me* warily. He feared *me*... "Are you up to walking, or should we wait for whoever's coming?"

"I don't especially like knowing that someone I don't know is coming up behind me."

"We can't exactly hide," he pointed out, and I scoffed.

"Put the light away, and we can."

He nodded, then looked at Kem. "One of your friends finally catch up?"

Kem shook his head. "I don't know. I doubt it."

"Why?"

"They don't like coming through here."

"Imagine that," I muttered, then lifted my voice a little. "If he takes the horses ahead, whatever noise they make won't give us away. You and I can lay in wait."

"Or it's his friend, and they'll trap us between them. Or he'll just take the horses and leave us here. Why don't you go with him? I can handle this." His eyes held mine, and the iciness they held made me shiver. He trusted me—in this instance, at any rate—and he didn't trust Kem. If Kem betrayed us I may very well have to kill him. But Kem was afraid of me...

It was both an unnerving and interesting situation. "All right. Keep the light, in case you need it."

He nodded. "You've got the other one," he said, telling me indirectly that Kem didn't know about the third. "Be careful."

"You, too." I found myself looking at him, looking into his eyes and sensing strange things I couldn't even begin to understand. Apprehension pushed me abruptly to my feet and I steadied myself against the wall.

Tanris stood, too. "You going to be all right?"

"Fine."

"Liar."

"Braggart," I shot back, and things settled into a familiar, comfortable pattern.

Kem rose more slowly and made his way to the front, tying the reins of my horse to the saddle of the one he led while I took up the leads of the packhorses. He didn't notice Tanris handing me the war axe. I hefted it experimentally. Then Tanris squeezed my shoulder and went to work his way past the packhorses and into the dark. The cat leaped delicately after him. Good riddance. The witchlight winked out. I waited a moment until the disconcerting sensation that accompanied loss of vision settled, then clicked to the horses, urging them forward.

"I'm fine, in case you're interested," I informed Kem, a little dizzy, a little prickly, but nothing worse.

"You are not fine."

"How do you know?"

"Letters and symbols written on the wall came to life, wrapped around you, lit you like a bonfire, and made you scream and babble strange things. For a long time."

That explained why my throat hurt. I looked down at my invisible hands. At least I wasn't glowing any more, though I couldn't help being curious about what it had looked like, and if it was actually real or some strange product of the cave. "Did I hurt you?"

"No."

"Did I do anything to you?"

"No."

That wasn't quite the truth. I pressed him. "I scared you."

"Yes."

Somewhat surprised by the honesty of his answer, I fell silent, counting off about two hundred paces that included a snakelike bend in the passage. "All right, stop. We wait here."

Wordlessly, he came to a halt. I considered having him join me, but frankly I preferred having the horses between us. As strange a mood as he was in, I didn't know what he'd do. It would have been a simple thing for him to either take the lead horse and keep right on going, or leave the troublesome thing and make a run for it, and I listened intently lest he try sneaking away. I decided that he must be more afraid of the Ancestors than of me. Neither one of us said anything, and I imagined him straining his ears just the way I did, waiting for something from the passage behind us that might indicate what was happening with Tanris. It took considerably longer than it ought, but Time was a slippery thing here.

In an effort to distract myself, I mulled over the perpetual puzzle of Duzayan's letters. Clearly he was planning a seizure of power, else he wouldn't need soldiers and ships and pirates. If the missives from the priest were in code, I had yet to decipher them. Of what use to a coup was a pile of musty books? Spells, perhaps? Details to a successful historic plan he wished to use again? The intervention of the gods?

The glow of the witchlight reflecting on the walls as Tanris rejoined us seemed almost cheerful, and I edged past the horses to meet him. I did not expect to see the light held straight out in the trembling hand of the girl we'd saved from Kem and his friends and then left behind in Uzuun Village.

— 14 —
Goose Bumps

"What's *she* doing here?" I exclaimed. No one, apparently, had told her that the Ghost Walk was a scary place to go alone—or with other people, for that matter. Even in the fragile witchlight she was white as a sheet.

"I don't know," Tanris said, coming along behind her. He'd kept a good distance between himself and her and walked with his sword drawn, which startled me. Was he afraid of her? Or... was she real? "All she did was squeak when I surprised her, and then she sat right down and cried. Hasn't said a word."

"Are you crazy, girl?" I asked.

She gave me a distressed look, then hurried forward, thrusting the light at me. I barely caught the thing and held it up to appraise her. She wore ill-fitting men's clothes and a knapsack, her face was smudged and her eyes red and puffy. I wondered how much of her time in the passage she had spent in tears, and what she might have seen or heard. She'd had no one to reassure her or to warn her what was happening.

"What are you doing here?" I asked her.

She pressed both hands tightly over her mouth, and for a moment I feared she might vomit, but she just cried more. That girl spent more time crying than anyone I had ever known. Granted, her folks had suffered a tragic ending, but crying wouldn't bring them back or pave the way to a better existence, and she had no idea at all what keeping company with us entailed. Given the choice, *I* would avoid us. Vigorously.

"You can't come with us," I explained. "We told you that before."

"We can't just leave her here," Tanris said, just as I'd known he would.

Kem hung back behind me, as silent as the girl. I turned my head to study him for a moment. The emotions wafting off him weren't nearly as strong as

125

the girl's terror—not even as strong as Tanris's annoyance and underlying apprehension—though he was wary and curious and carefully reserved. "Got any ideas?" I asked him.

Kem rubbed his cheek. "I'd say it might help to have another person along, but if she can't hold herself together we're asking for trouble."

Lest I invite disaster, I didn't ask what kind of trouble he anticipated. "Did you hear that?" I asked her.

She nodded and cried.

I heaved a sigh of exasperation. "You can't cry. You have to remain calm. There are things in here with us."

"The Ancestors," Kem supplied helpfully.

"Ghosts and such," Tanris tacked on.

Sick and scared already, she couldn't possibly like what I had to say next. "We can't travel with lights. This kind—" I held up the witchlight, "isn't wholly reliable. The torches only last a couple of hours, and we have to use them carefully."

Her eyes widened in horror.

I sighed.

Tanris sighed.

One of the horses sighed.

"We should go," Kem said.

"Do you know your way around horses?" Tanris asked.

She nodded hesitantly.

"Good." His decisiveness was appealing. Annoying, too. "You can help, then. We could use somebody to take the extra horse. You lead it along. Keep it calm, and it'll help keep you calm. You *must* stay calm. Do you understand?"

She was mute, not stupid. She nodded and wiped her tear-streaked face.

"You follow Crow, and I'll come behind."

She nodded again, and we sorted ourselves out like a bunch of people and ponies on a string. I held the witchlight wistfully, then tucked it back in my pouch.

I do not know what time it might have been when we stopped. I know that my feet dragged, my eyes could barely stay open, and Horse kept bumping her nose against my back. Every time she did, I stumbled on for a while longer, and then my eyes would drift closed again. My exhaustion robbed me of concern about the narrowness of the way or the depth of the darkness. I was consumed only with the need to keep putting one foot in front of the other until we found daylight—and there *would* be daylight. It was a promise I held onto with savage need.

Ragged sleep wove a tapestry of dreams not my own. I knew this even as I dreamed, and I still could not escape. Some were mundane, consisting of things as trivial as building and nourishing a fire, walking through a mountain field, or talking with someone as I worked on building a wall of stone. Others terrified me. I dreamed of being hunted, now and then catching glimpses of the awful creatures chasing me—great, manlike creatures that towered over me and wore the heads of animals. I dreamed a darkness enfolded me, and out of it loomed a charred figure, features melting to expose one eyeball and his teeth, and I knew he was still unutterably dangerous. I dreamed of flames over which I held a great brass plate onto which I'd poured a measure of some sort of powder. The plate did not get hot to the touch, but the powder heated, melted, and became a glass surface in which I saw things—not just shadows reflected from my surroundings, but faces I knew. I saw *myself*. My reflection stared directly at me, and for such a length of time as to make chills run up my spine. Could it see me? Then my reflection looked away, determination stamped all over the familiar features. The scene shifted to a tall and beautiful white building, and inside the walls a horribly violent murder. I woke screaming.

After we settled the horses and ascertained that no one had died from the heart attacks I'd inadvertently instigated, I learned that my companions hadn't fared much better than I. We decided we did not wish to try to sleep any more.

We did not talk much as we walked. The darkness weighed heavily on us, sapping even the desire to converse. I do not know about the others, but numbness wrapped me. I was in such a daze that I didn't realize Kem had stopped until I ran into the horse he led. It stomped a foot and stepped backwards into me, swishing its tail and snorting. "Whoa, whoaa…!" I had to push my own horse backwards, prompting a chain reaction of indignation down the line. Luckily the line was short.

"Why did we stop?" I asked, peering uselessly ahead into the darkness.

"Two things," Kem said, his voice drifting eerily. "First, I can't stand your constant whispering any more. Second, I'm standing in water."

I wasn't whispering! What was he going on about? "I take it there's not supposed to be water."

"There never has been before." Even so, he sounded quite calm.

"Is it real?"

He kept silent for a little space. "I don't know."

"What's the trouble?" Tanris's voice came from behind, sounding very far away.

"There might be water." What a ridiculous thing to say. There was either water, or there wasn't. "Just go, Kem, and—well, it's just water."

And water it was. The passageway dipped downward here, and the further we went, the more obvious the incline became. The water made the going treacherous and slippery for both us and the horses, and what started out as an ankle-deep nuisance rose slowly to our knees, then our thighs and our waists.

From ahead came sudden splashing far wilder than mere wading necessitated, a gasp, more splashing, then swearing. Whatever had happened, Kem had not drowned. Were there things in the water? Where would they have come from, and what did they eat?

"Are you all right?" I called out to him, picturing some scaled creature with a mouth as big as a horse and lined with thirteen rows of knife-like teeth.

"There's a—" Indecipherable muttering filled in the sentence, and then, "ledge!"

Certainly a less worrisome outcome than the monster. I tried to decide if a mysterious ledge was better or worse than the magic that may or may not have attacked me. Or the giant scaled creature. "How deep?"

"Just a moment." More splashing followed, then a bubbling, unnerving silence, another splash and a gasp. I imagined Kem sinking or diving into the water to discover the depth and then resurfacing. How disorienting the black depths must be! "I can't find the bottom," he rasped. "There must have been some kind of shift. An earthquake or something."

My hand tightened on poor Horse's bridle. If an earthquake had changed the passage that drastically, did it even have an outlet any more? And how in the names of the plentiful gods were we going to get the horses turned around so we could get out again?

Tanris startled me, coming up alongside. "The passage is wider here," he said. "Maybe ten feet?"

That much? It was practically palatial. Fingertips against one wall, I stretched the opposite hand. I met no resistance. "We could turn around."

"Or see if we can still go ahead."

"See?" I laughed.

"You know what I mean."

We lit one of the torches. The cave wall continued along the right hand side, then disappeared past the light cast by the wavering flame. The ceiling dipped down low but the still, black water reflected the torch for a long way. To the left, both water and cavern extended beyond our line of sight. The floor descended into the water for about five feet, then broke off abruptly.

We argued about whether to go forward or back, and if we went forward should one of us first swim to the other side to ascertain conditions? And if only one went, should he take the horse too, and risk having no place to go? And that begged the question of whether it would be too far for a man to swim at all. The thought of the amount of time we might have lost made me ill. We couldn't afford to go back and take the longer route.

"I'll go," I said, putting an end to the argument.

"No, it should be me. I told you I'd show you the way," Kem protested, and I rolled my eyes.

"Fine, you go. By yourself. No sense risking the horse."

"Stay close to the wall," Tanris advised. "Just in case this space opens up further still." He was always so practical and so full of horrible ideas. If Kem kept to the edge, he could find his way around to where—hopefully—the passage continued. If he didn't, he might very well get lost and drown.

"Better yet," I said, pulling one of the witchlights out of my pouch, "take this."

He paused apprehensively, then nodded. "Thank you."

"Don't lose it. Make sure it's lit when we start across so we know where to go. They like to be warm."

After a moment's disbelief, he offered a strained smile. "Wish me luck."

"Luck," we echoed as he struck out. We watched the pale light bobbing along, lighting the wall next to him for a long way.

"Ceiling's awfully low!" he called back to us, and then there came some more of his elegant swearing and the light disappeared. We caught our breaths and held them until the light reappeared, then moved sideways. Faint splashes marked his progress, and I found myself leaning forward, straining to see something, anything. Past the ring of light our torch cast, it was hard to say if he was moving across or away.

"What's he doing?" I asked.

"Swimming," Tanris supplied with his usual skill at stating the obvious. The cat wound around his ankles. He bent to pick it up, cradling it in one arm while he rubbed its head. Incredibly brave or wildly obtuse, the fool creature purred noisily. "Think the ceiling comes down too low to go under?"

"We might be able to swim under water for a little way, but what about the horses?"

He grunted.

The light disappeared again. We waited. And then we waited a little more. Tanris rubbed the cat's head and regarded the girl with pursed lips. "What's your name?" he asked.

She shrugged and looked down at her boots.

"You don't know?"

A nod.

"You do, but you're not saying?"

"She's mute, Tanris," I reminded him. She just pressed her lips together.

"Surely she's got a name."

"Most folks do. Can you write?" I inquired. She shook her head and I held my hands palm up. What could we do? "She's a girl, I'm going to call her that."

"You can't just call her *Girl*."

"Why not?" I crooked my brows at her. "Do you care?"

She shook her head and shrugged her shoulders, a very confused—but still silent—expression.

"That's ridiculous."

"I suppose you could always try guessing."

He rolled his eyes. "That could take forever."

"You have something pressing to occupy yourself with while we're toiling across the empire?"

"Is it a common name?" Tanris asked.

She shrugged again.

"Hey, Girl, want a bit of jerky?"

She smiled and nodded.

Tanris snorted his disgust. I fetched her the jerky. I couldn't remember when I'd last had a dose of the antidote, so I took it out and administered the required two drops. Without looking, I felt the girl watching me curiously. Nervously. It was impossible to tell if she was frightened of the situation still, or of me.

"Kem?" I called out, fastening the stopper and tucking the vial away.

We waited a little more. The horses shifted and sighed and switched their tails. And then Tanris took a turn hollering, and I had to admit he had an enviable set of lungs. *"Kem Bohadri!"* The phrase echoed eerily.

The water worked with the uneven walls and ceiling to distort the reply. "I found it!" couldn't possibly be misinterpreted as an echo.

"Is it good?" Tanris bellowed, loud enough to make me wince.

Is it good… good… Came back to us. We looked at each other and waited. We received no answer, and we could not see the witchlight. Tanris rubbed his jaw consideringly, then tried again. "Kem Bohadri!" he called again, hands cupped around his mouth.

We were back to holding our breaths again. I ventured a glance at Girl. She peered anxiously across the water, her face pinched and pale. The walls and the water, and perhaps the cursed Ancestors as well, did strange and unearthly things to our words.

"It's good!" we finally heard. "Come ahead!"

I briefly closed my eyes, thanked a goodly portion of the gods, then squinted into the darkness. "I don't see the light."

"We might not from here. The roof is low and he had to go around."

"Right."

"Well, shall we?" Tanris asked.

I didn't want to get wet again, which was just silly, since I was already drenched. The flatbread was probably soggy, too. Ugh. "Girl?" I asked. "You can swim, can't you?"

For an answer, she waded out past me, tugging her horse along.

"Stay close to the wall," I reminded, "and stay out of the way of those hooves!"

One by one we dragged our equine companions into the unfathomable water, and their fear fluttered at me like the wings of giant moths, a circumstance just as unnerving as swimming alongside their great, thrashing hooves. It was quite a trick to stay close enough to the wall to follow it while avoiding their feet and directing the silly brutes. Tanris's cat, perched on top of one of the packs, growled and cried and carried on in a truly demonic voice. No amount of reassurance quieted the thing, and Tanris took exception to the notion of drowning it. After a very long way I found the lower portion of the ceiling with my head, and promptly went under, stars flashing in my vision. I could only imagine that Kem had done exactly the same, but he hadn't had to worry about being trampled.

I came up gasping and choked out a warning to the others. I had no idea where they were in relation to me, but I didn't have time to do anything about it as I had to deal with Horse's panic. "This way, stupid!" I ordered her, pushing myself to one side and tugging on the reins. She hit the ceiling. I heard the dreadful thump and I'm sure everyone heard the panicky whinnying and flailing and hollering the two of us engaged in. They probably heard it all the way back to Uzuun village, cave or no cave. Maybe the cave amplified it, for all I know.

Hysteria reigned until I caught and held a decent breath, finally bracing myself against the low ceiling until I got my heart mostly back under control. I had to physically drag Horse around in a new direction which, while being somewhat easier to do in the water where she couldn't get a purchase, was still no mean feat. Fortunately, the others avoided my same near-disaster, and we made our way along the ceiling.

The downward bulge took us a considerable distance to one side—much further than seemed possible. We could not tell if we were actually going sideways, going straight, or even going in circles, and I was haunted with images of the three of us swimming round and round. Eventually finding the floor beneath my feet again made me dizzy with relief. Pulling out one of the witchlights, I held it up high. Thank the merciful gods, we had not gone clear around to our starting point again. Some fifteen yards or so to the left a darker stain of shadow indicated the passage. Of Kem Bohadri, however, we saw no sign.

As soon as we reached dry land, the cat gave a horrendous shriek and catapulted off the pack and into the shadows. The horses shied. Tanris hollered. I hollered. It took several minutes to restore calm. The floor here was steep and rough, and that occupied our attention as we helped the horses up and over it, but several yards down the passageway once again became smooth and regular. Tanris called for the cat, but it refused to show itself. Magnanimously, I kept my joy to myself. I lifted the light to peer into the darkness overhead but the ceiling remained invisible—a circumstance which didn't hurt my feelings in the least. We called out for Kem, but he did not answer. We searched along the edge of the water and Tanris even swam out a ways, but we did not find him, nor any trace of him.

Tanris took me aside. "I don't like this. For all we know, he's waiting ahead to ambush us or he's gone on to join his friends, which is even more dangerous. Be on your guard, Crow."

We resumed our journey, a gloomy and sodden group. Distracted by morbid thoughts of Kem's drowning or betrayal, I found myself in the lead, Girl behind me, and Tanris bringing up the rear. The blind leading the blind, I mused to myself. The passageway resumed its former character, gently winding to and fro, and up and down. We had to contend with the frustratingly low ceiling again, taking gear off the horses to ferry ahead, then going back and dragging the poor, unwilling beasts through. I pulled and Tanris pushed, once getting himself kicked for his efforts. He grunted harshly and I felt the surprising shaft of shock at the blow, but he brushed it off and said he'd had worse.

Reloading our things did not keep my mind occupied enough to forget about the strange impressions besetting me. Had it truly been some magical spell that attached itself to me, or was I merely suffering some form of hysteria? I opted for the latter, wondered how long it would last, and forged ahead. My false optimism was short-lived. Rounding the very next corner, there appeared more of the foreign markings, clearly visible the very instant I came abreast of them.

"Don't touch the walls here!" I called out, careful to avoid contact. Whatever had happened to me, I did not want to repeat the procedure. Looking at them with much distrust, I passed them by.

They came with me.

— 15 —
Sensory Overload

The sensation reminded me of spiderwebs sticking and dragging across my skin. It was not limited to those parts of me that were exposed—my hands and my face—but affected me from head to foot. I froze. Horse bumped into me, and Girl bumped into Horse.

"Crow?" Tanris queried. "What's going on?"

"I'm not sure." My heart had leaped up into my throat, and I swallowed it back down. Turning in place, I took another cautious step. Fragile webs of light, some so fine I could barely discern them, stretched out from the markings on the wall to me. "More magic." I admired the remarkable steadiness of my voice and dragged my hand experimentally through the threads. A scratching noise filled the air, and I caught the shapes of words —*leaving... listen... all that remains... pattern... must be protected... enough... must be done now...*

"Crow!" The sharpness of the word jerked my attention back to the passageway.

"What?"

The whispering continued, like the wind through autumn leaves.

"I can't see you, and I can't get to you." There was a flicker of relief in his tone. "Is the passage blocked?"

The strange glowing strands draped across her face did not affect Horse at all. She shook her head a little, picking up on my own anxiety. I could sense that, too, though I did not understand how or why. Extending one foot behind me, I took a cautious step back, then another. The threads stretched out further and the voices kept whispering, growing neither more nor less frantic. As I continued to ease down the passage, the threads stretched and stretched—until they began breaking off and drifting away.

"No," I said at last, watching curiously as thread after thread disconnected and fluttered away. As they did, the whispering became quieter. "Look to the side, and you should be able to see the writing. You have to be looking straight at it."

I kept glancing backwards as I walked, but the inky darkness revealed nothing—not the symbols, and certainly not my companions. They passed the spot without any incident. "Did you see it?" I asked.

"Yes, but it's very faint. Is this the same thing as before?" In my mind's eye Tanris looked right at the things, his brow creased.

"Yes. You're not touching it, are you?" My voice went up an embarrassing notch.

"Not touching it," he said calmly. "And now we're past."

"Good. Did you—hear anything? See anything strange?"

"Just the marks on the wall, why? Did you?"

I got a firmer grip on Horse's bridle and tried to pick up the pace a little. "Probably just my imagination."

"Are you all right?"

"I'm fine, and I'll be even finer when we get out of here."

"Can't argue with you there," he muttered, but his voice carried.

I cannot say much about walking along in the dark for mile after mile except that I was exceedingly glad for a smooth floor almost entirely free of things to make man or beast stumble, though occasional strange pitches or loose rocks kept us on our toes. I hummed a song or two, and Tanris didn't complain. Girl didn't say anything, which came as no surprise. The horses plodded along cooperatively, however unhappily. Sometimes I heard other voices, but I elected not to tell Tanris. And then I perceived his sudden anxiety, brushing along my nerves and making the hairs on the back of my neck stand up.

"Tanris? You all right back there?"

"No," he said, his voice oddly strained. "Can we go faster?"

Girl squeaked behind me and I heard a smacking sound, then stomping and more squeaking and slapping.

"What is it?"

"Bugs." Tanris grunted. "I think it's bugs."

"Would the Ancestors have two of us experiencing the same illusion? Kem said it was different for everyone."

"Will you just *go*, Crow?"

My face tingled with their growing terror. The horses, too, were uneasy, pushing and twitching and making horsey noises. I pulled out one of the witchlights and abruptly wished I'd remained worried and ignorant and just gone ahead as fast as my little feet could carry me. A thick, fuzzy-looking web slanted sideways across the passage in front of me. All up and down the strands and across the ceiling and floor ran dark, eight-legged blobs the size of my fist.

Girl sucked in a terrified breath. A spider landed on my shoulder. A sudden wind sprang up from behind us, rushing wildly down the passage and sending the horses straight into a panic.

"Crow!" Tanris bellowed, though I really didn't need him to urge me to action. I ran. Granted, running straight into a monstrous spider web that probably came with a monstrous mommy spider wouldn't have been my first choice if I'd had any other. The strands caught at me, slowed me, and might have held me if not for Horse pushing me anxiously from behind. I staggered through and lit off down the narrow corridor like—well, like giant spiders were chasing me. The near darkness didn't hinder me, I'd spent a great deal of my life honing my ability.

However, running blind was not a talent the horses could claim. With nowhere to go but ahead, they bounced and scraped off the passage walls, whinnying wildly. Luckily, the narrowness of the way kept them from going any faster, else someone would have been knocked down, trampled, and their troubles with spiders and unearthly winds would be over.

Trailing streamers of sticky webbing, we left the spiders behind—most of them, anyway. The wind still followed us, though. Rank, stinking of rotten flesh, putrid with the decay of things I didn't even want to contemplate, it chased us, plucked at us and tangled around us. I had to press my arm over my mouth and nose, fighting the urge to vomit. Behind me, Girl was less successful, but I really couldn't stop to cosset her, even if I had been so inclined.

Ahead of me, the passage split into two in spite of Kem's assurances that it did no such thing for its entire miserable length. The putrescent wind went one way, and I went the other. I ran until I was sucking furiously at the air to fill my lungs and a stitch jabbed at my side with every breath. Then I had to figure out how to slow the headlong rush of Horse without getting plowed over in the process.

"Whoa!" I gasped. "Whoa!"

She was not much inclined to cooperate. I, unfortunately, couldn't run as far as she could. To make matters worse, the witchlight I gripped tightly in my hand flared crazily. I shouted in startled dismay. Magic pulled, the voices rustled. Horse jerked me forward and dashed around a corner. White gleamed ahead, and my poor pounding heart achieved new and painful levels of speed; at any moment it would make an emergency exit through my nose. *"Stop!"* I screamed at Horse, terrified of whatever new torture the Ancestors had devised.

The cloth over Horse's eyes blinded her to the new danger we hurtled into headlong, and I am not certain vision would have done anything to change her commitment to escaping the terrors besetting her.

"Stopstopstooooop!" I screeched as we burst into the all-encompassing whiteness. Beneath my feet the cave floor dipped suddenly. Fresh, cold air hit my face, right along with the knowledge that three more horses and two

people were about to crash into us from behind. My screaming did nothing to keep us from falling. Horse went down first, dragging me with her, and the ground went completely out from under me.

For a terrifying slice of eternity, I hung suspended in space. A heartbeat later—probably ten, given the speed at which it thundered along—I met the earth again as my entire right side crashed into it. Stunned, I dangled with a one-handed death grip on Horse's reins while she grunted and shuddered above me. Her heaving breaths echoed mine, but bigger and louder. I flailed around until I had both hands on the reins. Burning from fingertips to shoulders, but somewhat safer now, I endeavored to look around.

Blinking madly, eyes streaming, I realized I was face to face with rock, that the brilliant white mercilessly assaulting me was sky, and then, lastly, the ground was actually a good hundred feet below me, mostly hidden beneath a blur of greenery I could only assume was trees. My mind, working far more quickly than one might expect, supplied me with the awareness that the rest of the group would strike Horse any second, sending her over the edge, and that would be the end of the two of us.

But the gods who had deserted me inside the mountain had returned and I did not go plummeting to a horrible death.

"Crow!" I squeezed my eyes shut against a barrage of rocks and dirt. One vicious chunke smacked me hard in the cheek, adding insult to injury.

"Could you maybe give me a hand up?" I croaked.

"Thank all those crazy gods you worship, you stubborn, stupid, crazy son of a crazy cross-eyed donkey. I thought I'd lost you."

Gratifying as it was to hear Tanris's grasp on speech reduced to dull and insulting repetition, I had more important things to worry about. Horse's sudden thrashing underscored my plight.

"Stay there!" Tanris ordered, and scrambled out of sight.

"As opposed to what?" I asked rhetorically, and ventured a look at the trees below, which appeared a bit clearer now as my eyes adjusted to the light of day. Heights didn't generally alarm me, but I was a bit concerned about the results of falling such a distance, particularly since the only thing holding me up was a little leather attached to a terrified horse in obvious pain and distress.

The thrashing upstairs stopped, and an examination of the cliff face provided me with some tentative places to brace my feet, thus taking some of the pressure off my hands. I daren't let go the reins, in spite of them slicing steadily through skin and bone. I discovered a crack where I could wedge my toe and put my weight on it gingerly, then pulled myself up a little. Horse grunted and tried to toss her head, a feat I'm sure was made incredibly difficult with my entire weight dangling from the bridle. Tanris barked sharp orders, then Girl laid down across Horse's neck and peered down at me. She looked petrified, and I couldn't really blame her. Doubtless I wore the same expression.

Horse groaned horribly. Tanris appeared again, stretched out flat on his belly and holding his arm out to me. "Grab hold."

"You're not going to take advantage and drop me, are you?" It would be an easy way to rid himself of me for once and for all. Still, he didn't have the dragon's egg yet.

"Just shut up and grab on."

I pried one fear-cramped hand off the reins and took hold of his forearm. He caught hold of the back of my coat. Half climbing, half dragged, I soon found myself up over the edge. I laid on my belly in the dirt and rocks, catching my breath and waiting for the burning pain in my hands, arms, and shoulders to subside.

"You crazy idiot," Tanris complained uncharitably, his voice ragged.

"Hey, I found the way out."

"That was pure luck, and you know it. And more luck that you didn't just *die*."

"The hands of the gods are everywhere," I said, pushing myself up with a wince. My unexpected journey had torn holes in both cloth and skin. My wrists bled. Shaking, I made my way to Horse's side and knelt, murmuring sweet nothings to her, thanking her for helping save my life. Girl, who still laid across the beast's neck, stared at me as if I were a ghost. Tanris argued that the "flamin' stupid creature" had nearly killed me. He had little faith in the abilities of the gods. In order to keep himself safe while he helped me up, he'd secured himself to Horse with a rope tied to her saddle, and when I'd recovered sufficiently, we used it and one of the other horses to pull her around so she could scramble to her feet without being in danger of throwing herself off the cliff. The blindfold no doubt saved her some needless worrying.

While Tanris examined the mare for injuries, then cast about for some sign of our missing guide, Girl crawled a safe distance from both the cliff edge and the cave opening and had herself a nice cry. I collected some of the supplies that had been torn from the saddle and tried to work some sensation back into the hand and arm with which I'd gripped the reins during our acrobatics. My shoulder, ribs, and hip ached, but nothing appeared to be broken. Only a little worse for the wear, Horse suffered nothing more serious than some scrapes and bruises. Her mouth, Tanris said, was another story and he refused to let her wear a bit. He fashioned a hackamore for me to use instead, and then pointed out that we'd be walking for a while anyway. The way down from our lofty exit wound along a perilously thin track across the face of the cliff and then, evidently, along the crest of a wonderfully steep ridge.

It was a good thing I wasn't afraid of heights.

:-:-:-:-:-:-:-:-:-:-:-:-:-:-:-:-:-:-:

"Crow. *Crow.*"

I blinked as Tanris snapped his fingers in front of my face.

"Where are you?"

"Right here," I grumbled, a frown pulling at my brows. My head ached dully, and I couldn't banish images of a room hung with pelts and thick quilts to keep out the persistent chill of the season. A neatly made bed stood against one wall, and a table with two chairs near the other. The only source of light came from a crackling fire burning in the hearth. A kettle set over the flames promised a thick bean soup flavored with chunks of onion and ham. I would do just about anything for a bowl of that soup and for the comfort and aid wafting through my senses like a promise.

From the Ghost Walk, we'd come down out of the mountains without any incident and traveled east across the Kerdann Moors for days and days, shrouded in constant fog and mist. I had begun to doubt these parts guarded any kind of civilization at all. Even Kem had disappeared completely. Our supplies were so reduced that Girl rode one of the pack horses, silent as a sack but wonderfully obedient, doing whatever Tanris required of her, wrapped in an air of quiet, hopeless misery. I wondered time and again what had possessed her to follow us on such a journey. She had no idea of our destination, nor our purpose. How could she possibly trust strangers so blithely, and what did she think she could get from us? And when she'd joined us there had been one of her attackers in our company besides. I did not understand, not at all. Maybe she'd come for revenge, though she didn't look the sort. Had her quarry escaped before she could work up the courage to do him in? Killing did not come easily to everyone, I knew.

Tanris snapped his fingers again. *"Crow!"*

Speaking of airs, the one he wore was prickly with concern. I wondered, if I touched him would it sting?

"What is the matter with you?" he demanded, his face all scowly. "Are you sick?"

"I don't think so. Why?" I squinted at him in the lowering gloom. Dusk had fallen, though I was certain it had just barely been afternoon—a cloudy, cold, gray afternoon, to be sure, but with hours to go before sunset. A more depressing landscape I had never known. Tanris's cold hand touched my cheek, and I pulled away. "What are you doing?"

"Checking for fever. Your eyes look funny, staring off into space like you actually see something more than fog and scrub grass, and you keep talking, but not to me. Not answering me when I ask you anything, either."

"What are you talking about?"

The cat poked its head out from beneath Tanris's coat and gave me an inscrutable inspection.

"Is that your cat?" I asked, sluggishly disgusted.

"Yes. There's something *wrong* with you, you feather-headed fool."

I did feel lethargic and muzzy-headed, but I put it down to weeks spent traveling, a dismal variety of food, and lack of social interaction. I was just not accustomed to this sort of lifestyle. Still, I tried to humor him. "What have I been talking about?"

"Most of the time I don't even know." His lips pursed with patent disapproval. "You talk in some foreign language."

Girl watched me intently with that same pinched expression she'd worn since the Ghost Walk. I'd get no help from that quarter.

"I do know a few," I sniffed.

Tanris shook his head. "They don't sound like anything I've ever heard before."

"How do you know I don't know some obscure language?" I inquired, pulling indignation around me defensively. He crooked a brow at me and I sighed, letting go my annoyance. It took too much effort to keep it up. "Fine, I know two or three common ones. What about Girl, has she heard this chattering I'm supposedly doing? Or maybe the Ancestors followed us and they're playing games with your mind." As a joke, it fell pretty flat, and Tanris just gave me one of his trademark sour looks.

"She heard you, too. I asked her if she understood, but she didn't."

I'd had some awfully strange dreams, but they were just dreams, weren't they? "I am tired," I allowed. "Maybe I'm just talking in my sleep."

"And sleeping at all hours of the day?" His dark brows furrowed with real worry. "In the saddle?"

I smiled at him brilliantly. "When I fall off, then you can worry."

"You have. Several times. Why do you think I tied you on? You already beaned yourself twice."

"I did what?" I looked down and regarded the rope around my waist in astonishment. Panic fluttered through me and Horse did a quick sidestep, her ears twitching backward. Tanris held her lead rope.

He let out a sigh. "You've hit your head twice." He pointed to the ground which, while covered in thick winter-pale grass, showed a fairly abundant crop of rocks.

I lifted an exploratory hand and right away found a bandage on my noggin. A little judicious probing revealed a tender, swollen lump on one side and another on the back. No wonder my head hurt! "I don't remember..." I murmured, still astonished and not a little frightened.

"I know," he said glumly. "This has never happened to you before, has it?"

"No," I whispered. Images from my strange dreams lingered, even now. Why? Who were these people and what did any of it mean? "What happened in the cave—it wasn't just a dream, was it?"

Tanris said nothing, and that was answer enough. This time as we rode along it was him trying to engage me in conversation to keep me in the here and now. It horrified me that I had no idea of knowing whether it worked or not.

— 16 —
Things That Don't Bump In The Night

I am not certain how long we rode after that or if it was even the same day, but the knowledge that we were not alone slowly crept up on me, making me uneasy. Itchy. All the peering in the world could not penetrate the perpetual mists swirling about a barren landscape decorated only by scattered boulders and occasional thrusting knobs of granite.

"Time for a rest?" Tanris asked.

"No." The idea made my skin prickle even more. "No, we should move on. Quickly."

"Why?" Saddle leather creaked as he glanced about. Girl's horse, several paces behind, swiftly closed the gap and she stared at me from a face pale as the moon.

I didn't want to frighten her. If she panicked, she might run off and Tanris's contorted version of chivalry would demand we find her, thus consuming time I couldn't afford to fritter away. "I don't like it here," I prevaricated.

"Why?" He had to press, forever unsatisfied with my answers. "There's nothing here."

"No, there's some*one*," I spat, wanting suddenly to hit him. I didn't need to see him to feel his skeptical examination like it was a tangible thing.

"Did you see something?" he asked at last with the air of patience reserved for the gently demented.

"No," I admitted reluctantly. I hadn't seen anyone in the cave when Girl appeared either, but I had known perfectly well she was there. Senses keenly honed over the years have never included prescience, and this sudden certain *knowledge* without any apparent facts to support it alarmed me, but not everything could be explained away as an uncanny coincidence.

Tanris's gaze shifted again to our surroundings, dubious but unwilling to take unnecessary chances. That I knew how he felt without him telling me generated another wave of apprehension, but now wasn't the time for personal reflection and scrutinization of my wretched affliction. *Something* followed us, yet I still jumped when I heard a distinct thump followed by a muffled grunt and a low growling noise.

"Did you hear that?" I asked, pulling Horse to a stop. The mists distorted everything, so I could not be certain, but I could just make out a jumbled outcropping plenty tall enough for someone or something to hide behind.

Tanris halted his mount and looked sharply in the same direction. Nothing further came to our straining ears. Finally, Tanris flipped his reins against his horse's neck and started forward again. "Probably a rabbit or something."

A rabbit? My sanity was being threatened by a rabbit? I didn't believe it, but I certainly didn't want to go investigate the noise just to prove Tanris wrong and suddenly find myself faced with, say, a pack of ravenous moor wolves. Did such things really exist, or were they fictions told to scare children and unwelcome travelers? Perfectly willing to remain ignorant, I urged Horse to a quicker pace. Bound by rope, Tanris's horse came along, too.

"Crow…"

Girl passed Tanris up and fell in right behind me. She apparently didn't want to meet any moor wolves, either.

With a thump of hooves on the sod and the jingle of tack, Tanris trotted past to take the lead again, giving me an evil look as he passed. I was used to those and would far rather suffer his glares than fall afoul of trouble in the form of wolves, bandits, rabbits, or any of the many bogs that littered the area.

We met with one of the latter anyway. It was not the first we had encountered, and Tanris had proven his efficiency in identifying them before we rode into them and then leading us safely around. Like most of the bogs, this particular morass cleverly disguised itself with grass and low bushes—the conniving, treacherous things. What looked like a puddle or two frequently revealed itself as an extensive area of soft, marshy ground, following the margins to avoid falling in frequently took us much out of our way. This time it was the pack horse that slipped and flailed itself in so deeply it required all three of the other horses to haul it free.

Needless to say, it was a wet and muddy business.

Afterwards, we walked for a while, giving the horses a rest and taking a break from riding. The exercise helped keep me focused.

"Hey." In the sullen, boggy silence my voice made the horses shy. "I'm not dead."

"Look at him go," Tanris drawled. "Why, I'd bet he can walk and chew at the same time."

Girl, walking alongside me, restrained herself to a small smile.

"I mean it, Tanris. I haven't been taking the antidote and nothing's happened. I'm free!"

"Free to be an idiot. I gave you the potion, Crow."

I could only see his back, but I knew his mouth crimped in a grimace of contempt.

"Oh." The remains of my premature victory drifted like ashes around me. After a few steps Girl gave me a jab, then flapped her hand toward Tanris. "Thank you."

He just grunted.

The appeal of walking faded after a couple of hours. I remembered how sore I'd been the first week or so of our journey, and how hard it had been to ride or to walk after smashing my leg escaping from Raza's men. Raza and Marketh seemed like another world, another life now. I wondered if I would ever make it back, and if I did, would things just pick up right where I'd left them? Would Raza still be hunting me? Would my rooms still belong to me? And what of Tarsha? What would Duzayan have done to her?

I was still worrying about her when we made our camp for the night in a place between two rough hills where a single bedraggled tree offered miserly protection from the weather. Tanris and I tied our tarpaulin to the outstretched branches, then anchored the other side to the ground with iron stakes made for that purpose. "How much farther do you reckon we have to go?" I asked him, pounding a stake into the ground.

"Mmm…'Bout a week, maybe less."

"Less would be good. I'm more than ready to get this trip over with and get back home to Tarsha. You think she's all right? She and your wife?"

"She's fine."

"And your wife, too."

He grunted, but didn't comment. With typical foresight, Tanris had set us to picking up whatever wood we found as we passed by the rare trees dotting the moors. We would have a modest fire tonight, even if it only lasted long enough to make a little soup and a mug of kaffa for each of us. While Girl went to fill our water skins from a stream trickling between the hills, Tanris squatted beneath the tarpaulin and dug out a little pit for the fire.

"You ever see her dance?" I asked. A professional dancer, I had first set eyes on Tarsha at one of the more elite theaters in Ha'jani, a city neighboring Marketh. Her beauty easily captured my attention, and I'd made a point of seeking her out to watch her perform. When I'd met her later at a festival and actually spoken to her, I'd known immediately that the most remarkable jewel I would ever steal would be her heart.

She had not made it easy for me, waving me aside as yet another besotted admirer, but I had been persistent and clever in my romantic pursuit. I could not be like all the other men taken in by her charms; I had to be something more, which required an extraordinary amount of patience. I was not put off by her first refusal to let me call on her, and after treating her to three months of apparently casual interest, it had been she who had invited me to her rooms. I did not refuse and the rest, as they say, is history.

"Yes, I've watched her dance, Crow. She's a fine dancer."

"You don't sound very convincing." He grunted again, and I went to take care of Horse. Tanris joined me a moment later, leaving Girl to do the cooking. Silently, he took the tack off his mount and set about brushing him.

"I have never known a woman like Tarsha," I went on, applying a brush to my own horse's hide. "She makes me feel... I don't know. Complete. You know?" He didn't answer. "Have you ever been to Pelipa?" I asked.

"No, why?"

"It's beautiful there. In the islands, you know, but not so far away from the mainland that it's too far to go visiting the city every now and then. You know how women love to shop in the big city markets." I smiled, imagining a future that didn't include rain six days out of seven, Tarsha on my arm, and the bright city to revel in. "Can't go too far from them. I'm thinking of buying a house in Pelipa. Settling down. I think Tarsha would—"

"Forget Tarsha."

The harshness of his voice surprised me. I stopped what I was doing to stare over Horse's back. "Why would I want to do that? I love her and she—"

"Doesn't love you," he interrupted again.

"What are you talking about? You don't even know her."

Lips pursed, he turned his face away from me, a heavy reluctance in him. And anger. It both frightened me and made me curious.

"Yes," he gritted out after a short, unpleasant silence, "I do."

I shook my head, bemused. "How? You couldn't. I was careful." So very careful! I had enemies aplenty, but few of them knew who I was and no one knew about my connection with Tarsha. I had not survived this long by being careless in my habits.

"I followed you, you flappin' feather head. I followed you and I bought her." Darkness hid the expression on his face but I *felt* his roiling emotions and heard the way he dragged the brush roughly over the horse's hide. The horse didn't seem to mind. "You cannot be that blind, Crow, nor that stupid. I know you better than that."

"What are you talking about?" I repeated, dazed. "Bought her? Tarsha?"

"Yes, Tarsha. You were set up."

"No." A band of pressure tightened around my skull.

"Put the pieces together. They're all there."

I could not stop myself from replaying the last scene in her rooms as though it had just happened—her laughter and her welcome, her lovely bright eyes, the look of expectation... And like a nightmare conjured by a demon, I saw her evasions, the look of greed that should have been desire and, worst of all, the dawning comprehension that she had not locked the door behind me. She had not screamed for help or done a single thing to aid me. Busy with the guards and the demon, I had not noticed then what she'd done: I had pushed her out of the way of danger, and she had remained out of the way, watching as they took me down and beat me. And who had been holding the stolen pearl? Who had been close enough to slip the thing into my pocket when the commotion came at the door?

I dropped Horse's brush and turned to walk blindly into the dark.

"Crow…" Tanris called softly, ruefully behind me, but I did not answer. I felt Girl's eyes on me and her quivering fear, but I ignored that, too, and moved stiffly away from the impossibility of Tanris's words. Complete and utter disbelief robbed me of sense. It made breathing difficult. In a minute my heart would stop and the world I knew would cease to exist. Maybe I would, too.

I did not realize until that moment how I had pinned all my hopes for a bright future on the woman I'd fallen in love with. She was safety, she was promise. She was white picket fences on a sunny island. She was the end of long, lonely nights and the end of being hunted by Tanris and men like him. She was *everything* to me.

Abruptly, I whirled back, only to find Tanris right behind me. He jerked backwards as I waved my arms wildly, angrily. "Was it not enough for you to capture me? Do you need to carve my heart out of my chest as well? *Do you?* What are you waiting for? My knife? Here!" I yanked it free from its sheath at my waist and held it out to him, hilt first. When he would not take it, but backed away from me with both hands lifted and palms out, I threw it violently at his feet. It bounced on the turf, then lay still. "What, not good enough? You want me to fall on my sword? I don't have one, but you do. I'm sure you wouldn't mind loaning it to me." Contempt edged my words.

Apprehension turned swiftly to anger and Tanris stepped forward and slapped me, hard. The impact spun me to the side, face smarting and eyes watering. "Stop it," he hissed, grabbing hold of the front of my coat and jerking me up against him. "You're acting like a spoiled little boy, not a man." He shook me. "Who's the thief?" he demanded. "Who's always got a ready, cutting quip on his lips? Who always flies away free?"

I wanted to weep in anger, humiliation, and hurt, but he was right. No one stole from Crow and got away with it. It still didn't stop me from hating him for the part he'd played—not in capturing the thief he'd chased for years, but in smashing my rosy, domestic future to rubble. My jaw edged forward and my mouth curled in a snarl that went clear through me. "You *bought* her."

"She was cheap."

My fists jabbed hard into his sides and he grunted, but he didn't let go. "You *humiliated* me," I gritted out.

"You let me."

I punched him again. "You trapped me!"

"It was my job."

"Why?" I shouted at him, hitting him again, hating him, and hating Tarsha nearly as much. He winced with every blow.

"I'm sorry, Crow."

I had never loved anyone before her. I did not want this to be real. "Why should I believe you? Why should I believe any of this?"

"Don't believe me." It was not what I expected him to say. "Believe what you know. Who told you about the Gandil? Who wanted it more than anything? Who told you where to find it? Who challenged you and made you promises if you succeeded in getting it?"

"Shut up." The thought of how I'd let her play me like a fool made me sick. My chest hurt, and my brain was numb. I couldn't process a single useful thought and fell victim instead to a thousand dreamlike memories of Tarsha's smiles, Tarsha's teasing, Tarsha's kisses.

"Crow—"

"Shut up!" I shoved him as hard as I could and walked away. I could not share my grief with him.

"Crow, you can't go out there," Tanris called to me.

"Why not?" I hollered back. "I can do anything I please."

His worry pricked at me like sharp thorns. "You walk out there in the dark and we may never see you again."

"So?" I kept going. Then I heard him coming behind me—*felt* him coming. I didn't want to know what he felt, didn't want to hear anything he had to say. "Leave me alone, Tanris."

"Come back to the fire, and I will."

I snorted. Tussocks of grass hid in the dark to upset my pace and wrench my ankles. I didn't care. None of that mattered any more. Nothing mattered.

"Are you going to run away?" Tanris challenged, still following me. "Are you going to let Duzayan win?"

Those words halted my feet, and just as clearly as I'd envisioned the images of Tarsha I saw Duzayan's smug, knowing expression as he'd led me along.

"That's something else I did," Tanris said quietly a few paces behind me. "I delivered you to Baron Duzayan. I should never have done that," he admitted pensively.

"Oh, really?" Sarcasm gave my voice the sharpness of a knife, but its edge could not cut him deeply enough to satisfy me. "I tend to agree with you, but my reasons might be considered a trifle selfish."

"It wasn't supposed to be like this, Crow."

Was that *guilt?*

"No?" I spun around to jab his chest with my finger. "How was it supposed to be, Tanris? A quick and tidy hanging? A heavy purse of gold for you and a happy retirement with your darling wife? The bards singing your praises for finally cornering and dispatching yet another filthy, contemptible thief?"

"No." Misery came off him in waves. Brows crooked, he looked away and then back. It took a major effort for him to meet my gaze. "I don't work for Duzayan. I never did."

"Mm. And I suppose you're not really married, either. Pardon my skepticism."

"That part is true. You were just a means to an end, and it didn't hurt that I wanted you caught. Look, I don't want to talk about this out here. Can we go back to the fire?"

I stared at him. "You completely ruin my life, and you're worried about a little cold and dark?" Wet, too. Rain, always rain.

Tanris's jaw came out and he folded his arms over his chest. "Suit yourself." He turned away a little, looking back at the tiny fire and Girl. "About a year ago I accepted an appointment in the Emperor's Eagles."

I frowned. That explained the relative freedom I'd enjoyed from his particular brand of pursuit until recently. I was not sure exactly what the elite and much-vaunted Eagles did, but hunting down thieves—even one as talented and successful as I—seemed rather below them.

"It was kept quiet and some rumors were circulated about me. Rumors about me and my superiors having a parting of the ways, as it were." He pressed his lips together tightly and rocked back on his heels. Rainwater sluiced down over his features, shining brightly where the firelight reflected on it. "It was part of a scheme to get me close to Duzayan so I could report his activities and eventually gather solid proof against him. When it comes to criminals, Crow, he makes you look like a toddler."

He really needed to add insult to injury?

His steady eyes met and captured my gaze. "He is a murderer and a traitor, Crow. Those letters of his have names listed in the margins. They're crossed out because they're dead. He is recruiting allies from the empire's malcontents and plotting to overthrow Gaziah. He's already forming an army, and he is responsible for the deaths of several key government figures."

"He's what?" For about three minutes I'd believed my life couldn't get any worse. At least not until the poison got busy killing me. Now, assuming I survived that, my name would be linked with a *traitor*? When captured, traitors got a whole lot worse treatment than mere thieves. A dank, dark cell would be the least of my worries.

Tanris looked away again, his mouth briefly turning down at the corners. "I should have stayed in the city and finished my job. I left word with the commander that—" He stopped, clearly struggling. "That I had to leave. I can only imagine what Duzayan has been doing in my absence."

"Where do I fit into this?"

"You were my reward for being a good little soldier. For services rendered, Duzayan offered to help rid me of the one stain on my otherwise perfect record."

"That's all? What services did you perform, exactly?"

He shook his head. "I'm not at liberty to discuss that."

"Right," I snarled. "I'm just a worthless thief." Why I did not push his nose right through his head I do not know. Instead, I brushed roughly past him to stalk back to the fire.

"Crow."

"*What?*"

"He stole both our women. I want mine back, and I'd like you to help me."

I whirled around again. "Help you?!" I exclaimed, laughing in startled, humorless surprise. "Why in the names of all the gods would I do that? You didn't just arrest me, Tanris. You completely destroyed my future and made me a puppet to a madman."

He drew his lower lip between his teeth, reluctance making him consider his words carefully before he spoke. "I want my wife, I want Duzayan, and you want your life."

Yes, I wanted my life, which was far too dependent on Tanris, on finding the dragon's egg, on getting back to Marketh, and then on Duzayan's non-existent good will—never mind dragging the wretched emperor into the picture! What a steaming pile of horse manure. I had never actually wanted to kill people before, but there were three of them lining themselves right up and begging for it.

"You help me, and I will do everything in my power to help you find an antidote for the poison."

"Isn't that generous," I sneered, "considering that if not for you, I wouldn't even need it."

He struggled for patience. "I never wanted you to die, Crow. If you do, it will be my fault, and I don't want that on my conscience. This… rivalry between us has been an honest one, your wits against mine, and it's been a good fight. I don't want it to end like this, do you?"

"Don't be stupid," I growled, resuming my march back to the fire. The heat it offered was pitiful, but I didn't need it right now, I had fury to warm me. I did need him, and it galled.

Girl looked up at us as we returned, her eyes going from one to the other uncertainly. The cat half-sleeping in her lap looked up at us, too, its expression one of benign patience.

"Have we got a deal?" Tanris asked.

I picked up a stick and stabbed the fire, sending up a tiny fountain of sparks. Then I looked up at his tense features. "Tell me something, Tanris, and I'll know if you're telling me the truth, so you'd best have a care."

"Anything."

His offer drew another sneer. "I don't want *anything*. I just want to know if you're supposed to kill me after I get the prize."

He blinked at me, then shook his head slowly back and forth. A ripple of shock emanated from him—a ripple I did not want to feel. It absolved him of a slice of guilt, a portion of treachery. "No. I had no idea he was going to do this, I swear. I would never have put Aehana at risk, and I would never have agreed to poisoning you."

He was telling the truth. I didn't know whether to be relieved or to hate him even more for not being a back-stabbing swine after all.

There was nothing to say, so I said nothing. I did not sleep that night, nor the following day when we struck out again across the gods-forsaken uplands. The sensation of being followed eased somewhat, but I still kept a sharp eye out. Late in the afternoon, Tanris brought down some sort of bird. I did not ask, I did not care. Girl found some tubers and herbs and turned them into a bland soup we shared in silence. The rain continued unabated and the temperature dropped, bitterly cold. When we eventually stopped our travels, if we ever stopped, I suspected I would find mold growing in my armpits, behind my ears, and between my toes. With so much water available we ought to be fairly clean, but we stank of horse and leather and sweat and smoke and mud and wool and… putrescence. Complete and utter putrescence.

It was another reason for me to hate Tanris.

Our little fire hardly lasted long enough to cook our meal and certainly not long enough to warm us. The three of us watched it flicker and die, then I laid out my sodden, useless bedroll and curled up in the wet blankets. After a moment, Girl came to lay down against my back—not because she cared particularly about how I felt, but because it gave her a modicum of warmth. Before long, Tanris came to lie down on Girl's other side. The cat, soggy and smelling faintly mousy, thought it could curl itself up against my chest. The cat was wrong. Lifting it by its mangy scruff, I reached across Girl to deposit it on Tanris's chest.

He grunted. The cat purred. I closed my eyes and tried to focus on the soft patter of rain hitting the waterlogged ground. There were no night birds, no wind, no howling wolves, nothing. Though nearly impenetrable, at least the darkness wasn't the murderous black of the Ghost Walk. Small consolation, that. What a horrible place that was. I remembered all too clearly the way the stone walls closed in until they blocked the way entirely, wrapping around my body and holding me deep in the arms of the earth.

Eerie, fragile green threads wound through the memories of that darkness and made my skin smart. I tried to wriggle the phantom prickle away, but it persisted like that old saying about someone walking over a grave. Graves, caves, crypts… and rain. When I die, have mercy and cremate me.

Staring at the unyielding fabric of the night and trying to imagine that morning would find me on Pelipa's beautiful white sandy beaches, I watched a shadowy form slowly pick its way away from the camp into more and deeper shadows. Girl still had an arm around my middle, tightly pressed against my back. Maybe she'd freeze solid to me—another cozy thought to lull me to sleep.

Behind her, Tanris let out one of his hallmark snores and I caught my breath. If Tanris was snoring, who was that other fellow?

"Girl." I tried to move her hand, but she clung fast. *"Girl!"* I hissed, and she still didn't budge. I reached past her to smack Tanris.

He grunted and sat up suddenly. "What? What is it?" Thank the gods of reasonably good sense, he kept his voice low.

"Someone was just here."

"Who?"

Did he really expect an answer to that? I very nearly seized one of the more-than-plentiful rocks lying about to drop on his head. Instead, I shoved Girl's hand off me and sat up. She whimpered and sat up, too, hugging herself tightly. "Why don't I just go ask?" Knife in hand, I got up and set off into the darkness in the direction our visitor had disappeared.

— 17 —
Bean Soup

"Crow!" Tanris whispered. "What are you doing?"

Sleep clearly fuddled his brain, else he would *know* what I was doing. I had, after all, just told him. Duzayan had put Tanris in charge of defensive measures and there was a reason for this: namely, he was the big fellow with the sword. But you know what they say about warrior-types—all brawn and no brain, and so it fell to me to go creeping about in the darkness in search of trouble, armed with nothing but a knife. And a rock. I had a fine supply of those and may as well make good use of them. I was tempted to use one of the witchlights to perhaps locate the Visitor, but its glow would surely mark me as an obstacle to avoid. Or a target to kill…

So I made my way cautiously around the circumference of our little camp as best I could. Dark and mist hid it, but I could sense the presence and direction of my two traveling companions, waiting for me to return. I made a second, larger circle, but found only knobby humps of grass to trip me up, dips in the ground to twist my ankles, and puddles everywhere. I stopped several times to listen and peer into the gloomy surroundings, to no avail. Perhaps it had been my imagination, another dream figure from the Ghost Walk haunting me, and so I returned to our comfortless resting place.

Tanris was furious with me. I didn't particularly give a rat's tail. I got back into my abandoned blankets and worked on going to sleep, a feat made astonishingly difficult with one companion grinding his teeth and the other staring holes in the back of my head.

When the excruciatingly long night finally ended, we broke our fast with a minimum of conversation, and I couldn't help peering off into the fog-shrouded morning, looking for some sign of the Visitor. Afterwards, I walked around our campsite again, but the rain had washed away any tracks, so I went back and went through all my things.

The ropes and climbing gear were all in place and easy to verify. Clothes, yes. Everyday things, yes. I unfastened the ties on a folding leather pouch and checked my lock picking tools. All safe and sound. Another pouch that held sundry items like wax, string, wire and so forth was also accounted for. From the bottom of my pack I removed the letter tube, unfastened the end and peeked inside. Then I inspected the contents of the small box in which I kept certain drugs and herbs.

"What are you doing?"

"Inventory."

To my relief, I found the pharmacy undisturbed. While I had it open, I examined the little glass vials of Adamanta Dust and found them thankfully dry.

Tanris continued to watch me silently, mouth turned down, disapproval stamped all over him. "All of this because you had a bad dream?" he asked with the silent suggestion that I'd had a lot of bad dreams lately and I was no longer entirely reliable.

I just grunted and kept working, laying things out in neat rows the way I always did when I checked my gear. Girl crouched down nearby and watched. The cat came and sat beside me. "Shoo!" It didn't of course, but gleefully pounced among my things as if it had found the most delightful sort of toy. Girl rescued my lock-picking tools before the feisty feline could figure out how to loose the leather ties. I retrieved a jar from beneath the tussock of grass where it rolled. The cat, highly offended, sat on a rock with its back to us. I made a face at it and returned to my inventory. "Things would go faster if you got busy with your own gear," I pointed out to Tanris.

"I'm not going to unpack everything just to satisfy your delusions."

"Yes, you are."

"No, I'm not."

We would see about that. I checked my pouch last. Among the other odds and ends were my two remaining witchlights. Kem still had the third, curse the wretch. When I'd accounted for everything, both in my packs and on my person, I looked at Girl.

"Girl!" Tanris objected, and I lifted my brows in surprise. Thus far, he'd studiously avoided calling her anything at all. I felt a small sense of victory. She ignored him and got up to fetch her pack and dump everything out to examine one item at a time. When she finished, she shrugged and shook her head. Nothing missing. We both looked at Tanris.

"No." He folded his arms across his chest and glowered at us fiercely. He needed a shave, both noggin and chin. He was starting to look strange. Hairy. Less Tanris-like, not particularly friendly, and rather a lot like the cat. "Quit looking at me like that."

I eyed him for a little longer, just to make him squirm. When he stepped forward and uncrossed his arms in preparation of violence upon my person, I bent my head to finish packing my tools. He stopped, glaring daggers fit to pierce skin. Why was he allowed to glare, but not I? Finally, he went to saddle up the horses, and I straightened my bedroll, climbed back into the deliriously uncomfortable blankets, and started counting. How far would I get before—

"Crow!"

Gratification met his burst of incredulousness, though I kept it to myself.

"What are you doing?!"

"Sleeping. Shut up."

He made a strange choking noise. It was always a grand thing to rob him of speech. It was unfortunate that it never lasted, but if it did I would miss the sheer joy of repeating the experience. "We've got to get going. We have precious little time to waste."

As if he was the one with poison riddling his body, promising a hideous death. "Then quit wasting it. Go through your things and find out if anything is missing. I'm not budging until you do."

He treated me to a brief silence. "You're out of your flamin' mind," he grumbled, but he stomped off and soon I heard clinking and thumping and muttering. Lots of muttering. "It's all here," he announced after a time, none too pleased about it. I couldn't really say I was, either. "Are you satisfied?"

"Yes." I got up and rerolled the blankets.

"Why?" he asked, practically dripping suspicion.

It would have been much simpler if something had been missing, but I knew as certainly as I knew that Horse had a tail that there was something wrong, something I couldn't put a finger on, much less explain to Tanris. "Because now we know what didn't happen."

If one could hear looks being exchanged, the one that passed between Tanris and Girl positively hummed. I tied the bedroll to Horse's saddle and dragged myself up. I squished. I swear, I did. "Well?" I asked, giving them a look of exasperation. I didn't wait, but urged Horse off across the field.

Evening had fallen when we topped what Tanris declared was the last ridge before the Darya Mountains began. I don't know how he could tell by looking at a cloud bank. We had to dismount to descend the steep slope, and I cannot tell you the number of times I twisted my ankles. Thank the gods of footwear and cobblers, the boots Tanris had long-ago forced me into were sturdy enough to keep me from breaking, even if I developed a limp. The cat alone got to ride, watching the rest of us smugly from one of Tanris's saddlebags.

The wet ground made the going slick. It hadn't rained all day, but who needed rain when we had fog? It hung over us with steadfast determination and muffled the world. The silence nearly drove me mad. Girl didn't talk at all, and I didn't want to talk to Tanris. He acted completely, insultingly unfazed, and kept a close eye on our surroundings, our path, the nearby ridges and ravines, the trees, the horses… I don't know how he could see further than about thirty feet, but he certainly made it look like his eagle eyes could pierce right through stone. Fog? Ha! A mere trifle. He was a veritable paragon of guardianship. Besides being a stinking, rotten, no-good wizard, Baron Duzayan clearly possessed a very twisted sense of humor, else he would never have even dreamed of throwing the two of us together.

Stepping down onto level ground after a skidding, sliding, heart-pounding trip down the side of the ravine, I paused to look about, because of course a twenty foot drop in elevation would give me a much better view and I'd be—Wait. What was that? From above, the little tree had appeared as a shapeless dark blob, but now that I viewed it from the same level upon which it grew it appeared eerily familiar.

"What is it?" Tanris asked. He sounded suspicious again, and it occurred to me that perhaps I was losing my grip on reality, because Tanris *always* sounded suspicious—or scathing—and I must be out of my mind to expect anything else.

"A tree."

"At least we know your eyesight still works." Scathing, see? He brushed roughly past me, leading the horses. Girl followed him, but stopped next to me to look from my face to the tree and then back.

"We're not lost, are we?" I called after Tanris.

"Don't be ridiculous."

I couldn't help but bristle as I pointed to the tree. "I know that tree." I don't know how I knew it, but I did. It squatted down low in the ravine, one branch reaching toward the hill and then bent up like a crooked elbow.

"Don't be ridiculous."

"Don't treat me like an *imbecile!*" My voice cut through the mist, and Tanris turned to look at me with one eyebrow raised critically.

"Then don't act like one."

I wanted to growl at him and fling something, preferably something substantial. Instead, I stabbed my finger toward the tree again. "I have seen that before," I insisted, enunciating each word so the sharpness of it might get through the thick muscle wrapped around his tiny little brain.

He looked at the tree, then came back my way a little. "Have you been to the Kerdann before?"

"Never."

"Then you have never seen that tree." Flipping the reins up over his mount's head, he put a foot in the stirrup and hauled himself into the saddle. "Let's get moving. It won't be daylight much longer."

I looked past the tree where the ground rose a little. I *knew* this place. Just beyond the rise, the ground would dip again and curve gently to the right and then down to the left like a broad avenue sunk a little into the rocky hillside. A canyon opened up not far beyond, filled with bushy evergreens. "There's a house there," I said, and pulled Horse toward the place where my imagination filled in details I shouldn't know.

"There's no house."

"If you haven't been there, how can you say with absolute certainty it doesn't exist?" I shot back, resurrecting our old debate. I was getting some good mileage out of it.

Tanris heaved a sigh audible even over the distance between us. "Fine," he agreed, then hawked and spat. "Go take a look. I'm not the one with the hourglass measuring out my life."

I forbore to remind him that he had a wife awaiting rescue and kept right on walking. The cat bounded past me, then trotted along with its crooked tail in the air like a flag. As much as I hated it, I took a perverse satisfaction in its choice to side with me and leave Tanris glowering after us.

Past the tree the rise was a little steeper than it had first appeared, and then it fell away just as I had known it would, and the evergreens came down the canyon just as I'd expected. I could see no house, but I could smell smoke, though the plume itself was lost in the drifting mist. Tugging Horse after me, I set off down the other side.

"Crow!"

The house—no, it would be a cottage, old and gray and looking as though it had grown up out of the land—would be tucked in against the trees in the lee of a fold of earth protecting it from the worst of the winds that whistled like furies down out of the mountains. Sod would cover the roof, and probably at this time of the year there would only be a few straggly, faded streamers of grass drooping down like funny little fringes, somehow hanging on in spite of wind and water. The window boxes would be empty. The garden with the creek running through the middle would be asleep, all the remains of the vegetables from summer turned under to feed the soil.

...late again... Hurry, now, go fetch the bowls... Watch out, you'll fall!... Didn't I tell you? ...mind the door, please... snow before long... fine animal, truly... take this row and I'll get the other... have you seen him? seen him? seen him?

The voices followed me down, down and around the last corner, and my eyes revealed what I had beheld in my mind. Although I have always preferred comfortable, roomy apartments, this pretty little place felt strangely like coming home. In the growing dusk, the little windows winked at us like amber eyes, warmed from within. The smoke curling up out of the chimney crept along the sod roof and drifted into the nearby trees, and I could smell food cooking. My mouth watered.

"How did you know?" Tanris demanded from beside me, and even at a whisper, his voice made me jump.

I looked at him, and then to the cottage again. Next to the sturdy rock chimney another piece of the dwelling had grown up, leaning close to its older brother. In the summertime spears of greenery grew in front of the cottage—lush with broad leaves and pink flowers nearly the size of a dinner plate. An infusion of the flowers sweetened with a bit of honey made a good cure for coughs and chest troubles. The addition held a horse and a few milk goats. It was snug and warm in there and smelled like grass. Cozy and safe.

I didn't say anything, but walked up to the door and reached out to open it, barely catching myself to knock instead. The cat wound itself around my ankles, then sat down right in front of me, one foot resting delicately on my boot. Tanris dismounted, but Girl stayed on her horse and trembled like a leaf in the wind. It was a wonder that she didn't blow away, but maybe the dampness weighted her down. "How do you know this place?" Tanris asked again, loosening his sword in its sheath.

"The Ancestors showed me."

The door finally opened, the cat slipped inside as if it owned the place, and an elderly person looked out at me. I could not tell if it was a man or a woman, for it was bundled in layers of quilted fabric and wore an embroidered felt hat from beneath which protruded wisps of gray hair. A map of wrinkles marked the face, and dark brown eyes sunk deep with time gleamed brightly, curiously.

"Are you Serkan?" I asked.

The old one stared at me for the longest time, then slowly blinked and shook his—her—head. "No," came a voice like a rusty hinge, which didn't help at all in determining gender, "I am Jelal. Serkan is gone." The word carried the weight of portent.

"Where?" He should be here. This was his home.

"It has been many years since Serkan joined the Ancestors, Stranger," Jelal answered slowly, and the dark eyes narrowed even further as they studied me thoroughly inside and out. "How do you know of him? Are you of his seed?"

His seed? "No." I had no idea what to do or what to say, and I had no idea how I knew the name. "I don't know," I amended. The examination I received, together with the disconcerting knowledge I somehow possessed, made me uneasy, and I stepped back just as Tanris came up behind me, laying a hand on my shoulder and ruining all plans for escape. Even through my coat the squeeze he gave would leave bruises. "I beg you to forgive my friend," he said easily. "He's not quite right."

I searched for a witty comeback, but Jelal beat me to it. "But he is quite right." He—she?—seemed more curious than afraid. "He is lost, isn't he?"

"I've never heard it put quite that way, but yes, yes he is."

"I'm not." I elbowed Tanris indignantly. He didn't even have the good grace to grunt.

Jelal stepped back and opened the door wider, waving us in. "Come inside before it rains."

:-:

Jelal was a he. Jelal's home didn't have wind blowing through every cranny or rain leaking through the roof. Jelal also had lovely, thick, warm bean soup flavored with chunks of onion and ham, and he generously offered some to us.

"We really don't want to take from you," Tanris protested, and Girl whimpered softly.

"Yes, we do," I countered. I was a thief. I had no trouble at all with the idea of taking something from someone, especially nice, hot, savory soup. Tanris, naturally, gave me a withering look. "We'd be happy to repay you," I amended, and the look grew downright icy. He could decimate small villages with a single expression.

Jelal waved his gnarled old hand dismissively. "We have plenty, though I wasn't expecting that one." He pointed at Girl. She shrank and held the cat against her chest as though it might protect her, but the cat didn't want any part of that, so it wriggled away and went to sit by the fire, leaving Girl alone and unprotected from dire pronouncements by eccentric old men.

"But you knew the two of us were coming?" I asked.

"Yes, oh, yes."

"Are you a wizard?" The thought made the hairs on my neck stand up, but Jelal laughed out loud, showing he still had all his teeth. Quite a feat for someone of his advanced years.

"You have nothing to fear from Old Jelal," he said, not really answering the question. He ladled soup into big, deep bowls and passed them around. I watched carefully lest he administer another draught of poison, and waited for him to eat first—a herculean task with the delicious aroma wafting to my nose, tantalizing me. I nearly wept with the first bite, eyes closing in sheer bliss.

Tanris nudged me, spoiling the ecstasy of the moment.

While the four of us ate, the old man asked us questions about where we'd come from, what the weather was like, and what we had seen. Normal, inquisitive questions asked of travelers by regular people that stayed home to tend their hearths and farms and animals.

He had a grandson, apparently, who lived with him during the winter months. His name was Young Jelal, and he had gone to the village on an errand, though Jelal expected his return any time. I couldn't decide if Old Jelal was trying to keep us on our best behavior with a threat or if he really did have a grandson. Barring attempts to poison or enchant us, he was safe from me, for I had no particular desire to abscond with his felt hat, even if it was a lovely shade of emerald all stitched about with figures of stylized vines and birds. I thought I saw one of them looking at me, which I found vaguely unsettling, so I focused my attentions on my soup. Either his skills rivaled Mrs. Mayor in Uzuun, or it been so long since I'd had real food that anything hot and properly salted would taste divine.

Thick pelts and colorful quilts hung on the walls, drawing my eye, and although I didn't want to tuck any of them away in my pockets, either, I stared at them in fascination as I ate. They didn't exactly match those in my vision, but were awfully similar. Changed, perhaps, with the passing of generations.

Suppressing a shiver, I listened to Old Jelal's raspy voice and let Tanris do most of the talking, though one couldn't label him as particularly loquacious. The more I listened, the more I saw how vague he was, and I turned my attention upon him curiously. He had, I suppose, every right to keep our purpose private and I would have been very angry if he had developed a case of verbal vomit. He didn't lie, exactly, but slipped right past the truth with an astonishing ease. For weeks, nay years, he'd been honest and blunt and virtuous. What was this?

I got the distinct impression that he was avoiding looking at me altogether, and for some reason it made me want to laugh. It came out as funny little snorts competing with bites of the wonderful soup. Jelal looked at me. Girl looked at me. Tanris ate his soup and a piece of the equally spectacular bread Jelal had made that very morning and which reminded me of Tanris on the roof of the pretty baker's house and getting a batch of very good bread in repayment for his services.

"He's not right," Tanris said again, and tapped the end of his spoon against his temple apologetically.

"What am I not right about, Tanris?" I interjected, trying to get my giggles under control so I could properly contest his unfair and unfounded character assassination.

He met my eyes finally, with an air of deep consideration. "You're quite mad."

I snorted again. "One man's madness is another's genius and you, friend Tanris, don't have either."

His brows lowered in a familiar critical glare. "What's that supposed to mean?"

"You have to possess a brain in order to be either crazy or smart."

Girl snorted, too, and out of the corner of my eye I saw her duck her head and pay extreme attention to scraping her bowl clean. Humor fairly sparkled around her.

"Have I mentioned that you're a wooden-head?" Tanris asked with deceptive mildness. Irritation boiled in his eyes.

"Frequently. Usually when my wit outdoes yours."

A dry, rasping noise came from Old Jelal and his shoulders heaved up and down like a miniature earthquake. I stared at him in consternation, fearing a fit of some sort, which would be deucedly annoying if we were left with a corpse, though it would free us to appropriate his foodstuffs and yes, perhaps his hat. Tanris would object, but Tanris objected to nearly everything I did that wasn't in cooperative response to one of his direct orders.

"Sir?" Tanris got to his feet.

Jelal wheezed and gasped and shook his shoulders some more, and it dawned on me that he was laughing. No, he'd laughed before, this was outright hilarity, and I had to smile. So far away from civilization, he probably didn't get much to laugh at, and it didn't hurt me one little bit that his amusement was at Tanris's expense. He waved one hand weakly and used the other to wipe his streaming eyes. "I am fine. Very fine." He coughed and gasped for a moment, leaving us in uncertain suspense. "Young Jelal should meet you. Crazy outlanders." Reaching for Tanris, he used him to straighten to his unremarkable height. The top of his head barely reached Tanris's shoulder.

"Grab some of those quilts," he ordered, gesturing to the blankets covering the walls, "and I will show you where you will sleep."

The look of bafflement on Tanris's face nearly rivaled the soup in sheer wonderfulness, and I was still smiling when the old man showed us to the loft over the stable, filled with piles of soft hay and warmed by the heat of the chimney. Who knew one could find heaven in a hayloft? I kept right on grinning like a fool—until Tanris backhanded me in the chest.

— 18 —
Dem Bones

I didn't so much as twitch all night long, and when I woke it was to the certainty that the hay loft was more comfortable than any bed I'd ever slept in. It took me considerable time to work up the desire to pry my eyes open.

I groped for the silver cylinder on its chain around my neck and had to tug it from beneath my shoulder where it had slipped. I inspected it sourly. The minuscule leaves fashioned around both top and bottom made it attractive without being feminine. *Thank you, Baron.* I hated it. Hated the way it shackled me. I took my two drops. Hated the way it tasted.

The sun had long since risen when I finally crawled out of our marvelous, toasty, dry nest, and I wouldn't have left it at all except for the rumbling in my belly. For a miracle, Tanris hadn't jabbed me into wakefulness demanding we continue our journey. Immediately. To my further joy and astonishment, the sun had actually risen and shone magnificently. Oh, there were clouds, to be sure, but they were wildly outnumbered by rays of sunlight. Pack slung over my shoulder, I stood outside the door and gawked at the way the light shone on the scrubby hillside and glimmered from pools and runnels of water. It made my eyes hurt, it was so bright.

"You've brought good weather with you," Old Jelal commented, and I nearly jumped out of my skin. He sat at a little table up against the cottage wall, watching me, looking inscrutable the way only very old people who still possess their wits can do. And wizards. Do not believe I had forgotten how he sidestepped that question. *But he invited us in and fed us and gave us a warm place to sleep!* you may say. Ha. And I reply, *He lulled us with a false sense of security and bought our cooperation with treasures. His food and blankets were water to a man crawling through burning sands in search of*—Wait, no, not water. That was a terrible analogy.

"If that is true," I said, "I wish we had stopped long enough for it to catch up with us while we traveled, for we've had nothing but rain and snow and more rain."

"It is that time of year," he pointed out reasonably. "Fetch a chair."

"Where are Tanris and the girl?"

"Tending to the horses."

By "tending," I had no doubt he meant "saddling and loading." A wise idea, I supposed. We could ill afford to linger and soak up the sun. A fat lot of good sunshine would do me if I didn't have the cursed dragon's egg fetched and promptly delivered to his supreme lordship on time. "I should go help," I said, and went instead to get a chair and settle myself across from the old man just as he put the last of some small gray-brown disks with pictures carved on them into a leather bag worked with curious, much-faded characters. "What are those?"

"Your future."

He held the bag out to me and I took it, looking at him askance.

"Shake them out onto the table," he invited, palm up.

"You are a fortune teller?" Retired, no doubt. I couldn't imagine much in the way of traffic out here.

"No, I just read the bones."

That was a good way to get me to drop the silly things all willy-nilly. Two of them skidded off the table to the ground.

"Try again, but with a little more composure." Humor glinted in those dark, dark eyes of his.

"They're bones." I did not like dead things, I truly did not. Except dead rats and dead enemies, and I was perfectly happy to let someone else do the murdering and clean up the inevitable messes.

"Cross sections of sheep horns, actually."

"Oh, well that makes a difference. Why didn't you say so?" I asked drily, and with some trepidation picked up the disks to put back in the bag and shake again. This time they all stayed on the table, though one landed quite near the edge. Jelal leaned over to scrutinize it critically.

"This is one of those that fell the first time," he said, tapping it with a knobby finger. "It is your life. You are on a perilous journey."

"I'd have never guessed." I had to admire my utterly deadpan delivery.

"Then it is lucky for you the bones have spoken. You might otherwise have been doomed."

Did I perceive a twinkle in his eyes? What did he think he knew? "You said they were sheep horns."

He poured over the rest of the disks intently and put a finger on one. "Details are important to you."

"You can tell that by looking at a piece of horn with a little picture scratched on it?"

"No, I can tell from watching and listening. This," he tapped another disk, which bore a circle with lines coming out of it, sun-like, "is the light and knowledge that will drive away darkness and ignorance."

Very handy. I wondered if he'd mind if I took it with me.

"It can represent either friendship or the light of inspiration."

Inspiration came to me frequently—courtesy of the gods—which he would know if he was truly a seer. Was the old charlatan trying to trick me?

"You are lost," he murmured in his rusty voice, rocking back and forth a little. He'd said the same last night, and it brought a frown to my brow. Intense curiosity slowly replaced his look of humor.

"I know exactly where I'm going," I contended.

"Do you." Not a question at all.

My frown deepened. "What is that supposed to mean?"

He was quiet for long enough to make me want to wriggle in my chair, but I forced myself to meet his gaze and tried to conjure a way to break the standoff. Flip the disks, using one to make the other jump? Pretend to catch a fly (nonexistent at this time of year, but perhaps worth the effort)?

"You have been touched," he said at last.

The sudden breaking of the silence startled me. I sat back in my chair and pretended nonchalance, one arm hooked up over the back and one ankle across the opposite knee. "Hardly an uncommon occurrence," I pointed out.

"You do not know what to make of it, or what to do with it," he went on, and as he did he picked up another disk, this one with two narrow rectangles, parallel, and another across one of the open ends. Lines like rays came from the open side. "You will be given the means to understand."

Under his intelligent, knowing gaze I could not resort to flippancy, which put me at a serious disadvantage. Normally, I would resent that, but I suspected that Old Jelal had answers I could use to my advantage. "How?"

"Curiosity." He mused over his answer, then nodded. "I strongly recommend caution, but such advice tends to go in one ear and out the other with you young people."

I bit my tongue on a childish temptation to protest that I was not a child. "I'll take it under consideration, then. Thank you."

He gave me another look, and I wished I could tell what was going through his head, but he just smiled and nodded. The next disk was face down, leaning against another, and Jelal turned it over to reveal a zigzagging line. "This is important, very important. The Sword of Enshan, but overturned. The swift beginning or ending of a conflict through the use of force, though it may be a loss or a victory reversed. One cannot control the storm.

"And this," he said, indicating the disk the Sword half hid, "represents those gathered about you, friends or family. In this arrangement, either the conflict will ruin them or they will stand with you to shoulder the burden. Here," he went on, turning over another upside-down-disk, and I had to lean closer to hear his soft voice, "is Opposition. A lack of harmony with others, either because you do not accept society or society does not accept you. And this one, this is the critical piece of your future."

The carving on the new disk looked like bubbles to me. "What is it?"

"Riches."

"Does that mean success?"

"It is not absolute. It could mean success, or perhaps lack of restraint and self-control. A selfish action that brings about destruction. You must decide if the deaths of many are an acceptable exchange for your own desires."

"I don't kill people." None of this fortune-telling struck me as particularly promising.

Old Jelal shrugged.

As I pondered his words, doubt crept into my mind. Should I take this bone-reading as a gift of the gods or a farce? If the former, then the warnings could be critical. If the latter, but I took them seriously, I could fatally cripple myself. I had to be sure. "How do I know your interpretation is true?"

He smiled a canny little smile and nodded approvingly. "Do you know what this one is?" he inquired, pointing out another disk.

"It looks like a—a tree?"

"Yes. The Golden Tree. The symbol of fertility and creation and family." An insult against my manhood loomed here as well as a criticism about my oat-sowing habits. "Turned sideways like this suggests an estrangement, and sitting right here next to the Spear—see how the Spear points away?—I can tell that you are an orphan."

No one knew that. Gooseflesh crept over my skin and it took everything I had to remain still and quiet and outwardly unruffled. Inwardly, my heart thudded like mad. A charlatan could not divine such a thing, though a wizard perhaps might, or the unpredictable gods. They often delivered their messages in mysterious ways. I reached out to pick up the Golden Tree and turned it over in my fingers. Years of handling and banging about in the pouch with its mates had polished it smooth. "What else can you see in these things?"

Jelal regarded me silently for another too-long time. "You have been recently betrayed."

"Betrayal is an unfortunate consequence of my line of work," I countered. Jelal was not welcome to pick my sorry love life as a topic.

He picked up the Riches symbol and set it atop a nearby disk with a picture resembling a barrel with legs and a head. A horse, perhaps. "Thievery."

Well, that was disconcerting. "Transportation of goods."

"Embroidering your hat does not change the function."

It was a quirky and unexpected thing for him to say, and I couldn't contain a bark of laughter. "Do your bones have anything else to say on the matter?"

"Certainly, and on many other aspects of your life, as we have already discovered."

I could use all the help I could get, and I found myself liking the little man. "Tell me more. What's this one?" I picked out a satiny smooth depiction of a curling horn.

"Is this game going to take long?" Tanris asked. He stood at the end of the stable wall with his arms folded and a predictably disapproving look on his face.

"Friend Tanris! I am just getting some advice from Old Jelal about our upcoming business."

Displeasure segued to irritation. "Did he suggest to you that the day is not getting any younger?"

"Not yet, but I'm sure he was about to."

"Would you like me to read the bones for you, Tanris?" Old Jelal asked, gathering them up and slipping them into their bag.

No! Those were my future! My advice from the gods! What was he doing? "Wait!" I exclaimed. "We weren't done!"

"Now we are," the old man said, unruffled. "Tanris?"

"No," he said shortly, and then tacked on a slightly more polite, "thank you. Crow, we need to go."

"Not yet," I said, astonishing both of us. Jelal remained placid and curious as I pulled the waxed tube from my pack and uncapped it. Tanris reached for it, but I avoided his grasp. The Ancestors pushed and pulled at him, though not hard enough to be useful. At that, Jelal leaned a little further, studied a little more intently.

A shiver went right through my middle. While I had allegedly spoken with the Ancestors and credited them for things I felt and unexpectedly knew, I had never consciously witnessed a physical manifestation. It might have been the wind, but I knew differently, and so did the old man.

Hurriedly, I separated some of the papers from the stack. "Master Jelal, can you tell me what you make of these?"

"We don't have time for this," Tanris insisted, meaning that he didn't trust the old man as far as he could throw him.

"We don't have the luxury of neglecting possible resources."

Old Jelal chuckled and laid the documents out on the rickety table, one at a time to conquer their perpetual curl. "Do you see? Already the Bones are proven. Light and knowledge."

A smile tugged one side of my mouth. "I'm a quick learner."

"Also cocksure." Tanris smacked the back of my head. I didn't give him the pleasure of a reaction.

Jelal pored over the papers, marking his passage with a gnarled forefinger, pausing now and then to reread occasional phrases. His lips moved, but I could not make out any words. Tanris glanced impatiently toward the horses. Girl joined us, clearly puzzled but wonderfully silent. The cat appeared, and Tanris drew some comfort from it, holding the smelly creature in his arms and scratching its ears. It purred thunderously.

Eventually, the old man sat back in his chair.

"Can you read them?" I asked.

"No."

"How unfortunate, thank you for your time, we'll be on our way now," Tanris said, all in one breath.

"Most of the script is written in the language of wizards," the old man went on as soon as Tanris ran out of words. "I did not pursue my studies of it, but I do recognize some of the symbols. Those, together with some of the phrases I can understand, lead me to certain conclusions."

I smiled benignly at Tanris. "Please, whatever help you can give us would be most appreciated."

He nodded. One of the faces in his felt hat winked at me. I stared.

"The author disparages the use of charts graphed by Saint Cafel, but does not give a reason beyond abysmal stupidity. Apparently he did not like the person he was writing to. The recipient sketched out some calculations and projections. I assume the actual work appears elsewhere, for these are shorthand and incomplete."

"Who is Saint Cafel?" Tanris approached to look, though we both knew perfectly well that neither the script nor the symbols meant anything to him.

"A famous diviner, dead these two centuries." The old man heaved a sigh. "He has a reputation for being perfectly right or embarrassingly wrong. He also has the questionable honor of having a rabid cult named after him. The Cafelites. Perhaps you've heard of them?"

"The ones that tattoo their destinies on their scalps, and twirl around until they're so dizzy they can't stand up, then claim they're inspired by visions?"

"The very same."

"You ever see our mutual friend twirling?" I asked Tanris.

"No, thank all the gods."

"Indeed." Duzayan was still rabid, but bitten by another dog entirely. "What are they trying to predict?"

"Mmm..." Jelal rubbed his chin and stared at the drawings in the margin of the topmost letter. "A favorable time."

"For?"

"Why, a new endeavor, I suppose. Something involving birth, or perhaps rebirth."

"Like an egg?"

Tanris's forefinger was sharper than it looked. I know. He stabbed me in the neck and my arm went numb for several minutes. I tried to control a gasp of shock. Jelal looked at us askance, but neither of us offered an explanation. No need to involve him in our ongoing feud.

"It could be an egg," Jelal allowed, our interaction provoking a knowing smile in his eyes. "Spring has come. Eggs are laid. Eggs hatch. Life is renewed."

"Does any of this mention what sort of egg?" I rubbed my arm, but it just dangled from my shoulder like an awkward log.

"No."

"How about a date?" Tanris asked.

"The spring equinox, though it has passed already." He squinted at the letter again, then shook his head. "There is the suggestion of an alignment of power and a pathway. I'm sorry, but I cannot tell you more. I do not recognize the configuration. I might be able to understand better if I had the rest of the notes and calculations."

"Is it—dangerous?" I asked.

Jelal rolled the papers and handed them back to me. "Power often breeds abuse."

Tanris snorted. Maybe he'd do that so often his brain would explode from his nostrils. One could hope.

The old seer offered to read the bones again, and although my recent experience encouraged my willingness, Tanris would have none of that superstitious claptrap. Luckily, he was polite enough not to say that in front of Jelal, but the next thing I knew, we were on the horses and heading away from the cozy little cottage while Tanris grumbled about superstitious old coots and gullible halfwits.

"This is it?" I had to ask. Hasiq jum'a Sahefal looked nothing like I'd imagined, though the sun's slanting afternoon rays gave it a sweet, pastoral appearance. A convergence of several barely-distinguishable tracks led into one side of the village, and no road at all, just as Tanris had warned. The paths straggled along only one side because a mountain completely occupied the other, and the mountain came right down from the heights to create a towering cliff against the base of which stood, presumably, the Temple of Nadimesh from which Magister Mell-something had written. The main building was of a fair size, with an ornately tiled roof, and two arms extended to either side, encompassing a garden courtyard complete with surrounding wall. I made out a fountain inside, some sizable statues, and several picturesque trees. From this distance it appeared to boast all the amenities of any well-to-do temple located in any of the great cities of the glorious Bahsyr Empire—and next to the humble buildings surrounding it, it looked completely, astonishingly out of place. Such civilized elegance on the outside made me wonder what treasures it might house on the inside.

As if he was reading my mind, Tanris cuffed the back of my head, knocking my hat down over my eyes.

"Ow! What was that for?" I shoved the headgear back into place and glared at him.

"You're not here to rob the brothers."

As stupid things to say went, that one topped most of the lists. "You're right, I forgot. I have slogged miles and miles through constant, freezing rain with a completely insufferable companion who doesn't even try to hide the fact that he loathes me. I've had exactly two pleasant nights and no pleasant days in the last two months. I've been subjected to horrendous food right along with your bad temper and your refusal to ever be pleased by anything I do," I railed, my voice going up an octave and several decibels. I got some good arm-waving going, too. "Maybe, just maybe, I can take tea with the devout brethren, and tour their famous gardens. Do you think they'd mind? Is this one of the places with healing baths? I forgot to check the legend on the map. Perhaps I could prevail upon the good and pious brethren to let me take a dip so I might be miraculously cured of the poison eating away my very life, and then I wouldn't need to steal anything, which wouldn't help *you* a great deal, now would it?"

Tanris's face contorted in anger. He balled one huge fist and drew his arm back.

I leveled a warning finger at him and narrowed my eyes, every bit as angry as he. "Don't. Don't you dare hit me. It's bad enough you said something so abysmally stupid, but if you hit me and you break me who is going to be your cat's paw?"

His eyes didn't leave mine, but he lowered his fist and turned his head to spit into the dead grass at our feet.

Folding my arms to stem a sudden fit of trembling before it could get out of control, I studied the scene below, jaw set, teeth clenched. The layout hadn't changed; it was still an extravagant temple in the middle of nowhere surrounded by a scattering of extremely modest houses and barns. To the east beyond a hedge of trees was a large paddock filled with sheep, and a good many tracks leading to it from the fields and hills beyond. Besides the obvious dichotomy in architecture and affluence, something about the scene didn't sit right. "You're sure this is the place?"

"I'm sure." He did a bang-up job of looking and sounding sullen.

"Let me see the map." I held my hand out and waggled my fingers, gesturing for him to pass it over.

"There's nothing to see," he growled. "This is it."

"I believe you. Give me the map."

"Why? It isn't going to change anything."

I forced myself to patience I didn't feel. "Because I want to find out if there's something on it we missed, some clue about the–item." I still couldn't call it an egg, it was just too ridiculous. "Duzayan wouldn't have gone to so much trouble to throw us together and send us all the way to the edge of the world to collect something infinitely valuable for him without providing a way for us to even recognize it. Something he said or wrote must give us a clue."

Girl watched us with a puzzled, pained sort of expression while we debated. Crazy female. She'd probably be even crazier after we got done with her. Since she'd joined us I could not recall having spoken with Tanris about our quest—where we were going or why. There'd been no reason. It did not concern her and she did not particularly concern me beyond the practical issues of food, transportation, and personal safety. Tanris had let her come with us, let Tanris deal with her. She got on well with his cat; they were made for each other. At the moment talking to me was as attractive a proposition as chewing oyster shells. His face and his... *aura* conveyed his pain.

"We should probably worry that a powerful wizard didn't, or couldn't, or wouldn't make the journey himself," I observed. "What have we got that he hasn't?"

"I'd say you," he pointed out sourly, "but he's got you by the nose."

"A temporary condition, I assure you." The muscle in my jaw knotted.

"Sure it is."

I didn't like the insinuation I would either be dead soon or Duzayan would own me for the rest of my life, cooperation permanently assured with his blighted little concoction. "The map?" I reminded, waggling my fingers again.

Disgruntled, he reached into the depths of his coat and twenty-seven further layers of clothing meant to keep him warm and dry—and stilled for all of five heartbeats. He checked the other side. He checked up and down. He checked all his pockets, inside and out. "Crow..." he growled warningly.

I have yet to understand why he always blames me every time something doesn't go exactly the way he desires. "What have you done with it?" I pressed, eyes narrowing even further.

"*I* haven't done anything with it, you miserable snake! Hand it over!"

"I haven't got it."

"Don't lie to me." The look in his eyes promised a painful pounding, and clenched fists emphasized his intention. He took a step my way, and I took one backward.

"I *haven't* got it!"

"This is no time for one of your stupid games! You cough it up right now, or I swear I will do you a serious damage."

Unbelievable. I held my hands out to either side, empty, surrendering. "You've got me again, Tanris, congratulations. Now that we're only a mile or so from from procuring the one thing I can trade to save my life, I am going to steal and hide the map so neither of us can find the wretched thing. With any luck at all, it will take us another week to figure out what it is we're looking for and where exactly to find it. I will of course, do everything in my power to delay our success, because of *course* I want to die a dramatic and unbelievably painful death." I paused for a breath. "Are you out of your *mind*?"

He glared at me, sparks fairly flying from his eyes. Such a thing was not possible—or it hadn't been before we'd begun this miserable adventure. "Where is it, then, bird boy?"

"If I knew that, would I be asking you, dimwit? How could you lose the map? The *map*, by all the gods and goddesses! You – *Augh!*" I threw my hands up in the air. In my outrage I couldn't even begin to devise words to describe his absolute stupidity. Worse, he blamed me for his utter lack of responsibility. It was a rare thing indeed for me to be completely bereft of speech, yet all I could come up with to compare him to were farm animals, and that seemed grievously insulting to the unfortunate beasts.

He growled and stabbed my direction with one finger. "If you think I'm going to let you get away with robbing me and costing me everything I care about, I am more than willing to educate—"

"That's it." I stared at him in sudden realization.

"What's it?" His glower deepened, shaded sharply with suspicion.

"Remember the night I told you someone was in camp? And you didn't believe me?"

He still didn't believe me. "You can't really think I'm going to buy that story."

Half-a-dozen retorts surged to the tip of my tongue, but I bit them back. No sense wasting witticism on a brute. "You're right again," I said, turning away to go to Horse. "It would take all month to sell it to you, and I've better things to do with my limited time." I swung up into the saddle, settled my hat on my head, and urged the mare forward.

"Where do you think you're going?"

I pointed to the village, but I didn't look back.

— 19 —
Gifts Of The Gods

The buildings surrounding the temple were sturdily built, stone for the most part and with polished wooden plaques over the doors depicting runes and, in some cases, stylized pictures. I examined those we passed close to, and found an abundance of bucolic talent. The people inhabiting the village were stocky and solid mountain folk. They tended their animals and barns and ditches and fences diligently until we appeared, and then they stopped to stare. A few of them approached to give us greeting and a pair of strapping boys kindly showed us the way to the temple that we couldn't possibly miss.

A beautiful structure, it sprang right out of the mountainside as though a part of it, and up close it appeared even more incongruous than it had from afar. I had not at all mistaken the presence of fountains and statuary, and if the mountain people we had encountered had carved them I was a goat's uncle. The details, the design, the decorations—all of it had been transported directly from the south lands and did not match the construction of the surrounding houses. Where the cottages had straight, modest roofs, the temple had one that was flaring and ornate. Where the cottage walls were rough stone, the temple walls were exquisitely dressed. The cottage fences were simple and rustic, the enclosures around the temple were significant barriers boasting ironbound gates worthy of any southern castle's defenses. Two sturdy columns flanked them, on top of which perched a pair of fierce looking stone dragons. Over the entrance doors, tucked below the gable of a porch roof supported by a quartet of spectacular marble columns, sat yet another. Outspread wings looked as though they might lift the thing into flight, and its carved neck supported a head that hung right out over the path, gaping, toothy maw ready to snatch at unwary passersby. As we walked beneath, I could not help looking up at it and wondering what kept such a weight from falling. Or if maybe it sometimes came to life. And surely the dragons were not coincidental to our mission. An incongruous number of guards stood like statues all along the outer wall. Supposing they worked in shifts, three or four times as many lurked somewhere close by. The temple keepers were clearly on their guard against invasion by sheep farmers.

Inside, the reception area was worthy of any of the emperor himself. Stunning, clever insets decorated polished marble floors. The ceiling arched high overhead, its walls and ceiling pierced with long, narrow windows of imported glass. Fantastic paintings covered the panels between. Wax candles, not tallow, graced expensive brass candelabra in the shape of dragons with outstretched wings. A few choice items from the foyer alone would make me a wealthy man.

A guard hovered nearby as we gawked, but it was only a matter of moments before a servant escorted us into a spacious parlor where the magister awaited us. Ammeluanakar was tall and skinny as a stick, though not as old as one might expect of a man in his auspicious position. Both his Adam's apple and his nose were sharp enough to use as weapons, though extreme nearsightedness guaranteed he'd never see his opponent until it was too late. It made the temptation to purloin some of his possessions difficult to resist. He had some very nice possessions. Still, I did not want to raise alarms before we had what we'd come for, and there were a plethora of brothers available to blow whistles or ring bells or whatever they did when outraged, and no doubt they would be.

It took me all of five seconds to realize this was the same Melly-something, from Duzyan's letters. Not for the first time, I thought it might have been helpful had the baron told us a little something about what we were getting into. I cast a sideways glance at Tanris, but he either didn't recognize him or he was a more accomplished actor than I gave him credit for.

Along with Skinny Melly-whatsit there were five other brothers of the order, each with names I couldn't get my tongue around, much less keep lodged in my brain.

They gave us tea.

I gave them a false name. "I am Fajhal, and this is my niece Etana." Tanris was just a guard and not worthy of introduction. He didn't seem to mind. "We are overjoyed to find your beautiful village at last," I told them. "We somehow managed to get a little off track, and we feared we'd missed it completely."

"It is a bit out of the way," Melly agreed.

I looked at Tanris to make sure he remembered to stay in character according to the story we'd concocted on our way down to the village, but he pretended not to see me, instead choosing to watch his mangy cat make its way around the room sniffing at the walls made of (more) marble with borders of indecipherable runic symbols. Were I the cat, I'd have gone straight for one of the big, deep chairs on the other side of the room. Arranged around a fireplace in which a fire crackled happily, they sported thick, deep velvet cushions. We humans sat upon hard chairs around an admittedly beautiful teak table inlaid with mother of pearl, subject to a breeze creeping in between the panes of a real glass window. However had they got the glass to this remote location, and how much of the original shipment had broken to bits in the process? Just contemplating the cost staggered the mind.

"It is lovely, very lovely," I murmured, gazing about and letting my sincere appreciation show. "I'm quite sure I've never seen such a fine collection of dragon art before." I had seen pictures and carvings and jewelry, of course, but never so much of the same theme all in one place.

"It is an… homage," Melly murmured, and stirred his tea. The fellow sitting next to him added some honey to the cup, then patted Melly's hand, and he stirred some more.

"Oh?"

"We protect the dragon, and the dragon, in turn, protects us. We will never forget to whom we owe our daily lives," he intoned with great humility.

"Ah, I see." People across the world worshipped stranger deities. Some folk believed the mythical dragon represented courage or longevity or ferocity in battle, though none of these men looked to be particularly warrior-like. A few of them were downright chubby. "Do you perchance make and sell any of those exquisitely carved and inlaid dragon's eggs I've seen from time to time in my travels? I should dearly love to purchase one."

"No." Just that, no more. Not even a smile.

"How unfortunate. Well." The silence drew out, and none of the brothers offered to fill it. I took another sip of my tea and nodded agreeably. "It has been a terribly long journey," I said, continuing the story I'd already begun at the door, in which Girl—my niece on my mother's side —had been cursed on her wedding day by a rival for the groom. The wedding had been postponed for a year and a day to give us time to find a cure for the curse, which prevented her from speaking—a necessity when exchanging wedding vows and thus living happily ever after. "With each day that passes and each holy place we visit without success, Etana grows more and more disconsolate. There are days at a time when she cannot stop crying." I adopted an expression of sorrow.

Girl—Etana—pressed her hand over her mouth and looked at the floor demurely.

"We have been from one end of the empire nearly all the way to the other, seeking the means, magical or holy or otherwise, that will release this lovely, sweet girl from her affliction and free her to follow her heart."

Magister Melly peered in Girl's direction, and after a moment he cleared his throat. "What leads you to believe we have such an article?" he asked in a surprisingly deep voice.

"Hope, Your Eminence, only hope." I could tell he liked the sudden elevation in title. "It is all we have left."

"The Temple of Nadimesh holds many wondrous and powerful artifacts." He looked toward me, but missed meeting my gaze by a good six inches. "Some of them so ancient that their purpose has been forgotten. Some of them are too powerful to remain in places where they might be subject to thieves. Some of them," he smiled beatifically, "are simply beautiful works of art." And therefore also subject to the temptation of thieves. I should know. The table itself was probably worth its weight in silver, but as you know, I like my treasures small enough to fit comfortably into a pocket or even a pack.

"Such a remote location is a good first defense," Tanris observed.

"We have guards, of course."

"Of course," Tanris nodded. "So few of them patrolled the walls, I hope there are more in reserve."

I didn't, and he must have been joking. I do not particularly like guards. They tend to be a nuisance.

Melly just smiled and I found myself staring at him. Something about him disconcerted me beyond his inability to see past the end of his own very large nose. Staring, however, wouldn't answer any of our questions. "Do you happen to know if one of your treasured artifacts might be suitable for helping my niece?"

"Unfortunately, nothing comes to mind. I am terribly sorry."

Girl chose that moment to sniffle and, gods bless her, she was crying. It was the first time she'd ever cried when it was actually convenient and useful, but it made me outrageously suspicious of her other crying jags. "Now, now, dear," I murmured, patting her hand solicitously. Head bowed, she caught my hand in her own, clutching dramatically.

I gave Magister Melly and his companions my most beseeching look. "Perhaps we could just look...?"

One of the other brothers leaned forward a bit. "Magister Ammeluanakar," he murmured, and I had to hold my breath to hear what he said, "what if they are thieves?"

"It is well known," I pointed out, cutting off any reply, "that some Gifts are triggered by the mere presence of the, erm... needy."

"That is a myth," Brother Three declared with not a little derisiveness.

I crooked a brow. "Oh? Then you should perhaps tell that to Baron Dasuf. His son was half blinded in a hunting accident and forced to give up his soldierly habits. Brilliant young man. Went on to handle all the details of his father's finances and business endeavors. A priest from the Temple of Lishur visited the Dasuf holdings one day. The priest sat next to the young man at supper. Much to the astonishment of all present, the lad leaped up and exclaimed that he could see." I snapped my fingers for emphasis.

"There is also the report of Mildar Sirjin," I went on. "A great captain in the Emperor's own army, he was run through by a sword and lay dying in the street. One of his men ran to him. As it happened, this man was transporting some valuable artifacts that had been captured. The Amulet of Disrae was in a bag at his side. It came to life spontaneously and lit so brightly that it glowed through the leather—and Sirjin was healed."

I'd completely fabricated the first story, but the tale of Sirjin's miraculous recovery was something of a legend and who could know if it was indeed true? The stories had the desired effect on my audience, and they began a whispered debate that soon had them all hovering about good Magister Melly. Restrained as the group's arm-waving was, I fully expected someone to take an injury and witnessed several near misses.

I waited for a lull in the argument and clasped my hands in entreaty. "Surely it can do no harm if we simply look upon your collection, and it could do a great deal of good."

"What if they are thieves?" Suspicious Brother Two repeated, and he didn't whisper this time.

Girl covered her mouth and turned her face completely away, still sniffling.

Tanris glowered. Such a helpful sort...

The Second Position of Entreaty required me to put my hands out, palm up. It did not prevent me from subtly insulting them. "With such a valuable and dangerous collection as you claim to have, you can't afford to be too cautious. I understand completely."

I got to my feet and held my hand out to assist Girl. Even as I did, the pious brothers of the Temple of Nadimesh were working up their righteous indignation over the suggestion they had no treasures at all. "I am sorry, dearling. We had best be on our way and leave these good men to their work."

Tanris got up, too, in a rush of vexation to rival the brothers. "You cannot mean to just walk away without even trying!"

"I have tried." My tone was doleful and Girl's lip quivered pathetically. "I cannot very well force them to accommodate our small desires when they have the safety of the entire empire to look after. Come now, Etana." Ignoring the way Tanris stiffened, I tucked Girl's hand into the crook of my arm solicitously and headed for the exit, lowering my voice to her confidentially—but not so confidentially that my words would be missed entirely. "Perhaps your father will let you contribute the reward money to a good cause. Do you remember the dear children in that little orphanage in—"

"Perhaps you would like to stay here tonight. It is a long way to anywhere and we do have guest rooms," Brother Four offered, getting to his feet and smoothing his chubby little hands over his very well rounded belly.

"Oh," I paused, and I swear I could hear Tanris rolling his eyes. It was a terrible habit of his that made me look bad and made my job harder to do. I resented that and gave him a look to let him know it, which he utterly ignored. "We really don't want to impose upon you…" I lied to the dear brothers. Very smoothly. I'd had practice.

Brother Six didn't seem to be suffering from starvation, either, and heaved his ponderous weight upward. The belt barely visible at his sides completely disappeared in the front beneath his considerable girth. "It is no imposition," he countered as he rose. The rest followed him like gophers popping up out of their holes. Very pretty gophers in their fine woolen robes and painstakingly detailed felt hats and exquisite, expensive jewelry.

Magister Melly cleared his throat, the only one of the brothers still sitting. "Let us not be hasty." The others moved aside a bit so Girl and I had a good view of him. He'd produced a brass-rimmed monocle and peered at us. The monocle distorted his eye bizarrely. "My companions are quite correct in that the nearest habitation with an inn or hostel lies considerably beyond the few hours you have left to travel before night falls." He paused to give us an even keener inspection. "You certainly do not have the appearance of traveling aristocrats, but it is our duty, nay, our *privilege* to provide lodging for the few pilgrims that make the considerable effort to visit us."

I offered him a look of haughty reproach. "It is better, as I am sure you understand, not to blatantly advertise goods one is not prepared to part with."

"Quite so, quite so," he murmured, and his companions bobbed their heads in agreement. A waggle of Melly's fingers drew Brother Two from the crowd. "Brother Enmenkima will show you where you may rest and take care of anything else you might require."

Hands together, gratitude shining, I bowed. "Thank you, your Eminence, for your understanding and for your truly gracious hospitality."

In spite of his suspicious attitude Brother Two was not completely unapproachable, and it didn't take much to persuade him to tell us something about the history of the temple, the works of the good brothers, and so forth. I smiled and nodded at all the right places, murmured appreciative responses or ventured leading questions as the conversation required. Tanris was as talkative as a rock, which suited me perfectly. I had no particular desire to listen to him, and the attitude of silent-and-deadly guard benefited the circumstances. While he practiced being stony and Girl tried not to look utterly bored, I coaxed Brother Two delicately along by the nose until I got him bragging about the temple's fantastic collection of statuary, jewelry, bottles, scepters, carvings, pictures, weapons and the like.

I pretended skepticism.

He was surprisingly mercenary.

For the price of a generous donation, which I managed to convince him to suggest, I persuaded him to allow us to view the fabled treasure ourselves. Girl, I must say, played no little part in his seduction with her attitude of quiet despair and her occasional expressive looks of fragile hope. I would clearly have to pay more attention to her in the future. I might even have to consider sponsoring her career as an actress.

The Vault where the artifacts resided was, of course, underground—and dismayingly small. Walls of fine, polished marble of a pale gold enclosed the collection. A channel carved into the upper portion of the walls held burning oil, which lit the room very nicely. Brother Two told us in a reverent voice that the flame never went out. Unimpressive though the collection was, nearly every treasure sat upon a block carved of marble and draped with an embroidered cloth of rich gray velvet. A great number of the "treasures" were downright ugly, poorly made, or bore the appearance of common, everyday items. The Plate of Yousak, for example, was wood. That's it. Just wood. Plain, ordinary, undecorated, though highly polished wood. Apparently, under the proper circumstances, it would be filled with food the likes of which we had never tasted before, and once we ate that food we could run for days and not be weary nor hungry.

Brother Two gave me a disapproving look when I asked if he could show us. I didn't touch anything. I do not like magic, no, not at all, and I certainly didn't want to inadvertently activate something fatal. I wanted to postpone meeting the gods in person just yet. Keeping my hands to myself did not keep me from experiencing the strangest sensation as I walked slowly along. I prickled as though a tiny charge of energy scurried over my skin. It was most disconcerting and distracting, but I had work to do. Pasting a reverent look on my face, I admired a fuzzy woolen cap, a half dozen nearly identical statuettes Brother Two identified as likenesses of the famous, saintly Peyumi brothers. I'd never heard of them, but I nodded and encouraged a story from him. I nearly lost my composure when I came to a ratty-looking nest, slowly disintegrating into a pile of dust.

It didn't take us long to tour the room, and I looked everywhere for an egg, or an egg shape, but nary a single eggy anything presented itself for my ogling. We stopped in front of each piece so Brother Two could tell its miraculous—and usually long and boring—story.

While we listened and gawked and scoured the place for the slightest clue, a pair of guards each the size of a house followed behind, one of them carrying a loaded and spanned crossbow and watching us with depressing attention. It rather detracted from the reverent atmosphere.

And it made Girl cry.

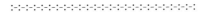

We had hardly closed the door of our room before Tanris spun, features intense. "That was the priest!" he hissed at the very same time I said, "That was Melly! The priest with the horrible name in the letters."

He nodded, mouth tight. "It has to be. Is that going to complicate things?"

"Hard to say," I shrugged. "We'll find out."

"You have something in mind?"

I brushed past him. "It's my job, let me do it."

The brothers had fed us, bathed us, provided proper tools for shaving, given us clean and dry clothes, and showed us to our rooms. Once again, Tanris and I were forced to share a space, but Girl got a blissful room of her own. The rooms—with or without Tanris—would have been nothing to get excited about except that I'd recently spent so much time lying on the cold, wet ground with ever more wetness falling on me. Though thin, the ticking on the narrow beds was warm and dry, and we even had small fireplaces flanked by little shuttered windows looking out upon newly worked vegetable gardens.

Evidently unimpressed, he cracked his neck, one side and then the other. "There was no egg."

"Lo, Captain Tanris of the good ship, *Obvious*. What would we do without you?" I didn't even try to keep the scathing tone from my voice. I needed viable ideas to solving the puzzle of Duzayan's egg, not repetition of what I already knew. Stretched out on one bed, I took out the Beisyth Web, turning the ball over and over in my fingers. Utterly quiescent, it gave me a good point upon which to focus.

"At least I'm trying to come up with a solution. Will you quit playing with that thing and help me?"

"Playing with this thing does not preclude thinking. Your pointless jabbering does."

"Do you have a plan?"

"Yes." I lied, but maybe it would get him to shut up.

"Does it include *resting* and changing your clothes?" he sneered, and it took a moment or two to recall where that had come up in our conversations before: right after Baron Duzayan had made his oh-so-generous offer to let me help him or die. After an eternity of torture.

"I would love to change my clothes," I agreed and plucked at my borrowed tunic. "These are all well and good, but I grow weary of such dull, practical garments, though I will have to admit it is nice to wear something clean and dry."

"And how is that going to help us?" Tanris growled. "Can you not be serious? If we can't find the egg, what are we going to do?"

"From my point of view things are fairly simple." I looked at the ball, a frown tugging at my brow. My fingers were tingling. I thrust the thing into my pocket and sat up, shoving one foot and then the other into disreputable boots that had been new two months ago. The coat I shrugged into was still damp, still smelly. "Things will be quite tragic for you, but I will merely die."

I let the door bang shut behind me and stalked down the hall. The door at the end of the hall slammed, too, and I stepped out into the cold. Sharp stars punctuated the ebon sky overhead, and my breath hung in clouds. I paused for only a moment before making my way down the path leading around the building. I could not think with Tanris whining at me and I did not like him this way. I wanted to keep the old image of him, the Tanris that followed me doggedly and did his utmost to catch me and stuff me in a cage; the Tanris that challenged me, and skillfully exchanged insults with me, and was strong enough to keep coming back in spite of numerous defeats.

I heard the door open and close again. The corners of my mouth turned down. "Go away," I muttered.

"Crow?" Distance and caution muffled Tanris's inquiry.

I was sure he saw me, but I hurried around the corner building anyway —and ran smack into someone else.

— 20 —
And It Was This Big...

We struck fairly hard. My automatic grab didn't keep us from going down and a grunt exploded from me as we landed. Having the wind nearly knocked out of my lungs didn't keep my eyes from working.

"You!" I gasped.

Kem Bohadri stared at me for a fraction of a second, then struggled to get free, but I had a good hold on the front of his coat and I wasn't going to let go. Not, that is, until he hit me. Twice. The fist that met my chin produced a shower of stars that had nothing at all to do with the sky. The other fist landed in my gut and very firmly finished the job of expelling my breath. My assailant leaped to his feet and sprinted away, and all I could do was lay there and suck madly at the too-cold air in the hope of filling my lungs again.

But, aha! Trusty Tanris, right behind me as I had rounded the corner, leaped over my prostrate self as gracefully as a deer, barreled after Kem, and flew into a tackle. The two of them went tumbling across the ground, eliciting more grunting, only it was accompanied by thumping, too, and I seriously hoped Tanris gave more than he got. Well... A good thump on the noggin would probably do him a world of good, but timing was everything and having him incapacitated right at this moment was not at all conducive to happy endings.

"You *skunk!*" The accusation was punctuated with another thump-and-grunt. "You lying, stinking, rotten—" *Thump! Thump!*

"Tanris," I wheezed, managing to roll up onto my knees.

"I ought to take your fool head off!" *Thump!*

"Tanris, don't kill him!" Had I just said that? The man was a lying, stinking, rotten *snake.* He'd deserted us, robbed us, and then attacked me, but

178

for all we knew he had twenty or thirty cronies stashed someplace nearby and we didn't need them making things difficult. I forced myself to crawl over to them. In the mud. So much for the nice bath and clean clothes.

Tanris straddled Kem, and Kem held his arms up defensively, wheezing and groaning something about stopping and letting him go. As if that were going to happen.

"Just hold him down, will you?"

While Tanris very ably tended to that, muttering some surprisingly dire things under his breath, I searched our erstwhile guide. I found nothing inside his coat, tucked in his belt, or under his jerkin. "What did you do with it?" I demanded. Wheezing still myself, I didn't sound horribly menacing, but neither did he when he croaked out a reply.

"I don't know what you're talking about!"

"What are you talking about?" Tanris parroted.

"The map!"

"I haven't got any maps!" Kem fought to free himself, but he didn't get anywhere at all.

Crawling around, I sat down (in the mud) and grabbed hold of one of his boots. He kicked at me with surprising vehemence, and removing the thing was a struggle that did not come without a price. I would very likely be sporting colorful bruises on the morrow, thanks to his flailing feet. When the boot came off, a folded parchment slipped out, a bright rectangle in the glittering starlight. Picking it up, I unfolded it and lo! there was our missing property.

"Ha!" I exclaimed and clambered to my feet to go wave the paper in Tanris's face. "*This* map! Does it look at all familiar to you? Didn't I tell you he took it? Do you believe me now, you self-righteous prig?"

"Fine! You were right! Is that what you want to hear?" He smacked at my hand, which freed Kem to smack at Tanris, and another tussle ensued. I brought that to a quick stop with the application of Kem's boot to his head and was rewarded with a satisfactory groan.

"Stop that," I ordered, completely put out with the pair of them. "I would also like an apology. And then I want to hear what our dear friend Kem has to say."

"I got nothing!" Kem spat and then swore when Tanris pinned one of his wrists beneath a knee.

"You didn't have the map, either," I pointed out, folding it up again and tucking it safely into my shirt.

"Start talking," Tanris ordered, winding his fists in Kem's coat and giving his battered captive a good shake. "Are you alone?"

"Yes!" With his one free hand, he clutched at Tanris's arm, though all the pulling he could do couldn't free him now.

"He's lying." I narrowed my eyes, and Tanris looked at me as though he wanted to argue, but he already owed me one apology.

"How many are with you?" he asked Kem instead.

"There's nobody!" Blood stained his mouth dark and he licked his lips.

"How *many*?" Tanris asked again.

"None, I swear!"

Tanris hit him. "Now how many?"

Kem shook his head and groaned softly, and Tanris raised his fist again.

"Wait," I said. Much to my surprise he paused, though he didn't relax. One arm pressed against my aching middle, I edged close and stared at our prisoner intently, silently. Moments slipped by, and rasping breaths settled into a more normal pattern, though Kem's were peppered still with little hisses of pain. Maybe Tanris had broken something. I didn't much care. Kem watched me apprehensively.

"What are you doing?" Tanris asked, finally lowering his fist. He was still sitting on the man, still holding a handful of coat, still leaning on Kem's wrist. That had to hurt.

"Do you remember what happened in the cave?" I whispered, not letting my evil glare waver for an instant.

Kem's eyes widened further and he licked his lips again. The fear radiating from him grew considerably. "Let me go. Please. I haven't done anything."

I bent a little closer. "No?" I whispered. "You brought me to the Ancestors. Do you know what they did to me?"

He shook his head back and forth violently.

"Do you want to find out?" I hissed.

"No. No, please..."

The smile I gave him was not meant to be reassuring, and indeed, it had quite the opposite affect. "Then tell me what I want to know."

He couldn't talk fast enough. "Three. There are three others! We've got a camp about a mile east of here and up on the side of the mountain. In a grove of trees."

"Where'd you get them?" Tanris asked sharply.

"On the moor. I found them on the moor when I was following you. They run with Kiral Stone's lot."

Following us... There *had* been someone there, just like I'd thought! I gave Tanris a tight-lipped look that he chose to ignore.

"Friends, then," he said.

"No—Yes!" Kem changed his mind quickly when Tanris raised his fist again. "I know them. I work with them sometimes. They were going to rob you, and I stopped them!"

Yay for Kem! Our hero! "And *you* robbed us instead," I pointed out drily.

"I—yes." Misery and fear bathed him.

"Why?"

Kem looked from me to Tanris. Open to speak, bloodied, his mouth trembled for a moment before he went on. "I wanted whatever you were going after."

"Where is it?" Tanris asked, teeth clenched and voice strained.

"I don't know!"

"*Liar!*" His hands wrapped around Kem's throat and squeezed.

I eased back a fraction. "You have a strange way of interrogating prisoners, Tanris. When he's dead, what will he tell us?"

With a snarl and a shove, Tanris let him loose, hands on his thighs and breath straining. I had never seen him so angry. I didn't much like this side of him, either, but as I crouched there looking at him, it occurred to me that the twin blows of having his wife taken and his prize captive freed—and worse, he was forced to cooperate with me—had been too much for him to take. It wasn't especially comforting to know that I was now partners with a man on the edge of madness.

"So, then, Kem," I said calmly, "let me see if we've got this straight. You left us in the Ghost Walk in spite of promising you'd guide us through in return for your freedom. You followed us when we left. You ran into some of your old mates and stopped them from robbing and murdering us—" I paused and crooked a brow. "Why *did* you keep them from doing that?"

Kem swallowed noisily. "Because—if they got the map I wouldn't get the treasure."

"Ah, you wanted it for yourself."

"Yes!" He spat and struggled uselessly against Tanris's weight.

"Jackal," Tanris growled.

"You got the map. What are you doing here?"

An ugly, sullen look crept over Kem's face and he didn't answer.

"Ha," I smiled, and levered myself to my feet. He didn't have the egg; didn't even know where or how to find it. Maybe not even what it was. "I'm going to go get some of those ridiculously huge guards. You can kill him now, Tanris."

No, I didn't want to have anything to do with the guards. They're a nuisance when I'm working, and they generally want to turn me over to the local authorities—a project they are especially passionate about when there is a chance of reward. However, Kem didn't want anything to do with the guards, either, and he was even less thrilled to be left alone with a violent and apparently homicidal Tanris. In short order, we knew everything he knew about the alleged treasure, where he'd looked, what he'd found out, how much his companions knew, and what he'd had for dinner.

And *then* I fetched the guard. We could not, after all, have Kem running about and getting underfoot, and we certainly didn't trust him to work with us on this venture in spite of his begging and pleading for us to save him from his partners, who would surely kill him when they found him. Alas, such were the consequences of choosing felonious friends.

On my way to collect reinforcements, I tucked the map safely beneath a flower pot next to the door into the building, and detoured to relocate my sack full of incriminating work gear and the letters. The room across the hall from ours was unoccupied.

The brothers listened to Kem's side of the story, of course, and he took the opportunity to cast all sorts of suspicion on us. A contrary breezed fluttered around us and when I listened intently, I made out a few words, but they made little sense to me. The judicious brothers searched our things. Girl cried. I kept her and Tanris company in the hall. He wore a tight, unreadable expression, certain we were about to be exposed. I crouched on the floor, hugging my abused middle and taking quiet pleasure in Tanris's suffering, but I'd already hidden the things that might give us away and made sure they found the plentiful coin they'd expect a nobleman of my alleged stature to carry. In the end, the brothers apologized again and expressed their outrage that guests had nearly been the victims of robbery on the very grounds of the temple. They were wonderfully horrified that the incident might have culminated in murder. And so the hulking guards took Kem Bohadri away somewhere until he could be turned over to the authorities—perhaps for a reward—and they made no objection when I requested that we might continue our sojourn at Hasiq jum'a Sahefal for a few days. I had been badly ill-treated by my attacker before I was rescued by the vigilant Tanris, and I had the bruises to prove it.

They gave me tea.

They gave me a poultice that didn't smell too badly.

They even gave me a room of my own so I could rest undisturbed.

The situation could not have worked out more perfectly if I had planned it myself. The gods had remembered me once more, and I thanked them. Profusely.

The temple's healer wrapped my ribs in a stiff fabric and hoped anxiously that I had not broken anything. I'd had practice feigning broken ribs before—had, in fact, actually suffered broken ribs and knew exactly how they felt—and the healer was not as difficult to deceive as I had feared. Wonderfully sympathetic, he shared his concern with his peers, and after he checked on me in the morning I had visits from the cook, the captain of the guard, and Magister Melly (again)—all of whom departed my company a little lighter for their charity. From the healer I purloined a jar of salve. The cook donated a handful of sweets from a bulging pocket. The captain of the guard was a veritable walking treasure. He had keys. "Had" being the operative word. Melly also had a key, but it took some toying with to figure out, as the key itself—which must be important to be hidden so cleverly— was part of an interlocking puzzle hidden behind a lacquered face. Coincidentally, it depicted a dragon.

Alone at last, I fetched the map and then my hidden pack so that I could make use of my tools to create a decent copy of the important part before Melly missed it, and then I sought him out myself. By then I'd smudged a little dirt on the pendant so it could support my story of having found it in the garden where I had seen Melly walking earlier. He was nearly speechless with relief and I convinced him to tell me its history. A symbol of his office, it had been handed down from Magister to Magister for hundreds of years. The dragon symbolized his position as a protector—of the astonishing treasure hiding in the Vault, of course.

Just as I was about to take my leave, something caught my eye and gave me pause: a tiny ivory figurine exactly matching the one I had taken from Duzayan's secret office. I am far too practically minded for such a thing to strike me as coincidence. "This is an exquisite piece of ivory," I said, reaching for the figurine slowly, so as not to alarm him. It was just as well, for my fingers tingled wildly, and green light limned them. Striving to mask my own alarm, I turned the reach into a waving gesture and tucked my hands safely behind my back. "What is it?"

Melly came to stand beside me and peer nearsightedly past my shoulder. "I have no idea if it was ever meant to represent anything special. I ran across it during my travels and it appealed to me, so there it is."

There it was, indeed, right along with Melly's bald-faced lie, and him a pious devotee of some remote, completely obscure god. And right there my thoughts began to spin into some truly dreadful patterns. Behind my back, I wriggled my fingers to make sure they were still in good working order. "Isn't it interesting how some little trinket can catch an individual's eye and become one of their favorite things, and other people completely miss the appeal in it?"

"Oh, indeed. I appear to have a taste for the peculiar, or so I've been told."

My imagination was likely working overtime, but his smile reminded me horribly of Duzayan's, and it was all I could do not to bolt then and there. Into what disastrous trap had the wretched baron sent me? Was Melly forewarned? "We don't know each other, do we?" I asked, feigning a conspiratorial little chuckle and trying to brace myself for what I must do.

"No." He peered at me, and when he did, he had to lean very close. "No, I don't believe we do…" he murmured.

Thank the gods of happy circumstance, he was telling the truth about that. Stepping away from him provided me with just the opportunity I needed. I patted his arm in a friendly manner. "If you should ever travel to Naziridath," I named a good-sized city as far off the beaten path as I could recall, "you must search me out and we can compare peculiar—augh!" I stumbled wildly, and as I teetered and fell, I grabbed onto him.

He was, of course, not prepared for such a clever display of apparent clumsiness, and he toppled over with me, squeaking in dismay. I flung a desperate arm around his neck and caught hold of the chain he wore tucked beneath his robes. It—and the heavy silver medallion it bore—came free and banged me sharply in the nose.

It hurt astonishingly badly when it touched my skin, tingling so sharply it made my eyes water, which was rather counter productive to the entire exercise. As Melly struggled to free himself from my clutches, I blinked madly to clear my vision. I wondered, if I lit up like a witchlight torch, would he run screaming out of the room or stuff me in a jar of some sort for investigation and experimentation? The silver medallion swung into view, revealing the shape of a triangle puzzle.

Melly was a wizard.

The healer could discern no obvious aggravation of my allegedly broken ribs, which relieved him considerably. It pleased Melly as well, for worse damage might have required me to stay much longer than the two or three days unenthusiastically recommended. A social, charitable lot they were not. As it happened, I did not particularly wish to socialize with *them*, and when I was released from the healer's care, I beat a cautiously hasty retreat back to my room, only to run into—figuratively this time—Tanris.

"What happened?" he asked, brows furrowed and eyes narrowing. Suspicious as always.

"He's a wizard."

"Who?"

"Melly." Inside my room, I abandoned the injured act and went straight to my bags to retrieve the letters I'd removed from Duzayan's establishment. Sitting down on the bed, I riffled through them while Tanris hovered in the doorway.

"How did you find out?"

"Come in and close the door, you fool," I ordered shortly.

The door shut with a decisive thump. When I glanced at him, Tanris sported one of those expressions that ought to kill instantly. Of course I ignored it. "I borrowed his secret key to make a copy, and not only did he lie about the figurine, but he—"

"Stop." He held both hands up and patted the air between us oh-so-gently. Such a strange man. "You stole a key from the magister. And he's a mage."

He caught on so quickly! "Yes."

"By yourself."

I looked from side to side. "Yes…"

His hands curled into fists. "And you are aware that he and Duzayan are not on good terms which, as far as we're concerned, makes us the magister's enemy."

"We still have to find the egg and steal it from him," I pointed out.

"Which we cannot do if you are dead, Crow!" he barked, catching himself and remembering to lower his voice. He growled and punched the air. "Do not ever go off on your own to do something so dangerous! You could have been hurt or imprisoned. Worse, you might have got yourself killed."

"That would have complicated things for you, no doubt."

"You're an idiot, you know that?"

"What, you care about what happens to me?" I laughed and shook my head in disbelief.

"Yes," he snarled this time. He'd make a good bear.

I knew he wasn't lying, felt it in the energy around him, but I still had a hard time believing it. "Huh. Well, thank you. I'm fine. Everything is fine." I went back to my search. He folded his arms, pressed his lips together, and steamed. To his credit, he didn't ask what we were going to do now, but maintained his silence while I searched through the papers. "Ah, here it is. This is from Melly to Duzayan. There's all this rubbish about plants and rivers and stars, ascendancies and descendancies, then a quote from some Corunni mage about smoke from a fire rising against the wind. Then Melly gets blunt:

"Your misguided attempt to use Brother Gedikcan did not go unnoticed. He has been dealt with. I would return your most recent squad to you, but they fell apart. You will never have what is rightfully mine, and the Blessing will be mine to use, mine to control. You will never be allowed, under any circumstance, to assume the power we have awaited for decades. Never."

Tanris sat on the end of the bed. "So the magister has in his possession— or will have—something so powerful that Duzayan will do anything to get it."

"There are far more guards here than there ought to be. Granted, the temple itself could provide plenty of material to scavenge and sell, but transportation is such a problem it's hardly worth the effort. The collection in the vault is barely suitable for rustics."

"You haven't seen many rustic temples, have you?"

I ignored the criticism. "Why is Duzayan so eager to get his grimy little hands on this egg thing? And Melly so determined to keep it that he—a priest of the gods—will do violence to keep it?"

"We're talking about mages. I think they trump priests." He made a face. "With so much of his writing in code or in gibberish, we can't tell what else Duzayan has sent against him. He hasn't used an army yet, though he could afford one. Why?"

"Fear of destroying the egg?" I shrugged. "How about the difficulty of getting the army into this place?"

"Maybe fear of reprisal or even unwanted attention. Employing an army is not just expensive, it has political consequences."

"So he's secretly maintaining an identity as a wizard, utilizing the leverage of a noble title, gathering an army and allies, and secretly trying to obtain a magical item that will tip the scales in his favor when he sets his armies in place." Tanris had also mentioned that Duzayan was responsible for the deaths of several figures in Emperor Gaziah's government. "And we're helping. I'm so happy to be adding treason to my list of skills."

"I am not a traitor!" He stood abruptly, pacing to the door and back. "To the Dark with him. I will not help him. Not ever."

"What about your wife? You made a deal with Duzayan—the egg for her life."

"We'll figure that out when we know what the egg is and we have it in our possession."

I was glad I did not suffer the nobility required to save lives. I went to the little fireplace to stir the flames to life. "Where is Girl?"

"In her room, resting. Do we need her?"

I shook my head and held the letter out to the fire. The corner of the paper curled with heat then caught flame. I watched as it ate the possibly incriminating evidence, then dropped the remaining corner into the coals. I watched until it had disappeared completely, then stirred the ashes and considered what to do next. What *did* one do when caught in a wizards' game? Under the threat of poison, I couldn't very well run off and take up life in a foreign country; nor was I willing to let the poison run its course—or take my own life to avoid the painful death that had been promised.

In the middle of my rumination the door burst open without warning and Girl stood there, wide-eyed and white as the proverbial ghost.

Standing right next to the door as he was, the startled Tanris instinctively grabbed her. "What?" he demanded harshly. "What's wrong?"

She pulled on him, gesturing to me anxiously with her other hand. She did not need words to say "Come! Come!"

Out the door at the end of the building we ran, and I wondered what could possibly have her in such a state of agitation. At least she wasn't crying. Rounding the corner didn't reveal anything of catastrophic nature; no fire blazing, no army descending, no murder or mayhem in progress.

Then she pointed up at the sky.

There, gliding in lazy circles over the little sun-warmed valley, was what looked like a very real, living and breathing, *flying* dragon. Silhouetted against the bright sky it looked dark, but as it turned gently this way and that, I made out a glimmer of silver or white. I could not help but stare, helpless to express my utter astonishment. I briefly dragged my gaze away from the spectacle. Tanris gaped in open amazement, pale-faced. Did I look like that? I clapped my mouth shut.

The creature didn't really look very big, but the breadth of the sky didn't offer anything by way of perspective. It circled about several times before flapping its leathery wings and making a turn directly toward the mountain. Stepping out of the lee of the building, we watched its approach to the cliffside. Just when it seemed it must crash into the rock, it lifted its wings to brake gently and then disappeared from view. I looked fixedly at the place for a bit longer, and then I finally overcame my speechlessness. "Well."

My companions remained silent, and while not particularly unusual for Girl, Tanris generally had something to say. Their gazes remained glued to the cliff. "I don't think that was a bird," I jested, and then looked over the gawking pair more critically. "Are you all right?"

"Mm," Tanris said after a moment. "You?"

"Oh, certainly." I gave a dismissive wave of my hand and moved off. Neither shock nor hysteria were going to be of any help. "Tell me, do you think we could get supplies of ink and paper here in this remote hamlet?"

Tanris fell into step beside me, giving me a sideways look very effectively portraying his belief that I'd finally lost my mind. Girl came so close behind us she practically trod on our heels. "Do we need ink and paper?" he asked.

"I thought I should perhaps get started on that book you told me to write. I am, after all, about to meet a genuine dragon and that is the stuff of legend. The involvement of a couple of wizards adds a certain spice to the tale, eh?" I paused to frame a scene with my hands. "Handsome, cursed hero—that's me. A war between wizards. A fire-breathing dragon. A race to the death. All very dramatic and exciting."

"Aren't you forgetting something?"

"Am I?" I looked at him in surprise. "Oh, yes! The trusty sidekick."

He rolled his eyes. "You have something of a deadline, and you have yet to figure out how you're going to get up there—" he pointed, "much less how you're going to steal an egg from a genuine fire-breathing dragon and then get away from him—her—and get back to Marketh in time."

The gravel on the path crunched beneath our feet. A miasma of fear surrounded me, but it wasn't mine. Girl's was a quivering thing and Tanris's all cold and hard-edged. How easy it would be to let myself be caught up in the tide and pulled away from my purpose. "Has anyone ever told you that you're a really depressing man to be around?"

"Crow—" he started, and I waved a hand at him to hush, sizzling with irritation.

"I'll find a way." Me, not Tanris. We'd arrived at the point of crisis, and suddenly I was the one with the deadline and the entire weight of logistics and risk. Tanris's emphasis on the "you" part of the equation left no doubt I was on my own. I couldn't really say it surprised me. He may have got me from Marketh to Hasiq jum'a Sahefal, but stealing the blighted egg was the entire reason for my presence here. Angrily, I pushed aside the sensation of being hung to twist in the wind. I had no idea—yet—how I would deal with the dragon, and my sketchy memories of children's tales generally had the dragon winning all the encounters. But I was Crow, beloved of the gods. I would find a way.

"How?" Tanris had to ask.

— 21 —
Which Way Do We Go?

I didn't answer him, but pulled the map out of my jerkin and sat myself down on an ornate bench. Duzayan had bid us destroy the thing—a logical course of action to prevent anyone else finding his treasure, except that it was missing critical information. But, given what I had learned of Melly, I wasn't so certain that destruction was the right course of action. *This is a map to the dragon's lair*, Duzayan had said. *Memorize and burn it.* Not just a map to the village or a map to the temple, but to the *dragon's lair.* Did that not mean it held more than met the eye? I unfolded the parchment to smooth over my legs, noticing for the first time a strange sort of fuzzy, prickly sensation. I turned it sideways, upside down, and then backwards. I looked at it through eyes squinted partially shut, then I held it up to the sunlight— and paused.

"What is it? Do you see something?" Tanris asked, crouching down next to me.

"No." I got abruptly to my feet to hurry back to my room.

"Then what?"

"We haven't followed all the instructions."

"What are you talking about?" He trotted after me. Girl trotted after him. Catching sight of a pair of the brothers coming in through the gate, I slowed to a pace more suited to the woefully injured and pressed an arm against my side in pretend discomfort. Tanris put a solicitous hand under my elbow to help me along.

"Do you remember what he told us?" I asked, pulling open the door and striding down the hall a little more quickly once I was out of sight of any watchers. I slipped into my room with my little train trailing behind. "He said to burn it."

"Wait, no…"

"Yes." I went to the fire and crouched down. "We're already here, so the obvious instructions have already been accomplished." I held the map over the flames by opposing corners, and little wisps of smoke curled up around it. For a moment nothing happened, and then the center slowly darkened. As it did, pale lines appeared.

"What is that?" Tanris whispered in my ear, bending close.

We watched as the center continued to become darker and a new map appeared, just faint at first, then the lines grew thicker and more confident. My hand shook slightly and I held my breath, waiting. As the page transformed, the fuzzy sensation from earlier increased until my fingertips smarted as though needles stabbed each digit. I held on as long as I could bear, but the more it hurt, the stranger the coloring in my fingers became. With a hiss, I let the map go and staggered backwards.

Tanris gave a startled yelp and grabbed for the parchment. "Crow!"

"It hurts!" I exclaimed, holding my wounded hands against my chest.

"You didn't even touch the flames! What's the matter with you!?" He dropped the map on the little stone hearth and slapped out the flames eating away one corner.

Girl stared at me for a moment with her fingertips pressed over her mouth, then dropped down to examine my hurt. While Tanris dealt with the minor conflagration, the two of us watched my fingers go from a sickly greenish color to a healthy pink again. Mouth pursed and brows drawn in concern, she looked up at me. It was a tender and unexpected expression. I flashed a quick smile, then crawled back to the hearth. The new illustration had faded considerably, so I had Tanris hold it over the heat again while I examined a detailed map of the Temple of Nadimesh, including parts we had not yet seen and parts an ordinary visitor was never even supposed to know existed…

Long after the brethren—most of them, at any rate—and their servants had gone to sleep, the temple lay quiet and dark, just the way temples ought to do at such a late hour. A light shone in one of the upstairs rooms, but thankfully it was not Melly's. I didn't need some nosey wizard awake and alert to sniff out things he was better off not knowing. Predictably, the guards were stationed at unfortunately interfering intervals. They were, however, not wildly vigilant. An utterly reasonable development, given that the building they guarded was, after all, clear in the middle of nowhere. Rational, sensible people stayed on well-traveled highways and visited well-populated cities, or even towns, and visitors to the illustriously named Hasiq jum'a Sahefal had to be about as rare as snake feathers. And besides, I'd suffered a terrible injury, eh?

Getting into the temple was not as hard as it might have been in one of those well-populated cities where the guards commonly defend against criminals, vagrants, and transportation merchants such as myself. The cat made it a little trickier. Tanris would have had my hide for using it as a diversion, so I didn't tell him. Besides, I had no intention of hurting it or letting it be hurt. For whatever bizarre reason, Tanris liked the fool creature.

Once I'd put the thing in the bag I'd brought along exactly for that purpose—no mean feat, I'll tell you now—it quieted down. I suspected it would wait until I opened the sack and then leap to freedom, incidentally clawing my face to ribbons on the way by. I wore my coat for the padding it would provide as much as for protection against the cold, and I tied the sack across my back. The cat remained very still, but its low-voiced growling made shivers go up my spine.

The guards were stationed all the way around the temple and right up to the cliff wall, so up and over them I went. Traversing the face of a cliff is something of a different matter than going across the side of a building, but there were certain similarities, and I took my time. I only had to backtrack once before I reached the roof. From there it was a simple matter to use my knife to lift the latch on one of the dormer windows and slip inside.

I pulled the window closed and glanced around, pleased to note I'd correctly discerned its purpose as a storage room. A convenient stack of crates stood by the door, and I hurried to put myself behind them, crouching low so I could scoot out the door behind whoever might come to investigate the disturbance.

Moments went by, measured in heartbeats. I did not trust the silence and waited a while longer, until the cat squirmed once, suddenly, against my back. It startled me and I sucked in a breath, but it was only the cat. Quiet as a shadow, I made my way out of the room toward the main level. I had only discovered three sets of guards indoors; one pair at Magister Melly's quarters, one pair at the massive entrance doors, and one pair at the doors leading into the Vault.

The temple's main stairs stood at the back of the entrance hall. They were flanked by gigantic marble columns at the top of which fantastically beautiful sculptures of men, every one of them different, held up the towering ceiling which was itself a work of astonishing beauty. A man could get completely sidetracked studying the story told by intricately painted panels set into the domed ceiling and separated by slivers of glass. The first flight of stairs, shorter than the others but at least twice as wide as I was tall, ended on a landing overlooked by the statue of some glorious, haloed hero inset in a niche. The stairs continued on the right and the left, ascending into arched doorways and thence to additional wings. Even at night braziers burned, lighting the stairway, gilding the carvings and paintings, glimmering on inlaid jewels and precious metals. Such elegance did not belong in an obscure, remote temple, but who was I to doubt the sanity of the gods that allowed it?

The guards, thank the god of clever thieves, were stationed outside the fabulous, three-man-tall double doors to keep less enterprising burglars from entering. Wary of surprises, I crouched low next to the carved stone balusters and slipped down the stairs. Just as I reached the upper landing, the whisper of leather on marble announced the presence of one of the good brothers. Head bowed, he rubbed his face and shuffled slowly across the wide entryway. Three-quarters of the way, he stopped and came back. Behind the bulk of one of the columns, I breathed quietly, waited until he'd satisfied his curiosity and continued his journey, waited a few minutes longer, then glided down the steps to the entry floor. Left around the column brought me to another staircase tucked directly beneath the grand one, but much narrower. Eleven steps down, it met a landing and branched into two staircases, one left and one right, parallel to the front of the temple. A hall led off each stair, and another intersected them. At the center of that intersect was another hall leading toward the mountain—and the uninspiring Vault.

I tiptoed toward my goal, peered around the corner and, just as I'd expected, found the steadfast guards—and this was where the cat came in. Crouching down against the wall, I loosed the bag's tie and the cat sat up slowly, fur ruffled and eyes brimming with umbrage at the indignity it had suffered. Ears laid back, it glared at me fiercely. Wary, I took hold of the fabric and gave a tug or two to encourage the cat out. It stumbled a bit, then stepped delicately free of the bag, only to sit down and begin grooming itself.

I waved my hands at it in a shooing motion, but the cat ignored me completely, calmly licked its paw, and wiped its face. Scooting back a step or two, I flapped the bag at it, and the cat jumped away, then looked up and down the hall as if I didn't even exist. Tail held high, the very tip twitched back and forth carelessly.

I snapped the bag sharply, which inspired it to a piteous meow and garnered the attention of the guards. That was more like it, except the blighted thing still just *stood* there, looking right at me. I withdrew my blade, fully prepared to do it more than just a little insult—and the cat turned its head, looking down the hall toward the noise of an approaching guard. It padded toward the corner and peered around, froze, then abruptly shot across the corridor. I dropped down low and tight against the inside wall as the guard broke into a trot, chasing after the cat, calling foolishly after it. "Kitty! Here, kitty!"

I didn't have long at all to accomplish my task, and leaped to my feet to hurry toward the other guard. I had not become a successful thief on looks alone, though they certainly didn't hurt. Palming a vial of Adamanta Dust, I worked the stopper loose as I walked. "The cat!" I called out to him. "Have you seen it?"

He was obviously surprised to see me, but pointed helpfully back the way I'd just come. "Marjan just chased it that way."

I assumed an expression of annoyance. "But I just came from that way… It must have run around the stair. Blighted beast." I waved my hand in irritation—and tossed the powder from the vial right into his face. He blinked and sucked in a startled breath, which was just what I needed him to do and exactly the wrong reaction for anyone planning on defending the treasures of the Temple of Nadimesh. The powder stung one's eyes violently, I knew, and I was very careful not to breathe the stuff. The guard coughed, and when he sucked more air into his lungs, I blew the remainder of the powder off my hand and into his face. I caught him as he crumpled to the floor, quieting his fall. His weight pulled me over in the process and I barely grabbed his long and lethal-looking halberd before it clattered to the floor.

Across from the Vault were several small rooms whose purpose the map had not revealed. The first was locked, but the second opened up for me. Into it I dragged my unconscious companion, shut the door, then dashed further down the hall. "Kitty?" I called, letting myself be heard and peering into the few open doorways. Frankly, the torches decorating the walls did nothing to light the interiors of the rooms beyond, and I wouldn't have seen the cat if it was ten feet tall until it jumped out at me. "Where are you, cat?"

"Hey!" the returning guard hollered at me, and I whirled to look at him in surprise, then made my way back to him, another vial in hand.

"Have you seen my cat?" I asked, walking right up to him. "Well, it's actually Tanris's cat, but it ran in here and now I've lost it and he'll probably want my hide for it. He's brought the wretched thing across miles and miles —" I paused to hold my hand up in an innocently questioning motion, and gently blew the dust in his face. I did not want to kill the guards, but I certainly couldn't have them scampering about, alerting the other guards to the night's activities and trying to chase me down. They'd only get in the way.

I grabbed Guard Number Two's halberd and let him fall, then I dragged him into the room across from the Vault to lie next to his partner. I used the sashes they wore, torn into long strips, to bind and gag them thoroughly, removed everything of value that I could find on them —rings; an earring of fine pearl; another of the lacquered pendants, though this one was strung on a leather cord and didn't have a clever little key worked into the back; coins (not many of those); an ordinary key ring; and of course their weapons. I tucked the trinkets in my pouch and the knives into my belt, and then I took their boots. Barefoot pursuits are notoriously short-lived.

I checked the hall, then pulled the door shut, locking it with the very handy keys. With a few twisted, finger-length strands of fine wire shoved into the keyhole, I jammed the mechanism and used one of the smaller keys to push the exposed ends out of sight.

It was but the work of moments to employ the keys again, unlocking the great and heavy Vault door. I brought the boots and the halberds with me, then eased the door shut and locked it again, thanking the very powerful and unpredictable god of luck. As Brother Two had promised, the flame in the channel still burned.

A large, ugly urn received the boots as well as the cumbersome swords, and I hefted the halberds, balancing them against my shoulder. A fantastic triptych hung at the back of the repository, three carved panels in separate frames with the two narrower ones on the outside hinged to the larger one in the middle. The scene depicted a dragon in flight over a village—presumably Hasiq jum'a Sahefal—and all the little villagers running wildly, mouths and eyes agape and some of them on fire. It was rather disturbing.

According to the map the door into the Real Vault hid behind the center section. Some investigation proved that the middle and left-hand panels swung away from the wall, and behind the panels—more wall. Lovely gold squares of marble, polished to a glossy shine. The temple would work well as a museum of marble. Where all the varieties had come from I could only guess, and marvel at the cost of import. I held up the witchlight and examined the wall carefully, but its pale light didn't reveal the seams that must surround the door, and indeed, the stonework was so fine I didn't believe they *could* be seen. It was a magnificent example of masonry, but not really what I needed in my life right now. I swung the panel of the ravaging dragon wide and stepped back. I could discern nothing in the wall, no handle, no embellishment perhaps hiding a latch, no discoloration, no shadow indicating an indentation. The smooth stone floor didn't have any secrets to share, either. Knocking on the panels proved fruitless, so I pushed—and the heavy door slid back on well-oiled tracks. Thank the gods of expert construction. I had no time to admire the work, but slipped inside

Pulling the triptych panels closed, I went around the door to slide it closed again, then turned to look about for a way to jam the thing. It is a wonder my eyes did not fall out of my head. What I had first failed to notice was that the same sort of channel ran around the outside of this room as had encircled the pathetically small Fake Vault. At least as wide as the aboveground portion of the temple, this room extended a considerable distance further into the mountainside. The marble plinths holding up the exterior room's assortment of almost-valuable items were here as well—very, very many of them. Here were the sacred, the precious, the invaluable, the extraordinary. My slack-jawed admiration had to wait while I jammed the end of one of the halberds into a track and kicked it firmly into place.

Out of curiosity, I had once visited Gaziah's Imperial museum, and this room easily rivaled any one of the rooms there. Piece after piece of astounding beauty sat upon velvet cushions. Now and then there were some hideously ordinary things, but I discovered something as I explored —or rather, I confirmed something I had only guessed. Every time I reached toward one of the treasures, my fingers began to tingle. Some of them I could touch; the larger ones made my entire arm ache and my hand glow green.

What was this thing? What had happened to me? Moreover, could I get rid of it? Not only was it ridiculous and unattractive, but held the potential to ruin my career. It is a curious fact of life that while the general populace avoids wizards like they avoid stinking, rabid dogs, they are hopelessly enamored of magical things. I steal magical things for a living. Granted, I steal other items as well, but magical items earn me the most coin by far. How could I steal them if I glowed hideously and—worse—I couldn't even pick them up without experiencing terrible pain?

A particularly attractive dagger caught my eye, and I brought the witchlight closer to examine it. Cast all in one piece, a foreign, beautiful script marked the length of the blade. As I tried to place the style, I became aware of a whispering noise.

"Go away," I hissed, not wanting a repeat of the incident in the tunnel.

If anything, the whispering grew louder. Soon I could make out words.

Ours... ours... ours... Look! There it is. Can you see? Come look! Come! Come! The voices beckoned me to the right side of the room.

"I don't want to see! Go away!" Hefting my halberd, I marched down the aisle toward the back of the enormous room where the map indicated another door.

Ours! Can he take it? So long... So long! How is it here? ...stolen from the Hall... Who? Who? ...he touch it? Bring him. Come! Come!

"I can't *hear* you!" I called out in a singsong voice, and I would have covered my ears if not for carrying the halberd and the light. Even as I started to put the latter in my pocket, it dawned on me that it hadn't made me tingle or light up. I stopped and stared at it in mute surprise. "Hey!" I asked my invisible companions. "Why isn't this hurting me?"

Hurting! He is hurting! Help him. What can we do? Help... help... help...!

"No, no, it's *not* hurting me. Pay attention. Do you know why?"

Ours! It is ours... ours... ours!

"It is?" What did that mean?

Come! Come! the voices insisted.

"Who are you?!" I growled at them, lifting the witchlight and looking around. I had nothing for company but treasures. Two rows of plinths ran down the length of the room, and beyond them stood other, different displays. Larger items sat upon raised daises. The very largest items occupied niches all their own, and there were several fantastically carved statues, some of men and some of strange creatures that I would just as soon not meet in this world or any other.

A finger of suspicion tickled my spine. Aside from the very obvious question about where the elusive egg might be located, where had all these things come from and why were they here, on the very outermost edges of civilization? A king could not claim such mystic wealth, never mind an obscure order of priests. Baron Duzayan would turn a vivid shade of green with pure jealousy. Of course then he'd dispense with the brothers and their guards so he could take for himself an assortment of magical and historical gewgaws that would make taking over the empire as easy as slipping in cow dung. Such a collection in the hands of any one wizard—or even a group of them—nauseated me. What power they would have!

Come! Come! the voices kept insisting and didn't answer my question. I found myself standing in front of a large brass statue of a man with six arms, eyes of some sort of white stone glowing eerily, and a bejeweled tongue hanging out of his mouth. The jewels were appealing, the tongue not so much.

There! See? Do you see? Do you see? Do you see?

"See what? An ugly statue?" My skin tingled uncomfortably.

Not ours! No no no! Take what is ours! You can! You must! We will have it back and we will be heard again!

Each of the statue's hands held a different weapon—two blades, a flail, an axe, a spear, a crossbow. I would loathe having such a monster come to life and attack me. For all that it was decorated in jewels and fine metals and carefully groomed feathers, it wore about its neck a plain disk of some dull-colored material reminiscent of Old Jelal's bones. A symbol was carved into the surface, though I could not quite make out the details, and a plain leather cord with several beads to either side held it around the ugly statue's neck.

For no logical reason, I wanted it.

I propped my halberd nearby so I could step up onto the marble dais. I balanced myself upon one of the outstretched arms and—

—promptly found myself lying on the floor, staring up at a room tilting crazily back and forth while the panicked screeching of whispery voices echoed all around me. A very odd circumstance, I can assure you. Between me and the room was a strange greenish glow, and it took me several minutes to realize that it came from me. I was glowing. Excessively.

"What happened?" I asked, slowly sitting up. The witchlight had rolled away, coming to a stop against the base of the statue.

Magic! Magic! Eeeevil magic! Not ours, no, no!

Dizzy as a child's spin-toy, I could only sit there, squinting at the room until it finally settled down again. I crawled over to retrieve the light and tuck it away, and when I ventured to stand I wobbled alarmingly, as though every ounce of energy had been sapped from my body. I should have perhaps contemplated how this would further complicate my career, but instead I worked on figuring out how to get that pendant.

He can't reach it! What will we dooooo? the voices wailed.

"I can't think with you crying like that," I complained. "Hush." And they did. I blinked and looked about. As I did, I laid eyes on my discarded weapon, and couldn't help a smug chortle. It took a minute or two to work the pendant up over the statue's head, but I am a thief, and such dexterity is part and parcel of my profession. Careful this time, I reached toward the disk as it swung from my halberd. Nothing happened, except an impatience to hold it, to wear it, to possess it. "Is this going to hurt?"

Don't know… It is ours! He is ours… Take it. Take it!

I took it. As I settled it around my neck, a sharp prickle went through me from head to toe. Little wisps of green just like those from the Ghost Walk followed, and then disappeared. I moved my hands; they seemed to work just fine. I took a few cautious steps and, aside from the remnants of dizziness and weakness, I didn't have any trouble with that, either.

Is it well? Does it work? He can hear us…

"I could hear you before," I grumbled, "and I would just as soon not."

They said nothing, but joy practically glittered all around me. Holding it up to the light, I examined the amulet, which was indeed a slice of sheep horn polished smooth. The carving depicted two narrow, vertical rectangles with another horizontal one across their tops. Faint lines in a ray pattern decorated the lower edge. It looked uncannily like the disk Old Jelal had shown me. "What is it?"

Door, it's a door. Portal… entry… exit… passage… means…

"What does it do?"

A small silence and then the rustling whispers again, like dry leaves in the wind. The voices talked right over themselves, and I had to listen carefully, but I thought I could actually understand them better. *Allows… makes an opening… a passage… ours, ours, it is ours…*

Yes, that was clear as mud and just about as helpful. "Very well, then." I tucked the disk beneath my layered tunics, lying against my skin, warm and *right* somehow. It did not tingle nor make me glow, and it was mine now. I put the light away again, reasoning to save it for urgent situations. Halberd against my shoulder, I went back to the center aisle and finished my trek down the length of the room. Upon the back wall hung a magnificent tapestry. Another dragon. At least this one looked more heraldic than violent, though with those outstretched talons it was probably just me feeling wishful. Behind this tapestry, according to the map, I would find the door.

Behind the tapestry were *two* doors.

Duzayan didn't give very good directions.

Awkwardly, I gathered the tapestry in the middle to tie with a leftover piece of one of the guard's sashes. A portion of each door was visible to either side, separated by several feet. I stood in front of them and tried to impose my memory of the secret map on them, to no avail. How could I know which was the correct door? I needed to make a choice and soon. The men I'd drugged would only be unconscious for so long (hopefully), and eventually their replacements would come along. I needed to be long gone before that. Luckily, I am a very practically minded man. I tested both doors, and then, taking the two rings of keys—one obtained mere moments ago and the other liberated earlier from the captain of the guard—I searched for the one that would fit the locks. None of them did, which had me scratching my head for the space of a heartbeat or two, then I recalled Melly's secret key. A secret key for a secret door…

I had to hold the witchlight close to the opening of the door on the left, I studied it carefully. I couldn't help a smile when I realized that the lock itself was a deception. The hole was inset, and Melly's key fit perfectly into the depression, but I couldn't turn it. That required some thought, and it occurred to me that perhaps the pendant itself served that purpose. I had the guard's similar pendant. Fitting it to the hole worked like a charm. The latch clicked and I pushed the door open. The passage beyond yawned as black as pitch.

I ventured in a few steps to a landing of sorts, with a torch in a bracket and a half-barrel holding several more. Further, the passage turned left and became stairs going up into the mountain. But was it the correct upward-going steps? And did they have to be so narrow? Did the gods really believe that prolonged entombment would relieve me of my dislike of tight, dark places?

With a huff, I went back out to repeat the process on the other door. In a mirror of its mate, it possessed a small entryway, torches, and turned to the right. The hideously cramped stairs, however, disappeared going downward. I needed to go up, so I tucked my little light away and took the torch from the bracket, closed the door, left it unlocked, and freed the tapestry to fall back into place. The subtle signs I left marked my choice as the downward passage. With flint and striker, I lit a spark to set my new torch burning nicely. Bracing myself, I stepped into the left-hand passage, closed and locked the door, and began my ascent into the lair of the dragon.

— 22 —
More On Bearding Lions

I hadn't gone very far before I turned around and started right back down again. How could I possibly vanquish a dragon? It didn't matter how small it *looked*, I am a thief, not a warrior. A clever thief, you say, would have brought along the handy and oh-so-capable fighter who had been his companion for the last fifty-some days, and to be truthful, I had considered it because there was, as we all know, a dragon to deal with and even if he couldn't deal with it successfully, he would have made an excellent distraction. However…

I had not been certain I could get Tanris into the building with me, particularly if it was magic-warded. I am, as I have previously mentioned, accustomed to working alone and he had his own ideas about doing things. I can count on *me* implicitly, and I rarely argue with myself. And then Tanris would refuse to leave Girl behind; I would refuse to take her. I did not need another encumbrance, and she was unpredictable at best, particularly considering the danger involved. I would happily use her as dragon bait, but couldn't imagine Tanris condoning such a thing, and then he would protest leaving her behind to become a hostage when the good brothers discovered our absence—and they surely would. I didn't care about that, either. I had not asked her to come on the journey and didn't count her my responsibility. Rather than quarreling pointlessly, I had simply bid Tanris good night, promised to continue working on my plan, and retired to my room. The poor fool hadn't suspected a thing in spite of our association over the last decade or so. I slipped a note under his door, short and not too cryptic: *"Gone for the prize. Leave now. Will catch up or meet at original supply stop."* I didn't want to leave the name of the town, but Tanris knew where we'd planned to resupply for the next leg of our journey.

I had a plan for everything—and still found myself going up and down the secret stairs, dithering over my choice. I had been selected specifically for this job, and I was very good at what I did. Up I went.

I couldn't fight a blighted dragon alone. Down I went.

I would die if I didn't trade the egg for the antidote. Up again.

This time, I decided, I would go all the way to the top and then sit down for a while to go over the details rather than wasting my energy going back and forth, which wasn't practical at all. I prided myself on my practicality, and this ridiculous vacillating upset me tremendously. I had to take what was in front of me and do the best I could, period, no hesitation. I am no coward, but I could see nothing sensible in confronting a dragon face to face. "I am an expert thief," I reminded myself. "I have been in perilous situations before. I will simply slip in, nick the egg, and be out again before the dragon even knows what happened."

The ascent didn't take very long to wind me; even all the climbing we'd encountered on our trip didn't compare to the vertical route I now traversed. Inside the mountain, the distance covered felt like a great deal more than what it appeared from the outside. It was difficult to measure time and space on the winding stair, though much to my relief the stairway widened after a few turns. Landings here and there broke up the monotony, and I discerned openings leading off to either side and sometimes doors, as well as lengths of passage between stairs—and some of them, passages and stairs alike, opened into cavities of utter darkness. I wondered where the apparently man-made openings led and what lay within these secret places, but although tempted to explore, my curiosity was tempered by two things: first, time was pressing, and second, I am really, sincerely not keen on underground tunnels or chambers.

As I climbed, I found myself considering questions I had avoided whilst denying the existence of dragons and dragon eggs. Why did a dragon live in this region? Surely some enterprising hero ought to have made the tedious trip into this remote outback to rid the world of the terror and claim his glory and possibly riches. Was it protected?

Well, yes. I realized suddenly and with some chagrin that the brothers really were protecting it, but why? What sort of magic did dragons possess, and was their magic common among their kind, or did it differ from dragon to dragon? Was the egg alone magical, and was that why Duzayan wanted it so badly? Was he going to raise himself a dragon and—what? Somehow challenge Emperor Gaziah?

Amazing as a dragon might be, one single dragon in the face of all of Gaziah's vast armies seemed a pretty pitiful opposition, and I found it difficult to believe that Duzayan's new army could even begin to compare. Magister Melly had not razed the empire, nor even carved out a nice little kingdom for himself, and he obviously had access to his very own dragon. I could understand why no one would want a kingdom in this dreary, wet, stark locale, but that begged the question why anyone would live here at all, which was neither here nor there in the overall scheme of dragon things.

Back to Baron Duzayan and his egg-gathering.

What had he said about it? Not much, to be sure, but—except that I wasn't going to steal from another wizard, but from a dragon. Stinking, duplicitous son of a bowlegged cow! Even if Melly wasn't actually holding the egg in his hands, he certainly stood between me and the dragon, and Duzayan had *known* this, as his letter proved. As a wizard, he was naturally treacherous and deceitful, but he wanted this egg and had gone to great lengths to get it. But did he warn me about Melly? No, he did not!

I stomped up another ten steps, but fatigue swiftly put an end to such foolishness. Turning around, I sat myself down on the stone. Well-supplied by the brothers with torches and light, I contemplated the unhappy turn of events. What did it mean? Perhaps Duzayan didn't want the egg at all, but he wanted to put Melly out of commission. Why then, send a thief? But he hadn't, had he? He'd sent a highly skilled thief *and* a fairly efficient, but by no means famous, warrior.

Did he mean for Tanris to kill him? I couldn't imagine that happening. Tanris wouldn't kill in cold blood. He was a warrior, yes, but not a murderer.

I sat for a while longer, and while I came to no certain conclusions about anything, I did get a good rest. Thirsty, I refrained from drinking, afraid my flask of water wouldn't last for the duration of the trip. My legs ached already, and I had to wonder if I would be able to make the return trip. I could just imagine myself tottering along on wobbly legs, only to inadvertently pitch myself down the steps—probably at the longest stretch.

With a heavy sigh, I levered myself up and resumed my climb. The halberd made a pretty good walking stick, and I fantasized about using it to slay the dragon. I was going to have a hard time convincing anyone of the truth of my tale without witnesses. Maybe I should have brought Tanris and Girl along...

Up and up I went, and it came to me that it wasn't difficult at all to guess which of the brothers made this trip regularly and which chose to stay in the temple below to partake of the good meals provided by an adept cook. After an age or two, a small gleam of light ahead made me quicken my pace. The end was near! Keeping close to the wall to avoid tumbling into the depths of an open chasm, I turned the corner, expecting to see the dragon's lair opening up to the sky, preferably without the dragon.

There *was* more light, though not as bright as I'd hoped. Unfortunately, there was also Melly. Another brother accompanied him, number Three, possibly. He wore a look of evil glee as he nudged Melly's arm and pointed at me.

Melly's face twisted into a strange smile. "Ah, Fajhal," he greeted, recalling the name I had given him upon our introduction. "Or is it Crow? Or perhaps something else altogether?"

"Melly." I sighed. Of course this wasn't going to be easy, and Duzayan's pile of lies continued to grow. He might protest that he could not know Melly's intentions, but I would still hold it against him. Bitterly.

"I beg your pardon!" he exclaimed, his horrible smile segueing straight into an expression of astonishment.

I would have waved a dismissive hand, but they were both occupied. "If I address you by your proper name, will our relationship change?"

"Don't be ridiculous."

"Well then, Melly, what can I do for you?"

He blinked, clearly taken aback by my question.

"Cheeky rascal," Brother Three muttered.

"Duzayan is a short-sighted fool. He always has been, and sending you here just goes to show how desperate he's become. You can't really have thought we would let you get away with your ill-advised plan, can you?"

I resented being lumped in the same company as my tormentor in the planning business, but it seemed unlikely that Melly would sympathize and simply let me carry on. "Actually, I'd rather hoped you were completely oblivious. It always makes things easier."

"You must think me an idiot."

"Either that, or I am a hopeless optimist." I smiled.

Brother Three gasped.

Melly lifted both hands and said something I could not understand, but the air all around me crackled with little white and green lightnings. Abruptly, an army of ravenous, invisible ants was devouring my skin, inside and out. I couldn't breathe. Shocked, I stumbled back several paces. The whisper of voices sprang up all around me, but I couldn't focus on them through my panic, couldn't tell if they offered anything useful. As Melly advanced on me, chanting and full of dire purpose, I backed down the steps as quickly as I could, which did nothing to fill my lungs but provided me with a perfect opportunity to strike back. It didn't take much to pretend a stumble and a fall. I flailed for balance—and hurled the halberd wildly at the wizard. I did not care how it hit, only that it made contact.

Alack and alas for him, he had all the visual acuity of a cave rat.

Trailing behind him, Brother Three yelled a warning, but too late. The halberd struck Melly, his cry bringing an end to his chanting even as the weapon parted cloth and skin. The point caught in the shoulder of his robes. He tottered and yanked at the thing, which only succeeded in damaging him further and upsetting his balance. Brother Three grabbed at him. Melly screamed.

Over he went into the gaping hole, flailing his arms and legs and taking my lovely halberd with him.

"Master!" Brother Three cried, horror etching his features as he looked into the depths. I doubted he could see anything; I'd tried earlier, and the torch light didn't carry very far.

Leaning against the wall, I sucked in great breaths and thanked the gods of good fortune, halberds, fissures in mountains, air, and every other appropriate subject I could come up with, certain the wizard's demise had been far too easy and I had many, many gods to thank.

"You!" Brother Three screeched, turning a livid look upon me. "I am going to kill you. I am going to make you hurt in ways you've never even dreamed!" he spat, and he lifted his hands in exactly the same manner his erstwhile master had done, except his fingers curled into vicious claws.

"You aren't a wizard, too, are you?" I asked, and looked about for some sort of inspiration for dealing with him.

He didn't answer in words I could comprehend; he didn't need to. More white and green lightnings erupted around me, and they hurt. Horrendously. Whatever spell he cast at me hurt worse than Melly's, which had only frightened me and robbed me of air. Acute pain stabbed my gut, twisting and pulling and tearing. I screamed loud and long, until that, too, robbed me of breath.

Brother Three jabbed his clawed hands and stalked toward me, his voice rising in pitch until he screamed, too. The Voices shrieked through the passage and a violent wind sprang up, tugging at Brother Three's hair and robes and making the flames of the torch I desperately gripped in my hand dance wildly. "The torch!" I hissed. "Don't put it out...!"

The pain bent me over nearly double, and it was a battle to shove myself upright again. Twisted nearly in half, my free arm clutching my tormented belly, I forced one step at a time, faster and faster, closing the space between us. The wind howled through the chamber, but barely touched me. Painful green lightnings flared across my skin, bright enough to penetrate my clothes.

He did not pause in his incantation, but his own steps slowed, confusion dawning on his infuriated features. *What was I doing? Why wasn't I lying down and dying?*

In truth, I could not answer the latter except to say I was not just going to lie down and die for anyone, most particularly a hateful wizard posing as a priest.

Good intentions be as they may, I didn't make it all the way to my goal. Every step was more excruciating than the last and twisted my body in wrenching spasms of agony. I fell at his feet and lay there panting and making terrible noises in my throat.

His expression shifted again, this time to victory.

No. No, I refused to accept that. My lips curled in a snarl and I put everything I had into moving my arm. Just one arm. He laughed at my struggles, and the spell eased just a fraction. It was still harder than I expected to shove the torch along the floor in his direction.

Brother Three sidestepped. "Oops, you missed," he taunted. His talon-like hands jabbed more pain into me. I managed to roll away from the edge of the pit, but I could go no further; I couldn't even crawl away to anything resembling safety, so I just huddled there sobbing for breath while he laughed and laughed.

The voices of the Ancestors dropped to an ominous whisper, but Brother Three remained oblivious. His hands drew apart, and it felt like he pulled my innards with the motion.

Then the light on the wall sprang upward suddenly. Brother Three's laughter turned to screams. Light and the shadows carried out a tortured dance, dizzying me. I forced myself to focus on him. Thank the gods—all of them; the flames had touched the hem of his robes and sped up the fabric to light him like a bonfire. Unable to watch, I squeezed my eyes shut. I could not move, I could scarcely breathe or form a single thought.

The light disappeared with a strange whoosh, and then it was silent but for the soft, anxious whispering that filled the passage. *Does he live? Is it too late? What can we do? Who will help? Does he live? Does he live?*

And then even that noise faded away.

Consciousness returned in bits and pieces. I could not at once determine where I was, nor why I hurt so badly. Opening my eyes revealed only more darkness, and a tentative exploration with one hand gave me the knowledge of cold stone. I found the wall, too, and after some effort I managed to sit up enough to lean against it. The tools in my pack dug into my back. They were the least of my worries. Off to my right and up a little way the texture of stone walls revealed a source of light from higher up.

The familiarity tickled my brain until remembrance flooded me. I lurched to my knees and retched violently, which did nothing at all to ease the aching in my belly. The odor of burnt flesh tainted the air I gasped, and I pressed my hand over my face and mouth, trying not to breathe it in, trying not to remember Three's strangled, horrific screams.

I could not stay here. Getting to my feet, I staggered up the steps and around the corner. The passage extended gently upward for another twenty or thirty feet, then took an abrupt turn to the right into weak daylight. Was it dawn, then, or had I laid there unconscious throughout the entire day, and into night?

I stared at the splash of brightness for a long time. More than anything, I wanted to go up into the light and breathe fresh air, but at the same time I was in no particular hurry to go through the motions of another battle that would, given my current condition, likely end in my demise. Knowing the lay of the land—or cave, in this case—would be helpful, though.

After another moment or two in which I could discern no obvious lessening of the pain, I forced myself onward. I didn't want to contemplate what Brother Three had done to my insides, but having the wherewithal to walk heartened me, and even the ability to vomit gave me hope. If my innards had been utterly destroyed—well, to begin with I'd be dead, and I clearly wasn't, and I didn't particularly feel like I was getting any *worse*. All the way up the narrow corridor, I cursed the wizards for making my job even more difficult. They'd hurt me, and they'd taken my halberd and the torch as well. Interfering, no-good, black-hearted *snakes*.

It struck me that I had just defeated not one, but *two* wizards, and something like hysteria overtook me. I sank down on my knees and laughed until I cried. I stayed there for a little while after I'd finally calmed myself, but sitting accomplished nothing. So I struggled upright again and made my way slowly to the opening, which was just large enough to admit an average-sized man, though anyone taller than I would have to duck his head. On the left a fairly large cavern opened to the sky, but I could not tell if it was dawn or dusk. Haphazard piles of whitened bones littered the floor around the walls, and I shuddered. I did not want to add my own to the count. Of the dragon I saw no sign, nor of the egg but, as luck would have it, another passageway led deeper into the mountain.

Oh, the joy that filled me.

Would there never be an end to horrible caves and darkness? This one no doubt led directly to the lair itself, or the nest, or however dragons made themselves comfy. Perhaps it had a hoard of gold as a nice bonus.

I needed to go into that blasted tunnel, but not with the dragon inside if it could be at all avoided, so I chose a spot just inside the passageway from which I had come, and settled down to rest myself and wait.

I jerked upright, instantly tense and wary. I must have fallen asleep, for the bright rays of the sun filled the entrance. The Voices whispered in my ear, ever so soft a warning, and a moment later I made out a shadow crossing the doorway and then a scrape. I held my breath when I heard a coughing noise, deep and rough, another scrape, and then the shadow disappeared.

Rising carefully to my feet, I made my way silently to the doorway to take a peek. The chamber was empty. With considerable glancing back over my shoulder, I ventured out and to the ledge. The spectacular view revealed the moors spreading away to the southwest; a short, craggy mountain range extending a finger between them and the valley; and then the valley itself a patchwork of fields trimmed with trees and embroidered with ribbons of water. The dragon appeared from the west and circled back. I dodged to the edge of the opening and peered out, heart clattering wildly, but the beast only wheeled around the valley several times before beating its wings and heading northward to disappear behind the mountain it called home.

Relief surged through me.

It was tempting to sit there on the ledge and enjoy the view while I broke my fast, but hardly sensible. Back into the downward passage I went and took up a seat on a small outcropping. I pulled the antidote vial out of my pouch and shook it. Impossible to tell how much remained, but surely too little. The silver gleamed gently in the light. So pretty, so terrible. Apprehension sat like a weight in my aching belly as I tipped it up to take the day's portion. *Not much longer...* I stowed the vial again, polished off the remains of my scanty supplies, and gave my oblations to the gods, praying sincerely that the trip back down the mountain would be quicker—and safer—than the one going up.

Shifting my pack onto my shoulder, I reached into the pouch for one of the witchlights. I drew forth the Beisyth Web instead. It sent tingles up my fingers strong enough to make me wince. If I held onto it long enough, would the stinging stop, or might I somehow accustom myself to the sensation? I knew only one way to find out.

I held the thing lightly, turned it over a few times as I considered all of the gory details of what I might encounter in the dark, cursed Duzayan a time or ten, then started moving. As I walked, I breathed warmth on one of the witchlights. It seemed less bright than before, and for some reason that made me sad—a feeling completely apart from losing a very valuable item. It puzzled me, but I had no answer for it.

The passage, polished smooth, dipped down rather steeply as I went and then, after about a hundred paces or so, ascended again. My light held high, I could make out the ceiling only dimly, which helped to relieve the dreadful sense of tons of rock pressing down upon me. Here and there I spied little nooks and even one or two deeper niches that might lead elsewhere. I could not tell for certain, but I had the impression the tunnel wound ever-so-slightly as it progressed. It was longer than I had hoped, and after some time I became aware of a noise. Just slight at first, a niggling at my senses, then it sorted itself out as the steady dripping of water. The instant I recognized it, I became aware of a horrendous thirst.

Ssshhh... the Voices warned, shivering uncomfortably. *Sshhh, make not a sound! Do not go there. Dangerous, it is! Go back, go back...*

"Hush yourselves." I would go back as soon as I had the egg.

I came out of the passageway above an underground lake. A floor as smooth as glass led down to the black water, and around the edges as well. Further back, the walls arched steeply high overhead. My little light shone upon a marvel of tapering columns rising from the floor and, where the ceiling came down low on one side, more columns grew downwards from overhead. In some places they had connected. They gleamed with water and with glittering minerals, and I could only stare for a time in amazement before going on.

Down to the stony shore I went and bent to drink, laying the Web aside as I lifted a handful of water to sniff, then carefully taste. It was tepid, but sweeter than any water I could remember, though that might have been because I was so thirsty and because the only water I'd consumed for hours, perhaps days, had come from a leather flask. I drank my fill and felt considerably refreshed. Even my aching belly seemed somewhat improved, though I continued to feel faintly nauseous.

I refilled my flask, then rested another moment. Flexing my hand, I considered the Web where it laid, a pale knob by my knee. My fingers burned, ached. Moving them relieved the discomfort, though my fingernails glowed green. I tucked the witchlight away so I could judge the brightness, and was satisfied to watch the glow fade away as I continued working my hand. Collecting the Web again, I held my light aloft and looked about. One direction seemed no more obvious than the other, and for all I knew I needed to go straight across the water. I wasn't going to swim unless absolutely necessary, so I turned right to make my way around the shore.

A broad path carved the space between the columns, and the air was moist but comfortably warm. Comfortable enough, in fact, that I wished I could doff my coat, but I didn't want to carry it, as it might hinder me at the most inopportune time, and I couldn't just leave it. I would need it again on the journey back to Marketh. How far I walked I cannot say with any reliability, but my light grew more and more dim and I grew more and more troubled with its passing.

I was pondering this rather odd situation when a musky, bitter stench hit me. I had to press my coat sleeve against my face to breathe, lest I lose all the water I had recently consumed.

The whispering of the Voices picked up again, and little panicked zephyrs wound about me. They ruffled my hair and tugged at my clothes, shocking me into a surprised little dance step. "Stop that!" I hissed, but they moaned and shivered and kept up with their eerie plucking.

There you must not go, friend! they cried mournfully. *Danger, so much danger. Come back! Come away!*

"Will you be quiet?!" I admonished them between clenched teeth. Goose flesh crept over me in waves. From all around came the steady, drip, drip, drip of water. Had I heard something else? A scraping sound? I hid the witchlight beneath my open coat, then eased toward one of the columns and the uncertain shelter it offered. I waited. It was not the first time I'd been startled during a robbery, and experience had long ago taught me that I needed to remain calm and in control of myself, if nothing else. My breathing eased, my heartbeat steadied, and I didn't hear anything—not even the soft, worried whispers of the Voices.

After a while, I withdrew the light and advanced a little further. The nest was impossible to miss. Enclosed among a circular grouping of the tall, upward-pointed columns, bones comprised the outer layer and, woven between them, twigs and little branches and smaller bones. I stopped and stared. The light trembled violently, though whether because of the shaking of my own hand or the result of the wind-inducing Ancestors I do not know. I looked all around again, but everything beyond my faint circle of light was pitch black except for the gleam here and there of light upon sparkling stone. Some of those lights moved, else my imagination was getting the better of me.

I held still again, and when nothing dire leaped out of the shadows I advanced upon the dragon's nest. As high as my shoulders, at its widest it was perhaps half again the height of a tall man, and the supporting columns forced an irregular shape upon it. Bracing against one of the columns, I stretched up to get a better look. A layer of bracken and bits of fabric lined the inside, the latter of which made me curious, but I refused to dwell on where they'd come from. Right in the center of the nest the softer inner lining had been gathered and carefully arranged around the egg. It didn't seem like much. It was about as large as my head, irregularly shaped, and an indeterminate dull color that didn't cast back so much as the slightest gleam. Nowhere, alas, did I see any sign of gold or jewels.

I eased back down so I could search out a practical entrance. Picking my way over a rough portion of the floor, I glanced up now and again to survey my choices. I had gone perhaps a quarter of the way around when a noise came to me. It was that same hissing slide I thought I'd heard earlier, and it brought the distinct sensation of being watched. Slowly, slowly, I turned around, and in spite of that inner knowledge telling me I must remain calm and composed, the lingering belly ache increased until it had a stranglehold on my throat. The Ancestors held their collective breath.

— 23 —
Beloved Of The Gods

What would Tanris do, I wondered, if faced with a dragon? I chose to scream, but the sudden advent of bile strangled it. The witchlight cast the beast in shades of dark amber tinged with green. About the size of two or three horses, thick overlapping plates protected neck and chest; its long snout beaked at the tip, and from it protruded wicked canines both top and bottom. Sharp, bony ridges started atop golden eyes and turned into two sweeping, curled horns at its crown. I took several hasty steps backwards and the dragon gathered itself.

Think! Think! Think! I tossed the witchlight one direction and dove in the other.

A roar of flames followed the little light. Much to my astonishment, and probably the dragon's as well, the witchlight exploded. Violently. Chunks and shards of rock flew every which way, light arched outward in a thousand tiny flashes, and the dragon—Well, I didn't care what happened to the dragon. I ducked around behind the nest and threw myself flat.

No! I had no time to waste and I would never come up with a better distraction. Shoving myself to my feet, I vaulted into the nest, tucked the egg under one arm, and jumped right back out again to run like fury toward the exit.

The Voices screamed at me. *What are you doing? No! No! You cannot steal a dragon's egg! Give it back!*

The dragon's roar brought more light—which was both good and bad. I could see ahead, but the dragon saw *me*. I dodged to and fro between the columns and did not look back. Did not dare. From behind me came the scrabbling of massive claws on stone, rocks grinding and breaking, and a hideous growling. The entire cavern shook as the dragon threw itself after me, and I was hard put to keep my feet under me. Fire lashed out, and I skidded behind one of the upward rising columns. The heat singed my clothes.

Run! Run! the Voices shrieked, apparently having a change of heart.

"I *am* running! Do something useful!" I hollered back.

Whatever they might have done, it didn't impress the dragon. Its roar shook the stone and it crashed after me, periodically belching fire. I didn't waste time sheltering behind pillars that were just going to get flattened, but I did try to keep them between me and the flames. I crossed the distance between nest and lake in record time, leaped like a gazelle over a pile of still-settling rubble, and ran to the entrance of the tunnel. With any luck I could hide behind some of the protrusions and rock formations or— maybe—duck down one of the little side tunnels, though gods alone knew where they led. I skidded inside one of them just as another burst of fire toasted the place I'd occupied. That gave me a few seconds, as it appeared the dragon couldn't breathe fire continuously. I wondered what fueled it and desperately hoped it would run out quickly. I hoped, too, that its mate wouldn't come back anytime soon.

The dragon bounced off the passage walls as it came bellowing after me. Rocks fell from the ceiling. Tripping over one likely saved my life. The heat of flames scorched the air as I twisted to protect the egg. The dragon bounded toward me, and the only weapon I had was a lumpy whitewashed knob. I threw the Beisyth Web as hard as I could and hoped, without much conviction, I might knock the dragon senseless. I have a superb aim, but my opponent was a *dragon* and the knobby bits on the outside of its head probably indicated some considerable bone structure on the inside.

To my astonishment, and I spent an awful lot of time lately being astonished, the Web thunked into the mailed skull and burst into scores of long, sticky strings. Some of them wound around the dragon's head and others attached themselves to walls and ceiling. The dragon went down in a pile of screaming, steaming fury. A burst of flames freed its mouth but not the rest of its head. It flailed back and forth wildly, tangling itself further. Thank all the gods of web things and distractions...

I rolled up onto my feet and pelted down the passage as fast as I could go. I had the distinct sensation of being half-carried, but I didn't have time to examine anything closely. With the egg held tight, I fled, one hand on the wall to guide me. When I'd rounded enough corners and bumps to shield me, I slowed to take out the last of the witchlights. It shone brilliantly, and I had no need to encourage it to work, which surprised and unsettled me. There was far too much magic in my life these days. At least it didn't make my fingers hurt or my skin glow.

The bellowing of the dragon continued to echo behind me, the noise amplified by the shape of the cave. Not about to rely on Duzayan's "gift," I ran all the way to the end of the large passage, across the cavernous entry floor, and sped into the smaller way leading down through the mountain and back to the temple. I slipped and skidded down the incline and around the corner, where I collapsed into a heap, gasping and trembling and covered in perspiration brought upon me by both running and stark fear. My belly churned and cramped horrendously. Laying back on the cold, uneven stone, I waited for it to settle and for my breathing to return to normal. With a short prayer to the gods of water and cleverness, I took a long drink from my recently filled flask.

Finally, I sat up to examine my prize. It was, as I said, distinctly ordinary-looking, dull-colored, strangely leathery, and not particularly heavy. My hands didn't tingle when I touched it. I pushed at it with one finger, and then nearly dropped the thing when the insides pushed back. I pushed again on another side, and the innards pushed back again. "Oh, joy," I said with a distinct lack of enthusiasm. I suspected another complication.

"Can you hear me in there?" A stupid question, likely, for if I was bound up in a leather sack (and I had been once), I could hear what was going on outside it just fine.

The egg thing bulged, but it didn't say anything in return, which suited me perfectly. Bad enough I heard the voices of Kem's long dead Ancestors without having a talking egg to deal with as well. Unslinging my pack, I untied the top to put the egg inside, but then I found myself worrying that it would be uncomfortable. Or rather, I was concerned that my tools, namely the grapnel, might poke a hole in the casing. I scratched my head, and in the end I put the egg inside my coat, only then it kept working downward, and I didn't want to drop and injure it, so I loosed my clothes and put it in between my shirt and my outer tunic, tying the bottom secure with my belt. Looking down at myself, I perceived that I looked distinctly pregnant.

Duzayan would pay for that, too.

Sick, exhausted, and afraid that I might actually become accustomed to caves, the trip back down the mountain was no easier than the ascent. I clung to my little witchlight. With no one for company, I was left with nothing but the steady clump and scrape of my heavy feet going down and down and down—

Until the sound of voices drifted up toward me. Real voices. Several of them. As you may recall, occasional tunnels and alcoves and doors led off the stair. I had not looked into any of them previously, but now I had no choice but to dive into the space behind the nearest door. I dashed back up the steps to the closest and slipped inside, whisking the door shut behind me. Holding the witchlight up, I discovered I was in a three-sided wooden box large enough for perhaps two or three men to fit inside, with a pair of chains on one side descending through the ceiling and thence the floor. I had no sooner made this discovery than the box moved and the chains grated. I was going down. There were mechanical lifts? Is that what those little hourglass shapes on the map had been? Why hadn't the mapmaker put a more descriptive symbol? Think of all the time and trouble I might have saved!

Duzayan didn't give very good directions.

The box swayed and stuttered downward, and I looked frantically for a way to escape. No trap door marked the ceiling or the floor. I had no convenient tunnels to leap into. With a clang and a bump, my descent came to a halt. I managed to drop the light down my shirt before the door creaked opened.

I exploded out of the lift, successfully pounding the unfortunate door-opener in the face and knocking him flat. Catching hold of the edge of the panel, I swung my feet at the next man, knocking him right in the chest. His torch flew and he went down like a sack of potatoes. I leaped after him. If the fall hadn't incapacitated him, my knee in his stomach did. He grunted and turned a funny color, and I had plenty of time to remove a short truncheon from my pouch and smack him smartly over the head. Twice. I absolutely refused to take chances.

Only two brothers occupied the hall, praise be, but my first target sat up, his legs flung out haphazardly and his robes rucked up to reveal far too much of his skinny legs. I leapt to my feet to defend myself. He merely lifted both hands to his face, which bled profusely, and let out a long, tortured groan.

"What a mess," I commiserated, and he peered at me through bleary eyes that widened in sudden alarm. Alarm frequently led to action, and we couldn't have any of that, so I whacked him, too. Twice.

I stood there for a moment or two, looking up and down the corridor and listening for any sound of further company, then thrust my truncheon back into my pouch.

"Are you all right, Egg?" I queried, carefully kneading the protrusion beneath my shirt. It had been subjected to some awful bouncing and squashing, but to my vast relief some knobby part of the creature it contained slid beneath my inquisitive fingers. "Sorry about that. Couldn't be avoided."

May the gods please help me. I talked to rats, I talked to ghosts, I talked to eggs…

Shaking my head, I dragged first one and then the other unconscious priest into the lift and relieved them of the burden of their valuables. I hauled on the chain enough to bring the box up off floor level, then slid underneath. I paused briefly to wonder what sort of counterweight managed the box, dismissed it as wizard work, and hoisted my boxed brothers up even further. Set into the floor beneath the box I found a pulley wheel. I contemplated it for a moment or two, then inserted one of the brother's knives into a hand-sized link. Straightening again, I grabbed the chain as high as I could and put my entire weight on it. There came a lovely grinding, cracking noise, and the mechanism jammed.

Dusting my hands off, I stowed my witchlight properly in my pocket. It was the one thing—or three, as the case may be—for which I could truly thank Duzayan, though the counts against him far outweighed my sense of cumulative gratitude. I retrieved the discarded torch and collected another from a half-barrel near the lift. If I'd known about the presence of the torches perhaps I would have appropriated one to use as a club, but all had worked well in the end.

"So where are we?" I asked, looking about.

To my surprise, the Voices whispered at me. *We do not know. Deep, we are deep in the mountain! We will look. Shall we look? What shall we see?*

"Rocks, probably, but a way out would be lovely." I had absolutely no confidence in them. A fickle and nervous lot they were.

Out! Out! Out! they exclaimed. A brief, cool breeze preceded silence.

I could not decide which was worse, the absence of the Voices or the thought that I was only imagining them and in severe danger of losing my mind, if it wasn't completely gone already. One thing was certain: I needed to go "down" and I knew this passage led right back to the Real Vault.

Descending the interminable stairs, I contemplated the reception likely awaiting me. How could I get past it, and how many more wizards would be involved? My encounter with the other two did not engender in me any confidence about fighting or tricking my way out in spite of the happy conclusion. I wondered where the dastards had ended up, and if they would ever be found again. Chasms in the belly of a dark mountain make a really good place to dispose of bodies. I hoped.

"Are they dead?" I asked, half hoping for a response and half dreading it.

Who, Friend, who? Who? Who? They resembled a flock of imbecilic owls, but their prompt response proved they'd not left me, which I found bizarrely comforting.

"The wizards from upstairs." Responsibility I could not comprehend clung to the word "friend." It worried me.

We will see! We will find them!

Another chilly little breeze marked them dashing off, and then quiet reigned again. I trudged onward for at least two minutes before another rush of air swept over my face, swift enough to ruffle my hair and make me blink. My lack of concern was probably a sign of my exhaustion.

Out! Out!

"You found a way?" I could not help doubting.

Yes! Will you come? Come see!

"Will I fit and can I reach it?" My eyes narrowed further.

The Voices twittered and skirled around me, debating amongst themselves. *How big? Big enough? In pieces... Long, it is long! But no wizards there, no! No dragons!*

I liked the last two parts, but not the one about "in pieces."

Narrow, it is! He is narrow. Very narrow. Short! Not that narrow. Big enough! Come with us! We will show you!

They were enthusiastic, I'll have to admit. "All right, where is it?" I could not see them, but I swear they looped around the passage in elation, up and down and back and forth, and then they went shooting off. Without me. The gods did have their sense of humor. My witchlight and I continued our trek down the stairs, and I'd descended several levels before my ghostly friends rejoined me.

Where is he? Is he lost? No! He is here. He did not come! Why did he not come?

"I can hear you, you know," I advised them sourly.

He can hear us! Jubilation. *Come this way!*

"Which way? I can't *see* you! Gods protect me, I'm talking to invisible voices." I suffered an intense urge to cry, which was neither manly nor useful, so I suppressed it and stood patiently waiting for the Voices to direct me and tried not to imagine the look of disgust on Tanris's face should he bear witness to this.

This way… this way… careful of our Friend… so dear! …come this way! Turn left.

I turned left at the first opening, which required stepping up and ducking at the same time. I did not like that. Too uncomfortably like the Ghost Walk. I glanced back over my shoulder, reassuring myself that I could always come back to the main passage, and then I pressed on. I had to walk bent over awkwardly. My back ached after a while, then the Voices had me go down on my knees to crawl into an off-shooting tunnel. Kneeling, I wondered again about my sanity.

"Why should I trust you?" I asked.

There followed a moment of stunned silence which I found interesting and even funny. *You are the Friend! We need you. We like you! You are precious, yes, precious! Precious!*

That was kind of disturbing. "Why?"

To speak… share… help… advise. Yes! It comforts us. We comfort you. Lost! You were lost so long!

I frowned, remembering how Old Jelal had pointed out the same quality —or flaw—and announced that something had "touched" me, and I had the means to figure out the confusion. *Magic* had touched me in the Ghost Walk, and changed me somehow. "Who are you?"

The past. Counselors. Friends. Looking, looking, but now we have found you…

I sat back on my heels, considering. I could perceive other peoples' emotions and their presence. The voices in the Ghost Walk had not talked specifically to me, yet these did. When had they begun and were they the same? I closed my eyes and endeavored to remember. It had been in the Real Vault, when they'd directed me to the ugly statue. Clammy with dread, I fumbled for the pendant I'd taken. "It's this thing, isn't it?"

No! Yes! Sometimes. Not always. Not later.

"What does that mean?"

It is ours. You are ours.

I did not wish to be collared and owned; I had enough trouble with a miserable wizard thinking he could do that. I did not wish to be haunted. Pulling the pendant off over my head, I tossed it away. The Voices wailed pitifully.

No! No! Do not leave us! they cried.

Ignoring them, I crawled down the tunnel, pushing the torch ahead. The further I went, the more faint the whispering became. I let out a breath of relief and kept going. The tunnel twisted downward, but did not change in height or width. I bumped my head several times, until I sat down and wriggled my pack around to dig out my hat. Hopefully, it would cushion the blows somewhat. I checked the egg, and it moved in a sort of revolting manner. After a while, the tunnel branched. Both sides appeared to maintain the same level for as far as I could see. I rested there and studied them for a moment, queasy and wondering absently how long ago I'd eaten.

"All right," I surrendered. "Which way?"

I heard a rustling like dry leaves, but no words.

"Hello?"

Silence.

"Hello!" I called, a little louder. I didn't even hear an echo of my own voice.

Strange dread crept up on me. The darkness seemed heavier, the surrounding rock more oppressive, the egg I carried more sinister. And I was cold. In spite of the movement that ought to have helped warm me, I was cold to the bone.

Abruptly, I crawled backward. I couldn't turn around and I couldn't use the torch to light my reverse journey. I scraped my hands and knees and banged into the walls any number of times before I finally tumbled out into the larger passageway. Frantically, I cast about for the necklace, and when I saw the light gleam off its polished surface, I grabbed it up and held it close against my chest, panting in terror and relief. "I've got it back!" I shouted. "Don't leave me here!"

How pathetic was it to plead with ghosts?

Their very soft voices gradually wrapped around me, and I had to hold my breath and strain to hear. *Angry, he is... What have we done? Is he hurt? Frightened. Do we frighten him? Sorry! Sorry! What have we done? So sorry!*

The emotional and physical turmoil I'd suffered came out in tears to wet my cheeks. "I'm not angry. I'm not. I'm—" *Desperately afraid.* Not a wise piece of information to surrender to anyone, even apparently friendly ghosts. "I'm not used to talking to ghosts."

Ghosts! The air swirled with agitation.

Were not the voices of people long gone ghosts? "I am not—used to talking to people I cannot see."

Cannot see us… No one sees us. Kalinamsin! Where is Kalinamsin now? Gone, gone! Who is this one? Like him, he is…Does he have a name? He cannot see us! Woe! Woe! What is his name?

"Crow. My name is Crow!"

He is a bird! Can he fly? He has no feathers, how can he fly?

"Did you find the wizards?" I asked tentatively.

Wizards, yes. Dangerous no more. Bottom of the abyss. Broken to bits. Pieces strewn all up and down. Wreckage spattered—

"Thank you!" I interrupted. "That's good to know. I can live without the graphic descriptions."

Fragile. Delicate sensibilities. Like a bird. Crow!

On they went, their murmuring nonsense strangely comforting. I hung the amulet around my neck again, tucked it safely under my tunic, and set out to crawl back down the hideously small passage, fairly certain I was a raving lunatic and it would serve Baron Duzayan right should he happen to find some way to survive my wrath and bind me to him as his servant forever. When I came to the forked passage, it took a few tries to get the attention of my companions, for they were still arguing and debating over my name, my abilities, my relationship with Kalinamsin—whoever he might have been—something about a "door," and their awful invisibility. They directed me to the left side.

It descended sharply, awkwardly downward. I could not slide on my belly for fear of damaging the egg, and I couldn't crawl because I kept pitching forward. It was a long, long way down, and I was alternately exasperated, afraid, hungry, sick, hopeless, and hysterical. Nothing prepared me to fall out of the side of the mountain. I missed seeing it altogether. From my sprawl beneath the pines, staring up at the cloud-covered sky between the branches, I reasoned the torch had blinded me.

A pitchy, smoky smell assailed my nose and I sat up with a yelp. The torch smoldered against damp pine needles, and I leaped up to stamp it out before it became a blaze. Safe for the moment, I sat down on a fallen log, pressed one hand against my forehead, and laughed helplessly.

— 24 —
Burning, Looting, Squashing

I would have liked an end of going up and down. I would have liked to stop moving entirely, for my hands and knees were bruised and torn, my head hurt, my back ached, and my belly roiled. What I wanted most in all the world—aside from a cure for the horrible poison—was a hot bath and then a warm, soft bed in which I could sleep for at least ten days. How long since I'd had a dose of the antidote? I couldn't remember. Perhaps that was why I felt so ill and not what Brother Three had done to me. I had nothing but water to wash down my two bitter drops. I checked the egg, then forced myself up the nearest ridge to get my bearings.

I don't know why I didn't smell or see the smoke before I made the exhausting climb. I blame the torch. Unexpected fear stabbed me as I stared down upon the dragon's work. Whatever reason had kept the dragons from laying waste to the village before was now null and void. Houses and fields burned, and even the temple sent up a pillar of thick black smoke. People ran back and forth every which way. They were probably screaming, but the wind blew steadily at my back, taking their voices with it and tipping the column of smoke away east and southward from me. A group of people—the good brothers by the way they were dressed—ran to one side, bulging sacks under their arms and robes lifted high to keep from tangling in their pumping legs. They could only be looting, for the Vault itself with its walls and doors constructed of thick stone and marble would not burn. I had nothing against thieving itself, mind you, but a strict moral code forbids any such thing by priests, and looting is simply crass and vulgar. Wouldn't *priests* be doing something to aid and protect their people rather than hightailing it for safety with sacks full of plunder?

What had become of Tanris and Girl? Had he seen the message I'd left him and taken her to safety? Unexpected dread and dismay held me captive. What if things had gone awry and they had been detained? Bursting into motion, I ran down the hillside, slipping, sliding. *Dear gods, keep them safe,* I begged. A root sent me sprawling, shrubs stabbing and scraping, rocks bruising. I twisted instinctively, trying to protect the egg. My head fetched up against the trunk of a small tree and the impact nearly knocked me senseless. With a groan, I rolled over on my back and held my burning hands up to inspect them. Half the skin had been scraped away and a pound of leaves and debris took its place. I shook some of it loose, then froze. One of the dragons sailed past, a great, dark shadow. With teeth. How stupid to go rushing headlong down the mountain with angry dragons flying about. I glanced around for its mate, but saw nothing.

The gods, in their infinite mercy, had kept me from danger. Closing my eyes, I murmured a quick but heartfelt prayer of gratitude. Then I sat up cautiously, assured myself that I had sustained no crippling injuries, and set about picking the worst of the dirt and leaves from my hands before tearing strips off the bottom of my shirt to wrap them. The gods kept Egg safe, too; it remained whole and the little creature inside responded when I prodded.

My fall had taken me to the bottom of the ravine. I stumbled into the cover of the trees growing along the far side and made my way down the hillside. I had to find Tanris and Girl. I needed a horse—and food. Food would definitely be good. The only place I could get either was from the village, but the village was under attack by dragons eager to roast me.

Except for one little thing: I had their precious egg. It was an advantage I could use if pressed, but better to avoid any such situation. I had first to get the rest of the way down the mountain. The sun hid behind smoke and clouds, but judging by the light it was somewhere about midday, so I could not rely upon imminent nightfall to give me cover. I also had to consider whether dragons could see in the dark. They did, after all, dwell quite nicely in an unlit cave.

I kept an eye on the sky and minded my step lest I take another fall, careful to stick to the cover of trees and rocks. I had to stop and rest far too many times to make good progress. The dragons kept up their attack for some time. The devastation was terrible.

When I finally reached the little valley I found a safe place tucked in among the trees on the edge and waited.

I did not mean to, but I slept for the first time in a day and a half. Night brought cold temperatures and shivering woke me. I had to move. I had to find Tanris and Girl. My body protested with screeching, aching muscles. Movement tore open some of my scrapes and I wished I had salve for them. I had hardly finished the thought when I realized I did. I had the stuff I'd taken from the temple healer! Blessed gods be praised…

A well serviced several of the houses on one edge of the village. I washed myself as best I could, teeth chattering in the cold, attention darting to every imagined movement. I found the sting of the salve curiously reassuring.

Stealing a horse turned into a serious challenge. The village didn't possess a great number to begin with, and the attack of the dragons scattered most of them. The corpses of two laid on what passed as Hasiq jum'a Sahefal's streets, too well done even for a crow.

Fires continued to burn, most notably at the temple where figures passed constantly between me and the light. The guards had their work cut out for them, particularly considering that the brothers themselves had been making off with the goods. I wondered if anyone had noted Melly's disappearance or if people assumed he had perished during the attack. Nowhere could I find my own dear Horse with the white snip on her nose. Nowhere, in fact, did I find any horses, people, or even sheep, which made the village a disturbingly ghostly place.

It began to rain, which did not at all astonish me. I was glad for my hat. It no longer looked remotely suitable for the jaunty feather it had once sported, though it definitely boasted character. Coming to the sorry conclusion that I was not going to have a horse upon which to make my journey, I set about collecting what provisions I could carry, fashioning packs out of deserted blankets and a leather duffel that I discovered.

Finding food proved easy. While many of the houses had burned, and with them the owner's food stocks, the people had fled. My opinion of the intelligence of dragons went down. I could understand revenge, but how could they have known they wouldn't cook their precious egg when they lit the houses afire? Unless, of course, their eggs resisted the flames. An interesting concept I had no desire to test.

Nowhere did I find Tanris or Girl, nor their horses, nor any sign of them. I eventually discovered the missing villagers and some of their sheep at the temple where they had come together for the protection the sturdy stone walls and numerous guards. It made good sense if they still wanted to linger in dangerous territory. At the temple they had access to dragon-proof caves where they could hide, or perhaps even live. The temple's two wings and upper floor had suffered extensive damage, but the great statue over the door remained untouched. I wondered if the supports were still sufficient to hold it up, but that would be a worry only if I was underneath it when it fell, and I had no intention of going anywhere near. If Tanris and Girl had taken refuge within the temple, I could not get to them. At least they'd be safe. I watched for well over an hour, arguing with myself whether to stay or to go. And to think, I had once worried about the possibility of avoiding Tanris in such a small settlement. Finally, I set my steps to the trail leading south.

It took about a mile to decide I had far too much to carry, but what could I do? A heavy load would slow me down, but with one too light I would starve. And so I trudged on through the rain, mulling over how I ached, how long was the trek to the Le'ah River, and how utterly despondent I felt when I should be overjoyed to have accomplished the impossible and now only had to complete the difficult.

An enormous shadow lunging at me from the side of the path brought my heart to a screeching halt. Terror and a fine sense of self-preservation immediately got it going again. An abrupt reversal in direction to escape being rent to pieces by a sneaky, vengeful dragon sent me sprawling on my back, awkwardly propped by my bulging packs. The point of my grapnel dug painfully into a kidney, but I didn't even have time to wriggle free of it before my attacker loomed over me and lowered its enormous head, only to give me a whiskery sniff and a none-too-gentle nudge in the chin.

I pushed right back and scooted away as speedily as I could manage.

My attacker shook its head, stomped a foot, and whickered softly.

"You're a horse!" I exclaimed, and nearly suffered another collapse, this one inspired by sheer relief. It took a step closer and leaned down to sniff at me again. Happily, I rubbed its whiskery nose. "Praise the gods, who never let me forget how dearly I am loved."

A giant of a thing, the beast's back came clear up to my nose and it was at least as broad as the dragon. It wore no saddle, more's the pity, but the remnants of a broken harness. I tied it up out of the way, fastened my packs to it, and then looked about for a rock whereby I might climb aboard. Along with rain, the area had rocks aplenty, and when I'd mounted I steered my prize steed back to fair Hasiq jum'a Sahefal, where I concealed my new equine acquisition in one of the burned-out houses and collected a much better supply of foodstuffs as well as another blanket and a good oiled canvas. I also found a saddle, though it would need some reworking to be suitable for Horse Too. And then I was on my south.

As a point of further enlightenment, I must point out that dragons are completely indifferent to rain. I discovered this as I rode along on Horse Too's far-too-broad back, which already magnified my aches and pains. I learned just how my muscles had stretched to accommodate his back when I paused for a brief rest. Dismounting was a minor disaster. Luckily, when I fell I landed on my side and not on the egg still tucked into the front of my tunic where, incredibly enough, it helped keep me warm.

I walked for a while so I might exercise—or exorcise—some of the pain from my lower limbs. The rain continued, of course. My determination to walk did not last long, and I climbed back aboard the horse, who shall hereafter be referred to simply as "Too." Draping the canvas over us went a long way toward keeping us all dry and warm, and I didn't particularly give a flying monkey how unfashionable it looked.

Too possessed a bone-jarring but swift gait, and after a while of sitting it I managed a more or less cross-legged position on his back, balanced by packs of provisions. I could hardly keep my eyes open, I was so exceedingly exhausted. The kemesh I'd found did nothing to ease the queasy state of my stomach, giving the lie to the rumor about the drink's cure-all properties.

The clouds did nothing but get thicker and more generous in releasing their abundance of moisture. One could scarce mark midday for the darkness. Water ran off the canvas in streams, and poor Too's mane looked flat and dismal. A sudden cacophony of panic from the Voices yanked me out of my daydreams. I looked about wildly, dragging back the canvas blocking my view. Too twitched his ears at me and kept plodding.

"What? What is it?" I exclaimed.

Before they could reply, a dragon swept out of the mists, skimming around a low hill on my right and letting out a roar fit to crumble small mountains, including my horse.

Too whinnied and bucked and ran.

"Augh!" I cried, tumbling head over heels the other direction in spite of the gear heaped around me. I hit the ground hard and rolled ten or twenty times until I came to a breathless, groaning halt. As much as I wanted to lie there and die quietly for a few minutes, I had absolutely no intention of actually departing life just yet. I'd worked entirely too hard to get to this point.

The dragon fast approaching, I twisted violently to the side and staggered to my feet, minus my usual grace and style, and dove behind a pair of boulders. Fire singed the muddy ground in a stripe. A thump came from somewhere nearby, and then the dragon crashed, cartwheeling madly.

It screamed.

I screamed and ducked.

Someone else shouted.

The boulders behind which I'd taken cover served as a perfect way to curb the dragon's forward motion, and it slammed into them—and me— with enough force to rattle my teeth and send me sprawling all over again, this time with a dragon on top of me. It was not, thank the gods of unusual circumstances, the full weight of the thing, but my leg had become pinned between the newly arranged boulders. I could not move, though I tried with all my strength. Either my skin or the entire leg would be left behind, but when it came down to life or limb, I chose life.

The dragon thrashed and the rocks ground together. Someone hollered, and the dragon thrashed even more. Something struck me and I succumbed to oblivion.

"Crow."

The word came from a great distance, wrapped in wool.

"Crow."

More insistent this time, and it came with movement. A hand on my shoulder. Burning pain in my leg. The same leg, mind you, as had suffered when Raza's men chased us half a lifetime ago.

"I'm here," I croaked with a grimace. "What do you want?"

Someone let out a long sigh.

It was warm on one side of me, cold on the other, and the warm side came with the lovely snap and crackle of wet wood burning.

I sat up suddenly. "Egg! Where's Egg!"

"Relax, it's right here." At my side, Tanris examined me with a sour expression. Someone had propped Egg amongst my gear. Nearby, Girl had her legs drawn up and her arms around them, face as pale and apprehensive as usual.

A blanket covered me, and I pushed it aside to get up, but that didn't work out as well as I'd planned. I laid right back down again, beating my fist against my uninjured thigh until the staggering pain let me breathe again.

"It's not broken," Tanris offered, and held out my bottle of kemesh. With a great deal more care, I propped myself up to take a swig.

"The egg or my leg?" I asked, wiping the back of my hand across my mouth and handing the bottle back with a nod of gratitude.

"Either."

"Good," I breathed, "that's good. Are you sure?"

"Mm. I should have just let the dragon cook you."

"I'm extraordinarily glad you didn't. Thank you."

His brow twitched.

I looked around. A ceiling of rock sloped down to nothing, dirt on one side, rocks on the other, and open in the front. The fire burned between me and the darkness beyond. "Where did you come from, anyway?"

"The village. You remember it? The one you managed to burn down?"

"Why do you always accuse me of everything you don't like?" I had not personally lit the village on fire, and it was not my fault the dragons reacted the way they did. "It wasn't that bad anyway. There were still houses. And the temple. Sheep, too, I saw them. And I got the egg."

"Yes, and left us there to burn."

I *had* rather deserted them, though I didn't intend for them to die. And if Tanris hadn't found the message I left, he wouldn't be here with Girl. "I looked for you, but couldn't find you. I thought you'd left."

He gave me one of those long looks that said he didn't entirely believe me. Then he took a swallow of the kemesh and eyed me a little longer. "You went to the dragon's lair without us."

"Yes."

"You went off on your own again, in spite of the danger. Danger, I might add, that was so obvious a blind man could have seen it. Why?"

I closed my eyes against the memory of Melly cartwheeling into the chasm, then abruptly opened them again, unwilling to chance having the image burned forever onto my eyelids. "You know why." I didn't look at Girl. Neither did he. He just ground his teeth.

"Was it bad?" he asked finally.

"Could have been worse." I'm not sure how, but he would never believe me about Melly and Brother Three, never mind about the dragon and the Voices and climbing out of the mountain by way of a chimney-sized hole, so why bother?

"You look like you took a beating."

I snorted. There'd been three actual beatings, but who was counting?

"Those marks on your belly—what are they from?"

I had marks? I shouldn't be at all astonished, but I pulled my shirt up to look, and was astonished anyway. The light of the fire revealed squiggly black lines and a strange kind of bruising all over my abdomen. How nice that the pain and stiffness bore illustrations.

"One of the dragons do that?" he asked.

"No," I murmured, and pulled my shirt down again, realizing I wore only the one, and my tunic and coat had been replaced with a blanket. I shifted it aside and discovered myself bereft of anything but my smallclothes. My injured leg was wrapped up in the remains of a shirt. "You undressed me?" I did not like knowing I had been so vulnerable.

"You were a mess."

Girl nodded, the expression on her face worried. With a leather glove she lifted the pot on the fire and held it up questioningly. It smelled good.

"Soup," Tanris said. "Want some?"

"Maybe a little."

"When did you eat last?"

"I don't know."

He grunted. "I brought your things."

Nonplussed, I looked about. Sure enough, there was my pack, and I should have recognized my extra shirt even if it didn't look the same wrapped around my leg and slightly bloodied. "Thank you."

He grunted again, which I assumed meant something like *You're welcome, see how I look after you?*

Girl filled a mug and handed it to me with a spoon, shifting to move my useless saddle behind me so I could lean against it. She looked at my face critically, made an adjustment to a bandage wrapped around my head, and sat down beside me. I blew on the soup, then took a few ginger sips. "So what became of the dragon?"

"Girl shot it."

"Girl?" I stared first at one and then the other.

Girl's beam transformed her thin, wan features completely. She looked like a real person rather than a sad waif who might blow away in a strong wind. She looked proud of herself, and well she ought.

"Remarkable. So tell me what happened."

Tanris looked at Girl. Girl blushed and looked away, so he shrugged and told the story himself, illustrating by drawing lines in the dirt. "Here's the village. There are three paths leading south. We were circling across, like this," he bisected the lines he'd drawn with one finger, "looking for any sign you'd been through, though it wasn't easy because of the rain and the mist. Then we caught sight of someone and followed in case it was you. Saw the dragon coming, so we ran to help. I handed Girl my crossbow. She shot it, and I finished the job with an axe."

Girl opened her mouth wide and pointed inside, eyes positively sparkling.

"You shot it in the mouth?" I asked, astonished yet again.

She nodded vigorously and Tanris actually smiled. "Right down the throat. While it was flaming."

"And flying." I was impressed. "Are you always that good?"

She shrugged and smiled.

"After that, we used the horses to pull the dragon off you. You got lucky. You should have been dead."

The gods did love me. "And you killed the dragon." Why did he get a witness to his heroics and mine had to happen in a hole in the ground?

"Me and Girl did, yup."

"Well." I dredged up a smile for them both. "Amazing work. Thank you."

Much to my surprise, Girl leaned over to kiss my cheek, then patted my leg and went off to do Girl things.

:-:

My leg was a terrible mess and quite bruised but, as Tanris had assured, not broken. And he had found the salve I filched from the healer at the temple. My pants were ruined, my coat needed mending. While I'd slept, Girl had tended to the coat and Tanris managed to make the saddle into something actually useful for holding packs, and we now had four horses, for he'd managed to come away from the village with his steed, one of the pack horses (which Girl now rode,) and my own Horse. Glad as I was to see the mare again, it would be some time before I could mount her without help.

Tanris was moody. He didn't like the look of my leg, didn't like Too, didn't like Too's name (though it made Girl smile), didn't like that I'd stolen Too—even if stealing had only required accepting his presence—didn't like the rain (who did?), didn't comment on the extra supplies I'd furnished, didn't like me carrying Egg… When it came time to leave Tanris jutted out his bullish jaw, pressed his lips together tightly, and summarily took possession of the egg, stuffing it into one of his saddle bags.

I seethed, but what could I do? I wouldn't survive a physical altercation with him—not then, and maybe not ever. To my surprise, Girl intervened. She marched right up to Tanris, looked him in the eye with a severely scathing expression, then simply took Egg out of the bag. While he stood there dumfounded, she brought Egg and handed it up to me where I sat aboard Horse. To have it in my possession again was a relief I could not explain, however short-lived. I gently prodded the leathery surface, but nothing happened. It did not feel warm any more, and it did not push back. Only the gods knew what it had suffered in the terrible tumble I'd taken from Too's back.

"Hey," I whispered to it. "You still with me?"

Tanris stared, but he did a lot of that and I was fairly immune by now.

Girl gave me a worried look. I gave one back. Then I poked Egg gently again. Still nothing. "I think it's dead," I frowned.

"So?" Tanris swung up into his saddle. "All we have to do is deliver it to the baron. He didn't specify what shape it had to be in, and I don't know how you can tell, anyway."

I began to explain, then changed my mind. He didn't believe anything I'd told him thus far, and arguing now would serve no purpose. I put Egg under my tunic again and belted him in.

Two days passed before Egg moved again. Two entire days in which I kept the thing warm and safe against me, refusing to give up possession. The bump against my belly was so slight that it took me several of Horse's patient steps to realize I'd actually felt it. "Egg?" I whispered hopefully. I put one hand beneath my coat to rub the thing tentatively, then gave it a little push. It pushed back.

— 25 —
Scrambled Plans

The journey to the river took forever, but then the entire trip bore a striking resemblance to a never-ending nightmare. I was sick and growing daily sicker. Two drops a day I took of Duzayan's antidote, but it did not ease the nausea or to stop the painful spasming that had begun shortly after I'd awoken in the care of Tanris and Girl. They became greater and more painful, and twice made me lose what little contents my stomach held. Tanris asked if I wanted to stop and rest, but I told him no and took two more drops of the medicine.

Tanris took the egg. For safe keeping, he said, but I knew he was just waiting for the opportunity to leave me. Maybe the threat helped me to keep up with the two of them longer, but there came a day when I opened my eyes upon a shadow-shrouded room smelling of dirt and grass. Uneven bars of faint light marked the outer boundaries,.

"—shouldn't be more than two or three days," Tanris was saying as he buckled saddle bags and slung them over his shoulder.

"Where are you going?"

Both pairs of eyes turned to me. Girl looked relieved and came to kneel beside me, rustling my bed of hay.

Tanris frowned. "To find help."

"Help? For who? *From* who?"

"You're sick, Crow," he said bluntly.

I wanted to protest, but I knew perfectly well that it was true. "I know. We need to keep moving, we're losing time."

"How long have you known?"

I shrugged. "Since I was in the temple caves." Irritably, I pushed myself up and Girl reached out to steady me. To my horror, I needed it. I had all the fortitude of a newborn calf.

"What happened in the caves?"

"I went up. I got the egg. I dodged the dragon. I came back down."

Tanris moved fast. Dumping his bags to the ground, he was on one knee next to me with his fist wound in my shirt faster than I could blink. "What happened in the caves, Crow?" he demanded, hauling me upward until his nose nearly touched mine.

"Nothing," I lied, lifting my chin and twisting my face away. I braced my hands to either side, for all the leverage it gave me against someone his size.

He gave me a shake, and Girl gasped, tugging on his arm. She had as much affect on him as the rain had on the dragon. "The truth!" he demanded in a low growl.

"You don't like my truth." My voice was just as hard and cold as his. "Let go."

"Try me."

I glared at him. He could beat me if he wanted to, and perhaps he did. I didn't really want to test his patience. "Fine. Let go."

His mouth curled into a sneer I hadn't seen in a long time, and he held me up for a moment, making sure, I assumed, that I understood who was in charge. Then he let go with a little shove and rested his forearm over his up-drawn knee. I pulled my shirt straight and resisted the urge to glare, spit, or otherwise make my life any more difficult, including fabricating stories about what I'd done. I gave him the bare bones of the entire tale from the moment I'd left him and Girl sleeping and only left out all the chatting I'd done with the Ancestors. He listened silently, even through the account of my battle with the wizards, though it made his mouth tighten and his eyes take on the telltale expression of skepticism. Girl, bless her, watched with steadily widening eyes and a hand pressed over her mouth.

"That's it?" he asked when I had finished.

I regarded him with patent disgust.

"The truth," he repeated.

Hadn't I predicted as much? He didn't believe me, nobody would. Except Girl. Tears glimmered in her eyes when she looked at me. "Are we done now?" I asked. "Can we go?" I suited my actions to my words. Or I meant to, anyway. The room—barn, it was a barn—wobbled horribly when I got to my feet and my stomach churned a chaotic protest. Tanris stood as I did, his hands going to my shoulders. I tried to brush him off, but he wouldn't let me.

"You're in no condition to go anywhere."

"I'm not in any condition to *stay*, either! It'd be so much easier for you if I just gave up, wouldn't it?" My attempt to rein in my temper disintegrated. "If I would just lie down and die like a good little victim!"

The tears Girl had been holding back flowed. Worry, fear and confusion came from her in waves threatening to mingle with my own and overwhelm me.

Tanris remained sober. Angry. "Do you want to know the truth?" he asked, stabbing me in the chest with his finger. And then, thank the gods of personal space, he moved back a step.

"Oh, the *truth*." I waved one hand in the air. "By all means, let us hear the truth."

He didn't answer right away. Finally, he nodded. "All right. I don't want you to die. You're the one man that hates the baron as much as I do, maybe even more. I want you to help me get my wife back—"

"Which you can do oh-so-easily with me out of the way," I pointed out bitterly.

"—and then I want you to help me completely and utterly destroy him."

Well, that caught me off guard.

"And then you can die, if you're so determined."

My eyes narrowed. "What gives you the impression I can help?"

"I know you. I didn't chase you up and down the length of the empire without learning anything." His next words had to cost him dearly. "You're smart, you don't think like other men do, you're very... talented."

I wanted to stretch the moment out, take the time to memorize the expression on his face while I enjoyed what should have been a victorious moment. Instead, my muscles convulsed hard enough to double me in half. Tanris caught me and eased me back to the makeshift bed, his face a mask of concern. I ground my teeth against the pain and prayed for it to pass.

"You're too stupid and stubborn to die now, Crow. Stay with me."

"I th-th-thought you just said I was smart."

"You're going to hold that over my head forever, aren't you?"

If I lived. "Y-you know it."

Tanris knelt beside me, patiently rubbing my back until the seizing died down into violent shivering. "You're going to make it," he told me.

"You b-believe me about Melly and—and whatever his name was?"

He pulled the blanket back up around my shoulders. "I believe you. Just going to have to call you Wizard Bane now."

I barked a sharp laugh. "You don't, either."

"There's a sizable town not too far from here," he said, pretending he wasn't changing the subject entirely. "I'm going find someone to help you."

"You know there's no one. You heard what he said."

"And I know wizards lie. I have to try, Crow. Girl will stay here with you."

"And the egg."

He snorted in annoyance. "I'm not going to leave you out here."

"Don't want anyone in town to s-s-steal it," I countered, teeth chattering.

He lifted a hand to rub his face, scraping rough whiskers. "No," he admitted and sighed.

"It's not like I'm g-going anywhere," I pointed out sourly. "Girl could hold me down with her little finger."

She blushed and looked worried at the same time. Somewhere between the argument and now she'd filled a cup full of water and held it, waiting.

"I'm leaving her the crossbow."

"Please don't shoot me, Girl." As a joke, it failed miserably.

Tanris pulled the egg out of his bag, set it down beside me, then got to his feet and moved away. "Just remember, I caught you once, I can catch you again."

"That was an aberration."

"One of many."

"I n-never make the same mistake twice."

"Hang on, you hear? I'll be back in a couple of days." The door bumped closed. He always did have to have the last word.

Girl cried a great deal over the next while. I wanted to, but I was too exhausted by spasms that had become nearly constant. I couldn't tell any more if I felt sick. Nothing remained in my belly and whatever contractions my stomach might have engaged in simply blended with the rest of the agony. I shivered violently with cold. Holding the egg close helped, and even Girl agreed she could feel some heat from it. She dug out a hole in the floor of the barn and built a little fire, but the flames did little to help. She spent the night lying next to me, trying to keep me warm. I much doubt she got any more sleep than I did.

By morning, the spasms came with surges of green. I do not know if the bursts could properly be termed "light," for it was more a pulsing discoloration surging through whatever muscles were cramping. Interesting, yes; pleasant, no. All the while, the Voices nattered at me like demented things, doing an outstanding job of observing the obvious: I was sick. I was in pain. I was dying. I was green. I was afraid. I was angry. I'd been cursed by a wizard. Another was needed to reverse the magic—and on and on until I croaked furiously at them to stop. With absolute certainty, I didn't want the interference of another wizard, living or not.

Frightened, Girl went to sit in the corner.

I concentrated on recalling every curse I'd ever known and applying it to Duzayan, and when I couldn't remember any more, I made them up.

Late into the second night after Tanris left, I finally slept. All too soon, consciousness returned to me. I ached abominably and grit filled my eyes. After a bit, Girl came to crouch down and study me intently.

"I'm still here," I rasped, and she nodded. Her thin face was pinched and dark circles marked her eyes. Inquiry into Tanris's whereabouts brought only a shrug, and asking where we were was just ridiculous. She had some broth for me, for which I was grateful if only to moisten my lips and mouth. It had an odd tangy flavor to it. After that I slept again.

Movement awakened me. It was small and erratic, but accompanied by a tearing noise and then a sharp stinging sensation across my belly. I would not have thought I had energy enough for yelling and leaping, but I burst up out of the comfort of my makeshift bed with surprising alacrity. There was no one in the little barn with me; I don't know where Girl had disappeared to, but she'd taken her crossbow from its place by the door. I understood that even as I collapsed against the far wall, too weak even for adrenalin to keep me up.

Heart pounding in terror, I pulled up my shirt. Among the black marks on my abdomen—faded somewhat now—two irregular cuts bled. I thought at first that Brother Three had planted a demon or some other sort of monster in my belly and it was digging its way out, but then my bed rustled. I crawled to my pack and drew my knife, sweating and shaking with weakness, ears ringing, lips dry. With the tip of the blade, I flipped back the blankets to reveal the egg. It wriggled fitfully, scraping and rocking. A ragged opening marked one side, and from it protruded a sharp little beak.

Egg was hatching.

"No!" I exclaimed. "No, no, no! You can't hatch. Don't do that!" I couldn't stop it; waving my hands and protesting frantically certainly didn't work. Tiny, dagger-like talons ripping through the tough covering followed the appearance of the beak. A thick, whitish substance oozed from the holes, and I gingerly moved the whole production off my bedding. Sitting down close by, I watched helplessly. Tanris would be livid, and I couldn't even entertain anticipation for watching him yell and flail about. No egg meant no cure for the poison; with no cure for the poison, there would be no Crow.

Under normal circumstances, I might have paced. I couldn't do that, so I sat on the floor and rubbed my head and watched the baby dragon's emergence into the world. There had to be a way around this disaster, and somehow I would find it. I lived in a world of possibility. Nothing came to me immediately, but the hatchling made a fine mess out of his previous home. On the off chance that the casing might still serve some purpose, I scooted closer and used my knife to make a cut far cleaner and easier to repair. Mindful to keep my fingers out of the way of the hatchling's continued efforts, and with my blade and a spoon from our cooking gear, I eased the edges apart. Slimy, filmy stuff covered the hatchling, but it blinked up at me with curiosity and utter fearlessness.

"Come on, then," I urged, and the little beastie tilted its head back and made minuscule creaking noises. With the spoon and a glove, I got it out onto the floor where it wobbled and stretched out sticky wings experimentally. I watched in faint disgust and then used some of the hay to wipe the thing off. It didn't work very well. Girl had left a pot of water on the coals, and with a piece of the fabric that had been wound around my head I managed to bathe the thing. Egg—only it wasn't "Egg" anymore, was it?—

creaked and wobbled about. Holding it got me a cut across the back of my hand for my efforts. That beak was sharp! Luckily, I had armor in the form of my leather gloves.

As nonexistent dragons go, it was rather engaging. It couldn't walk straight to save its life. What had been bony ridges and horns on the heads of its parents were merely bumps from beneath which peered golden eyes with slitted pupils. Its hide was an odd color, sort of coppery and green with no sign of the plates that had covered the adult's neck and chest, though the coloring was lighter there. No horns, either. It creaked at me and staggered about, and after a bit I thought to offer it some broth. I had no idea what baby dragons ate. Hopefully not people. It had some trouble with its long tongue, but didn't waste much time figuring things out as I poured little spoonfuls of soup into its mouth. I fed it until it wouldn't take any more, and then it sat there gazing at me sleepily, eyelids drooping.

"That looks like a good plan," I said. A little more hay made a nice nest, and then I took to my own bed. Hatching a dragon was exhausting work. I'd hardly closed my eyes before I had company. The dragon curled up against me, let out a tiny, contented sigh, then laid still. I debated pushing it away, but I'd grown rather used to its presence, and moving it seemed like altogether too much effort. I was reminded of Tanris's cat. At least Egg—I couldn't call it that any more—wasn't hairy. What had happened to the wretched feline? I drifted to sleep with images of dragon appetizers dancing in my head.

:-:

Girl screamed. Well, not a real scream, but more like a hiccuping gasp accompanied by an unsuccessful juggling of the wood she'd gathered for our fire. She kept hold of one piece, and in spite of having the crossbow slung over her shoulder, her weapon of choice was a two foot branch still dangling a couple of leaves. She leveled it at me—at us—menacingly.

"It hatched," I said, and she stared as if I'd lost my mind. I sighed and rubbed my face. I really needed a shave, and while I had never realized it before, I was apparently somewhat obsessed with cleanliness. "I couldn't exactly stop it, you know. I don't suppose you have any brilliant ideas you'd care to share?"

She lifted her branch threateningly.

"That's one possibility," I nodded, "but I'd like to exhaust all others before we resort to killing our only salvation."

Warily, she picked up her scattered wood and stacked it by the fire, then peered into the soup pot and gave a satisfied nod. Wait until she discovered I was sharing it with Not-An-Egg. Conversations with Girl were challenging; I had to limit myself to yes-or-no questions. Had she seen any sign of Tanris? No. Was she all right? Yes. Were our supplies holding out all right? Yes (and well they ought, for I had eaten nothing for days). Any sign of other people?

She branched out with her conversation skills to hold up three fingers and shrug, which I assumed meant they'd passed by without giving any trouble. Then she pointed at me and held both hands out.

I looked at my hands. Caught up with the excitement of hatching, I'd given them no thought at all. How glorious to find them looking quite normal, the abrasions fairly well healed, and with no traces of green. They trembled, and although that was only to be expected after my ordeal, it did not reassure me. Survival had always demanded that I be fit and in control.

A few more carefully worded questions to Girl did nothing to fend off exhaustion, and before long I found myself nodding off. The hatchling snoozed through the entire exchange, and didn't wake until nearly dusk. Then it staggered about the floor investigating everything, tripping over its tail, overbalancing with its clumsy wings, and landing on its snout repeatedly.

"It's a boy," I pointed out during one of its attempts to flounder upright. That it could ever grow to resemble the deadly, graceful creatures that had attacked the village seemed amazing. Girl's attitude softened as she watched, and she even smiled once or twice at its—his—antics.

She apparently took her job as guardian seriously, for she continually peeked through the cracks in the walls, and when noise outside heralded the arrival of a rider, she had the spanned crossbow in her hand and pointed at the door before I could even put down my bowl of soup and reach for my knife.

Tanris stepped in, brows and empty hands lifting. "It's just me." He regarded me for a long moment with an expression I could not readily interpret. "I couldn't find anyone who could help. Doesn't look like you need it. You're better."

"Mm," I nodded, and resumed my meal. I could call it that, though I didn't typically find broth particularly satisfying. I was at least no longer directly in the middle of expiring, though I felt like death's leftovers.

He shed coat and weapons, and Girl ladled some soup out for him. "Have the fits stopped?" he asked her.

I resented his choice of words. It made me sound like a lunatic, and I didn't much like to contemplate how close that might be to the truth.

She nodded, and he pinned a scaring gaze on me. "What happened?" he demanded.

I blinked at the accusatory tone of voice. "I am getting better. So sorry."

"It just seems flappin' strange to me. You've had what? Three magical attacks?" That many? I made a grimace of distaste, but when I opened my mouth to speak, Tanris continued. "No, four. First Duzayan in Marketh. Then the Ghost Walk, that statue in the Vault, then—well, I suppose if we counted both wizards, you're up to five."

"Who would have imagined I would be so popular among magicians and so cunning at escaping their wiles?" I quipped.

"I don't know if I'd call it escaping."

"Duzayan's poison didn't kill me."

"Yet. We don't even know if your sickness is from that or one of your other encounters."

Logical, I supposed, but a tad depressing. "The symptoms matched what he predicted," I said sullenly. He'd missed my bouts of turning green and talking to the air. I was pretty sure Girl wouldn't tell him about that, but she shook her head, wriggled her fingers, and then pulled at her assortment of layered shirts until she found a greenish one and pointed at it enthusiastically. Whose side was she on, anyway?

Tanris eyed me narrowly, but questioned Girl. "He turned green?"

She nodded. Loudly. Could have heard it in whatever village Tanris had gone traipsing off to, no doubt. Then she made an opening and closing motion with her hand, fingers straight.

"And talking. To himself?"

More loud nodding.

I grimaced. "I wasn't talking to myself."

"Then to who?"

This was going to sound good. "The Ancestors."

Tanris nodded slowly. "Dead people."

"Well… yes. I suppose so."

He nodded again, then sighed and set his empty bowl aside. "You want to tell us what's going on? You've been acting strange ever since the Ghost Walk. You hear things, see things, say strange things. You know details you can't possibly know on your own. What is this, Crow?"

"I don't know why you're asking me, I know as much about magic as you do." I glared fiercely at no one in particular and tipped my bowl up to drain the contents.

"You couldn't do any of this before that—magic or whatever it was went into you?"

"No." I wondered why I told him anything at all.

He sat quietly for a bit, thinking, rubbing his thumb up and down his jaw. He needed a shave, too. Again. "Maybe your experience in the Walk did something to your mind."

"Made me crazy?" I snorted a laugh. "Don't you think I haven't considered that?"

"How can we trust it, Crow? How can we trust you?"

"After all the years you've spent mistrusting and doubting and condemning me, *now* you want to trust me?" How absurd.

"I don't have much of a choice, do I?" Angry, his volume increased with each word. Off to the side, Girl sat very still and silent, hugging her knees tight and looking more pale by the instant. "If I don't work with you—and that requires some sort of trust—I don't get my wife back. I assure you, it is a temporary condition," he growled, tossing my own words back at me.

"Well, thank the gods!" I exclaimed with some heat. "I wouldn't want to have to like you or something!"

"You've never liked me, why start now?"

"Not true." I emphasized with a sharp jab of my index finger.

It was his turn to snort. "When did you ever?"

"Clear up until you collapsed in a heap on the street in front of Duzayan's mansion. And that might have been endurable, understandable, even, but then you went and got completely, uselessly, stupidly drunk. How such nonsense ever—Augh." I tossed one hand in the air in a gesture of disgust. "All right, fine, I never really did like you, but I respected you."

"Really?"

I gave him a Look with a capital "L," eyes narrowed. What did he expect from me? More to the point, what did I want from him? Nothing. I would not have minded at all if he had stayed behind in Hasiq jum'a Sahefal to help the wretched villagers recover from or escape the ravages of the dragons. I didn't need a trail guide. I had only to head southwest and I would eventually come to the Le'ah River, where I could put myself on a boat and speed south and thence to Marketh. Except... Tanris and Girl had certainly come in handy when the dragon had attacked, and I hated to consider what might have become of me in my illness had they not been there to tuck me away in a little barn and feed me broth. I could not know if the sickness had passed completely or if it would strike again between here and the city. Besides, Tanris *did* want to help me annihilate Baron Duzayan, an endeavor which might actually require, if not a partner, then a modicum of cooperation. Putting forth a little effort to assuage his self-image couldn't hurt. "Yes, Tanris, I did. Do." *Could*, if he kept himself pulled together.

A little creak came from behind me in the blankets, a rustle, and then the hatchling came lurching out like a drunken sailor. He paused to yawn theatrically, and Tanris stared.

"That's a dragon," he said.

"Yes, I noticed that, too."

"Where did it come from?" Alarmed, he looked about for the egg, the remains of which I'd tucked near my things. I'd persuaded Girl to wash the shell out in case we could figure a use for it. "How did that happen?"

Had he really just asked that? I made a little scratching motion with my finger. "First by scraping a little hole and then making it bigger and bigger. I intervened before the casing got completely ruined and used my knife and a spoon to get the baby out the rest of the way. Easier to sew or glue back together if we need to."

Tanris stared from the little dragon to the empty egg casing and back, his face transforming into a mask of horror. "What—"

"No," I said very firmly. "Do not ask what happened. You know perfectly well what happened. And do not ask what we will do now. Believe me, I have pondered the same question. Do not try to kill him, either. Most likely he is exactly what Duzayan wants, and if it was instead the egg itself he needed, we can try to bargain with it or threaten or—or train the wretched beast to attack him and peck his eyes out." Could one train a dragon to do anything? And how long did it take for one to reach full size?

"We can't take this back to him!"

I crooked my brows. "Can we not? We will bring the dragon and we will bring the casing, and it was you yourself who pointed out that the baron did not set out what shape the egg had to be in, merely that it arrive within the specified time."

"He'll kill us."

I gave him a scathing look. "And that changes things how?"

He opened his mouth, then closed it again and shook his head, still watching the dragon teetering one way, then tottering the other.

"He's kind of cute, eh?"

"Cute?" His face contorted. "Are you serious?"

Wisdom prevented me from mentioning the cat, particularly as a tool for ridicule. Hitching myself closer to the fire, I poured some more soup into my bowl and then added a little water to cool it, wondering if dragons were born with the ability to breathe fire, and if hot soup was actually a problem. Tanris watched in morbid fascination as I donned my gloves, put the baby in my lap, and proceeded to feed it broth.

"Is it going to eat much?"

"I suppose if we don't feed it properly we'll stunt its growth."

"And that would be a shame." I detected a definite note of sarcasm. "How are we going to get a dragon from here to Marketh?"

"We should probably purchase a cage," I suggested. "And a sturdy cover."

"And a wagon," he nodded. "This isn't going to be easy, you know."

I crooked a brow. "Remind me which parts have been easy thus far?"

He scratched his chin. "There was the mayor's house in Uzuun."

"The one bright spot in this whole adventure," I agreed. "And I did like Old Jelal's loft."

"You? A loft?"

"I am that desperate for a soft, warm, dry place to sleep."

"This one's not too bad."

"Except for the constant draft blowing through."

"It won't be long now," he murmured.

Relatively speaking, I supposed he was right, and the knowledge brought both relief and terror. The horrible journey would end, but would I be able to enjoy all the freedoms I had once known? I highly doubted Duzayan would give me the antidote. Why would he? It would be to his advantage to either keep me in his employ and dependent on him, or kill me outright. Did I still need the antidote? There was only one way to find out. I would stop taking my two daily drops, and if I became ill again, why, then I would know.

— 26 —
Well-Earned Respite

Dumpy and gray, the ugly town of Irfan squatted on the bank of the river like a lazy old woman who took no consideration of her appearance. She had bad breath, too. The heavy scent of fish both fresh and rotten—and other putrid things I had no desire to identify—hung in the air, an intrinsic by-product of the mud-filled streets. They twisted this way and that, curled, ragged, unkempt. Even road-weary, we were still cleaner than Irfan, and that alone drew attention.

"I told you it wasn't a good place to stop for bed and a bath," Tanris muttered, hat pulled low over his brow and one hand on the hilt of his sword. He'd planned our arrival for morning so we would have time to tend to our business and depart as soon as possible, preferably before we drew too much attention. A pair of hard-looking youths followed us for too long to mean well or be possessed of simple curiosity. I turned in my saddle and watched them like I hadn't eaten for days and they looked like they'd make a passing fine meal.

"Stop trying to pick a fight with the locals, Crow."

"I'm not doing anything more than they are."

"You're challenging them."

He must think I had just fallen off the potato cart. Most thieves and bullies, if they know that you know they're there, will quietly disappear. It is a matter of self-preservation not to be identified. Assassins and murderers, most especially, do not wish to be seen. While their plans most certainly include someone's extinction, there is always some slim chance, some unpredictable interference from the gods, that may preserve the lives of the victims and bring the would-be criminal to an end. I faced forward again, and Girl squeezed between us, making progress up the street considerably more difficult. The barbed edges of her uneasiness prickled.

"I just want them gone," I grumbled.

Gone... gone... gone... echoed back at me. Through me.

"We'll stick to the busier parts of town."

"Oh, I like that idea. Let them herd us right into place. Make it even easier for them. Thieves like few things better than so-called "average" strangers. There's no one to—"

"Stow it, Crow, I don't need a lecture."

Of course he didn't. He knew everything. Ahead of us, a cart pulled out across the way and immediately caused a small traffic jam, leaving an obvious and easy way around it to the right. "Go left," I said, and suited action to deed, reaching out to grab hold of Girl's reins and pull her along with me. "Quickly."

"What are you trying to do?" Tanris protested. We had to squeeze one-by-one through the opening between the end of the cart and the corner of a building. A tall man stepped into my way to wave his arms and holler about the lack of room and what was I doing, crazy fool, but I urged Horse forward. Ears back, she shouldered him out of the way and trotted ahead a few steps. With Girl right behind me, the man had no choice but to step out of the way, but he let us know in no uncertain terms that we had less than the usual capacity for brains. Tanris made it through as the cart driver urged his animal into motion. Backwards. That didn't look at all suspicious, now did it?

Nevertheless, Tanris's temper simmered. "Do you even know where you're going?" he yelled, guiding his horse up next to me and forcing Girl to fall behind. It made her nervous.

"I know where I'm *not* going. Look behind and tell me there aren't three boys now. Third one's a little fellow, but he's quick."

"What—" Glaring, he turned in his saddle. Sure enough, three boys now followed us. I couldn't hear over the noise of the horses, but I'd have bet good coin that Tanris ground his teeth.

"Watch. One of them will run off. *Watch*," I ordered when he would have turned back. "He's going to go down an alley or through a building and run ahead to set up the next ambush." I knew exactly when it happened just by the way Tanris stiffened. "Now we'll go the other way. Just keep an eye out. You've got a perfectly good pair of them."

The hatchling chose that instant to bump about in my saddle bag, where I'd had to put him not only to protect myself from sharp claws, but to keep him out of sight of the locals. We'd hoped he would stay asleep until we'd purchased a crate for him and arranged transportation down the river. I waited until we'd gone down the new street a little distance, then called out to my companions. "Stop here!" Slipping from the saddle, I had to hold on for a moment or two to keep my knees from buckling beneath me. The exercise, small as it was, made me lightheaded and suddenly clammy. When I could stand straight again, I settled my disreputable hat on my head and watched our shadows out of the corner of my eye while I made a show of refastening some of my gear. During the course of the task, I tipped a few grains of Adamanta Dust into the saddle bag.

"What are you doing?" For a man that had lectured me about trust, Tanris was awfully suspicious.

"I'm just putting the baby to sleep."

"What?"

"Sleep. Drugs. You've heard of them?" I refastened the buckle, then struggled back aboard Horse.

"What did you use?"

"If I told you, would it make you feel better?"

"Maybe," he said dubiously. "Is it safe?"

"Is having the baby out and about safe?"

He gave me one of his long, inscrutable looks, this one threaded with distaste. "You are the most unprincipled blackguard I have ever met."

"I have principles."

"Whatever is yours is mine?"

"That's one of them, but do you really want to discuss this here?"

Another long look, then he moved away, turning back to point at me with his highly dangerous index finger. "It better not be d—" A simple crook of my brow changed what he'd been about to say. "Ruined."

While he guided his horse into the street, I searched through the crowd until I found our shadows again. I pointed from my eyes to them. The dry rustle of Voices stirred around me.

Gone… gone… gone… they said.

"I wish they were."

Danger…

"Yes." Those boys and their cronies had the possibility of ruining everything, of having us robbed, if not killed, and detained, if not imprisoned.

The Voices gained volume, chattering and whispering so many things at once that I could not follow what they said. I made out a few words: *peril… death… hurt… cursed… fear…* A chill air whisked around me, flipping up Horse's mane, pushing the brim of my hat, tugging at my clothes. Horse danced a few nervous steps, but the sense of *presence* sped away down the street. Flying leaves and debris marked its passage, and then it whirled wildly around the boys. It looked like nothing so much as a dust devil, but I had felt that chill and I watched the boys covering their faces and screaming. A few others got caught in the uncanny wind, and they moved away hastily, but the wind closely followed our shadows as they tried to stagger out of its path.

I could not help but laugh in surprise at the spectacle. "Enough," I said, and the wind broke apart, skittering here and there up the street, snatching at skirts and cloaks and hair, chattering, strangely agitated.

Tanris watched with a perplexed frown. "Did you do that?"

I gave him a disparaging look. "The wind is my fault now?"

"That was passing strange," he murmured.

I glanced back over my shoulder. The youths hurried away down the street, casting glances back over their shoulders, faces white. "Passing," I agreed, and urged Horse into motion. We rode on again. The dragon creaked and bumped about for a few more minutes, then fell quiet. Asleep, I hoped.

The three of us did agree on one thing: we did not want to spend any more time in Irfan than strictly necessary, an opinion only strengthened by interactions with the people living there. While Tanris went to secure us passage on one of the riverboats, Girl and I purchased a suitable means of conveyance for the dragon. We ended up in possession of a small crate with narrow slits in the sides, which hid more than the bars of a cage would. For our return to civilization—or Girl's introduction to it, as it happened—I purchased new clothing. Ours bore a distinct resemblance to rags and, worse, had assumed an odor I much doubted would ever surrender to soap and water. Irfan was not a town where fine made apparel saw much use, so I settled for some practical things—shirts, tunics, pants, stockings, and even new coats, fairly sure that the season promised more horrible weather, though we perched on the very edge of spring at last. In an expansive mood, I even bought Girl some scarves. She modeled them for me, giddy with pleasure, an attitude I had not enjoyed since Tarsha had—Well. Better not to go there. Tarsha was a lying, scheming scab. A very beautiful scab...

But Girl's smiles and delight kept my mind off the wicked past, and the surly shopkeepers kept me on my mental toes. I haggled prices only enough to appear disgruntled without venturing into "livid." They portrayed well-practiced outrage, and the dealers took on particularly smug postures as they baldly cheated us, which bothered me not the slightest, as I cheated them right back. One shirt turned into three, two pair of stockings into four, and a new belt as well as a pair of gloves made their way into our parcels without any additional exchange of coin.

Keeping watch over our horses and possessions complicated the entire operation, but we took turns. Girl was at first shy about picking out new items, but after she'd done so the first two times and we traded places so I could go inside the store and pay for them—and come out with nicer and more numerous items—she recovered quickly. One of the shops had a little closet in which we exchanged old for new, and in spite of the dregs of illness, I found myself much cheered. None of this kept Girl from looking at me from time to time with a mystified expression on her face, and twice she made so bold as to look into my purse.

I laughed at her antics. "Our employer is paying us well for this trip," I explained.

She held up the bag and shook it. I bent close to murmur confidentially in her ear. "I don't keep my coin where any pickpocket could easily make off with it."

She regarded me quite seriously, then tapped a finger against my chest, pointed to her eyes, held up a coin, and then gave me a look so sly and conniving that I nearly laughed out loud.

"No," I said, shaking my head.

She gave me a greatly exaggerated frown nearly as comical as the sly look had been, then her fist thumped her chest.

"You want to learn the trade?"

A nod.

"Why?" I asked.

She plucked at her clothes, pointed at the pocket where I'd tucked away my purse, then mimicked eating.

"For a livelihood?"

Another nod.

"You could just get married."

Her face pinched a little more, and she looked… afraid. *Felt* afraid. Then her mouth bent into an expression of exasperation and she held her hands out and looked around.

"Choices will be better in Marketh," I pointed out.

She digested that for a moment, then brightened and tapped my chest again, smiling.

"What?"

A repeated gesture between the two of us made my brows lift. "You and me? Oh, no. No."

She held her hands out and gave me a questioning expression.

"I've sworn off women. Besides, you're too young."

She shook her head, then mimicked sewing and cooking and kissing, the latter of which nearly prompted another smile from me.

"Can you count? How old are you?"

All ten fingers, then seven.

"Too young," I repeated. She'd never been so animated. She almost looked pretty. "Besides, you're already cheating me, and that's a poor way to start such a relationship."

She grabbed my arm as I turned away, her brows knit in puzzlement.

Her action brought us very close. I looked over her unprepossessing features and let my gaze settle on a mouth that could be surprisingly mobile and appealing. "I believe you have a voice, little chick," I murmured to her, deliberately pitching my voice low and cool. "Refusing to use it is robbing me. Idle chitchat I can live without, but sometimes—" I touched my finger to her lips. "Sometimes you keep critical information from me, and where you might be helpful you are instead a dangerous burden."

Shock rippled through her. Tears abruptly filled her eyes.

"Don't," I said, glaring a warning.

Her mouth quivered, but she nodded and drew herself up.

Rejoining Too, I proceeded to toss the old, ugly, stinky clothes out onto what passed as a boardwalk and replace them with our new things.

Girl puzzled me. She was a strange creature at a strange time of my life— and I didn't need any more riddles to solve. Could I use her in my war against Duzayan? Possibly. *Would* I use her? If something useful came to mind, yes, without a second thought. I had been cast out on the streets at a much younger age than she, and I had managed just fine, even prospered. Survival on the streets required strength and cunning. *My* strength, *my* cunning. I worked hard and sported the lumps to prove it. I owed no responsibility to a girl foisted on me by Tanris's misplaced sense of duty and a wizard's abuse! I coveted my talent and my knowledge. Why teach her my methods? Let her learn for herself the pain and loneliness involved in such a life. I wanted none of it! I needed no cook—I cooked just fine for myself.

Why, then, I asked myself, had I bothered to buy her new things with my own coin? She was nothing to me. *Nothing*, I repeated to myself.

I kept an eye on those around me as I worked, buckling buckles and retying ropes. The entire thing would need repacking when we had time; Tanris would do it, necessary or not. Busy work, in my estimation, but if it kept him happy I didn't care. I looked in on the dragon, and I saw his little sides move as he breathed, so I fastened the bag again and went to untie the horses from the post.

"If you can ask me properly," I said, handing Girl the reins to her mount and then moving to climb up on Horse, "I'll consider it." I struggled to drag myself into the saddle. Thank the gods of transportation, sitting was a necessity in this particular form of locomotion and I needn't exert myself. I tugged on Too's lead rope as I set off, and he gamely followed along.

I was aware of Girl standing behind me still, staring. Likely, she had her mouth open, which was not at all attractive or useful. Joy burst through her completely out of proportion to my insane offer, and a moment later she trotted along beside me, smiling like a fool.

Tanris pushed himself off the side of the ramshackle building where he was sunning himself and waited for us to approach, one hand lifted to shade his eyes. "It's about time you got here. I found a buyer for the horses, but he's not going to wait around much longer."

"Why do we need a buyer?" I inquired, perfectly happy to remain sitting for a little longer and not at all opposed to watching Tanris squint in the light of the glorious sun.

"To pay for our passage on the *Empress of the Le'ah*." He gestured toward the end of the wobbly dock and a boat that looked at least as dilapidated as the building.

Empress? The thing looked more like a fat old washerwoman with most of her teeth missing. The hull listed to one side, and the masts went the other. "If that's an empress, then I'm a butterfly, and if you're going to risk your life on that death trap you're crazier than I thought." I turned a curious look on him. "And you'd sell the horses? Our *friends?*"

"You don't have any friends, Crow." He rubbed his forehead.

"Of course I do."

"They're horses, not friends."

"We've been through a horrendous ordeal together, how can you say that? I have slept with Horse, eaten with her, crept through a long and terrible cave with her, run for my life with her, and dangled off a cliff with her. If you ask me, that's a pretty intimate relationship."

"Says the man who killed my cat."

"I did no such thing!" I retorted, then paused. "It's dead?"

"She was trapped in a burning building, what do you suppose happened to her?"

I almost blurted that I'd last seen her in lower reaches of the temple. Truly, I thought it was probably alive and well, much too lucky to get eaten by dragons, and with at least six more lives to go through. It would have made a very small and unappetizing mouthful anyway. "What about that boat over there?" I asked, pointing to one that looked sturdily built and probably six hundred years younger.

Tanris heaved a sigh. "I told you, this is the best we can afford, and only if we sell the horses. Crow? Where are you going?"

"To make a better deal."

The captain of the *River Star* clearly did not hail from Irfan. He was clean, and a pleasant enough fellow, even if he did overcharge us for passage. "It is a hazardous trip at this time of year. The spring floods make it a high risk," he explained, which fooled me not one bit. If it was so chancy, neither he nor any of the other six or so ships' captains docked in Irfan would be plying their trade this far upriver so soon in the season, but it gave me a good way to strike up a conversation about risks and challenge him to a game or two of cards.

By the time I rejoined the others, Tanris had had time to notice Girl's new clothes and to rifle through the admittedly sloppy packs. When he laid eyes on me in my new gear, I feared he might burst a blood vessel.

"What is this?" he asked, flipping his fingers against my nice new quilted coat with a high collar to keep rain off my neck. No silk, to be sure, but the color was a nice forest green I liked. "A coat." I waved at Too, who apparently didn't mind standing about with heavy packs and a small crate on his back. "We got you one, too, and some clothes to replace those awful things you're wearing."

"And how did *we* pay for it?" he inquired in a voice peculiarly tight.

"In the usual way." Usual for me, anyway. "I got the colors you like. Boring black and gray and brown and such."

His jaw worked. The vein in his forehead throbbed. "Where," he said, and "tight" went to "strangled," forcing him to start over again. "Where did you get the coin to pay for all this? And the passage, too, I gather?"

I smiled reassuringly at him. "From the coin the baron gave us." And the jewels and artwork and such that he and his guests and subsequent bystanders had donated at the beginning of our trip. No need to go into vulgar detail.

"We spent all the coin on the horses and supplies," he said in a rough, low voice. Girl hovered nearby and watched us with a typically worried expression. Tanris doubted, Girl worried. It was just the way they were.

"I went back, and he gave us more." In a roundabout way. "You wouldn't remember, you were drunk." I clapped him on the shoulder and went to collect Too's lead rope.

"And now you've just spent all that, haven't you? We still need to get from here to Marketh City, in case you've forgotten your geography."

"I am keeping that in mind, my friend. I have traveled once or twice before in my life." I started off to the *River Star* with Horse and Too in tow and Girl hurrying to keep up. If Tanris handled most travel arrangements this way, it was a wonder he got anywhere, and I couldn't for the life of me figure out why Duzayan had given him that misplaced authority. Granted, Tanris knew about horses and packing and roving through the wilds, but he had absolutely no concept of comfort.

Once we'd stowed the horses and Tanris survived the extra cost of ensuring that they were properly fed, we retired with saddle bags and crate to our cabin. The *River Star* was just a river boat, and didn't have the generous rooms one might expect on a sea-going vessel, so we were, perforce, required to share the space. Girl claimed an upper bunk and stretched out with a happy sigh. I set Not-an-Egg's crate in the corner, then chose the lower bed opposite Girl's and sat down gratefully. The shopping trip and haggling for our places on the boat had completely worn me out. Mindful of my head, I removed coat and boots, tucked my pack up against the wall, and laid down.

"What are you doing?"

Tanris either liked annoying me, or the simple things escaped him. "Lying down," I replied with deliberate patience.

"We have work to do."

"Yes." I sucked in a breath and let it out in a sigh, tucking my arms behind my head and closing my eyes. "And such a trial it will be, lying right here and only moving to take care of necessary bodily functions."

"What about all that—that *rubbish* you bought?"

"I don't buy rubbish, but I assume you're talking about our supplies. What of them?" I knew exactly what he was getting at, and I had no intention of dealing with it right now. I had, bless the gods of miracles and fortunes, recently survived practically dying, and fully intended to take the opportunity given to me in which to recover.

"They're a mess. We need to reorganize them."

I shifted so I could rearrange the bed's itchy wool blanket to cover me, which required opening my eyes again. "Do you like sick people, Tanris? Do you like cleaning up after them, providing for them, and carrying them around because they're too ill to move themselves?"

He had elevated his glowers to an art form, and he possessed an entire set. This one expressed the opinion that I was harassing him unjustly and perhaps attempting to hoodwink him. "No."

"I didn't think so. In an effort to stave off certain death and the likelihood of even further distressing you by becoming grossly ill again, I am going to sleep. I don't know about you, but I have had exactly two good nights' sleep since we left Marketh months ago. If you will take a moment to recall your geography, you will know that it will take us approximately three days to travel the length of the river. We sail in the morning. If you would like to square away the packs now—" I waved one hand, "then by all means, help yourself, but I feel confident that our things will travel quite nicely just the way they are, and they won't mind at all if we take a well-deserved rest for a day or two."

"You're very smug about this."

"Smug? No, I'm tired. I have been sick for days. My head hurts, and I still need to figure out how to deal with Duzayan. You want your wife back. I might die any moment. Let me do it in peace." Yanking the blanket up over my shoulder, I turned my back to him.

"And the thing?"

"He's not a thing."

A moment's silence, and then, "I suppose you're going to give it a stupid name, too."

"Yes," I said waspishly, "that's quite high on my list of important things to remember. Now go away."

Much to my surprise, he did.

— 27 —
Because We Weren't Wet Enough

"Like this. Use the fleshy part of your thumb to hang onto it, see?" I gestured casually at Girl and then flipped a few of the cards lying on the bed, using the hand with the coin tucked in my palm. "You need to relax your hand, not hold it stiffly, or everyone will know there's something wrong. The more you practice, the more natural it will look. Do other things while you're holding it, so you get used to having it there."

I held my hand out as though to shake hers, and when she took it she came away with the coin. A smile tugged at her mouth and she nodded. Setting it down again, she copied what I'd shown her, her face intent with concentration. Her fingers were stiff and she looked like she was having a cramp of some kind, which made her giggle.

"Practice," I said, and picked up the cards, tapping them into a stack. "Have you ever played Blind Path?" I asked, shuffling the cards and then laying them out in a solitaire pattern. She shook her head. While she practiced palming the coin, I played a few games, and then I showed her how to turn her one coin into two. It was a silly parlor trick, but it provided a basic foundation for learning further skills, and in the meantime it entertained us both.

I'd slept through the first day and most of the second, and Tanris saved his repacking until I could help him, so we worked on that for a good part of the afternoon. He probably hoped he was inflicting some form of torture, but I asked questions and he showed me how to economize on space and how to balance a load. It was very much like what I did on a regular basis during my own work, but on a much larger scale. When we finished I rustled up a game of cards with a couple of the crew members and came away with a modest amount of coin to offset the cost of our passage.

My stomach continued to threaten biliousness. My muscles ached like I'd taken a beating, but the sickness didn't grow worse. I didn't take the drops.

The third day gave me more of the same but with less sleep, and I replaced lessons in packing techniques with teaching Girl tricks with coins and cards. "Put the hand with the coin over theirs like so, and use the other to pretend to pull a coin out of the air," I demonstrated. "Waving your hand around dramatically will hold their attention. They're not expecting you to have a coin in your other hand. You point as you drop the coin in their hand and then *poof*, there's two."

The dragon, who had been sleeping on the bed beside me, yawned. After a moment he got up and stretched, catlike, then sat down and licked his snout while watching us blearily, tail curled neatly around feet. He had a considerable appetite and was already growing. Providing enough food to keep him happy had proven to be a challenge. In the first place, we weren't certain what it *could* eat, and so tried to stick to soft things, at least for now. In the second place, we had to keep its presence a secret and so had to sneak in meals. The captain laughingly asked if we had stowed away a midget, to which I replied by patting my belly and telling him I had been ill and once I'd started eating again, I couldn't seem to get enough, though I was beginning to wonder if I would ever attain my former stature, which just made him laugh more and made Tanris roll his eyes. Luckily, we only needed the deception for a few days. Lucky, too, that the dragon didn't roar, but slept most of the time.

Beside me, he made a funny little noise in his throat, then belched a spurt of heat that put a burn mark in the sleeve of my tunic. "Hey! Ow!" I slapped at the scorched spot lest it turn into a conflagration, and the dragon looked back attentively. Girl clapped a hand over her mouth to stifle laughter.

"Not funny," I grumbled, and shook a warning finger at the dragon. "Do not do that again, you hear?" He opened his mouth and creaked. It wasn't a croak, and it certainly wasn't a growl. I glowered pointedly, then went back to instructing Girl in coin tricks.

Only a moment later, her eyes widened and she pointed. I looked back to see the dragon chewing contentedly on my cards. The last of one rectangle disappeared with a flick of a long tongue and he held another, already missing half, in a tiny claw. I opened my mouth to protest, and he paused, looking at me questioningly, the very picture of innocence. With a sigh, I picked up the rest of the cards and put them away in my pack. "I think it's safe to assume he wants to eat something more substantial than soup."

Without warning, the boat lurched and there came a grinding noise and then an audible crunch that did not bode well for buoyancy. The dragon flailed wildly, which would have been funny if Girl hadn't fallen on me. Instinctively, I put an arm around her to balance her, and the boat rolled and crunched the other direction, sending all three of us tumbling to the floor. I pushed the pair of them off me and struggled upward, bracing myself against the pitching. Our packs had fallen to the floor, and some of Girl's things had spilled out. I shoved them back in and thrust the bag against her chest even as I hauled her upright. "We've hit something. Get up on deck. *Now!*"

I had never seen her move so fast. She pushed the bag's flap closed, threaded the belt through the buckle, and ran out the door before the next surge sent her skidding sideways.

I threw my own bag over my shoulder. Scooping up the frantically creaking dragon, I tossed him into his crate and smacked the lid down, only to be thrown back onto the crazily tilting floor. It took far too long to get the clumsy oiled canvas around the crate and cinch the rope gathering the corners together, and I feared the dragon would drown if we went in the drink. My efforts were orchestrated by crashes and scraping, thumping and yelling from overhead, not to mention the screaming and pounding of the frightened horses.

By the time I got out into the corridor, the boat had stopped bucking so violently, but tilted at a severe angle. I clambered up the companionway and nearly fell right back down when the boat rolled again. One arm through the steps saved me, and then I found my footing and sprinted up the remaining distance. Chaos ruled the deck. Crates and barrels had been torn loose of their moorings and the smaller mast had snapped, leaving lines everywhere. A partially unfurled sail dragged in the water. Escaped chickens flapped to higher ground, squawking and leaving trails of feathers. Girl hung onto the rail on the upper side and I hurried toward her.

"You all right?" I called over the noise, and when she nodded I looked around for Tanris. At the other end of the boat, he hacked at something with an axe. All around us muddy river water roiled wildly. Trees floated past us, part of a roof, and someone's cow, lowing mournfully. There was much shouting and pointing going on. Tanris's end of the boat had become fouled in a partially submerged tangle of trees and the vessel was taking on water. "Stay here," I told Girl, handing her the canvas-wrapped crate. "And don't lose this."

I danced and slipped my way to the other end, grateful for years of practice that had taught me how to run over uncertain surfaces, leaping away from one unsteady perch to the next before I could get in trouble.

"We need to cut her free!" one of the hands shouted.

"We do that, we're going to swing right into the bank!" the captain yelled back. The bank at that point had an unappealing pile of boulders lining it.

"If we don't, we're going to go down!"

"Can we tie it off so it stays steady?" I asked, sizing up the situation.

"Got no way to get to the shore. If we put a rowboat over the side, it'll get caught in the undertow."

From the top of a wooden box, I looked over the arrangement of boat, rocks, trees and shore. "I can do it."

"What?"

"Get me a line." I dropped down to the deck and unslung my pack. From it I withdrew a lightweight cord and the grappling hook.

"Crow, it's too far." Tanris's face was creased in worry, his clothes soaking wet. It didn't take too long for mine to achieve a similar state. The water ran so hard and fierce that as it hit the boat it splashed upward a good ten or fifteen feet.

I refastened the pack around my waist and braced my legs wide. Looping one end of a cord through the railings, then through an iron ring in one of the hatches, I shoved some of the cargo over the door itself to hold it down. The other end was attached to my hook and I looked around. "Back off, and where's that bleedin' line?" I didn't have a great deal of room to swing the hook. The first few times around were to let out the cord as far as I dared and find my balance. Crewmen yelled and ducked and scattered as the hook whistled overhead. Two more turns at speed, and then I let fly. It arced across the water and clattered against the rocks. I yanked back hard, and when it stuck I gave a few more pulls to test the hold. Keeping the cord taut, I went to the hatch ring to tighten my line and knot it securely.

A crewman skidded toward me dragging the requested rope, a thick and heavy thing far more suited for the job of mooring a boat than my slender cord. He dropped it to the deck. I grabbed an end and jammed it through my belt, gave it a turn, and pushed it through again. "I'm going to take this over there," I pointed to the shore. "Make sure it doesn't tangle or get snagged. When I get it secured, you boys know what to do."

"We're going to need two. Three, if there's time," the captain pointed out, shoving wet hair out of his face and looking toward the other end of the boat with a worried expression.

"Fine, then get more rope. I'll be back as soon as I can." Tugging my gloves on, I went over the railing, dragging the heavier rope along with me. "Tanris, make sure I've got plenty of slack, and keep an eye on that cargo door."

"Crow—"

Ignoring him, I slid my hands out along the cord, leaned out over the raging water, and then swung away from the boat just as it gave another groan, slipping and jerking. There was no looking back and no looking down. Hand over hand I went until I had sufficient space to swing my feet up over the rope without hitting the rail. I missed the first time—how long had it been since I'd done this, and how much time had I spent riding and being sick instead of practicing? Shouts of alarm punctuated the air, but I didn't know if they belong to Tanris or the others. Another swing and I was up, ankles locked together and dangling upside down. I let out a hoot of laughter, then shimmied toward the shore.

Twice the boat shifted, each time carrying me close to the churning flood. Someone bellowed a warning, and the water in my eyes nearly kept me from making out an obstacle bobbing at me from upstream. All I could do was turn my face away and hug my line. Branches from an uprooted tree scraped at me and sought to drag me into their embrace. The rope snagged and I let go with one arm to grab for it. More branches scratched at my arm and threatened to tear the rope away from me, and me off my cord, but I held on tight. I won the brief tug-of-war, though it was a near thing. It took several moments to work the rope back into place, and then I had to go more slowly, for it was not as secure as it had been when I'd started out. My arms and shoulders ached already. Tipping my head back to check the distance, I was delighted to find land close by.

A fierce tug came on my cord and it strained beneath my hands, relaying the boat's movement. Tanris was out of view, and then suddenly the cord came loose. With a startled yell, I twisted my body hard to meet the rocks feet first. I didn't hit too hard, and then the slack in the cord was taken up again, but I had already reached my destination. Pulling myself to safety, I sprawled on hands and knees for a moment, panting and uselessly wiping water off my face with a wet sleeve.

In order for our plan to work, I had to make my way up the shore a short distance. Where the original shore had been I had no idea, but boulders formed part of a longish ridge, and at the upper end trees marched right down into the water. The rope secured over one shoulder, I dragged it against the current to where I could wind it around the bole of one of the trees. I fumbled several times before managing a satisfactory knot in the wet, heavy rope. I waved at the crew, watched them fasten their end, then hurried back to where I'd left my grappling hook and line. Much to my astonishment, Girl was on her way over from the boat.

My heart somersaulted.

It was one thing to do it myself, knowing that I had done similar things hundreds of times before. It was quite another to watch her—untried and so prone to tears—determinedly making her way across the chasm between boat and rocks. The river was so rough and so wild! All kinds of flotsam littered its churning, seething waves. Some of the lighter stuff merely floated past; more substantial branches and refuse beat at the boat, and it would beat at Girl if she lost her grip or if the constantly assaulted vessel moved too far. I scrambled down the rocks and braced myself, reaching out for her.

She inched along, her progress a painful misery of stopping and starting. When she caught sight of me, her thin, terrified features lit.

"Come on!" I called to her. "You're nearly there."

She nodded and went back to creeping slowly along. I kept looking up the river, searching for the next disaster, and I almost wished I hadn't. There was another roofed something, banging and spinning off the rocks that made the new shore.

"Girl!" She paused to look at me, and I shook my head, gesturing for her to come, come! "Hurry. You must hurry. *Now!*"

She froze.

I swore.

Looking across the water, I saw Tanris watching helplessly. "Cut the cord!" I hollered at him, and made a chopping motion, the edge of one hand against the palm of the other. He spun away, and I half fell, half scrambled downward, glancing up every few steps to eye the length of the cord between Girl and the rocks. "Hold on tight!" I shouted at her.

The Voices chittered wildly, the strangely familiar chill of them whisking around me. "Hush," I demanded. "Unless you can help, just *hush*." I had to go into the water. It was cold and strong, and my foot slipped, dragging me down until my knee slammed into something, stopping my sudden descent. I floundered upright and looked up at Girl just as Tanris cut the cord. She didn't even have time to scream as she crashed into the water, instantly dragged under and swept right toward me.

I grabbed her with both hands, hauled her into the air, and promptly discovered that the second rope was knotted around her waist. The gods of quick wits did not desert me. Dumping her unceremoniously on the rocks at my feet, spluttering and coughing, I yanked my knife from its sheath and sawed madly through the rope. I did not look at the oncoming roof, for I could not afford the distraction.

Girl tried to hold onto me. "Let go! Let go of me, let go of the rope!" I barked at her, and my knife bit through the last fibers. I had no time to sheathe the blade. I clamped it between my teeth and yanked the cord out of poor Girl's hands to tie it around the larger rope. "Out of the way." The knife distorted my words, but an ungentle shove got her moving. I ran back the way I had come, to where the remains of my cord still dangled from the grapnel lodged higher up in the rocks. Leaping as high as I could, I caught hold and half pulled, half ran up the rocks. Throwing myself over the top edge of the ridge, I rolled and sat up, hauling my cord—and the attached rope—up after me.

The broken roof crashed against the rocks, crunching and grinding, grabbing at the rope, dragging relentlessly. I put all my strength into pulling harder. It freed suddenly, and I fell over backward. Unbridled cheering floated across the waves. I would have cheered, too, but my work was not yet done. Hoping I wouldn't snap my blade against a rock, I jammed my knife into a patch of dirt. When it held, I wrapped the cord around the hilt to secure the rope, then made my way back to the edge to look over the side.

Girl sat below, out of the water, her head in her hands, visibly shaking.

"Girl?" I called out, drawing her attention. "You all right?" She nodded, and I grinned. "We did it."

She pointed up at me, brows knit.

"I'm fine. Can you make it up that way?" I pointed back upriver, where I needed to go tie off the second rope properly. At another nod, I went to it and my gear, then jogged toward the trees again. I chose one standing a good twenty feet from the first to help balance the load, waved at those still aboard the *River Star* to signal success, then picked my way to dry ground. The sides of my mouth hurt where my knife had nicked them, and I explored the damage with my tongue. It stung, but so did numerous scratches on my face and wrists.

Girl met me, running the last few yards. She stopped just short, dismay in her eyes. Her trembling fingertips touched her lips and she looked like she might burst into tears again. "Don't cry," I ordered gruffly, and instead she reached out to touch my mouth, then my cheeks and one eyebrow. Her fingers came away bloody. She pressed her lips together, gave a noisy sniffle, then threw her arms around me to hug me tight.

With two ropes to hold the vessel steady, the men on board made quick work of fastening a third, lowering a small boat over the side to ferry the crew back and forth to the shore. They rigged up a pulley system, cut the *River Star* free of the snag, then dragged her to the edge of the river where they proceeded to unload her. Our animals came first, and I had a serious fright when I realized that the dragon had been left unguarded. Tanris brought the canvas-wrapped crate off with some of our other things, thumped it unceremoniously on the ground, then stalked off again. While he fetched the remainder of our gear, Girl and I proceeded to set up a camp and attempt to dry out. Again.

Within the confines of a makeshift tent, I unwrapped the dragon and found him curled up in the corner of his crate, wide-eyed, shivering and utterly miserable. In pathetic relief, he climbed right up the wooden walls and anchored himself with his claws in my clothes. "Ow ow ow..." I complained, and he licked me. "No, don't do that! That's disgusting!"

Trying to peel a clinging, licking baby dragon off oneself is more difficult than it sounds, and Tanris didn't help matters by standing in the doorway, managing to smirk and look disgruntled at the same time.

"You could help me out here, you know."

He stepped inside, tweaking the tent flap closed behind him. "The boat's ruined," he said without preamble, taking a seat on an upturned cask.

"Oh, what a surprise. More riding." Freeing one set of claws from my coat had no real effect; there were still three more. The daft creature even tried to wind its clumsy wings about me, creaking softly and licking everything it could reach. His happiness confounded me, but then, I'd be really relieved to escape drowning and be freed from a dark box, too. I gave the beastie a little pat of reassurance and tried to pry him off again. "Have I expressed yet how utterly weary I am of riding?"

When Tanris didn't answer, I had to look up at him. He wore a very strange expression, and more emotion than I could decipher clouded his aura.

He shook his head. "No, you haven't. Not in so many words."

"That bothers you?"

One finger rubbed his eyebrow, and his mouth curled in a grimace. "No, I suppose not."

Ridiculous if it did. "Then what's the trouble? Do you want me to complain? I can complain. I can do a fantastic job of complaining. I can complain day and night until we stuff Duzayan's smug face down his throat, and then I can complain a little more. Will that make you happy?"

Some of the confusion faded and disgust snuck in. I could see it in his eyes, feel it in the air surrounding him. "You make it really hard to offer a compliment."

To say I was surprised would have been an understatement.

Tanris slipped out the tent door. "I'll go see if I can rustle up some food."

"Wait," I called after him. "You were going to offer a compliment?"

"You'll never know, will you?"

— 28 —
Aplomb Restored

We spent the night in modest comfort. That is to say that it didn't rain, we weren't wet, and the temperature was almost bearable. Lying with the dragon curled up against one side of me, Girl against the other, and Tanris beside her, I felt almost warm. I didn't sleep particularly well, even so. When I finally had a bed to myself (and no life-threatening injuries), would I be able to sleep at all? I spent the better portion of the night considering how we might travel through the city with a real, live dragon, and how to get the antidote from the wizard before I killed him. I was plagued, too, by the puzzle of how I would safely accomplish his murder. The Voices finally lulled me to sleep, and I had unsettling dreams of a doorway glowing with an unnatural purple light through which paraded a host of shadows.

The morning's view of the river was disheartening. Swollen and turbulent, flotsam from further upstream congested its width. One of the sailors suggested that the dam above Irfan had broken, and it seemed entirely possible. It would be days before boats plied the river. I contemplated what bowleggedness would do to my career and went to have a little chat with the captain.

As I'd known he would, Tanris had our gear all sorted out, loaded and ready to go when I returned to our campsite. Silently, I tossed a purse at him and went to mount Horse.

"What's this?"

"Partial refund of our passage." The saddle creaked, and behind the saddle, under his cover of canvas, the dragon creaked too.

"And you're giving it to me?"

I knew how he fretted about expenses. Call my action payback for the compliment he didn't quite give me. Call it a preemptive strike against a future insult. Call it a generous turn on my part, it matters not to me. "Unless you don't want it?"

He looked hard at me for a moment. Trying, no doubt, to figure out what sort of trick I had up my sleeve now. Then he stuffed the purse into his shirt and swung up onto his horse. He led the way out of the camp leading Too, and Girl rode beside me, smiling like she knew a secret. I refused to be driven to distraction. One day's travel by boat we had before us. I didn't want to consider how much longer it would take us to make the trip by horse, but watched the debris swiftly passing us by as we rode alongside the river.

The countryside continued to grow prettier, less harsh and less wet. Three days on a river swelling with spring rains and winter melt had carried us quickly to warmer climes, and I tried to dredge up some appreciation for it. Look how much faster it had been than our journey into the wilderness! I was haunted, though, by the likelihood that this would be my last Spring, and I wouldn't even get to see it in full bloom. I wasn't going to get to dance with pretty girls during the harvest celebrations, nor go sailing in the strait. There would be no more basking in the sun on Pelippa's pretty beaches. No Tarsha. I had planned to marry her, to have a family with her, but she had ruined everything.

I did not blame Tanris for purchasing her loyalty. I did not blame Duzayan for turning her against me. If she had truly loved me, she would have turned them both away, but she had lied and lied—and now my pretty dreams lay in broken fragments beneath the carelessness of her greed. It made my stomach turn, and every time it did I wondered again if today would be the last day of my life. I *must* have the time to exact vengeance on her and on Duzayan. I certainly wouldn't have the time to write my life story, though by all the gods it was going to have a spectacular ending.

"You look glum."

I hadn't even noticed Tanris watching me. "So?"

"Thinking about Duzayan?"

"Mmm."

"How are we going to get rid of him?"

It probably indicated something profound that he was leaving the entire plan up to me. "I don't know."

He rode in silence for a little. "You killed two wizards and survived how many magic attacks? And between us, we killed a dragon."

I wanted to cover Not-An-Egg's ears, but he slept peacefully across my lap, the sun gleaming on his greenish hide. He didn't even twitch. "You and Girl did that. I just made a nice distraction."

"You're good with those."

I snorted. "I don't think distracting Duzayan to death will work."

"It might," he said, dubious.

It came to me that he'd just offered an actual compliment. "Thank you."

"What?"

I refused to explain myself. Oaf. "How is distracting him going to kill him? Never mind, that's a stupid question. The only way he's going to be killed is if he's distracted, but what can we distract him *with?*"

"A dragon?"

"You are going to use a baby as bait?" Incredible. He was worse than an oaf. "Even I wouldn't sink that low."

He had that stare of his again. "It's a *dragon*. You know, carnivorous? Big? Dangerous?"

"He's not big."

"Yet. He will be. Can you imagine keeping a dragon? They're not exactly well known for their friendliness, never mind feeding the thing. They're hunters, predators, Crow. They're magic, and you hate magic. And big. Did I mention big? They eat little birds for snacks."

"You don't—

He interrupted me with an expressive wave of his hand. "And do you know they're valuable for their parts?"

"Parts?" I echoed, and my stomach turned yet again at the vision of little Egg chopped into pieces for his parts. It didn't take a lot in the way of instigation to upset my stomach. "Who would do that?"

"Wizards, bonehead. Wizards use their valuable and rare parts for their infernal spells." The flailing arm directed a cuff to my ear that nearly knocked me off Horse.

A sudden wind leaped into existence, swirling and nipping and noisy with indignant Voices. *Hit him, he did! How dare he? No right! Is he kindred? Cannot be! Who is he? Kill him? Maim him?*

Death might be a little extreme, but I was not averse to the idea of Tanris suffering for a moment or twenty for threatening Not-An-Egg and for clouting me upside the head, so I did not leap to his defense.

"Crow!" Tanris shouted, putting his arm over his eyes to protect them from grit and bits of vegetation.

He could not see that the wind didn't affect me, though it made Horse run a few steps ahead. Not-An-Egg lifted his head to creak his alarm. One set of talons curled into my leg and another went into the saddle. Good thing nothing went into Horse. Behind us, Girl's mount stopped dead, and Too pulled on his lead, trying to turn away from the sudden dust storm. Tanris's horse tried to run, too, but the packhorse pulled in the opposite direction.

"I had no idea you were so afraid of a little wind," I said in perfect innocence. Very protective of me, these spirits, though a bit unpredictable. The wind they could stir up was certainly startling, but they'd have to whip up a veritable gale to be truly dangerous. What an intriguing idea. Surely I could figure out a way to use that to my advantage when it came time to meet Duzayan. I would have to—

"Make it stop!"

"You want me to stop the wind?" I asked incredulously, brows lifted. I did feel sorry for his horse. His attempt to turn in frantic circles played havoc with the lead.

"I saw what you did in Irfan," Tanris snarled, ducking his head low and squinting against the buffeting while he tried to pull Too close. "I'm not stupid."

No, I would never call him that. I debated letting the torment continue for a bit, but it distressed Girl, and Too carried supplies we needed. No sense wasting that or losing them. The Voices had obeyed me before. "Stop," I whispered, and the little storm around Tanris gradually died. It gave me a crazy sense of power that lasted a whole thirty seconds, and then Tanris gave me a look that, were I a lesser man, might have deprived me of my hide. It gave a whole new meaning to the word "withering."

"Bet that's galling." Roughly, he scrubbed his face.

"Beg your pardon?"

His smile was thin and woefully unattractive. "You. A wizard."

"I am not!"

"What do you call someone who wields magic?"

"I didn't do anything!" I protested. In truth, I had not! Surely saying "stop" didn't constitute the use of magic.

He growled at me. Growled! A steady hand on his horse's neck calmed the beast, and Girl moved up warily to help with Too. "All right, then," he demanded in a none-too-friendly voice, "explain to me how a wind just happened to spring up when I smacked you, and how the same sort of thing happened to those boys in Irfan. And then explain to me how you get some random notion that someone's close, and someone really is? And how about telling me how you knew about the old fortune teller's cottage? And while you're at it, you can clear up how you were so sick you were dying until you came over all green and miraculously recovered. And wizards, Crow? How *does* a mere mortal thief go up against flamin' wizards and survive?"

Up and up his voice went, and I could only stare at him in growing horror. Some little memory from my past reminded me that I could not let him see the affect his words had on me, but I struggled to maintain something even vaguely resembling a calm façade. "You have—"

"Tell me this, Bird, and I want the truth: Why in the name of all the gods did you let Duzayan get the better of you? Did you? Or are you just another lying, two-faced—"

"NO!" I could interrupt him as well as he could interrupt me! All around me the Voices shrieked and shivered and gusted all over again, only it pulled at me, too, flapping the brim of my hat, twisting my collar, and even fluttering Not-An-Egg's wings. Afraid, he tried to crawl into my coat, which was awkward as well as painful. One wing slapped me across the face and stuck there. Horse bucked a little and trotted off down the path, scaring the spit right out of my mouth. I held onto the saddle with both hands, completely blind.

"Crow!" Tanris roared. "You idiot! Stop it before something really stupid happens!"

I could sense him and Girl coming up behind me along with their nervous horses.

"I can't just—" But it really had worked before, so why shouldn't it work now? "Stop! Stop!" I cried out. It didn't. "Are you listening to me?! Stop it!"

Frightened! Angry! Threatened!

"Yes, I'm angry, but—Stop. Just stop, will you? You're not helping anything!" With one hand I tried to uncover my eyes and with the other I searched for the reins I'd dropped. "Whoa, Horse! Whoa!" She refused to stop, but at least she wasn't running, and the wind died away abruptly. "Tanris, help me get Egg off my face!"

"You have so got to be joking."

Must keep our Friend safe! Safe! Cannot lose him!

"I am fine! Fine, do you hear? Except I can't see, and Egg's digging his claws into my head!" It hurt. A lot.

Then Horse stopped moving and someone touched my arm. When Not-An-Egg's wing was pried from my eyes I saw Girl, which came as no real surprise. Her face was pinched, which was also no surprise. She put one finger to her lips, then proceeded to gently stroke Not-An-Egg's back, soothing him the way she soothed the horses, and she was pretty good at it, too. Before long the dragon let go of my hair and settled on the front of the saddle. Tanris said some very unkind things about him as he dabbed at trickles of blood on my ear and neck. I pushed him away.

"You're bleeding."

Warmth ran down my scalp and the cuts stung. "No kidding. I just had dragon talons stuck in my head. And my leg, too, don't forget that."

"Which you wouldn't have if you ever listened to me." He reached toward me with his crimson-stained cloth again and Girl slapped his hand away. Glowering fiercely, she stabbed her forefinger toward Too, then made an unmistakable shooing motion.

"You're not taking his side," Tanris declared.

Girl's eyes narrowed. I should have felt some sort of victory, but it gave way before confusion and fear. The new holes in my skin were fairly distracting though, especially the way they kept leaking. Thank the gods of vanity none of those claws had touched my face. The last thing someone in my profession needed was wildly identifying scars.

While Tanris dealt with the horses, Girl made me get down so she could clean my wounds. She sat me down on a rock and Not-An-Egg crawled into my lap, looking up at me with the most woebegone expression imaginable. The Voices whispered and murmured, upset. Little bursts of wind continued to blow.

Tanris came to watch the painful process of Girl sewing my skin back together. She cared about me, which is more than I can say about Tanris, and had brought me a wineskin, which I partook of generously. "I am not a wizard," I declared sullenly, emphasizing with a shake of the skin.

Girl pushed my arm down and shook her finger in front of my nose.

"What do you call it, then?"

"An infection. A possession. I am not a wizard."

"But you do magical things."

"I am a victim here, Tanris. I didn't ask for this, I don't want it." Magic was wrecking my life—a life shaping up to be unfairly and dramatically short.

He fell quiet, and I could almost hear him thinking. Disgruntlement and suspicion oozed off him, and although that was probably a very reasonable thing for him to be feeling, I resented it. I am Crow. Just Crow. I did not like him accusing me of being a filthy wizard.

"It could be useful."

"Aye?" I asked, my tone biting. "How?"

"You did alert me to Girl coming up on us, and even Kem. You knew about the cottage. Maybe you know some other things, too."

I knew I had developed a walloping headache. I took another drink of the wine and Girl waited patiently, then resumed her stitching.

Tanris folded his arms over his chest. "Maybe you can talk to that dragon of yours."

"He's not mine."

"Right."

Not-An-Egg tenderly licked my chin and creaked.

"What am I supposed to say to him?" I asked, pushing him away.

"Maybe he knows how to defeat Duzayan."

I stared at him, nonplussed. "Even if I did speak dragon, he's a baby," I pointed out.

"Yes, a magical baby. Maybe you can enlist his help. Get him to work with us to defeat the man who plans to use his guts for magical garters."

Tanris could be so bloody-minded.

"What about your ghosts?" he went on. "Can they help?"

"They make wind." I hesitated. They'd also discovered the way out of the mountain, directed me to the amulet I now wore, verified for me the deaths of Melly and his cohort, and attacked people they anticipated might hurt me.

Girl giggled.

I had no idea why. "Do you remember how Kem told us the Ancestors caused us to argue? That different people had different experiences in the caves?"

"You heard humming when there was none." Tanris nodded slowly.

What good ghostly humming might do against Duzayan completely escaped me. "If these are the same Ancestors…"

"They could do the same things," he nodded again, and his eyes gleamed with a light I didn't really like. "They could haunt people and stir up all kinds of trouble. We could use that to our advantage."

Silly me, I worried about technical details. "Only if I can control them somehow."

"Can't you? Didn't you set them on those boys back in town?"

"Nooo…" I said, wondering if I actually had. Inadvertently, to be sure, but I had been wishing the pests gone. Wouldn't it be lovely if I could wish Duzayan gone and *poof!* the Ancestors would whisk him away, never to be seen or heard from again? Maybe they could make a really strong wind and carry him off to drop him down the same chasm his peers had fallen into.

"You did," Tanris contradicted as though he could read my mind. "I'd bet coin that you did, whether you meant to or not. And if you did it accidentally, you might be able to do more if you tried."

Me using magic? What was the world coming to? On the other hand, what could be better for defeating a mage than magic?

Cunning wizards. Slippery like fish. Say one thing, mean another.

Could they hear my thoughts? "Not me."

"Not you what?"

Had I said that out loud? I hid my surprise, refusing to give him any sort of advantage. "I didn't try, but I will." Of course I would. I am a Crow, and a Crow is a very cunning bird. We use whatever tool is at hand to achieve what we desire. I could not overlook the fact that the gods had blessed me with talent and wits, and they had been with me at every turn of my life— minus the stay in Duzayan's dungeons, and I can only assume they meant me to learn something by it—and in spite of the fact that the magic infecting me felt like an intrusion, it might in fact be a blessing. Strange, but a blessing nonetheless, and I was not one to refuse gifts from the gods.

"What's going through that head of yours?"

I blinked at Tanris. "The gods love me."

Predictably, his eyes narrowed in suspicion. "Does this mean you're going to give away more of our coin?"

"What a good idea!" I exclaimed, gathering Not-An-Egg to my breast and getting to my feet. Girl jumped up out of the way, looking at me worriedly. Nothing new there. "It has been too long since I've had the opportunity to show them proper gratitude. We can't afford to have them thinking we're unappreciative."

"Appreciate them with something other than the last of our coin. We need it to get back to Marketh."

"You have no faith. The gods will sustain us." Confidence filled me in a rush of familiar warmth. It was the first time in months that I'd felt it so strongly and it gave me a burst of exhilarating hope.

"What about your potion? Have you got enough left to last?"

I beamed at him, then made my way to Horse's side. "I no longer need it." And if I had doubted a moment ago, certainty filled me now.

"What? How?"

Changing my mind in mid-stride, I went back to Girl and kissed her cheek. "Thank you, Girl. I feel better already."

In my arms, Not-An-Egg lifted his head and creaked. Girl just looked surprised, then turned a lovely shade of crimson.

"Crow." Tanris was glaring at me again. He should have been pleased that I wasn't keeling over and leaving him to defeat the evil wizard all on his own.

"I wonder if Girl could shoot Duzayan in the mouth while we distract him." Not-An-Egg had learned all about horses and saddles. When I set him atop mine, he clung to the front, wings outstretched while I put my foot to the stirrup and swung aboard. Isn't it funny how one can be aboard a ship or a horse, and they are nothing at all alike?

"Crow," Tanris repeated, a warning note in his voice. "What do you mean, you don't need the medicine?"

"I haven't used it since I woke up sick in the barn." That, too, filled me with a sense of exultation. How long had it been? Five days? Six? And I was not getting worse as Duzayan had predicted. "Won't the Baron be surprised?"

"You just stopped taking it?"

"Yes."

"Why?"

"I couldn't keep it down any more than I could keep real food down. Besides, it tasted terrible and I didn't need it anymore."

He flexed his fingers and the Ancestors rustled apprehensively. "That's it." His voice didn't raise like it ought if he were posing a question.

"Truthfully? I don't know. The magic from the cave was green, and I turned green when Melly and his friend attacked me. I think what they did triggered something about the Ancestor's magic, which made me turn green all over again." I paused to reflect on the poetry. "Literally and magically. And then there was the dragon. The big one."

He growled. "You could have died, you flaming idiot!"

"I'm deeply touched that you care so much. I had no idea." Hand to breast, I sucked in a breath of bracing air and let it out in a dramatic sigh, my aplomb restored. The world was a bright and wonderful place, and the gods truly did love me. Gathering up the reins, I turned Horse downriver. "You should know by now, Friend Tanris, that I have no intention of dying just yet. Even if I didn't have some pressing unfinished business, there are things I still want to do, places to see, people to meet, coin and pretty baubles to liberate..."

"You could have died," he repeated, angrily stabbing the air. Incredulity accompanied every movement.

"But I didn't, did I?" I turned in my saddle as Horse walked on. Baron Duzayan's rules had declared I would die without the stuff, but his poison was bound to me by magic. Whoever, *whatever* the Ancestors were, they had purged me of it, and Tanris—dear, dear Tanris—had reminded me who I was. "Aren't you glad? I would kiss you, but you'd likely hit me again."

"From here all the way back to Hasiq jum'a Sahefal," he said with startling fervor.

It made me laugh.

— 29 —
First Things First

"Are you listening?" I whispered. I felt silly. Tanris and Girl slept, I'd made sure, and I'd crept far enough away from camp that I wouldn't disturb them. The sky was a blanket of deep velvet sprinkled with lovely stars. I loved stars. It had been far too long since I'd had a regular view of them, but admiring them was not what I'd come here to do. "Hello?"

Nothing. Did ghosts sleep?

"Hello!" I said a little bit louder. "Um... Friends? Ancestors?"

Still nothing. That was a fine thing. Now what was I to do? Did it take a particular set of circumstances for them to hear me? I distinctly remembered them associating my ability to hear them with the pendant they'd made me rescue. Drawing it out from beneath my clothing, I examined it in the starlight. Shadows hid the etching. The spirits had called it a portal. A doorway. A doorway to what? Some sort of afterlife? A parallel world? My head ached with the swell of too many possibilities and with the knowledge that such things were too far-fetched to be real.

"Do I have to be in danger to get your attention?" I asked.

Still nothing. The only lives I could discern were those of my companions and the horses and the dragon. I chewed on my lip while I tried to recall the things the spirits had said to me during the course of our brief acquaintance. A confusing lot they were, and I wish they'd communicate things more clearly.

"I am Crow," I announced to the darkness, feeling more foolish and more helpless by the minute. "I am kin to Kalinamsin!" I had no idea if I really was or how that might be true, but that was the name the spirits had spoken and they had alluded to such a possibility.

A little zephyr ran up my back and tangled my hair. I jumped in spite of myself. "Hello?"

Crow... Crow! Friend Crow!

"Yes," I said, vastly relieved. "Where have you been?"

Here. Always near. We angered you. We displeased you! Wanted only to defend you. Keep you safe, keep you near.

"Always?" I suppressed a shiver.

Always. Always. Always...

Gods protect me—or did they? The gods work in mysterious ways, I knew, but it would certainly be nice if they'd just tell a person what they were up to, or possibly send them a letter now and then. Devout as I was, surely I'd earned such consideration?

"Who are you?"

There came the slightest pause and a sense of amazement, then they all spoke at once. *Keshava. Brystani. Xuchai. Cimara. Darinan. Mesuk. Galen.*

It took a moment to realize the gibberish was actually their names. Ghosts had names? I supposed they must, for they'd had names when they'd lived and while I was certainly no expert on the afterlife, there was no logical reason why they shouldn't still have them after they'd passed. "That's not what I mean." I waved my hands in the air as though that might stop them. Much to my astonishment, it did. Anxious, unseen fingers tugged here and there at my clothing. It made me shiver. "What," I asked, choosing my words cautiously, "beings are you? Are you... people?"

People. Yes. Once. People like you.

"What are you now?" I asked, not sure I really wanted to know.

Guardians. Protectors. Advisors.

I tried to imagine explaining to my associates how I talked to spiritual guardians. I found it a little disconcerting that they rarely spoke in sentences, and their words continually overlapped. It made them difficult to comprehend, particularly when the entire group got going.

"How many of you are there?"

Some. Several. Many. A few.

They weren't presenting a very convincing argument for their collective sanity, but I didn't quite dare contradict them. Schooling myself to calm, I explored the backs of my teeth with my tongue and wondered just what the gods in their infinite wisdom and mercy had got me into.

"Who," I started, and my voice trembled unexpectedly. "Who am I?"

Ours. Kin. Dear. Son of sons. Friend.

An unexpected lump formed in my throat. "Are you saying that Kalinamsin is—was—a relative? A grandfather?"

Grandfather! they exclaimed jubilantly.

I had a grandfather? Silly question, of course I had a grandfather. I had to come from somewhere. "And Kalinamsin was—" What were the names of the tribes Kem had told us about? "He was of what tribe?"

Mazhar. We are Mazhar. You are Mazhar. Ours. Son of sons. Friend.

They kept using the word "friend" as if it had significant meaning. "What does it mean to be a friend? *The* Friend?"

All of the little winds rushed at me and *into* me at once, prickling and eager and completely overwhelming. And by "overwhelming" I do not merely mean "amazing" or "spectacular." I mean I was completely taken over to the extent that the physical world in which my body resided was lost to me. Images flashed through my mind, and a deafening roar in my ears eventually became words and sounds. The first few images were familiar scenes of domestic life in the mountains—hunting, working the land, exploring, creating tools and artwork. It was the very existence of an entire people encapsulated in heartbeats. Those images were swept away by a struggle to survive starvation, drought, monumental battles. There were layers and layers of history, learning, nuance—and then the caves in which hundreds, perhaps thousands, of people had died. *My people...*

So very many, but not all. No, not all. Three groups of them had formed a protective magic—a magic to preserve and to defend—and these became the Guardians, dedicating themselves to the protection of those few who survived. Some of the Mazhar escaped the Ghost Walk, though I did not understand how, and some of the Mazhar had never entered that terrible place. Among those survivors were a few chosen receptacles, men and women with whom the Guardians could communicate in order to protect both the people themselves and their great heritage. Something about the magic changed those chosen, and that change was passed down from generation to generation.

It had been passed down to me.

Gradually, I became aware again of the glitter of stars in the night sky, the ground beneath me. In the wake of such a powerful event, the world seemed a strange place. My entire life had changed in a matter of minutes or perhaps hours. I did not know how much time had passed.

Is he dead? Is he hurt?

"I'm not dead yet, though you might have warned me," I complained. The vision—was it really true? If so, what did it mean and how would it affect me from this point forward? I did not especially want to be a Receptacle that had regular chats with long ago people, relatives or not.

Not dead! He lives! He breathes! He knows! The Ancestors were utterly jubilant. I just had a headache. Perhaps my head had found a rock in its precipitous descent to the ground. Sitting up slowly, I rubbed the back of my head, reassured to find no sticky, warm evidence of damage.

Do you see? Do you know? they inquired, happy and excited.

"It's a lot to take in." The ground was as hard as memory said ground ought to be, and my body ached as though I'd been struck by lightning. Not that I've ever actually *been* struck by lightning, but I have heard stories and I possess a marvelous imagination. Look what it has got me. I desperately wanted to lie back down again, but it would probably be better to make my way back to the camp and thus avoid upsetting Tanris and Girl, who would be full of questions I could not answer without them further doubting my sanity, particularly if they found me gone in the morning and had to go looking for me, only to find me sleeping in a ditch somewhere.

Tanris! I had very nearly forgotten what I had set out to ask the Ancestors! "So." I rubbed my abused noggin and licked dry lips. My mouth tasted curiously, unpleasantly of sulphur. "If you are here to guide and advise, can you help me?"

We will advise… share… aid… reunite… A sense of eagerness filled the air.

"Can you find someone? Can you find Tanris's wife, Aehana?"

Who? Who? Who? asked my flock of invisible owls.

"Tanris. My traveling companion. The man with the dark hair and the perpetual frown."

Tanris Grimfist! Wicked! Hurt Friend Crow! Not one of us. Cannot see! Cannot hear! In no time at all their voices pitched into a jumble of papery whispers.

"Quiet!" Much to my surprise, the Voices fell immediately silent, eagerness replaced by a sense of skin-prickling apprehension. I rubbed my arms in an attempt to dismiss it, and the pendant bumped against my chest. A hiss brushed against one cheek. "Can you find his wife?" I asked as gently as I could manage, profoundly glad no one else lurked about to watch me talking to the air. *See the crazy man? He talks to himself, but he's mostly harmless.*

There came a rustling and a murmuring as they consulted among themselves. *Tanris wife? Who? Where? … do not know of her… do not know of him. Who is he? Grimfist! Why? More, tell us more.*

"She is Tanris's wife." Nothing like restating the obvious. What had she looked like? "From the city of Marketh. An average-looking woman." Very average. Average height, average looks (what I could recall of them through tears and bruises).

Average, average… the voices whispered back in some confusion, and I could not blame them. *Whose daughter? Whose claim?*

"The wizard hurt her!" I cried. "She was there in his house. I saw her!"

Show us! Who? A wizard? Black wizard! Stay away! Danger!

"You are not helping!" I had no idea how to show them things I held in my own head, but after what they'd done to me, I thought it might be possible. "Go to Marketh. Wait." I didn't want all of them taking off at once. "Some of you go to Marketh. Find the house of the wizard, Duzayan. Can he hurt you?"

Hurt us! Wizard!

In typical fashion their answer neither affirmed or negated. "You can sneak in, can't you? If I can't see you, then he can't hurt you, right?"

Sneak! Stealthy and sly we can be! Furtive. Quiet.

"Yes, good. You can sneak quietly. Search all through his house and—

and use your talents to find her. Get the servants to talk. You can do that, can't you? Make them see things and feel things?"

Visions. Tales. Stories! Sing to them, we will. Persuade them… Beguile them…

I shivered. "Find Aehana, Tanris's wife."

Tanris wife… wife… wife…

Something touched my leg and I nearly leaped out of my skin. I whirled about, knife in one hand and the talisman clutched in the other. The sudden motion made my head reel and pound. "Who's there?" I challenged. My heart beat so loudly it drowned out everything else.

A creak encouraged me to look down, where slitted eyes of gold looked up at me. Not-An-Egg voiced an uncertain greeting, gently flapping his wings.

I nearly collapsed in relief. "Don't do that!" I reprimanded severely, pointing my knife at him in warning. "Don't ever, ever, ever sneak up on me again, do you hear me?"

Were those tears welling in his eyes? Unbelievable. Head and wings drooped and a dismal fog of misery surrounded him.

"Don't do that, either," I said gruffly, sheathing my knife and dropping down to one knee to rub his knobby little head.

"Crow? Is everything all right?" Tanris's voice made me jump again.

"Fine." I offered his dark bulk a fake, reassuring smile hidden by the dim light, which was just as well.

"What are you doing?"

"Bringing Not-An-Egg back to camp." Gathering the little dragon up in my arms, I proceeded to do exactly that.

"What was he doing out here? Are you going to keep calling him that?"

I ignored the first question in favor of the second. "Why not? He's not an egg, is he?"

"It's a stupid name."

"You're one to talk."

"What's wrong with my name?" he asked indignantly.

"Do you know the Corunni tongue?" I asked, naming a country along the coastline, north of the empire.

"No." He told the truth, edged with the usual sense of doubt and distrust.

"In Corunn, your name means flatulence." It was true. I would not lie about such a thing, no matter how tempting. Except under special circumstances.

"It does not."

"Ha."

:-:

Soaking in the view of the city, I took a sip of my delightful, civilized Taharri Red wine in its beautiful, sophisticated crystal goblet. It was good to be home. I could not remember Marketh ever looking so beautiful. The afternoon sun shone sweetly, new leaves on the trees gleamed green as they reached for the sky, the first flowers bloomed, and marvelous life filled the streets. There was so much to absorb, so much to appreciate. Such was the contrast to what I'd suffered that I could not help feeling philosophical, feeling hopeful.

I had brought Tanris and Girl to the apartment I kept in the Sunhar District, a very nice place with a lovely view of the palace. I would regret having to let it go, but now that they knew of it the move was inevitable. We'd reached the capital in the middle of the night, hungry and tired but blessedly not cold or wet—for which I deeply thanked the gods—and none of us had been in the mood to expend another hour looking for someplace to stay the night. Apartments rate among the disposable things of life. We had wanted little more than to clean up and rest (in real beds!) after our ordeal. In another life I would have stayed in bed until at least noon, but the rigors of the road had imbedded new habits, and necessity compelled action. The day after our return, and most of the next, had been spent gathering information and filling in details. Tanris, forced to wait on my decisions, chafed.

"Do we know what day it is?" I asked.

"Three days past your expiration date." He could have said *Three days past when we were due to report*, but Tanris was out of sorts, and with good reason. He'd grown more tense with every day we neared the city and, now that we'd at last arrived, every delay keeping him from his wife frustrated him further. Arms folded, face set in a firm glower, he stood on the balcony next to me and stewed.

Remembering his wife, I remembered lovely, lying Tarsha. The two of them with their teary countenances always appeared in my imagination together, for I only met Aehana once—if the term "meet" can be stretched to describe our brief encounter.

"Are you ready yet?" he asked.

"Nearly so."

"It's been two days already, not to mention the entire four months before that." He looked much more like his old self now, clean and with head and chin shaved. I could not imagine deliberately choosing bald-headedness, but it was a good look for him. It gave him a forthright and uncompromising appearance without giving away his semi-noble streak.

"More than half that time was spent trying to figure out what we were actually looking for and how to acquire it, surviving weather, bandits, bad luck and—and so on. And for a considerable time afterward I was not in my right mind," I said with some asperity. Magic did that; it robbed one of his senses. Clearly the reason wizards were known for their dementia.

"You never had a right mind," he shot back.

Unkind! "I agreed to help save your wife." If she still lived, which had yet to be established. "Is this the way you're going to treat me?"

His hands curled tight. "I saved your life!"

"My *life* wouldn't have turned out this way if not for you." I had him there and he knew it. "Why, if not for you, Grimfist, I—"

Girl—who cleaned up quite nicely, though I found her too thin and too straight up and down for my tastes—appeared out of nowhere and gently pressed a hand over my mouth. I immediately pulled it away to protest both her treatment and Tanris's unappreciative attitude, but she gave me a quelling look. She'd been practicing it for weeks.

"Ha," Tanris said, promptly earning a quelling look of his own. He responded with an unexpectedly sheepish expression, and I merely pursed my mouth and waited for Girl to go on. At least she wouldn't raise her shrewish voice at us as was typical among women who believed, without knowing or understanding all the facts, that men were misbehaving.

Lightly, Girl wrapped her fingers around mine and tugged me to my feet to drag me over to Tanris. It was not a far distance on the modestly sized balcony. She held her other hand out to him expectantly, and had to cuff his chest to get him to comply. He did so gracelessly, and she put my hand in his and pumped them up and down. It was rather like shaking hands with a sack for all the effort he put into it. Girl rolled her eyes and promptly took my goblet for a drink, then she made a waving motion.

What did that mean?

Flexing her arm, she gestured to her bicep with her—my!—drink. Aha. Time to get to work.

Tanris yanked his hand to safety, folding his arms again. I looked from one to the other, then out at the view of the palace. Contemplating new living quarters did not protect me from the attentive and pointed regard of my companions. Girl—well, she was just Girl, and although occasionally surprising and therefore sometimes interesting, she and I did not share the same length or depth of connection as did Tanris and myself. In spite of the stinging banter in which he and I often engaged, things between us had changed radically in the months we'd spent together, and it could be no better evidenced than in the fact that he was counting on me now. I could not ignore, either, the fact that I did not feel entirely unwilling to continue with him as a partner. In this one thing we had a common goal, and nothing would turn us aside. However, while Tanris wanted to rescue his woman, I wanted to exterminate mine. And Duzayan, of course. Hidden from them by my body, my hands tightened violently on the balcony railing. What I wouldn't give to have them wound around Tarsha's pretty neck.

"Crow." Tanris wrenched me back to the present.

"I do not know where Aehana is."

Brief silence met my announcement, and then Tanris joined me at the rail. I eased my grip lest he notice and make injudicious assumptions.

"Have you asked the ghosts?"

A little whisk of wind raced between us, cool and earthy.

"Yes. They cannot find her, Tanris. They don't know enough about her. You could tell them, perhaps it would help."

"Me?" He blinked in surprise.

"She is your wife," I pointed out. "You know her best."

"I can't talk to your ghosts."

Again, the little huff of wind. This time it came with a prickle of vexation.

"They do not like being called ghosts, but you can certainly talk to them. They can hear you quite well, even if you are unaware of them."

His jaw worked, and he turned his gaze toward the shining palace of Emperor Gaziah. "You really believe you're talking to them, don't you?"

I did not blame him for doubting. Claiming one hears voices prompts unavoidable and unkind conclusions the world over. I have made those conclusions myself. The gods, in their humor, find wicked ways to teach us lessons. "Fine, then tell me about her." I folded my arms in mimicry of my companion and turned my back to the view, looking instead at Girl, who had taken my seat and my wine and sat listening attentively.

"Tell you?"

I suppressed a sigh of irritation. "You want her found, yes? Best we do it before dealing with Duzayan lest he choose to do something spiteful. It is up to you, of course. If you do not wish to talk about her, I have some things to attend to."

He didn't answer me. Reluctance and pain emanated from him. It was not a pleasant thing and I had gathered myself to take my leave when he began in a gruff voice. "I met her about three years ago. It was summer..."

— 30 —
An Abundance Of Booty

The Priests of Ishram devote themselves to the care of the sick and injured, and they spend many years studying healing techniques. The tests required to advance within their order are quite strict, and those who do not progress tend to the more basic needs of the patients or to growing the materials used in some of the remedies. Their farms and gardens dot both city and countryside, and they are usually quite beautiful. I have tried to limit the time I spend with the followers of Ishram, as being tended by them generally means I've taken an injury and tending *to* them is unprofitable. They possess little in the way of riches unless one is in the market for herbal collections.

I did not expect to find myself outside the Mapar Hospice and stood across the street for some time, looking at it with loathing and revulsion. Even from that distance I could smell the odor of sick bodies and the strong herbs the priests used as both cleaning agents and to attempt to cover the stench.

"Here?" I asked for the second time, because Mapar Hospice was in a very poor district, and the poor districts notoriously produced more sick and injured than the rest of the city and could be counted on to stink more. The Voices chittered at me in a most unsettling combination of excitement, dread, and curiosity. Imagine, if you will, standing in a crowd of people all whispering at the same time. Some of the voices are stronger than others, and some easier to hear simply because of proximity. So it was with these, and I could only catch bits and pieces of what they said. They searched for someone as yet unknown, both fearing and hoping to find him or her. It was not Achana of whom they spoke, I was fairly certain. They shared remembrances of pain and sorrow, memories of loved ones and hopes for reunion, though the latter seemed an unlikely event to me. Now and then they touched me, reassuring themselves and, strangely, reassuring me. It was an odd sensation like a tiny, cool breeze carrying with it a scent reminiscent of the woods in autumn.

I wondered if I would ever get used to it. I wondered if I would become accustomed to the way my clothing moved on its own accord when they caressed me. The motion was, of course, much more obvious indoors, away from natural breezes. I had caught Tanris looking at me strangely on more than one occasion, even when I wasn't saying things to which he could take exception.

I spent several moments offering prayers and supplications to those deities most appropriate to the occasion. Not only did I want to find Aehana quickly if she was truly in this place, but I did not want to inadvertently contract any of the diseases abounding there, though it crossed my mind to wonder if I might somehow purchase one and use it to infect Duzayan. Finally, mustering my considerable fortitude, I boldly crossed the street and went in through the tall double doors.

The miasma that greeted me nearly knocked me right back out again. Eyes watering, I covered mouth and nose with my crooked arm, for all the good it did me. The stinging of my eyes blurred my vision, but there appeared before me a green-robed priest exuding concern and amusement. To my vast relief, he pressed into my hand a sweetly scented kerchief, though he himself went without. How in the names of the many gods could someone become accustomed to such a horrific odor? Sickness and death oozed through the place and it took some effort to resurrect my aplomb.

I explained that I was in search of a relative, but the astute priest pressed for more information, upon which I fabricated the story that Aehana was my brother's wife. The two of us had returned from a journey, only to find her missing. The more truth one can insert into a false tale, the easier it is to believe. I provided the obliging priest with such particulars as Tanris had imparted to me, giving her name and a detailed description.

Alas, he shook his head and held his hands out in apology; too many patients might fit the bill.

Might I take a look around, just to be certain? I would never forgive myself if she was lost on account of my lack of diligence.

He took a little convincing, but at last I wandered through the wards, looking at groaning, moaning, and occasionally heaving nearly-dead people in hopes I would not actually find Aehana here. Gods protect me from a slow and painful death. People of every age and ethnicity rested upon thin little straw pallets on the floor, covered with thin little blankets that had clearly seen better days. Green robes stood out here and there, gently bathing brows and bodies or offering sustenance from sad little wooden bowls. It was pathetic and awful, and I wanted nothing more than to leave as quickly as possible. I had my own green robe following me, though I could not imagine what he thought I might want to do to these pitiable people.

"Where is Aehana?" I asked the Voices in a whisper muffled behind the kerchief.

Their direct path would have had me walking on the sick and the dying which, aside from raising the immediate ire of both the patients and their green-robed attendants, would certainly have inspired me to lose the contents of my belly. I picked my way around the bodies and the Voices gave me new directions to compensate. Eventually they brought me to a rail-thin woman with lank, unwashed hair that might have been a pale brown when clean. She laid on her side, knees drawn close to her body, hands fisted, eyes tightly closed. Quiet groans wracked her and between bouts of stiff tension she trembled uncontrollably. An awful, unnatural shade of gray tinted her skin.

"Aehana?"

She did not respond, but the Voices assured me that this was indeed the body—er, woman—I sought. Tanris was not going to be happy. As I pondered whether he would be more unhappy if she was never found or if I brought her corpse to him, I saw a fragile chain wrapped around one fist. She held something very tightly and I, curious Crow that I am, wanted to have a look at it.

"Aehana, it's me, Fajhal," I murmured to her, taking her hand in mine. Of course she would not know the name; we hadn't exactly met. "Tanris is looking for you. He is most desperate to find you."

Her eyelids fluttered and she moaned. I could not tell if pain inspired it or my presence.

"What is wrong with her?" I asked the priest, but he shook his head helplessly.

"We do not know. She was left here about a week ago, vomiting but without a fever. We have fed her broth, but she cannot keep it down. When there is nothing in her belly, she suffers terrible cramps. Whatever the sickness, it is affecting her muscles as well."

"How long?" I whispered.

Again, he shook his head. "It is a wonder she is still with us," he murmured softly, respectfully.

Bracing myself, I tucked the kerchief into my shirt and took Aehana's hand in both of mine, talking to her quietly as I massaged her fingers loose. I tried to breathe through my mouth but it didn't help. Thank the gods of loquaciousness, I managed to carry on a fairly convincing, albeit one-sided, conversation with her while I worked the bauble partially free of her death grip.

Seeing the familiar silver vial nearly robbed me of words. It matched exactly the one Duzayan had given me. I kept chatting while I maneuvered the cap off. One whiff confirmed my suspicion. Our vials held the same antidote, though hers was empty. He'd poisoned her.

"Can you—" A fit of coughing interrupted my question, and I had to press the scented cloth over my face until I recovered. Eyes watering, I turned to the priest. "Can you help me get her to a hackney? Let me take her home to her loved ones," I pleaded.

He searched my face intently.

I didn't need to manufacture tears, and wondered about the existence of gods of malady and rot.

Finally, he nodded. Patting my shoulder, he straightened and left to make arrangements. I waited until he was a good dozen or more paces away, then withdrew my own vial from beneath my clothing. A drop of it on her lips made her shudder, and another brought her eyes open.

"Who—?" she croaked in a terrible parody of a voice.

"Hush." I smoothed her hair back from her face. Little more than a skeleton, her skin was so frail it ought to disintegrate beneath my touch. Tanris was really, really not going to be happy. "I am going to take you to your husband."

"More," she rasped.

"Soon," I agreed, and wondered if I was only prolonging her inevitable death. There were drops sufficient only for a week or so, and I was somewhat irked to find myself once again in the position of needing to bargain for the blasted antidote. I could take some small comfort in the fact that at least I wasn't the one dying; at least not in this particularly odious manner. No doubt Duzayan had plenty of other revolting curses up his sleeve.

I had little alternative but to take Aehana back to the apartment with the view. A knock revealed the fact that Tanris and Girl had not yet returned from the errands I'd given them, and I had perforce to set on the floor the knotted up bundle of bones I carried. Reassured by the locked door, I still sent the Ancestors to have a look around and make sure there were no thugs lurking about and no evidence of pesky wizards. Not-An-Egg slept soundly in his box. He did not even twitch when I brought Aehana inside. Clearly he needed a lesson about overconfidence in one's security.

I tucked Aehana into Tanris's bed and then I paced. If the potion only stopped further growth of the poison, was she in fact doomed? Had the stuff already destroyed her body beyond repair? If so, I had surely done her no favor. If Tanris saw her like this he would be completely useless. I may as well go out right now and buy him a barrel of kemesh in which to drown himself, and that would leave me completely on my own to wreak vengeance. I have every confidence in my own talent and wit, and in the fact that I am beloved by the gods, but there are some fates one simply does not tempt. Common sense dictates that one doesn't stand on the roof in a lightning storm, nor jump willy nilly off a cliff, nor aggravate a wizard. Those are stupid things and the gods do not love stupidity.

What had I been thinking to bring her here? I could take her back. No, I would have to take her to another hospice, else rouse suspicion. If my most excellent memory served me well, there was one just to the west a great deal nicer than poverty-stricken Mapar. I even had a little Adamanta Dust in my things still, and could use it to ease her journey to join the Ancestors. Given her condition, it probably wouldn't take much. Rare and costly as it is, I could do no less. It would be a kindness, no?

She would go to sleep, never to awaken again, and perhaps when Duzayan was no longer a problem I could tell Tanris what had befallen her. From a distance. A *long* distance. In fact, I thought I would send him a letter.

I had no sooner stepped out into the corridor again than a key turned in the lock. Curse the luck! I hastened to the entry to greet Tanris, safely tucking the Dust into a pocket. "Did all go well?" I inquired smoothly, going to the sideboard in the parlor to pour myself a drink.

"Well enough," Tanris agreed, following me into the room as I'd hoped he would, Girl trailing behind him with an assortment of baskets and packages. "I got the message and the packet to the commander," he said, referring to the letters from Duzayan's allies we had decided should be turned over to people with armies to command. "I couldn't find that fellow Dambul in the Greenmarket, but you'll never believe who I did see." He had that accusing look about him that suggested I'd deliberately sent him on a fruitless errand, which was not only unkind but untrue. I really did want to find Dambul. He was the merchant most likely to be able to replenish the Adamanta Dust, and I wasn't above throwing an entire bag of the stuff at His Royal Loftiness, the baron.

"Who was it?" I asked, momentarily alarmed when Girl left with her things and made her way down the hall, but she headed into the kitchen and a moment later I heard dishes rattling.

"That red-haired fellow that gave us the exciting send-off when we first left the city." His eyes narrowed even further.

"Who?" I repeated, mustering an expression of ignorant curiosity. Granted, I hadn't practiced it much in the last few months, but I was hopeful that my natural skill hadn't faded.

"Don't even try to play innocent with me, Crow. He followed us for a little while, but I lost him in the Saddlegate."

I did not visit Saddlegate often, but the name swiftly conjured the smell of leather and horse ointments. "I have no—" Tanris had been keeping up his ability with his glare, and he pinned me with it like a dart to a board. "Maybe he's a criminal you've run into before. I hope you haven't dedicated your entire career to catching me."

He snorted his derision, then frowned. Deeply. "Are you all right?"

Had I left some careless bit of evidence lying about? No, how could I have? I had brought home with me nothing but a bag of bones wrapped in my own cloak, which hung on the hook by the door right where it belonged.

"Of course." I quirked a questioning brow. "Are you?"

Coming near, he reached out with one finger and hooked the chain upon which I carried the silver vial, then looked at me searchingly. "You sick?"

"No. No, not at all," I smiled at him, careful to temper the expression with a little curious amusement, all the while mentally kicking myself around the room.

"You're sure?"

"Quite. Are you sure you lost that fellow tailing you?"

"What are you wearing this for?" The predictable dog with a bone.

"I always do," I defended quite truthfully, even though I usually kept it out of sight. Habit or reminder, I knew not. I resisted the urge to tug it away and drop it back down my shirt. The last thing I wanted to do was look suspicious. He didn't need encouragement.

"Hidden."

I nodded and tried an expression of patience.

"So today you decided to display it for all to see." Look at him! Suspicious!

As best I could with him still holding the chain, I struck a pose. "You don't like it?"

"No. Did you use it?"

"No." Also true. Aehana had been the one to use it.

"I can smell the stuff."

"Really? Sorry." I smiled and rescued the chain, tucking it back into my shirt. "There, better?"

"You'd better not lie to me, Crow."

"Would I do that?"

"In a word? Yes."

I rolled my eyes. "You're in a mood. Did you miss a meal or something?"

"No. Get your cloak. It's time for us to go pay a visit to the baron. You've been avoiding it long enough."

"Avoiding? I've done no such thing. I've been planning." Storming a wizard's castle in an attempt to claim something one knows the wizard won't willingly surrender wasn't something a person did on a lark. It took careful scheming and expert timing at which, luckily for Tanris, I was an expert.

"Right." He smiled thinly and turned away, but rather than going to the door, he headed toward his room.

Ack! No! Did he hear the sudden clamor of my heart? "Are we going now, then?"

"Soon as I change my shirt. Just in case Red did manage to follow me, I don't want to make things too easy for him."

"Tanris, wait." What was I going to do? I couldn't very well volunteer to go get a shirt for him, since he was perfectly capable. There was nothing for it. "Duzayan poisoned your wife," I blurted.

Silence. I should be used to this.

"With the same thing he put in me," I added, hating the squeak in my voice.

More silence. It did not escape me that his silence was good for my health. It meant I wasn't in danger of a trouncing. Still, Tanris stared at me as though I had turned into something hideously loathsome.

"Tanris?" I ventured, and mentally calculated the distance to the door and my chances of getting out before he caught me. Perhaps I should attempt the window instead. I could get out the balcony door and up onto the roof in a flash.

"Is she—?"

"Not yet."

He stared at me a moment longer, then turned away, slowly dragging one hand down his ashen face. "Where—" he started, swallowed, then tried again. "Where is she?"

"She's in a bad way, Tanris. Very bad," I said softly.

"Where is she, Crow?" he repeated, carefully enunciating each word.

I bit my lip and nodded toward the door to his room. Astonishment flickered in his eyes.

"You brought her here?"

Was that a bad thing? Well, as it pertained to me and my—our—plans, yes. As soon as he caught sight of her he would turn into a great, useless blob of jelly. "Yes," I affirmed, inserting more confidence into the word than I felt. "Yes, of course."

All sorts of emotions quavered off him. Fear, dread, wonder, hope. Bright, bright hope. He seemed to glow with it, sudden and fierce, then he hurried to the bedroom door. Briefly, I wished I didn't know what he was going to find on the other side.

"Tanris," I tried to slow him for a minute without actually chasing after him and dragging him to a stop. "I gave her some of the potion, but I—fear it didn't help much." My voice dwindled away as he disappeared. Silence reigned for a moment or two, then came a soft murmuring. I heard him quietly crying, just as I'd predicted. I looked up at the ceiling. "This would be a really good time for a miraculous intervention by the gods," I pointed out. Unsurprisingly, I received no reply. "Is anyone listening?"

Not even the Ancestors answered.

Girl poked her head out of the kitchen and gave me a sharp look. Not-An-Egg waddled over to me, creaking questions I could not interpret. If this was the answer the deities had for me, I didn't understand and I didn't find this particular riddle amusing. For a truth, I felt more than a little sick at heart.

"Did you hear any of that?" I asked Girl.

She nodded and came another step or two down the hall.

"I'm going back out. Keep an eye on him." I did not wait for her agreement, but loosed Not-An-Egg from my leg, went to my room to change my shirt and collect a few small items, then I was gone.

— 31 —
Strategic Transportation Of Equipment To An Alternate Location

Flying over the rooftops of Marketh has always been one of the greatest freedoms I have ever known. It is a challenge, to be sure, to meet the varying slopes of roofs, the tangle of chimneys, rooftop gardens, windows, statuary, clotheslines... Vaulting from level to level and leaping over the chasms between buildings has never failed to fill my heart with giddy exhilaration. Leaving the apartment, I wanted more than anything to find that release—and I could not. Yes, I could climb and I could run and I could jump, but I felt keenly the effects of four months travel, and of beatings and hunger and poison and deep melancholy. My flight through the city lacked the thrill I craved, but sufficed to clear my head sufficiently to deal with the business laying before me.

I had not fruitlessly wasted all my time since we'd arrived in the city and had, in fact, discovered exactly the information I sought. Working my way back to the Sunhar District, I did not go to my apartment but to another two streets down and further along the hill. It, too, boasted a view of the emperor's palace, though not as good as mine. I judged for myself after I picked the lock—a skill that had not waned in the least—and let myself in. The rooms were sumptuous. Elegant. As one might expect in such refined quarters, a fine assortment of costly ornaments and treasures adorned many of the surfaces. I selected a few I found particularly appealing and migrated them to the pouch I wore at my waist. Nary a tingle of warning did I receive from any but one, and you can imagine my caution. From room to room I went, learning the layout, exploring the floor for squeaks, oiling the door hinges with lamp oil I found delightfully scented for discriminating noses, and otherwise arranging things the way I liked and preparing the stage.

From the window of the sitting room I watched the sun reflecting on the palace's golden roof and marveled at what a jewel it was, what a triumph of architecture. If I stood at the far right side of the glass and leaned close I could see my building and—yes, my own balcony. I would never find accommodations equal to those. From there one could enjoy the view of the palace's dome as well as the needle-like towers surrounding it. One could even see the tops of the trees rising up over high walls of beautiful, creamy white trimmed with blue and gold tiles.

Even while I admired the view and joyfully recalled my occasional visits inside the palace (there are ways even a beggar can get in to see the fantastic structure), I kept an eye on the traffic in the street below and listened closely for the key in the lock. "Tell me," I requested of the Ancestors as an extra precaution, "if anyone approaches the door."

No one did, not until the sun had begun to color the sky in glorious shades of amber and rose. I watched my target, in the company of a plainly dressed maid, alight from an open carriage, brush her elegant skirts straight as she waited for the maid to retrieve some packages, then disappear from view as the pair of them approached the door of the building. My earlier exploration of the apartment allowed me to choose an advantageous hiding place—an unoccupied bedchamber next to m'lady's. By the door, I waited and listened as the pair entered, chatting merrily about the day's shopping adventure and preparations for this evening's dinner engagement. When the maid was dismissed to heat bath water I opened the door just a crack. The maid's back retreated from view and I slipped out into the hall.

The mistress of the house was so comfortable in her security that she'd left the bedchamber door open. It was kind of her to be so accommodating, though a locked door would hardly have restrained me. I closed it quietly behind me and leaned against it, watching the woman sitting at the dressing table. She'd donned a robe of embroidered red silk —my favorite—and was brushing her long, black hair. Humming to herself, she was, and the afternoon sunlight filtering in through the windows bathed her perfect skin in a tender glow. So entranced was she with the image in the glass that she did not at first observe my approach. She had a lovely visage, to be sure, her face perfectly proportioned, eyes black as coal framed by elegantly shaped brows. Those glorious eyes widened as she caught sight of my reflection and she moved to stand.

"Did you miss me, my dove?" I asked, settling my hands on her shoulders and pushing her right back down again.

"Crow!" lovely Tarsha gasped, her cheeks draining of color. "What are you doing here?"

I gave her a chiding look in the glass. "Is that any way to greet a long absent lover?" I took some satisfaction in the knowledge that I'd surprised her right out of a glib, convincing reply.

"You can't be here." She could deny it all she liked, but her opinion didn't change the facts.

"Oh, but I am."

She tried to stand again. I pushed her back down, then drew her hair back over her shoulder to run my fingers through it. So rich and thick and silky... But trust my wild Tarsha to be unafraid. Alarmed yes, and already conniving. I could feel it moving through her, twisting and turning.

"It's not safe here, my love. Tell me where you are staying and I will come to you."

I could imagine all too well how that would turn out. "Do you promise?"

"Nothing could keep me away," she vowed, and this time when she rose I let her. Turning to me, she wrapped her arms around my neck and kissed me quite, quite warmly. I could hardly protest, could I? Her kisses were everything I remembered and the warmth of her body against mine pure delight. "Where can I find you?" she whispered breathlessly. "You must leave at once, Crow. Sayanna will return any moment. I've missed you so!"

"Sayanna... Your maid?" I murmured back, reacquainting myself with her completely enchanting shape. There was no fault at all to find in her face or form. "Lock the door."

The reluctance she feigned in breaking off our kiss did not match the irritation I sensed. She smoothed her hands down my chest and sighed, fluttering her lashes demurely. "We can't do this, not here, my darling."

"It's been so long," I protested, seeking her lips again.

"Crow, no. I—I'm married now." She blushed prettily and held me off, but only lightly. A token protest.

"You're what?" Two could play this game and I adopted a suitable expression and caught her upper arms, pushing her away to stare in feigned shock.

"I had to!" she declared with admirably wide eyes. "I'm carrying your child."

"Praise be to the gods!" I gushed, drawing her abruptly against me and then pushing her back again. "It's a miracle!"

"Oh, Crow!" she laughed. "Hardly a miracle considering your... appetite."

"A miracle," I pronounced, "as you were very certainly not pregnant when I was taken. Let me count." Releasing her, I held up my fingers to illustrate. "A little more than a month in Duzayan's lovely dungeons in the company of naught but rats—believe me, I'd have remembered if you snuck in to visit—and one, two-and-a-little-bit months getting to our destination, plus one and a little bit more getting back; that puts us at five-ish months since I've seen you, which means we are indubitably the subjects of divine intervention. Doesn't it?" I beamed at her.

She opened her mouth to speak, but I interrupted before she could. "I didn't just fall off the turnip wagon, you know. It must have been quite the whirlwind courtship. You and—what's his name? Jackal?"

"Jashel," she provided, tight-lipped. "*Lord* Jashel."

"Yes, yes." I waggled my fingers dismissively. "Betrothed some two weeks following my precipitous departure from Marketh and wed six weeks later."

"You know?" Was that a blurt? Not from my lovely Tarsha! So uncouth! "How long have you been back? Duzayan doesn't know you're here, does he." The last was no real question at all. Already, the toothy little cogs in her head turned. Wasn't she quick and clever?

"Of course I know. The High Houses are slightly more discreet with their gossip, but your friends at Even Street and the Rare Stair and the Anchor Moon and—I cannot recall the other, but they were all abuzz with the story. The marriage of an aristocrat to a dancing girl, no matter how beautiful, is the subject of very juicy gossip in circles high and low," I reminded her, wagging a finger.

Glaring, she slapped at my hand, which I easily avoided.

I chuckled and played gently with a lock of her lovely hair. "Jashel, as everyone knows, is the only son of Baron Maruban who, coincidentally, enjoys a position as one of Duzayan's bosom companions. Nearly as rich, too, I hear. Quite the coincidence, this sudden marriage to dear Jashel, isn't it?"

I did not like to think of Maruban as a wizard but, given the company he kept, it was an awful possibility—one that cast suspicion on his son as well, in which case my presence in the apartment of his new bride could prove quite dangerous, if not fatal.

Color blossomed in Tarsha's cheeks and something distinctly unattractive flitted through her dark eyes. "The baron told me you were dead! What was I to do, Crow? Wait for a ghost to return to me?" Perfectly timed tears trembled on her lashes.

"Mm. I would have liked if you'd not had such a willing hand in arranging for my demise."

"I did not!" she exclaimed. A few of the Spirits flitted around the room and the draperies stirred, though Tarsha appeared unaware. "How could you say such a thing?"

"Oh, it might have something to do with your interaction with the guards at your apartment that night. Or *maybe* the way you slipped the baron's pearl back into my pocket for them to find after all the work you went to convincing me to steal it for you. Or it *could* have even been the way you did absolutely nothing to help me.

"Do you know, riding through miles and miles of empty wasteland gave me plenty of time to reminisce, and one of the things that stood out in my memory was you, my dear. I recalled your tragic, teary countenance upon our last meeting, when the baron brought Tanris and me to see you. And eventually I recalled how you asked what would happen to *you*. You had nary a word of concern for me. Not a one… You didn't even romantically scream my name when the guards dragged me back out."

"I can scream now." Her dark eyes flashed with the threat, banishing all trace of subterfuge.

"You could," I agreed, "but then I'd have to resort to violence, and although I would find that a trifle annoying and possibly even anticlimactic, it wouldn't bother me very much at all. What you are going to do is come over to the door and tell Sayanna that you've decided to postpone your bath and take a bit of a nap. You can feel a headache coming on and you don't want it to ruin your evening. You'll hesitate, and then you'll tell her to take an hour or two for herself. Perhaps she'd like a walk in the garden."

"She won't believe me."

"Of course she will. You're a kind and thoughtful mistress, are you not?"

Her chin lifted. Very well, she wasn't *that* kind and thoughtful, but it hardly mattered.

"Come along, now." I shifted my hold on her hair to grip the lot of it and give her a little turn, pushing her toward the door. As I did, I unsheathed my knife.

"I won't do it," she said defiantly.

"If you do not, I will chop off all your beautiful hair," I promised without the slightest trace of rancor. "Really short."

"You wouldn't."

It was pointless arguing with her. A tug and a slice and a little flip, and a hank of hair drifted to the carpeted floor. "Won't I?"

She squeaked in dismay and tried to twist away. I was not the only one inordinately fond of her raven locks. Her struggles resulted in another severed lock before I had her pushed against the wall, my body holding her there firmly.

"Do you believe me now?"

The tears in her eyes were real this time. She wept more for her hair than she had for me. Chin trembling, she nodded, and I eased away, still holding my knife up to her precious locks.

"Careful," I warned as she opened the door.

"Sayanna?" she called tremulously.

It was a moment or two before the maid's voice came from further down the hallway. "Yes, mistress?"

"I—I think I'll wait to take my bath. My head is beginning to hurt. I'm going to lie down and take a nap."

"Would you like me to bring you a cup of tea?"

"No. No, thank you. Why don't you take an hour or so to yourself and go sit in the gardens?"

There was a hesitation and a flicker of surprise. "Are you certain, my lady? I have some mending I could tend to."

"Make her believe," I murmured. "Make her believe…" The cool caress of the Spirits touched my cheek. Tarsha must have felt it, too, for she shivered perceptibly.

"I'll be fine, Sayanna, and I'm sure you'll enjoy the sunshine."

The faint whisper of dry leaves came from beyond the door. "Yes, my lady. Thank you!"

"Smile," I ordered, and Tarsha pasted a grimace on her face that lent credence to her claim of poor health, whether she'd intended it or not. "Don't close the door."

"Now what?"

"Wait until she's gone."

It was several long minutes before we heard Sayanna leave and the grating of the key in the lock. Was it my fault there was a little sand in it? Well, maybe.

"How long until your husband returns?" I asked, turning her about and steering her toward the dressing table again.

"He'll be home any moment, and then you'll be sorry."

I thought about shivering in my boots. Instead, I guided her down onto the chair then tugged gently backward on her hair until she was looking up at me. "If you are going to lie to me, sweetheart, please put a little more effort into it. Your assumption of my stupidity is insulting."

"What am I to expect after your laughable display of gullibility!" she hissed and, in a display of ingenuity and perhaps desperation, she swung her hairbrush at my face.

I twisted my head out of the way but her elbow caught me a blow. I had her chair to protect my groin, but she struck my side then she grabbed with her left hand at something on the dressing table and spun about to strike me. Alas for her, I still had a perfectly good hold of her hair and I propelled her bodily to the floor, bringing the hilt of my blade down hard on her wrist. Her scream of frustration was cut off by my knee in her back. She was nothing if not a spitfire. I twisted her arm until the wickedly sharp hair stick she'd attempted to employ as a weapon dropped to the floor, and all around us the Voices hissed, kicking up such a stir that draperies and bedclothes fluttered and a few scarves that had been carelessly hung drifted to the floor.

Tarsha's eyes went wide and she stiffened beneath me, her sudden fear a palpable thing.

"Are you afraid?" I asked, taunting her.

"No!" she lied, and pitched into a bucking, struggling fit to get away.

My hand in her hair still, I smacked her head against the floor. The carpet served as a cushion, but the blow was sufficient to jar her. "Enough!"

"Or what?" she spat back, trails of loose hair half obscuring her face. Her breath heaved and the billowing air was electric. Threatening. I flipped her onto her back, only to have her spit and claw at me. I shoved my knee into her soft belly and pressed the point of my knife against her throat, which subdued her in a hurry. As she laid there gasping for air and trying to hold herself still, I searched her face for the woman I had believed loved me. She had all the familiar planes and curves, the same beautiful wildness in her, but those fantastic eyes held not a trace of concern for anyone but herself. She was afraid, and that was an emotion I could use. I found myself feeling strangely sorry for her husband, even though I suspected he'd had little say in the marital arrangement.

"Will you kill me?" Tarsha challenged, lifting her chin.

I snorted derisively. "Because that is what you would do—what you *tried* to do? No. Not just yet, anyway." I enjoyed the doubt flickering in her countenance, but I let my eyes wander a little further south to where her creamy skin lay exposed to my view, the pretty crimson robe all askew. "Undress."

"What? No!" With her free hand she tried to pull her robe up to cover herself. "You can't mean it."

I gave her a faint, patronizing smile. "There is nothing about your person I do not know intimately, my little wildfire, and nothing that could interest me less."

Fury shone in her marvelous eyes, but it was tempered. Nervously, she darted a look to the assortment of belongings circling about us in the wind. None of it touched the two of us.

"Can you hear them?" I asked in a whisper just loud enough for her ears.

Her gaze jerked back.

"I shouldn't make them any more angry if I were you." Keeping my hold on her raven locks, I used the tip of my knife to flip the lethal hair stick under the bed. Then I got to my feet, dragging her with me, which made her clutch at her abused hair and cry out. "Now lose the robe."

Hands shaking, she pushed the fabric away. The wind whipped at it and blew it to one side, which was very helpful. "Thank you," I told the Voices and let her believe I was talking to her, but other than a quick look at me, she kept her eyes down. It was a little late in our acquaintance for modesty.

"Easy, my friends," I murmured, and the wind died down a bit. "Now take off the earrings," I instructed, "and that gaudy thing Lord Jackal gave you."

"My ring? But why?" she asked in a voice nearly plaintive.

"Take everything off. The ring, the bracelets, the necklace, the anklets, the toe rings, and—" I pulled her around until I could view her front side in the mirror, "that pretty stone in your navel."

"You're jealous," she smiled almost slyly.

"Yes, I always wished I could wear such feminine, garish jewelry," I mocked, and the smile disappeared. I didn't care a whit about the jewelry, but I did care that it might have some sort of spell attached to it and I wasn't going to take any chances. The last thing I needed was another demon attaching itself to me and screaming fit to wake the dead as well as the City Watch. When she'd finished, I pointed to the bed and gave her a little shove. It was gratifying to see her eyes widen and her face pale again. "Put the jewels under the mattress, down near the foot of the bed, and then do the same with the hair."

Involuntarily, she lifted a hand to her ragged locks. She had a lot of hair, so the few missing bits weren't immediately obvious. Tears glittered in her eyes, but at another wave of my knife, she did as I'd requested. That task accomplished, I steered her to the dressing screen and gestured to the drab colored clothes I'd earlier procured from the maid's room. "Put those on."

"They're not mine. And they're ugly."

"I don't really care," I said pleasantly.

With a derisive look, she took them and moved behind the screen. Sturdy as it was, constructed of wood panels inlaid with mother of pearl, it still toppled easily when I kicked it.

Tarsha gasped and whirled upon me, clutching the clothes to her breast. "Am I to have no privacy?"

"You're already naked," I pointed out reasonably. "And call me silly, but I have no wish for you to discover another hair stick or something equally useful and attack me again."

Features tight, she leveled such a glare of fury at me that it was a wonder I didn't burst into flames. Apparently deciding I wasn't going to change my mind, she donned the servant's clothing. Sayanna was apparently somewhat more slender than Tarsha and a little shorter. It was not really noticeable in the body of the *lural*—a long sleeved, high-collared garment whose hem reached the knees—but the sleeves were too short and too snug.

"Been putting on a little weight, have you?" I observed aloud.

"I thought you weren't interested?"

"Academically, only." I watched her button the high-collared shirt. The bosom was also too tight. Such a shame. "If five short, pampered months could affect such a change, imagine what a dumpling you'll be in a year."

"I had no idea you were such a student of human form."

Student? I was a master. "There's a great deal you don't know about me." She wriggled into the loose, pleated trousers and I canted my head to ascertain if the tapering legs would also be too tight. She took the opportunity to hit me again. I merely lifted my knife, catching her along the outside edge of her hand.

"Crow!" she gasped and cried out, shocked. The casual hurt came as such a surprise to her that all she could do was stare as blood seeped from the cut and dripped onto the carpet.

For a truth, I wanted to stare, too. I had never hurt Tarsha before, and for all the hours I had fantasized about various ways to extract my vengeance— ways that included nearly everything from throttling her to tossing her over a cliff—it struck me that I'd never imagined having her blood on my hands. Tersely, I tossed her one of the plentiful scarves. "Wrap it up, braid your hair in a tail lie the maid's, and put on a pair of slippers."

It is curious how often completely separate paths and reasons weave together. At this moment I did not particularly care what Duzayan might do to Tarsha, or if he would. I needed only for her to be someplace where he wouldn't find her, and for him to have no idea I was responsible. Independent of that, I wanted to test what I might do to her. Neither need had anything to do with the other, but they were both met in one place and time.

"You can't get away with this. My husband is a powerful man."

"Actually, it's his father who is powerful, and I have a plan." I smiled at her. She gave me a murderous glare. It was not one of her better looks. "You're going to visit your brother."

She looked at me all uncomprehending. "I don't have a brother."

"You do now. Want to see?" From beneath my tunic I withdrew a parchment and unfolded it. Well-used, it had been written on, then scraped —a practice of the lower middle classes who, while they can read and write, can't always afford new parchment.

"It won't work," she protested, but doubt colored her words.

I held it up so she could see her name scrawled in a heavy hand across the front and proceeded to read. "Sister, I noe you told me not to kontact you like this, but I must—" I turned it so she could read along. "I underlined "must," and spelled some of the words wrong so it would be more convincing, since you and your dear sibling didn't have the blessing of a proper education," I explained, then went on. "I *must* see you rite away. Am in trubble and fear for my life. Bring munny. 3,000 gold or ekwal. Sorry. I will make this rite. Come to our place withowt delay. Yr loving bruther."

"That is—" Her mouth opened, but she seemed unable to finish the sentence.

"Brilliant?" I supplied. "Clever? Ingenious?"

"Augh!" she cried out, beating her fists against her thighs.

"I've helped you out and collected the gold you had in the blue vase. I'm surprised you didn't have more, but no trouble. I also added the Kalebri necklace, a few of your unmounted jewels—I suppose you use those for your navel?—and the jeweled dagger you keep under the mattress. I'm guessing Jashel doesn't realize it's there?"

"Augh!" she cried out again and picked up a bottle of perfume to hurl at me. It sailed harmlessly by my head and rolled across the floor.

"You've yet to see my masterpiece," I said, pretending to ignore it. I had another missive tucked away where the other had come from, and this one was written on Lord Jackal's own fine vellum and perfumed with one of Tarsha's scents. "I found some of the letters you've written to your husband. Very sweet and romantic. Did you know he keeps them in a box under a floorboard in his study? Also very sweet and romantic."

"I hate you."

"That's been obvious for some time, my dove. For a little while the opinion was mutual, but then I decided you weren't worth it. I'm too mild-tempered to hold onto such exhausting emotions and you really aren't worth losing sleep over. Do you want to hear what you wrote to Darling Jashel?"

"No."

"Suit yourself," I shrugged, "but it has a very apologetic and imploring sort of explanation, and I did a fine job imitating your hand." It hadn't been too difficult. It had been I, after all, who taught this lowly dancer how to write. Who could have foreseen the advantage it would be? "Enough small talk. Shall we be off?"

"What are you going to do to me? Where are we going?"

"I want to show you something."

The little purse I'd chosen to hold the aforementioned jewels—along with a few other choice items I'd brought along especially—had a long strap which would, when worn, cross the torso to hold the bag at one's hip. Of course Tarsha refused to put it on and I was required once again to threaten her with bodily harm. She did not make a very good captive, and I could not help but wonder if this shrewish nature she now displayed was normal, and the adoring looks and actions with which she'd fooled me before were nothing but a farce.

I took Tarsha into Marketh's streets, leaving by way of the building's back door in case we should happen to run into her dear, unsuspecting maid. The hold I kept on her arm would leave bruises, and I promised her that if she so much as opened her mouth or looked sideways, I would ruin her pretty little face, leave her with a collection of goods stolen from more people than the dupe she'd married, and make sure she found herself in a very real, very dark prison cell. If I had any influence at all—and I had the wherewithal to obtain it—I would find a way to guarantee that she was completely forgotten. She must have believed me, for she kept quiet. Little trembling breezes from the Ancestors caressed me now and then, and if they did the same to her, I would thank them for it later.

— 32 —
Nothing To Crow About

"Crow, you're hurting me," Tarsha ventured at last in a tremulous whisper. By then I was propelling her roughly up the stairs to my apartment, my temper growing all out of proportion. There was a certain irony to be found in her complaint. What was a harsh grip on the arm in comparison to being beaten, jailed, frozen, starved and poisoned?

"You'll live."

"Crow!"

She pulled at my grip and struck me with her fist. The noise we made coming in the door brought the others. Girl waited inside, brandishing a broom, and Tanris—pasty and red-eyed—had his sword in his hand as he came down the hall. Not-An-Egg, too, had come to investigate and stood in the parlor door, wings outspread.

"What is going on?" Tanris demanded.

I slammed the door closed and dragged Tarsha past our startled audience. "Get out of my way." If she saw the dragon, she did not have time to react to it.

"Why did you bring her here? What are you doing?"

I did not answer, but continued with Tarsha down the hall and into Tanris's room. Tanris yelled, Tarsha fought and shrieked curses at me. "Look at her. *Look at her!*" I ordered my erstwhile love, and this time I got one hand around her neck and caught that convenient braid with the other, forcing the dark-haired beauty to see what was left of Aehana. Tarsha struggled some more, but could not escape my wrath. The Ancestors careened around the room, wailing and chanting, and it wasn't until much later that I learned they were countering the curses she spat at me.

"What do you want from me?" she screamed.

"I want you to *look* at what you've done! Have you forgotten her? Have you?" I shook her.

"I don't know her!" Tears streamed down her anger-ravaged face.

"Her name is Aehana. She is Tanris's wife. She is *dying*," I snarled into her ear, my own anger bitter in my mouth. "Your precious wizard gave her the same poison he gave me. *This* is what you would have done to me, and for what? A pretty house? I have a pretty house. See?" I jerked her head up so that she could get a look at the room.

"*What?!* I don't know any wizards! Crow, stop! Please stop!" Tarsha's hands clawed at my arm, but I didn't even feel it.

"Don't lie to me!"

"I swear, I don't know anything!"

"You want money? I'd have given you money, Tarsha, more than even you could spend in a lifetime. Power? That's what money's for." I was so very angry. "But no, you took the one true and good thing you had and broke it all to pieces!"

"I don't know what you're talking about!"

"Crow," Tanris protested again, uncertain whether to interven or not.

"No, you don't, do you?" Even to my own ears my voice was curiously strained, as though dragged over the edge of a very sharp knife. My grip on her throat tightened. "I would have given you everything. I looked at you, and I didn't just see the pretty dancer that all the other men lusted after, I saw fire and passion for life. I saw hope. I saw a future I'd never hoped for before. And it was a *lie!*"

"Crow, that's enough. Let her go." At my side, Tanris gave my shoulder a little shake. He was right. I shoved Tarsha away from me and she fell on the floor, choking and gasping, holding her throat. Girl stood in the doorway, so I went to the window and looked out on the street, fists clenching and unclenching at my sides. No one said a word. No one knew what to do. The Ancestors hovered, whisking this way and that, shivery and cold.

Finally, I turned back to them. "Get up," I told Tarsha.

She looked pleadingly at Tanris, but he said nothing, only shifted his grip on his sword. Hand to her neck, she staggered to her feet and followed me out and down the hall to a room set aside for bathing. I dragged the single bench it held out into the hallway and the basket of linens as well, leaving nothing but the tall brass tub. Tarsha's apprehension followed me like a dog.

"Don't do this, Crow," she whispered hoarsely.

"I can think of several less pleasant alternatives." A tip of my head directed her inside. "Now *stay* here." I shut the door behind her and turned the key in the lock, leaving her in the dark. There were no windows. Locks were easy to pick, so I fetched a pair of the wooden wedges I routinely used in my work for discouraging the opening of doors and hammered them into place. Girl and Tanris watched me silently

—for which I would have to thank them later, too—and Not-An-Egg followed me about plaintively.

"Now," I said when I was finished, "I'll see the baron."

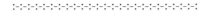

The message was straightforward: we had returned to the city and would meet the baron in the Yasmin Gardens which, being located in one of the larger market districts of the city that never sleeps, received a goodly amount of traffic both day and night. Tanris wanted to add a pointed reminder to bring the antidote, his words something along the line of *"bring the cure for the poison or I'll rip your beating heart out through your throat"* which, although charming, I thought not altogether wise, as we didn't want to provoke the wizard before we had our prize. I left that part out, confident he would remember the terms of our agreement. He had, after all, gone to considerable lengths to catch and coerce me.

After attending to the delivery of our message we went to the indicated market and did a little shopping. Tanris fretted and grumbled until I wanted to box his ears. It was too long until the meeting, he said, we ought to just march right up to Duzayan's door. The market could be a trap. What were we doing buying an entire cart of melons, and what were the Yudizan peppers for? Why did I waste time and coin on a bundle of burlap sacks? Did I really need to stop at another beastly temple and give away even more coin?

I didn't even bother to respond to his irreverence and disrespect. He was, after all, under a great deal of strain, which wouldn't improve if I reminded him of the improbability that Duzayan would be inclined to let any of us live. If I were to have any say in the matter, and I am occasionally persuasive as well as decisive, Duzayan's plans would be drastically changed. When I transferred our preserved dragon casing (filled with water now and sewn up quite neatly) to one of the sacks and tucked it into my belt, then put Tanris to work stuffing single melons into the remaining sacks, he caught on fairly quickly.

Right on schedule, dark had fallen when Duzayan made his way to the table I'd chosen. A huge, hulking brute in armor accompanied him, bristling with weapons.

"I hope you'll forgive me if I don't stand." I smiled ever-so-faintly and dabbed at my face with a much-used-looking cloth. I perspired freely, thanks to the peppers, which were pungent enough to put hair on a man's chest, or so the rumor suggested. I would soon discover for myself. I had of course dressed for the occasion, and sported a stylish tunic of blue, gray trousers, and sturdy but lightweight boots. I'd oiled my hair to give it a lank, unwashed look, and the hands that gripped both sack and kerchief shook fitfully. I held the top of the sack close against my chest, teeth clenched and stifling groans not altogether counterfeit. All of this in order to preserve the appearance that I was suffering the affects of his monstrous poison and might keel over at any moment.

"I feared you had perished," Duzayan said, sitting down as gracefully as though he were in one of the finest parlors in the city. The Brute stationed himself just behind, fondling the hilt of a humongous sword and looking at me with some of the coldest eyes in existence.

"The potion is gone," I bit out. "Did you bring the cure?"

I found his smile distinctly unpleasant. "I knew you'd watch out for yourself. Of course I brought it. Did you bring the item?"

I gripped the sack tighter, and my other hand came down to protect it. Moisture dripped conveniently from my nose. "Give it to me."

"Let me see what you've brought me," he said, his tone perfectly equable.

"Have you ever seen one? Do you know what it looks like?"

The Ancestors fluttered about nervously.

Duzayan's glance flickered away and then back, irritation glittering like frost. "Of course," he said. "It is about the size of your head. Drab colored and leathery. Unprepossessing."

"Like this?" I pulled the top of the sack down a little, giving him a glimpse of the egg.

His lips twitched ever so slightly; a precursor to victory. "Exactly like that. I'm glad your reputation wasn't completely exaggerated. You've accomplished quite a feat."

Exaggeration, my eye. I could take insult by that. "Yes, and I want the remedy for what you did to me, baron. Now."

"We'll trade."

"I don't think so."

"I beg your pardon?" Up winged one brow and patent surprise mushroomed in his aura.

"You seem to have forgotten part of our agreement."

"Oh, really?" he inquired, smooth as snake oil.

"Where are Tarsha and Aehana?" My hand trembled badly as I blotted perspiration from my face. My skin felt hot enough to glow, and the fiery pepper in my belly suggested I might have to make an unscheduled dash. On the other hand, puking on the baron's fine boots would be wonderfully vindictive and only serve as further means of convincing him I was on the verge of dying.

"Where is Tanris?" he countered.

The game of answering questions with questions might have amused me in other circumstances. I gave my adversary a sickly smile. "As you said, I watch out for myself."

He laughed in appreciative humor and I squeezed the sack as I struggled with another mostly fake cramp.

The amusement disappeared as quickly as it had appeared. "Careful," he hissed, sitting up a little straighter.

"Oh, I have been, believe me. Have you any idea what I went through to get this thing?" I twitched and jerked a little. "Of course you do, which is why you wouldn't go after it yourself. Where are the women?"

"In good time. Were you followed?"

Yes, by a dragon, but a mere girl killed it. I resisted the temptation to share the thought. "The time is now."

He shook his head. "You'll give me the item," he said, temper showing around the edges.

"No. No, I won't. You're not thinking clearly, baron. Give me the antidote, and you'll still have something I want dearly. *Don't* give me the antidote, and I will die and you'll never have this... item."

He laughed, all shaded with disbelief and crackly anger. "Come, Crow, you are not the kind of man to sacrifice yourself for anything. You know it. I know it. Women are cheap and plentiful." He gestured toward the passersby.

"I don't want other women." I started to get to my feet, and a very real cramp took hold of my belly. The gods of fortune smile upon me. Sack clutched against me, one hand balancing me against the table, I gave up the contents of my stomach.

Brute grunted in disgust and took an involuntary step backward. Duzayan was hardly less nimble getting his robes out of the way. People nearby made appropriate noises of sympathy and aversion, and opened a wide margin around us that I knew would quickly fill with people who had not witnessed the incident.

I drew the back of my hand across my mouth, spat, and bowed extravagantly. "I'll bid you good evening and goodbye, you braying chunk of garbage. May the gods visit upon you a thousand terrible curses."

I had hardly begun my disappearing act when Duzayan's chair scraped behind me.

"Wait."

The baron had proven himself an exceedingly treacherous man, so I did not yet allow myself to entertain any sense of victory. I would need all my considerable wit about me to win this battle. Fortunately, some of that wit was already in motion. Plenty of people in the crowded market had proven quite willing to accept a free melon from a generous crazy man— though I much doubt Tanris would take kindly being called such—and dozens of replicas of my sack peppered (ha!) the marketplace already, just as planned. Slowly, I turned back to Duzayan.

He stood, fiddling with something at his waist, his expression truly frightening. Around me, little huffs of wind tugged at my hair and clothes.

Wizard! Wizard! the Ancestors whined and squirmed. *Why did we insult a wizard?*

I *had* warned them. My attention skipped to Brute, who had his sword half drawn and determination writ all over him. I hoped he would not come after me, but I was prepared to run and, being experienced as well as clever, I had a plan. Plans within plans, even. I had, after all, had months to consider all the dark and twisted ways Duzayan might thwart me. I could not know exactly what he would do, and so I would have to be as difficult for him to catch as the wind.

He studied me narrowly.

The residue of pepper in my belly—perhaps I had eaten too many of them—made my gut spasm again, and I clenched my arm against it. Such nonsense might complicate the idea of running. Finally, the wizard held something out. A crystal vial glimmered in the reflected light of the lamps around the marketplace.

"Put it on the table," I instructed.

"So untrusting." He did as I said, and moved back when I made a little shooing motion, though Brute snarled at me. He did a very respectable job, too, quiet but full of promise I did not take lightly. On the bright side, the table remained between them and me.

"Let me think," I pondered, cautiously advancing to take the vial. It made my fingers sting and I quickly dropped the thing into the pouch at my waist. He'd attached a spell to it. I knew he would. No doubt he meant to follow me, but I had a plan for that. "You've given me exactly zero reasons to trust you and you're deeply in the debt column where it comes to reasons to *like* you."

"You should take the dose right away. You don't look very well, Crow."

"No doubt. All of it at once?" I asked, and as he nodded I backed away. Brute edged around the table after me. Duzayan made a little motion with his fingers and another prickle ran over my skin. "Don't," I warned, and held my sack out to one side. "I won't just drop it, I'll smash it to bits."

"Shall we meet here again tomorrow? The same time?"

"I'll let you know. If this doesn't work the way it ought, you can kiss your—well. Whatever fits." The fury growing in him should perhaps have frightened me, but something more underlaid that, and it drew my curiosity. I thought I recognized appreciation, but it was probably my imagination. I could spare no time for puzzling it out. Spinning away, I darted into the crowd.

Duzayan shouted.

The Voices whistled and—something I had not taken into consideration—whipped wildly through the market. Sudden chaos ensued and, standing at the center of the commotion, Duzayan wouldn't look particularly innocent, and wasn't that a pity?

I did not look behind me. I sprinted between tables, vaulted a low railing, and ran straight toward the candlemaker's shop, which set my course at a slight angle away from the cart where Tanris dispensed his melons. Girl waited in the place we'd arranged, a bright red scarf tied to her head like a beacon. As soon as she knew I'd spotted her, the scarf came off and fluttered to the ground to be trampled underfoot. I bumped into her deliberately, handing her the sack with the egg while I took her melon, then careening off into the wild tangle of stalls that made up the ever-changing scenery of the market while Girl dodged away down an alley to whisk the egg to safety.

I took a quick glance back as I rounded one of the three-walled stalls. Brute pounded after me. Just as expected, a dozen or so of Duzayan's minions loomed into view, having previously hidden in the crowd until their master called upon them. I zigzagged this way and that, coming around in a semi-circle until I was more or less behind Brute and his cronies and the panic they left behind. Ducking out of view beneath a cart piled high with fruit, I peeled off my tasteful blue tunic and stuffed it out of sight atop the wagon's axle. I had another shirt on beneath it, rough gray and quite common looking. From the bag Girl gave me I drew a hat and shoved it on my head, then I took a quick look around.

The Minions grabbed my unwitting accomplices left and right to check the contents of their sacks. You can be certain such action did not win any accolades from the populace. A high wind whipped through the gardens and a section of the market bordering them. Tent flaps, flags, banners, and textiles randomly wrapped around the faces and limbs of the pursuing Minions. Praise be to the god of strange legacies. I could not see Duzayan, which made me ill-at-ease but was not at all unforeseen. If he'd been conniving enough to catch me, he was clever enough not to get himself caught in the middle of the busiest marketplace in all of Marketh.

From the pouch at my waist I withdrew the new vial Duzayan had given me and another a little big bigger. It hurt to hold his, and I worked quickly, transferring the liquid from one to the other. Sharp little green sparks stabbing at my fingers only complicated the job, but I have performed successfully under more strenuous circumstances. Swiftly, I tucked my vial back into my pouch and wriggled from beneath the cart to pitch the wizard-cursed crystal high into the air toward Duzayan's last position.

I was not quick enough.

I still had my arm up when the demon dove at me from out of nowhere. Well, not "nowhere," exactly. We all know perfectly well it was there at Duzayan's behest, and I am sure you realize I had planned for just such a contingency. Even so, it came as something of a shock. Clawing, beating at me with its leathery wings, shrieking fit to wake the dead as well as the City Watch—the latter of which, to my dismay, arrived somewhat tardily on the scene.

I had very much wanted to garb myself in thick leather or armor against such an eventuality, but that would have looked a trifle out of place. The demon sank its claws into the flesh of my arm which, while it made me shriek right back, was thankfully not my face, which is generally their preferred target. I swung my arm hard at the side of the wagon and succeeded in cutting off another wail, but the thing hung on like—well, like a demon. As you can imagine, I had no desire at all to waste time with the wretched thing. Aside from being annoying and inflicting pain, demons had the unfortunate habit of drawing attention to one like a bonfire in the middle of the textile district, and I didn't want that, either. But forewarned is forearmed, and while I could have used four arms about then, I settled for rapidly beating the little beast breathless. Their tough hides turn aside most blades and they are extremely hard to kill or I'd have done it in a heartbeat. Grabbing a small fruit from the cart, I crammed it into the demon's mouth and succeeded in temporarily gagging it. Upending my burlap sack, I sent the melon rolling and wrapped the bag around my arm to conceal the nearly senseless demon. Right after having them screaming an ear-splitting alarm, there is nothing quite so obvious an indicator of guilt as having a demon decorating one's person.

Even with all the other chaos going on, the noisy beast had garnered a share of the attention. Four wide-eyed spectators gaped at me. I promptly reached into my pouch to disburse some more of Baron Duzayan's wealth. I did not give it to them, no, I tossed a handful of the glittering coin into the air and left them scrambling for it while I ran. By now the crowd swirled wildly in all directions, so it was easy enough to adopt one of the fleeing throng and "help" him escape to safety. A middle-aged fellow of some girth, he never noticed how I kept him between me and the tardy City Watch.

Abandoning my shield at the mouth of a convenient, albeit somewhat crowded alley, I surveyed the score or so people dashing its length. With no Minions in immediate view, I put on some speed. You will appreciate the fact that I had not only to get completely out of range of Duzayan's men, but to rid myself of a demon that would shortly regain consciousness and the use of his considerable lung power. My impromptu traveling companions seemed set on keeping to the straightest route away from the marketplace. Unencumbered by such narrow logic, and extremely averse to taking such an obvious direction, I ran along with them for a couple blocks and then ducked into a little space between buildings.

The demon squeaked and dug its ugly little claws into my arm. I reciprocated by smacking it two or three times against a wall. When it was quiet again and my arm satisfactorily numb (a better alternative than debilitating pain), I headed down the passage. It took a turn that plunged me into nearly absolute darkness, and I had to grope my way along. The noise from the marketplace was thankfully muffled. I touched my hand to my chest, pressing the Mazhar medallion against my skin.

"Hello?"

Hurry. Not safe. Pursuit...

While dying in the attempt to be heroic might sound tragic and romantic, it was also premature; we still had a villain to destroy. "I know. I need some of you to go make sure Girl is all right. And Tanris," I added.

One of the unfortunate side effects of having a bit of a breather was in becoming aware again of the *other* side effect: namely, the abundance of pungent Yudizan peppers I'd consumed. My lips, throat and belly burned. I came around another turn, relieved to see light at the end of the narrow way. What I really wanted was a nice mug of soothing milk, and you could bet I would find a place to acquire one just as soon as I had gotten completely away. I had no sooner made the end of the passageway when a dark shape blocked it. There are times when I wonder what lessons the gods feel I must learn. This was one of them.

"Well, well, well..." a familiar voice drawled. I could not immediately place it and dim quarters provided no help. "Look what we have here."

"What is that, boss?" asked a second voice. "A mockingbird? A jay?"

"Rooster, maybe. Where have you been, bird boy? I've been looking for you."

Every word brought me closer to recognition until—"Oh, it's you, Raza. What a thrill to see you again." Rather like meeting the tax collector or one of the city watch.

"You owe me." He came into the little alleyway and I retreated.

"I doubt it, but how much are you imagining to gull me for?"

"Oh, a life. Maybe several."

"Sorry, not handing out lives today." Whirling about, I dashed back the way I had come, Raza Qimeh and the stalwart Yahzir hot on my heels. So hot, in fact, that I didn't quite make it around the first bend. Raza's hand in my tunic jerked me backwards and when I twisted to shed myself of it, his fist clipped my jaw. Stars blinded me as he shoved me bodily into the brick wall.

"Did you really think you were going to get away from me?" he asked, as though I hadn't already done so enough times to have lost count.

"Still do." The gods would present a way.

"Definitely a rooster," Yahzir decided. "Can I hit 'im, boss?"

Of course he couldn't. Not there in the narrow alley, anyway. Raza did it for him, smashing a fist into my gut. I would have warned him, but he gave me no opportunity, and in a heartbeat he was wearing what remained of the contents of my belly. I would much like to have taken a moment for self pity, but I hadn't time to spare. Raza staggered backward into Yahzir and I, more or less holding onto him, went with. All three of us went down in a pile and look! I was wearing a demon! Semiconsciousness had loosed its grip a little, but it still tore my arm as I ripped it free and thrust it into Raza's face. It shrieked. Raza shrieked. Yahzir hollered and pushed at both of us—and I scrambled to my feet to hightail it down the alley. Around the corner the passageway narrowed enough that I could scramble upward, feet braced to either side and bloody fingers searching for purchase in cracks and protruding bricks. It was a feat I'd performed many, many times, but I was so shaky that I feared I might not make it. The other two—three, counting the demon—made such a racket they didn't hear whatever noise I made as I struggled upward. I threw myself over the edge of the roof just as they fought around the corner. The noise of the demon of course attracted immediate attention. There came shouting and the clatter of weapons, Raza's bellows of innocence, the demon squawking...

Laying under the pale starlight, I held my bleeding arm against me and waited for the noise below—and my stomach—to settle. The gods do love me. They'd not only helped me to acquire the antidote for Tanris, but to escape the marketplace as well as Raza, then arranged for Raza to be jailed into the bargain. What man was more blessed than I?

— 33 —
Not The Way It Was Supposed To Go

Tanris and Girl were both waiting for me by the time I returned to my apartment. Girl catapulted herself into my arms and hugged me tight, nearly knocking me back into the stairway. "Ow... ow..." got her off me in a hurry, and then she dragged me into the kitchen to tend to my wounds. Tanris, impatient as always, wanted to know if I had the antidote.

"Yes, I have the antidote. You are welcome. Am I hurt? Well, just a bit, but I hope to recover. All in a day's work, but this day is starting to feel extraordinarily long. You wouldn't—"

Girl put her hand over my mouth, and when I tried to continue, she gave me a threatening look. Just a look! Luckily Tanris had taken the vial and gone already and did not witness the deterioration of my previously unshakable character. It would not do at all to have it get out that I could be silenced with a mere look by a mere girl.

"Do you—"

She shook her head and went to set a lantern on the table nearby.

"I was just going to ask if you have the casing."

She nodded and pointed to the corner, where Not-An-Egg had incongruously curled up with the thing as though guarding it—and him hardly any larger. The little dragon watched me so intently I wondered if there was something wrong and how I might go about asking him, or interpreting if he happened to respond.

The cutting away of the remains of my shirt sleeve brought a gasp, and I winced when I beheld the damage. Girl gave me a slightly terrified look. Wriggling my fingers proved difficult and painful, and I was suddenly more terrified than she. I needed that hand! Those fingers! What if nerves had been damaged? And—other parts critical to my profession?

For a moment we all just stared. Then Girl wrapped my arm tightly in a cloth and pulled me to my feet. I didn't need for her to tell me we were going to visit the Priests of Ishram. I had long suspected they were magic users in disguise, which bothered me deeply. Priests should be priests and wizards should be wizards, but... these particular priests served the god Ishram, the deity of health and healing. They have done much good in the world and are disinclined to political power or riches. More often than not they will cure wounds and sickness with practical sense and herbal remedies, but there are times when those cannot suffice. Such a patient is always heavily sedated, and who can say whether magic is used or if Ishram happens to be particularly benevolent to his devoted followers?

Alas, I have never managed to discover the truth and this time proved no exception. The good brothers tranquilized me, skillfully tended my wounds, and then tucked me into bed to sleep the night away under their protection—a thought that makes my skin crawl, even now. If some scoundrel bent on murder should happen to breach their walls, what exactly would the kind, gentle brothers do to stop him? Love him into a coma?

As I have previously mentioned, I try to avoid such exposure. I may not have mentioned that I occasionally make donations to their cause. It strikes me as a good practice. Precautionary. They did not decline the gold coins I offered them, and they have never asked for more. A curious lot...

Upon leaving the hospice, I ventured into the Sunhar Market and purchased myself a new shirt. A lovely shade of emerald, the sleeves were loose enough to fit over my bandages. Naturally, I ventured a look beneath. The marks were pink and puckered and would no doubt leave scars. I disliked having such an obvious mark on me, but at least I could conceal it beneath my clothing. I was not just lucky, and I knew it as sure as I knew the sun rises every morning in the east. I made my way to several of the local temples, taking time to offer the appropriate gifts and gratitudes. One must never forget where their blessings come from, lest he find himself suddenly left alone in a brutally vicious world.

At the market I picked up some fruit, some fresh-baked bread filled with lovely sweetened cheese, and a jug of kaffa, then made my way home. The scene that greeted my arrival was in direct opposition to the sunny, ebullient mood I harbored. In spite of the parlor's open draperies, I was met with a distinct and overwhelming impression of sorrow.

"Tanris? Girl?"

Not-An-Egg lurched up to me, wings and expression drooping. He wrapped his arms (or are they called legs since he generally walks upon them?) and his wings around my leg and cried.

"What is it?" I asked, setting down my things and coaxing him from my legs into my arms. I could not help grimacing as sharp claws bit into my skin. He was like a cat except with bigger hole-pokers. I contemplated outfitting him with boots and he pressed his teary, knobby face into my neck.

Hearing a noise behind me, I turned about, completely ready to fling Not-An-Egg at my attacker, but it was just Girl. Tears reddened her eyes and nose, made her face puffy, and her hair was a mess. She waved for me to follow and took me to Tanris's room, where he sat in a chair beside the bed. His face looked like Girl's only worse, though he'd stopped crying and just stared across the room.

A chill struck my bones. "Tanris?" I whispered.

"You said you gave her the antidote," he said, his voice toneless.

"It was. It's what Duzayan gave me last night."

He swallowed two or three times. "She's dead."

"What?" The fears I'd entertained on our journey came rushing back to jab us all viciously in the gut. Tanris didn't answer; he didn't need to. Aehana lay still and silent upon the bed, her ashen features so bony and ravaged that it looked like she still must hurt, though not a breath disturbed her form.

"He tricked me," I breathed. "Again." I almost laughed. Hysterically. "He meant it for me, Tanris. He'll kill us both if he has his way."

I sensed a hardening in him. A fierce resolution. "He can't have his way."

"No," I agreed.

Girl stood at the end of the bed, crying all over again. This time I could not be annoyed with her. Gently prying Not-An-Egg from my shirt front, I set him on the bed and went to Tanris. He turned his face away. I wondered what people said in a time like this, and I had not a single word of comfort or condolence to offer him. Drawing my lower lip between my teeth, I watched his profile for a moment or two, then put my hand on his shoulder. Much to my surprise, his own lifted to cover it and he squeezed tightly. I hoped it helped him feel better. My "better" had fled the moment I walked through the door, and in its place grew a steady, resolute anger.

"This ends now."

I went to Duzayan's mansion.

For a long time I crouched on a nearby rooftop, watching the comings and goings—and there were enough of those to conclude he was looking for me and his precious egg. It takes a particular breed of man to plan physical or spiritual damage to another, to set such things in motion, to take pleasure in the pain he causes. How it must wither and blacken a soul, until nothing remains to be redeemed. How blind are they who trade their eternal spirit for a few short years of miserable, petty mischief.

Duzayan had tricked me, stolen from me, hurt me. He'd humiliated and used me. He'd desperately wounded Tanris, a man who had patiently toiled at my side and given his best to keep me alive in spite of the odds and my own independent nature. No doubt Duzayan still meant to kill me—to kill us both—and then forget us like yesterday's bath water. If I did not want us to die I must kill him first, and pray to the gods to preserve my soul.

But what of the law? you ask. Men like Duzayan make and own the law, I tell you. Let me pose you another question: While Duzayan bribed and threatened his way to power, what of the Tanrises and Aehanas of the world? Duzayan wants a bauble? Well, then, by all the powers Duzayan *gets* his bauble, and what matter the backs and spirits crushed beneath his careless feet? I am neither hero nor champion. I have no such aspirations, but if I know the disease and if I have a chance—better than just a chance —of eradicating the problem, is it not my responsibility?

For a truth, I resented every pain and every indignity suffered at Duzayan's hands. By my own choice I would have had my vengeance on him, oh yes, but until I stood in the hall with Tanris and had to tell him his wife had been poisoned, and then I had to hear those dreadful, needless words that she had died, I did not fully comprehend the meaning of hatred, and *that* education birthed further resentment. I have never hated anyone, never felt the need for such extremity. I will not be made over in such a way. *I will not...*

Something about the whole situation continued to gnaw at me, but I could not grasp the problem. I needed to separate myself from the issue at hand, as I had always done with the jobs I took. *Never get personally involved.* It was one of the cardinal rules, but I was involved right up to the eyeballs. It had started with Duzayan's wretched plan to catch me and force me to do his bidding.

No… I shook my head slowly, it had begun before that and its beginning had nothing to do with me. I was merely a tool used to gain a particular prize—and a disposable tool into the bargain. Such a thing could rankle, for I had some pride and disliked the notion of being incidental, but there was something more here. What was the prize? A dragon's egg. What did one do with a dragon's egg? The common man might destroy it, cook it, preserve and mount it, sell it to… a wizard, of course, and what would a wizard do with such a thing? Not being a wizard, I had no idea. I recalled that the letters I'd taken had made mention of a particular "Blessing" (with a capital B), and how "the time" was drawing near. Four months, Duzayan had given me, but he would not have created a schedule so tight he had no room to maneuver, especially when it came to preparations for something momentous.

What was it? I got up to pace back and forth, then promptly ducked down again before someone spotted me. Thank the gods of thieves and avengers, no outcry arose. Settling with my back to a convenient chimney, I returned to my rumination. What heavenly or earthly elements were especially significant within the next week or so? Never one to put much stock in astrology, I had no idea, and the clues included in the letters were not of much help to one as ignorant as I on the subject. Duzayan's hidden chamber had held star charts; did they contain notations detailing the event? Clearly, I would have to go back and see for myself. What other treasures might the room reveal now that I knew—more or less—what to look for?

Another incongruous detail bothered me. Duzayan had killed Aehana, would most likely kill Tanris, and had already killed me, at least for all practical purposes, for the poison in the vial had been meant for me. If not for the magic of the Ancestors I would be dead. Once the pawn was no longer useful, it was discarded. With extreme prejudice. But what of Tarsha? She was a puzzle. Her role had thus far been minor: seduce and deliver me. She still lived, and Aehana, who only happened to be married to one of the key players, had perished. She had, in fact, been punished far in excess of what her circumstantial role deserved. Clearly, Tarsha's part in this play was not yet finished.

Abruptly, I got to my feet and made my way down to the street, going into the building through a window and then taking the conventional path down the stairs. From there I went directly to the nearest temple, where I spent the remaining hours until dusk making my devotions—and never had I been more serious, more committed to the path I would take. If there had ever been a time in my life when I needed the blessings of the gods, it was now.

And… well, possibly when I was being chased by the dragon. Twice.

I returned to my apartment to collect my gear and to change clothes, and did not seek out Tanris or Girl. Not-An-Egg followed me about, taking occasional short, hopping flights with wings outstretched. I needed to pass undetected, which is trickier in the light of day, and so I assumed the guise of common laborer, which required another stop or three in Marketh's magnificent markets where a man can find anything he needs at any hour of any day. The judicious application of a few rips and smears of dirt had me looking as common as a brick, and the city was full of those. My leather tool bag went into an unimaginative canvas sack, and off I went.

I made my way again into the Litares District without incident. Several houses away from the baron's I ascended to the rooftops, which allowed a speedier journey, though I had to be careful when I crossed the narrow garden areas between the stately homes. My arm still ached. I worked it for a few minutes, mostly to convince myself that it still functioned properly and I would be fine, just fine.

Finally, I cast a grapnel out to hook one of the many decorative gargoyles standing watch on Duzayan's roof. When none of them came alive, and nothing untoward happened, I fastened my end of the rope to a distinctive ornament, then checked the traffic below. I'd chosen the side of the building cast in shade this time of day, and when all was clear, I shinnied across the space, thankful to the god of crows that I was quick and agile and not afraid of heights.

I did not immediately climb to the rooftop but, holding my breath, I reached out cautiously to touch the building itself, testing whether a magical barrier protected it. The shock when my fingers made contact nearly sent me tumbling to the ground. Green pain shot through my arm and set me to flailing. Thank the long list of gods watching over me, my legs tightened instinctively and I was merely left dangling upside down, swinging back and forth and casting savage aspersions upon Duzayan's parentage. Whispering, of course, lest I draw unnecessary attention.

Evidently he had taken extra precautions. Fine. I couldn't go in that way, but plenty of people went in and out on the ground floor; guards and servants and guests—who also had servants aplenty, as I'd observed from the rooftops. One more servant equalled one perfect disguise.

Still smarting, I hooked my arm over the rope and hitched back until I regained the opposite rooftop just in time to witness a pair of guards entering the garden. They took their sweet time meandering through, poking dutifully at the shrubberies with the ends of their weapons and stopping several times to chat. It was hard to believe the Baron's Best didn't look up and check windows, but their apparent security in the wizard's spell was telling. They knew perfectly well a wizard employed them. The pay must be incredible. If not for a certain difference of opinion and a string of vile insults to my person and my intelligence, I might have reconsidered my choice to remain self-employed.

When the Baron's Sluggards disappeared around a corner, I reclaimed my grapnel and hung my gear down a chimney. Thank the god of spring, warm weather put all but the kitchen chimneys out of use until evening at the earliest. The situation called for an alteration to my plans, and I wasted no time contriving and executing one. As it turned out, I didn't masquerade as one of the visitor's menials after all, but one of the baron's own servants. Their numbers made it easy to purloin the required livery, and they kept quite busy running back and forth and, in some cases, apparently in circles as well. I joined a modest throng of my new associates unloading baggage from a recently arrived carriage, taking a load that mostly blocked my view and therefore everyone's view of me—and also nearly capsized me with its sheer weight. Someone relieved me of the topmost chest and we made our way up the grand staircase and through several halls. A vigorous valet issued directions and clapped his hands to encourage haste. I contrived to be the last one out the door, and took the first opportunity to fall in with another knot of servants going down another hall. I'd spent considerable time traversing the baron's residence when I'd searched for the women, and I made my way to the stairwell with the hidden door without any trouble at all, though a few housekeeping tasks briefly diverted me.

All those riches lying about—and I forced myself to resist them in spite of itching fingers, fantastic finds, and the ridiculous ease of acquiring them. I had a task to accomplish, and it would do me no good whatsoever to raise suspicions. With the business of the manor in full swing, the stairs were not as busy as they had been that fateful morning. I didn't even need to create a diversion to give myself time to clamber up behind the familiar suit of armor, run my fingers over the dimly lit wall behind it, and find the catch to open the door. Chills ran over my skin. Evidently the spiders occupying that particular nook still reigned unchallenged. Such sloppy housekeepers the great baron employed! I waved my hand back and forth through the air, but it didn't do any good. A strong desire to leave at once nearly overcame me, but I resisted. I had a mission to complete. I looked about but didn't see a single spider. No rats, either, thankfully. Invisible, web-spinning rats would have been more than I could handle.

— 34 —
A Little Help From My Friends

The door sprang open only a fraction, just as it had previously. I glanced up and down the stairs, then pushed into the little corridor and thus to the faintly lit interior. The witchlights still hung upon hooks fastened to the bookshelves, but this time I had to stop and press my hand against my chest as a strange knot formed there.

Ours... Ours... the Ancestors breathed. *We must free them! Let them go. Release... Release...*

"How are they ours?" I whispered, as if anyone could hear me in this vault of stone. Everything about the room held magic, a natural result of what Duzayan practiced there. Predictably, it made my skin prickle and itch worse than if a score of spiders skittered over me. I scratched. I shook out my arms. I looked down my tunic. Still no spiders.

Old magic. Magic of the Mazhar. Not his.

"It's his now," I pointed out drily, scratching my head with vigor.

Not his! they repeated. *Stolen. Acquired. Strategically relocated...*

So odd to hear them use my own words and phrases. "How do you know?"

Patterns. Influence. Origin.

My following had grown, I could tell by the weight of them, which seems a silly thing to say about either voices or spirits. "What do you suppose he uses them for?"

They didn't answer, and I doubted Duzayan used witchlights solely for illumination. Nothing was ever straightforward with him. And speaking of *him*, I knew I had best hurry to find what I had come for before he paid a visit to his cozy little library. Taking one of the witchlights, I went to the door in hopes of locking it. The latching mechanism was quite simple, which begged a question. "Why isn't this room guarded or even locked?" I asked.

Warded. Yes.

"It is?" If that so, what was I doing inside it?

Dissuasion. Small. Modest. Uncomfortable.

That explained my earlier urge to flee, though I couldn't imagine Duzayan doing anything modestly. I turned my attention to my task, knowing the exploration was going to hurt. Steeling myself, I started with the maps and star charts stored in leather tubes. Blessedly not magic in nature, I had no difficulty opening them, and I searched as swiftly as I could through the collection, the witchlights illuminating my task. The little breezes indicating the Ancestors brushed across me now and then, ruffling papers, and I had the distinct impression that two or three of them looked over my shoulder. No astrologer, I was uncertain what I sought. A sense of movement accompanied the impression of a new presence beside me. Soft whispers banished questions and confusion, and I set aside charts without conscious decision.

"There."

There.

The eerie echo made the hairs on the back of my neck stand up, but I could not let it distract me from my purpose. The diagram at which I gazed had notations in the borders that I could clearly understand, along with pictures and formulas I most assuredly could not. Their author was a wizard, after all, and well-educated. And I? An erstwhile street rat who had managed to find a way to steal his own rather limited tutelage. Knowing I faced a brilliant mind with the teachings of all sorts of scholars and magic at his fingertips gave me a moment's deep and icy pause. But... Duzayan was not beloved of the gods.

Shrugging off the unwelcome sense of impending doom, I pointed at a figure depicting two narrow, vertical rectangles with another horizontal across their tops and faint lines extending from the bottom in a ray pattern. "This looks like the engraving on my pendant." The pendant I wore even now.

A portal.

"What does it mean? A doorway... where? To what?"

The Ancestors did not know, though they recognized a few of the other symbols. *The old seer*, they murmured. *Jelal fir Baris. A pathway. Power. Danger...*

Putting the extra cases away, I pushed Duzayan's things aside to spread my find out on the table, and kept it from curling up with carefully chosen weights. A look at the floor-to-ceiling, cram-packed shelves filled me with despair. "I don't have time to look through all these. I'm not even certain what I'm looking for!" I moaned.

The chill, moist touch of the Ancestors brushed my cheek, then riffled papers and scrolls. In an instant they turned the room topsy-turvy. Books flew off the shelves, thumping and banging, pages flapping; small items crashed to the floor; herb bundles tied to the ceiling beams swayed and burst apart; a handful of feathers tipped out of a bowl and whirled in the sudden maelstrom.

"What are you doing?" I squawked, throwing my arms up to protect my face.

Searching. Reading. Looking! Finding!

One massive tome came barreling from behind me and landed atop the chart with a puff of dust and a panic of pages. Another skidded across the floor and crashed into my foot. One page turned, then another and another.

"Stop!" I hissed, horrified at the instant disaster. "How are we going to put all this back the way it was?"

Not, came a whispering chorus of refusal. *Look. See. Learn.*

"And then what?"

Run.

"Oh, very helpful!" I snapped, assaulted by nightmare images of my impending death. Flicking a feather off my chest, I glared at the open pages of the volume sitting atop the chart I'd pinned down. In the center of the page, very nicely decorated in a frame of curling vines, was an artful rendition of the portal. It almost made me jealous.

The Wycked Gate, Derivation of the Ancient Portals, I read. *The discovery of these alternate passages came about as the result of experimentation and expansion upon an old work. The result is a gate or a doorway to an alternate plane. Thus far, it appears to be connected to a specific location. Repeated exercises result in a view of the same plant and animal life, though the latter departs extremely from the familiar. Hadelfia's research on the demons inconclusive. Of the dozen demons drawn through to our side for study, four died of unknown causes, four were executed, three succumbed to common poisons, one escaped. A later, large-scale trial by Parabrach of Vadrima proves the beasts intelligent and quite hardy with exceptions as noted below. Conflict ended in disaster for both parties. Succeeding studies suggest the possibility of control by way of intimidation; most effective in the case of "Ragnus Cruendithar." Use of the Wycked Gates was subsequently banned, various sources citing extreme hazard, lack of usable dragons, Gate instability, utilization of prohibited blood magicks. Ingredients for preparatory elixir as follows.*

"As follows" included items listed in an unrecognizable language. Little fits and spurts of wind continued to ruffle the disarray. Other than that it was silent as a wretched tomb. Did Duzayan plan to use Egg for control or an ingredient in the spell? I reread the words twice, then found an innocuous reed pen to mark my place so I could look at the cover. *Compendium of Theurgic Formulae.* "A what?"

Collection. Treasury.

"Yes, yes, a collection of formulas. What kind?"

Sorcerous. Wizardly. Dangerous arts.

I flipped the thing open again and took a step back, considering. Crouching, I had to squint to read in the shadow cast by the table.

"He's... going to open a gate to another world and let monsters through. Is that even possible?" Unbelievable, certainly. This was the stuff of fable, and I was caught in a horrible dream. By the immediate reaction of my invisible companions, it was no joke.

Deceiver! Madman! Ruin in his hands! Loss! Loss, oh loss! they wailed, shrieking wildly around the room in such a frenzy that I fell to the floor, arms over my head to protect myself from injury. Images flashed through my mind's eye, filled with promises of terror and devastation. I struggled to find my own voice, to shout at them to stop, stop! And they labeled Duzayan mad...

Even when they stilled, their agitation quivered through the air, weaving through me. I lay there trembling with distress.

I know not how long I lay on the floor before another book came fluttering across the room like an awkward, weighty bird. It landed in front of me, scant inches from my protective arms. A few pages turned, then it settled. I stared at it a moment in trepidation, then slowly sat up, wiping a hand over my face and then attempting to restore tidiness to my person and equilibrium to my senses.

Dragons possess a natural immunity to wizard's magic. The contents of an unhatched dragon's egg, combined with an as yet unknown ingredient of the Anneraen species of flowering plants, is used to create a magically enhanced concoction which it is said (in the tomes of Rothak Korsis the Great, which have been recently uncovered and translated) will make a wizard invincible.

Invincible? Wasn't he formidable enough already?

Bracing myself against the sting of Duzayan's magic, I tore the pertinent pages loose from the books and rolled them up with the chart. I stuffed them all into one of the map tubes and slung it by its strap over my shoulder. Why did I believe the sibilant, agitated voices whispering in my ears? I did not, entirely, but they had not yet lied to me. Duzayan, on the other hand, had done little else. Clearly, he would do anything at all to achieve the power he sought, no matter the innocents he destroyed along the way.

I looked about for some sort of sack, but nothing presented itself, so I went about the room touching various small chests until I found one that wasn't too painful to bear. Emptying its contents on the floor, I transferred all the witchlights into it. "Is there anything else here I should take?"

The Ancestors rustled a bit, but offered nothing intelligible. Fastening the chest shut, I looked about for something to use as fuel. I spied an entire collection of bottles in which floated various nasty things: little eyeballs, bones and wings and leaves and berries (possibly) and all sorts of objects I could not even begin to identify. I didn't want to. With a sense of extreme revulsion, I picked the emptiest and least noxious-looking jar I could find and carefully pried the stopper free. The smell of the preserved berries (surely they were berries...) made me choke, but the preservative in which they floated was exactly what I needed: alcohol.

Grimacing eloquently, I emptied the contents over the books and papers. It was a gag-inducing, eye-watering experience. I followed that dispersal with another, generously—nay, gleefully—soaking all kinds of arcane parchments, charts, books and paraphernalia it must have taken a lifetime to collect. Maybe several if Duzayan was as profligate with other men's lives as he was with ours. The alcohol ran into some other liquid from one of the broken bottles and produced a cloud of pink colored vapor that sparkled and snapped and twisted. Clearly, it was time to vacate the chamber.

I hurried to the door to peek out. The crackling of the sparks was noisy and made it difficult to listen for anyone on the stair. All seemed quiet, so I set the chest down near the door and returned to my task. Making use of a fire starter box on the baron's table, I struck sparks over the alcohol-soaked papers—which went up in a flash that nearly scorched my eyebrows off. I stumbled backward.

The strange pink cloud billowed overhead and slammed against the ceiling. Dust fell. The Ancestors literally picked me up and shoved me toward the door, and I hit the ground running. Grabbing up the box of witchlights, down the stairs I galloped, careened around the corner and—nearly ran smack dab into his Royal Pain in the Backside, the Baron himself. My heart hurtled up my throat and straight back down again.

Duzayan's eyes widened. "Crow!" he gasped, displaying fine observation skills as well as a talent for coordinating surprise and speech.

The first of my list of rules was to avoid direct confrontation. The second, when the first could not be helped, was to evade capture, and the third advised setting the opponent off balance. That was easy. On the stairs I had the advantage of elevation. Of course he reached for me, as any opponent worth his salt ought to do. Years of training and practice came to my rescue. I ducked instinctively and twisted aside, slamming the chest at his groin as hard as I could.

Pain and *shock* made me stumble, and my own surprise nearly undid me until I recalled that neither feeling belonged to me.

Duzayan gasped and doubled over, his fingers catching in the tabard I wore and dragging me down. Were I a bigger man, and had I remained inside the loose cloth, my story would likely have ended in an instant. The chest tumbled out of my arms and crashed against the wall. I crashed against the hard stone of the landing, wriggling out of the tabard and nearly losing an ear in the process. The strap from the tube didn't make things any easier. I kicked out violently. Something crunched. A strong desire to survive kept me in motion. I clambered to my feet, grabbed the chest, and pelted up the stairs through the strangely tinged and horrendously malodorous smoke pouring out the door that was no longer hidden.

"Fire!" I screamed when I rounded the corner and encountered someone else coming down. A clerk of some sort, perhaps. I did not stop to ask, but sprinted right past him and kept running.

:-:

"Do you know these symbols?" I asked, laying out on the table the fresh parchments upon which I had copied Duzayan's charts.

"No," Brother Ozan lied, looking them over swiftly and shaking his head.

He'd been one of those who'd worked to heal my arm. An evasive lot in general, I'd still hoped they could accomplish a simple translation without me having to resort to threats of violence. I heaved a sigh of disappointment and glanced down the length of the refectory. It was empty but for a few workers at the other end, one mopping the floor and the other scrubbing a table. Evening meal had ended and the good priests of Ishram had already gone back to their business. The sick kept notoriously bad hours.

"It is probably idealistic of me, but I had hoped that members of your house were actually honest," I murmured.

"I beg your pardon? Are you accusing me of lying?" Of all the nerve!

"Yes."

He got abruptly to his feet and stepped over the bench, long robes artfully managed. "I'll have to ask you to leave."

"You can ask. You can even insist." I did not move, but watched him most seriously. "I might respond by loudly proclaiming your dishonesty and, by association, the dishonesty of your peers." Doing so would help the Ishramites not at all, for the prosperity of their healing centers depended not only on their talents, but on their reputation for modest living—and honesty.

"You would not be the first to insult us. We have survived the injury of vindictive tongues before."

"Yes, I suppose you have." I mused for a little space on how the relatives of those whom the brothers tended might dislike occasional unfavorable results. "Let us dispense with this ridiculous game, Brother Ozan. You and I both know what the Order of Ishram is and it is pointless to argue."

"We are healers," he said with utter conviction.

"I know. Have you and your brethren also survived accusations of wizardry?"

His hesitation was so brief I nearly missed it. "Of course not. Who would believe such things?"

I shrugged. "People who dislike wizards, and there's an awful lot of them. Why else hide what you do?"

The muscles around Ozan's mouth tightened, angry and uncertain. "You have no proof of any such activity."

"Do I not?" I pushed up the sleeve of my shirt, revealing the scars the demon had given me. "Wounds like these do not heal overnight on their own, nor with the help of salves or physics, no matter how rare and wonderful they may be. You recall treating me, I hope?" It had been only a day, and I knew he had not forgotten me any more than I had forgotten him.

"Clearly they have." He assumed a stubborn demeanor to keep his growing fear at bay. An admirable stance, but I was determined. There was a great deal at stake for both of us, whether he knew it yet or not.

"You gave me an elixir—"

"You can hardly call that magic."

"No," I gave him a smile of understanding and patience, the latter of which was fast waning. "But the following morning when you brought me food to break my fast and checked my bandages, you used a small spell."

"Ridiculous." He did a fine job of hiding a stab of fear. "I recall quite clearly that you had some sort of muscle spasm when I checked your wounds. No doubt a result of the elixir. It happens sometimes." Another lie.

"You wanted me to forget what happened during my stay, and you wanted me to resist the temptation to look under my bandages and see what you'd truly done."

"Supposing what you say is true, you are remarkably ungrateful."

"No." I shook my head. "I left a very generous donation for your help then, as well as my silence, and I'll do it again today—if you help me."

Ozan looked at me as though I had recently come from a cesspool. "I can be of no assistance to you, sir," he informed me stiffly.

Who could have guessed that biddable and humble Ozan could be so obstinate?

I collected my parchments and pushed myself up from my seat. "Walk with me."

"I would rather not."

"I want to show you something, just outside. I have no wish at all to hurt you, Brother Ozan, nor your good name, nor the character of your order. I also have no wish to waste valuable time, which we are doing with every passing moment. Just come and look out the door."

Reluctantly, he inclined his head in agreement, and the pair of us made our way to the door and thence through the garden a little way. He kept his distance.

"Look," I said, pointing northwest to a distinctive glow of pink-stained amber in the night sky. The blaze still burned, and I could only imagine how the fire had spread with unnatural swiftness and to extensive proportions. It really was a shame that the neighbor's houses burned, too, but I suspected that *they* had suspected Duzayan was a wizard, and I had come to the conclusion that it served them right. "Do you know what is burning?"

He did not answer me, but shaded his eyes from the light of surrounding torches with one hand and peered in the direction of the conflagration.

"That is the residence of a wizard," I informed him, and decided to make use of my recent history in the north. "Two of his associates, also wizards, are dead."

"You—" Ozan flinched, then swallowed and licked his lips before he tried again. "You are from the Star Tower?"

I crooked a brow, neither admitting nor denying anything, although it was a severe temptation to ask what the Star Tower was.

"Come inside," he said tersely. My uncanny ability to read people had not failed me; I had chosen the appropriate response.

Thank the god of—well, perhaps the one of healing and health would be appropriate, as Ozan served that deity. I would have hated to drag him into an alley and beat him up. The order's benevolence was the reason I had chosen it—and him in particular—over any of the known wizards in the city. Ozan led me through the hospice and down a hall off of which lay several small rooms. Those on the left were used for storage and those on the right had their doors closed, except for a small library. The few brothers we passed looked at us curiously, but did not venture to engage us in conversation. Ozan opened the door to one of the rooms and I followed him into a chamber with one high, wide window, a cot, and a table that took up the entire wall opposite. The surface was crowded with parchments, books, and containers of herbs and other medicaments. He flicked the draperies closed.

"You understand the position you're putting me in," he said, turning up the wick of a low-burning lamp.

"Yes, I'm giving you an opportunity to help countless people. Save lives, even."

He gestured me to one of two chairs and took up the other next to the table. "What do you want from me?"

I laid the parchments down before him again. "I want you to translate these for me and help me make sense of them."

"And then what?"

His question gave me pause. What might someone from the Star Tower actually do to him or with him? Something fairly awful, apparently, at least in his opinion. "I already told you I have no wish to harm you, Brother Ozan. Please, look at the papers and tell me what you make of them."

With an air of weary resignation, he took them to regard intently. Not wishing to interrupt him and make things more difficult for either of us, I held my silence. "This is all... rather random," he murmured. "As if it were bits and pieces of a greater whole."

Shades of Old Jelal paraded through my head. "I have other information. Can you put this together to make any sense?"

"Perhaps, but will it be the right sense?" Ozan remained quiet as he studied the symbols and notations, moving a few things aside to spread my papers out on his table. "These symbols," he pointed, "involve the alignment of stars and sun, and specifically reference the solstice, the longest day of the year—and the shortest night. The sun's power is at its highest point and tremendous amounts of energy are released. It is a time of strength, of will, of passion. The position of the stars on that day indicates there is profit to be had in using aggressive—bold—energy."

Oh, Duzayan was bold all right. I couldn't argue with that.

"This," he pointed to an odd mark surrounded by a broken, spiraling circle, "is the symbol of Pheryn, the goddess of travel."

"It's a bird." Stylized, but obvious now, and logical given all the signs that Duzayan meant to open a gate between worlds. The sheer arrogance of reordering nature so radically raised my hackles.

Ozan nodded. "And these are—"

"Sorix and Onuial, the gods of the afterlife and of war." Elbow on the arm of the chair, I tapped my fist against my mouth and considered the fullness of the tale. This tapestry of demons and dragons, wizards and war gods, magic and mayhem did not appeal to me in the slightest. The easiest and most sensible thing to do would be to hop aboard the next ship sailing out of port and never look back. My, would Tanris be angry...

Ozan moved one of the charts aside. "Logically, one would want to take every advantage of the position of the sun, but the time marked here is midnight."

"The traditional time for calling on dark powers."

The priest shrugged. "There are two schools of thought on that. Midnight, when shadows are deepest, or twilight, when night conquers day. Even so, if one were to call on the greatest powers of the dark, one would do so at the winter solstice, on the longest night of the year. Let us say, though, that some unknown timetable prevents that and the spells must be performed now. Why, then, would the author choose the day, or night in this case, before they happen? He's obviously made an error in his calculations."

If only it were so easy! "No, he wouldn't do that. There must be another factor we've overlooked."

"I don't know," Ozan murmured, looking through the documents again. Once he'd consented to examine them, the mystery had drawn him in completely. "There are references to spells, but they have to do with opening locked doors, protection, and control. I'm afraid I am no expert in those fields." He smiled apologetically.

"The stars marking the path to a doorway might not line up on the same night as the solstice occurs," I mused out loud.

"That's certainly possible."

"Then there you have it." I blew out a sigh and slouched a little further in my chair.

Ozan pulled his lamp closer. Laying a straightedge against the chart he'd chosen, he scribbled some quick calculations on an empty parchment. "I think I can pinpoint the doorway."

"Really?" I sat up, eagerness tickling me.

"Hush."

I hushed while he did complicated math, referred to a book full of equations and diagrams and illustrations, flipped back and forth between charts, and plotted out the sketch of a map. The finished product was understandably rough, and Ozan less than pleased with it. "It's here in the city, somewhere in the Litares District."

Right where Duzayan lived. I huffed a laugh. "Of course it is."

"There's a mention here," he turned the documents until he found what he was looking for, "of the Cruendithar constellation—the Dragon—but it doesn't match the other diagrams, and the trait it signifies doesn't appear to have anything to do with, well, anything."

"What is it?"

He wrinkled his brow. "Those born under its sign are rumoured to be good with money."

Rich as he was, I suppose that applied well enough to Duzayan, but how was that important to opening a Gate?

"There's also the Arthon constellation, the horn. It represents a figure from a tragic myth and those born under it are said to be hopeless romantics."

The only person Duzayan loved was himself.

"Aside from that, we have symbols of Houses, of gods, of historical figures—nothing that makes particular sense, unless these are tied to something you know already?"

It was a good ploy to try to access information I didn't have, regretfully. "The Solstice is the day after tomorrow. I have work to do." I got to my feet.

Ozan, too, stood, gathering the parchments, rolling them, and tying them together neatly with a strip of cloth. "The night your wizard has chosen is tomorrow."

Tomorrow... Perhaps it was a good thing I didn't have much time to develop my sense of terror. "One more thing: do you have access to Adamanta Dust?"

"In small amounts," Ozan hedged.

"I need all of it. Now. And be quick about it."

"You can't—"

"Oh, yes, I can, and I will. I will do whatever it takes, and you will help me, do you understand?"

He wasn't happy about it, but apparently even lowly priests dream about being heroes.

— 35 —
Let The Conjuring Begin!

Nothing remained of Duzayan's huge, beautiful mansion but a blackened ruin, smoking still in places. Looking at it, I wondered how much worse the strange potions and magical items had made the conflagration. A fire will do much damage on its own, but the enchantments had set off something dire, and the resulting explosion made an impressive crater. The upper floors had crashed down into the cavity. Farthest from the blast an ell-shaped section four floors high still stood, partially intact. There was something surreal about rooms whose walls had been sheared away, leaving the remains of smoke-blackened contents exposed. The opposite corner had nothing left but a tenuous skeleton merely suggesting walls. All ruined... All the beautiful, thick carpets, the paintings, the fantastic artworks collected from the length and breadth of the empire. The coin. Jewels. I could not help but sigh at the terrible waste, but if I had it to do over again I would not hesitate.

Upon first inspection, the ruins were deserted, but I knew better. Duzayan would have to come here. This is where he had gathered his power, and he was connected to this place just as surely as he was connected to his own heart. The Ancestors believed it and Brother Ozan had confirmed it. The wizard did not have either the dragon's egg to make his spell of invincibility, nor the dragon to control the demon mob, but he had too much invested in this undertaking to walk away now. If he could not have his empire he would have revenge.

Tanris would like a bite of that particular dish, and that struck me as a wrong thing. A man as good as he should not be forced to such a miserable, low state. While his grief and anger would be useful in fighting against the wizard, I worried how it would affect him in the long run. When I'd left him at the apartment—me to tend to final details and him to organize the timely arrival the army, he had worn a veritable cloak of grimness. It had nothing of his usual air of efficient, detached purpose, and he'd lost his habitual glower. No, he *burned*. For his sake, I hoped the army would sweep in and finish the odious baron off before he could even draw his sword, and sooner would be better than later.

How long had I been waiting? Impatience filled me, and worry tugged at my nerves. The later it grew, the more likely were the chances that Duzayan would attempt to create the Wycked Gate, and the more complicated things would get.

The sound of crying drew me, though I did not at first identify it as such. It came to me as a small noise and emotion blended together, a soft murmur bearing a terrified helplessness. I picked my way slowly toward it, listening and pausing to ascertain the proper direction, on the lookout lest there were some of the baron's Best lurking about, or wretched little demons hidden in the ruins waiting to leap out and raucously proclaim my presence while they battered, bit and clawed me senseless.

The closer I came to the edge of the crater, the better I could hear—and see. Creeping up a thick, fallen wall, I peered over the edge. The heart of the crater was ringed about with hooded torches illuminating the interior without casting much light behind or above them. A clever design, but the uses must be quite limited. There were only four of them, and a little study along with the subdued whispering of the Ancestors revealed that they were placed at the four cardinal points. The floor of the area had been cleared, and two figures occupied it. The first, wearing a robe of some dark, faintly glittering fabric, was easy to guess: Duzayan. He held a goblet in one hand, and in the other a knife. He appeared the very epitome of every evil wizard described in children's tales, and the scantily clad figure at his feet only completed the scene.

It was a woman, of course, bound to iron stakes pounded into the stone floor matching the positions of the torches. Between one foot and the other, a distance of perhaps five feet—which could not have been at all comfortable for the woman—a shallow, rough channel had been carved into the floor. The wizard, who had his back more or less to me, was talking or perhaps chanting, while the woman tossed her head this way and that, crying quietly and with heart-rending sorrow. Duzayan's robes mostly concealed her, but I thought she'd been gagged, which not only went hand in hand with the Evil Wizard Sacrifice Scene, but made perfectly good sense. Screaming—even coming from a recently burned-out building—bore the obvious risk of drawing attention that any wizard worth his salt would want to avoid like an attack of sudden charity.

He'd already begun. My heart thudded painfully in my chest as I realized I must intervene, and quickly. Favored of the gods, I *had* killed two wizards already. I had the Ancestors... I could do this.

However, the plan for stopping a dangerous wizard and actually executing the endeavor were two entirely different things, no matter how well I'd tried to think things through. Lacking omniscience or the ability to prophesy, I had not planned for the woman, which put me at a disadvantage. Still in the shadows behind the torches, I crept down the tumbled stonework, keeping my eyes on Duzayan, hardly daring to breathe for fear of drawing his attention and ruining my nebulous new plan. "Sshhh..." I cautioned the Ancestors in a whisper when they skittered through the ruined chamber. The torches flickered.

Duzayan glanced about, but he did not stop speaking, chanting. The foreign words slid over each other and across my senses like slimy worms. I wanted to cry out, but clamped my lips shut, holding still as a statue. After a moment he moved toward the woman's feet, stepping over her delicately. The torch light shone on his robe again. Closer now, I could see it was heavily embroidered with metallic thread, though I could not make out the designs. Wizard sophistication at its best. Holding out the goblet, he waved his knife over it theatrically several times, muttering to himself, then poured the rich, bright contents out into the channel. A vivid, glowing pale orchid color, it hissed when it hit the stone.

Then, quicker than you can say "Blast that scheming wizard!" he bent and slashed at the woman's nearest ankle. The gag muffled her scream; her body bucked wildly against the restraints. Duzayan stepped between her legs and swiped again.

Thank the god of quick thinking, I was already moving. Grabbing up the nearest fist-sized chunk of rock, I hurled it at Duzayan and picked up another. The first struck him in the shoulder. He took a startled step backward, which should have landed his foot in the channel, but with an awkward twist he avoided it. The knife-wielding hand flailed about for balance, then the tip of the thing suddenly pointed at me and Duzayan's head turned my direction, spearing me with twin bolts of sheer fury. I pitched the second rock at him. Years of practice, a good eye, and the love of the gods had made me a very good aim. My missile clobbered him right in the forehead and over he went.

I wasted not a second of precious time, but leaped down the incline and ran to the moaning, crying woman, drawing my own knife as I went. One slice freed her hands, and then I—paused. "Tarsha! How did you get here?" I asked incredulously, and at once I knew that Duzayan had never intended she should live. Like Tanris and myself, she was nothing but a pawn.

She could not answer, of course. Another sharp hiss, a crackle, and an indescribable *snap!* drew my attention to the channel, except it wasn't just a channel any more. Tarsha's blood flowed into it and mixed with the potion, somehow creating a towering arch of pale purple that snapped and crackled like fire but looked very much like liquid. I had not the slightest inclination to touch it and find out. The purple bled into a dark, completely opaque center. Where I should have been able to see the floor and broken masonry behind it, there was only a cloudy, roiling surface.

Stark fear lent me speed. I could not allow her blood to fuel Duzayan's spell. I cut through the ropes binding Tarsha's bare legs, idiotically wondering where her darling husband might be at the moment. The awful light revealed a deep cut, blood spooling out in a black ribbon.

The gods had not deserted me. Grabbing up the fabric of Tarsha's gossamer gown—and deliberately not wondering why she wore such a frivolous thing in such a place—I cut off a piece. She, in the meantime, dragged at the gag. Down on one knee, I bound the cloth quickly about the cut on her leg. The delicate fabric promptly turned crimson, too fragile to serve as a bandage. That was no help at all. Casting about, Duzayan's robe caught my eye. He didn't move, so up I leaped to cut off a strip of the stuff, dash back to Tarsha's side, hoping as I bound the freely bleeding wound that the robe wasn't imbedded with magical incantations that would somehow set all my efforts to naught. Of course it took only a second or two for my hands to begin tingling fiercely.

"Crow!" Tarsha sobbed, struggling to sit up.

"Not now," I responded curtly, and swept her up in my arms. The entire crater was bathed in pulsing, eery orchid light that played strange games with the shadow and made footing treacherous. I had barely reached the outer edge and the first rough chunks of erstwhile wall that we needed to ascend when there came a horrific moaning roar behind me.

"Cccrrroooowww!!!" Why couldn't Duzayan stay unconscious—or even dead—while I made my escape?

Something struck me hard in the leg. I stumbled and dropped Tarsha. She gasped, and her arms tightened around my neck as she dragged me down with her. "Go. Get up. Run!" I hissed, scrambling off her and yanking her to her feet to push her unceremoniously upward, bleeding leg or no. She could hobble to safety or she could die. Either way, Duzayan would be bereft of a key ingredient. She gave me one wide-eyed, terrified look, then clambered up the side of the crater on hands and knees.

I would very much have liked to do the same. Unfortunately, Duzayan demanded my immediate attention, and he was fairly determined about it and unwilling to let Tarsha go, besides. Something whizzed past my head and she gave a little scream. Rocks clattered down around me, and I could only guess that she was scooting upward as fast she could go, which left me to deal with the regrettably conscious wizard.

The whizzing thing turned out to be a demon—a pair of them, even. Big surprise there, eh? Could a wizard have any less imagination? I wondered, though I was wildly disinclined to offer any suggestions. More shrieking and gasping came from further up the incline, but I could do nothing for her. Frankly, Tarsha was lucky to be alive at all, and she could just take care of herself from here on out. She'd got herself into this mess, after all.

I could sense the Ancestors darting about in sharp, quick little dashes, and I heard a thump and a funny little squeaking noise just as the second miserable demon flung itself out of the darkness and directly at my head. I squawked and went down in an inelegant heap, nearly twisting an ankle as I fell. I would thank the appropriate god for saving me in a minute or two. For the moment, I was slightly preoccupied with the leathery creature attached to my face, wings wrapped around my head. This was becoming an annoying trend.

"THIEF!" it screamed at the top of its lungs, also nothing new and not really appropriate to the moment.

My fall tumbled the pair of us down the slope with the demon flapping and shrieking and generally made a nuisance of itself. Burning lines opened up in my scalp, flying dust scraped my eyeballs.

"Quiet!" Duzayan hissed. How a single word could make my ears hurt so, I do not know.

I helped enforce the order with another chunk of debris aimed squarely— and repeatedly—at the demon's ugly little head. Bashing it senseless took some serious dedication. When it lay still, I smacked it once more for good measure, then turned to its master.

I had not gotten a good look at him before now. He was a monster out of the worst of nightmares—and I suddenly remembered the exact image, plucked from the visions that had plagued me in my travels across the continent, only I had not recognized him then because he so little resembled the man I knew. His nose was pushed violently to the side and his face, oh, his face! A disaster of bruises and raw, terrible burns created a ruin scorched beyond recognition. The entire right side of his visage had melted like wax, leaving his teeth exposed and his eye naked and red. I wondered if he could see out of it at all. I recalled kicking him when we'd struggled on the stairs, and I could only guess that I had been responsible for the wreckage of his nose. But the rest? He must have gone into his secret room while it burned! How he had not been incinerated when it exploded remained a mystery and still, blasted and ruined as he was, he was opening the gods-cursed Gate.

Gripping the rock tightly in my hand, I got to my feet. "You are insane." My voice held a peculiarly hysterical note I found dismaying.

"No, my thieving feathered friend, I am completely sound of mind." His voice was mild and tender, but his terrible smile sent shivers up my back. "What have you done with it?"

I wondered for a moment if the Ancestors had deserted me and why they would do such a thing right then, but no, I could feel their uneasiness. They roiled silently, warily all around me. And then I wondered if maybe, gods willing, they had some plan of action to which I was not privy. When this ended, we were really going to have to work on communication skills.

"Done with what?" I backed carefully, slowly away as Duzayan continued to stalk toward me. Warm blood trickled down my scalp. Thank the gods, none ran down my face to blind me.

"Please don't play the fool with me. I know you better than that."

"You know me!" I echoed, and laughed mirthlessly. "Forgive me if I have missed the part of our lives where we spent time talking and sharing and working together, getting to know each other! How utterly careless of me to have failed to notice! Either that, or you have somehow managed to accomplish an inherently cooperative project completely on your own."

"Sarcasm does not become you."

I spun about, leaping nimbly atop a wall-sized slab of rock. Thankfully my brief tussle and tumble had not robbed me of my agility. I turned to give him an extravagant bow. "Sarcasm is my middle name."

"Where is the egg? Do you want me to hurt you, little bird?"

"Want you to?" Pursing my lips and folding my arms, I looked about in search of an answer to the question. In reality, I was looking for Tarsha, and found her lying on the topmost edge of the crater, one hand just visible and her torn gown—a strange pink hue in the light of the Gate—fluttering gently over the edge. There was no sign of the other demon, but she was not moving. Unfortunate, I supposed, but I could not really find it in me to care. At least she was out of easy reach and Duzayan wouldn't hurt her in order to try to make me behave. And if he did, they were both in for a surprise. "No, I don't want you to hurt me, but that hasn't stopped you from doing just that—without my consent at all, I might point out—every single time we've met. No, you deal out pain as if you have some sort of divine right, which definitely counts against your alleged sanity."

His expression changed, but I could not decipher it. He made a gesture with blackened fingers, and I was struck with an overwhelming impulse to go to him. I took one surprised and unwilling step forward. Then another. Little green lights began to sparkle all over me and I braced myself, resisting the compulsion. The Ancestors helped me, their cool touch pressing me back, reassuring me.

"Come to me," Duzayan crooned, and if he noticed the play of contradictory magic, he did not show it. "Tell me what I wish to hear."

I regained the steps I'd lost with an effort and sneered, though it was not likely to win me any favor. The Ancestors brushed my face and ears. With a vague crackling noise the spell fell away from me. "You wish to hear where I've concealed the egg. You *wish* me to aid you in your rise to power. You *wish* me to bow down to you and dedicate my life to you. Well, let me tell you something: I will never bow down to you, Duzayan, and if you use your vile magic to force my body to bend to your will, then the obeisance will be a meaningless lie worth less than nothing. As for the egg—" I made a motion with one hand. "There is none."

Do not tease it! the feathery Voices pleaded. *Do not tempt it!*

319

Strange they should refer to Duzayan as an "it."

It—er, he—hissed, the pretense of patience evaporating. "Do not insult me, and do not lie to me!" He made fists of his hands and pulled. Magic tugged at me. I stumbled forward, then resisted. Disbelieving, he pulled harder but the spell frayed and fizzled. Like a great bloody vulture, he stalked across the space separating us.

I lifted my chin. Took several steps back. "I've no need to lie. You sent me too late. All those charts, all those calculations, all the meticulous planning —" I snapped my fingers. "Wrong! Stupendously, embarrassingly wrong!" He had certainly been wrong about the dragon, and I could do worse than to convince him that his calculations involving the opening of the Wycked Gate were in error.

No no no!

"Impossible."

"Do you honestly believe you never make mistakes?" I inquired in astonishment, crooking a brow.

"Impossible," he repeated, the gross interpretation of a snarl contorting his features.

"You chose me," I pointed out, pressing a hand to my chest. I took the opportunity to palm the little jar Brother Ozan had given me, working the stopper loose with my thumb. "Specifically. I would like to say that was your first mistake, but the papers and letters I took from your study and your— what *do* you call that dreadful little hole where you kept all the books and magical odds and ends? It's right here, isn't it?" I asked, waving at the walls of the crater. "Those things tell a different tale."

"You are impertinent and ignorant," he growled, "and you have no idea what you have done. None!"

I wanted to argue that I did indeed, but his charred hand tightened into a fist and he moved as if to throw something at me. Invisible, the spell punched me like a fist, knocking me head over heels off my perch and sending me skidding carelessly across the uneven ground. I lost my rock-turned-weapon. I lost the jar of Adamanta Dust. Stones and broken bits of masonry dug at me, tearing my clothing and skin. The edges of my vision flickered with bright green flashes of light. I had expected something like that from him before, and he'd only sent the demon, but still I lay gasping for air like a beached fish. As a means to distract Duzayan while I thought of a good—or even marginally successful—plan for stopping him, the situation left much to be desired. He was distracted, all right, but my own thought processes wholly focused on two priorities: breathing and not getting clobbered again. Once he finished toying with me, he'd get right back to the business of opening the Gate. I had to move, had to get out of his reach. It is said that being forewarned is being forearmed, and this might have been true, but an uncooperative and overwhelming part of me decided breathing was of tantamount importance and the escaping part could wait a second or two.

Not so!

If I had hastened to escape immediately, I might have had a moment in which to draw a breath or ten. Duzayan made another fist, little black threads of energy like some strange sort of reverse lightning gathering around his hand. I only had an instant to note it before he let loose and pummeled me again, sending me spinning willy-nilly across the ground. I would have to worry about the scraping and bruising later. What he did reminded me of how Melly and his colleague had attacked me, but without the twisting agony of my innards, for which I was profoundly grateful and not about to argue the difference. At the same time, I devoutly wished I had a handy chasm down which I might drop the loathsome creature.

"Do you—" I gasped and wheezed as I tried to sit up. I had no idea lungs could hurt, but mine certainly did. When he knocked the breath out of a body, he meant business. "Do you see? You're doing it again. I—I tell you a truth you—dislike and you—you start in with the hurting." I waved one hand and coughed. Licking my lips, I tasted copper.

Damaged! Wounded! the Ancestors cried, kicking up little whirlwinds.

Duzayan's approach heavily favored one side, but determination filled every hobbling step.

"You're not going to be reasonable about this, are you?" No doubt hoping for reason from a madman, particularly at this point of the game, was a waste of time. I looked about for some means of distraction or, better yet, defense. Struggling to my feet, I grabbed up the end of an extinguished torch buried under a bit of debris, spun about, and lobbed it at him.

My aim is good, but his hand came up to block it and it flew away into the darkness without ever touching him. Against all the laws of physics, it reversed in midair and whipped at the back of his head. He screamed in pain and rage as it knocked him to his knees, then the thing flew straight at me. Should I duck or grab? It dipped down and I opted for the latter lest it knock me over as well. It was a good weapon, after all, and with it in my hand I launched myself at Duzayan, fully intending to beat him senseless.

He was having none of that, of course, and another burst of black energy bowled me over. I nearly beaned myself with the torch, and then Duzayan leaped upon me. How someone in his condition could move so quickly escaped me, but he poised over me with both hands extended and gleaming horribly. The Ancestors protested with shrieking wails and a sudden furious gust of wind. Dust and gravel pummeled us and pulled violently at our garments, for all the good that did.

"Where is my dragon egg?" Duzayan thundered, and introduced me to the full force of his anger, this time complete with the gut-twisting pain his sidekicks at Hasiq had used on me. I screamed. The Ancestors screamed.

"It hatched!" I cried, convulsing in agony.

"LIAR!" He jabbed me so enthusiastically I was convinced that my insides would soon be my outsides.

— 36 —
Turn About

Through the flying debris came a dark shape to wrap itself around Duzayan's head. I don't know which of us was the more surprised, but his shock led to the suspension of his debilitating spell, and I scrambled for the dropped torch, wheezing and moaning and crying. I could hardly see. On my knees, I spun about, aiming my makeshift weapon for his legs while he screamed and cursed and tried to pull the flying thing off his face. I thought at first it was a demon with a powerful streak of vengeance, but then I heard it creaking and hissing. Not-An-Egg!

His timing couldn't have been better, but horror filled me. How had he found me? He was supposed to be safely locked away in my apartment! "Get away!" I cried at him, certain Duzayan would rip him to shreds. The dragon did a fine job doing some ripping of his own, talons and beak slashing savagely at Duzayan's head and face while I beat at the wizard's legs frantically. Jagged black energy crackled. Not-An-Egg made a terrible noise and fell away. My heart, had it not been beating wildly, might have plummeted to my belly in sheer, terrified dismay.

"Gods curse you!" I screamed, and with the dragon out of the way I had no qualms about thunking Duzayan about his ugly, evil head. He had hurt my—I do not even know what the dragon meant to me, but he had become dear, and he was just a baby besides. I cannot be certain, but it seemed to me that the Ancestors themselves lent me strength.

Duzayan refused to surrender. Black sorcerer that he was, he raised his arms protectively over his head and from beneath them made strange, guttural noises that swiftly became hurts. Each one lanced through my very brain, shocking me and causing my limbs to spasm painfully. Reeling, sobbing, I fell away. My body continued to jerk and twitch as the wizard got slowly to his feet. Not-An-Egg's attack had wreaked havoc on his terrible countenance. Blood streamed down his torn and ragged face, but he was *laughing*. It was a terrible sound.

Picking up the torch I had dropped, he examined it, then turned his ghastly smile on me. All around us the wind roared. I wanted to close my eyes against the dirt and grit lashing my face, but I dare not. Duzayan staggered and swayed as he came to stand over me and I, unable to find any kind of control over my convulsing muscles, could only watch helplessly.

"I am going to kill you," he said, just in case I'd missed out on the obvious. "Slowly."

I gritted my teeth against waves of pain and helplessness.

"The dragon was supposed to be mine, Crow. I have waited decades for him. I have planned and I have sacrificed. And you—you my talented little thief, even managed to get past Ammeluanakar and the others. Tell me how you did it."

I didn't want to tell him anything. "K-killed them," I said anyway.

He glared at me for a long time, the wind of the Ancestors whipping at his hair and his torn clothing. Torchlight played havoc with the shadows, casting him in the shape of some grim creature from tales meant to frighten the faint of heart. It worked.

"You?" he asked at last.

He had not loosed the spell torturing my body, each paroxysm prefaced with bouts of helpless shuddering. My jaw clenched too tightly to allow words, but it didn't keep horrible, betraying noises from escaping my throat.

Duzayan's features moved in a hideous grimace. "Excellent. I wanted the library and the treasures at Hasiq for my own, but Ammeluanakar and his allies have proven stronger than I expected. Who could have guessed that a noisy little bird would be their undoing?"

What?

Duzayan prodded me none too gently in the chest with the end of the burnt-out torch. "He was the guardian, you know. It should have been me. He was a wizard of mediocre talent and an extremely spineless man. Think of what could have been done with all that knowledge, all that power he kept hidden in the vaults beneath the mountain. He would never agree that we should use it. Instead of being relegated to the status of swine by people who do not appreciate our skills, we would have been lords and rulers." The noise he made might have been laughter. "*Will* be. Tonight I become emperor, Crow, no little thanks to you. You deserve some sort of reward for the part you've played."

His words turned my brain to a solid block of ice around which a few little frantic thoughts oozed. I had killed a Guardian? I was not an assassin, I had only been defending myself! What had I done?

Leaning on the torch still supported by my chest, he mused for a little while, which was no small agony. "I'll tell you what. I will let you live to witness it—and it will be glorious, I promise you—and then I'm afraid I'll have to kill you. While I admire your thieving and assassination skills when they're put to good use, I can't have you stealing from me or trying to kill me, and I'm not sure we'd be able to work out our differences amicably."

A small scraping and creaking noise came from a pile of rubble nearby, and Duzayan turned his head to look. The movement bathed his face entirely in shadow, which was a reprieve for my eyes, at least.

"The dragon..." He heaved a long, rasping sigh. "Have you any idea how important it is?"

I could only imagine how having a dragon at one's side might influence one's power, particularly for a wizard. An emperor wizard, even. Mute, I shivered and jerked and glared useless daggers at him.

"I was meant to bond with it, and I should have been the one to call on its strength."

Bonded? I knew nothing about any bonding, unless one counted the way Not-An-Egg liked to curl up near me to sleep, or the way he expected me to feed him. He liked Girl nearly as much, though he generally tended to avoid Tanris. As if *any* of that mattered now. All the little habits and quirks marking our days since we'd fled Hasiq seemed far away and dreamlike.

"I very much doubt I can change that now, Crow. Such a terrible waste." He thumped the end of the torch against my breastbone, provoking a gasp and another racking convulsion. "I'll likely have to kill it, too."

"*N-n-no!*" The word came out in a ludicrous, stuttering protest. The prospect of my own death terrified me, but it was worse to contemplate Not-An-Egg's. Panic galvanized me. "Help me!" I screamed at the Ancestors, and struck out at the length of torch as hard as I could. Duzayan tottered. I knotted my hands in his garments and pulled. The Ancestors shrieked and pushed and tore—and Duzayan fell across me, provoking agony beyond words. I grunted under the impact, which came with the revolting stench of burned flesh. I could reach neither my knife nor the charred torch that clattered away as Duzayan lost his hold on it, but I could punch and tear—and I put everything I had into it.

The pair of us rolled back and forth across the destroyed chamber, bashing and ripping at each other in a wild struggle for survival. Finding a rough fragment of stone beneath one hand, I seized it and struck at him. The blow glanced off his shoulder. His opposite fist slammed against my cheek. Bright light exploded across my vision, but I didn't need to see my opponent. I reached out, closed my fist, and pulled. He screamed as my hand came away full of hair and skin—an event I would find disgusting if I happened to survive the moment.

Duzayan threw me away from him bodily and came to his knees, black energy snapping and crackling around his hands and from the top of his head, making what remained of his hair stand on end. A violent wind tore between us and Duzayan fell over sideways. I wanted nothing more than to lie still, but I could not. Forcing my tortured muscles into motion, I hurled myself at him. If he used his magic against me again, I was done for. My shoulder struck his chest as he rose and we went tumbling again. What we did to each other was visceral and utterly barbaric, but I could not let him kill me and thus kill the little dragon. Somehow he managed to gain the upper hand, coming astride my chest and pinning me down. I can only surmise that his awful magic gave him strength; my own reaction to it had the air sparking wildly, eerily green, and every instance of contact hurt not only my body, but my very soul.

Black-sheathed hands rose and fierce triumph shot through him. I really was going to die this time, but I had every intention of taking him with me. I had no other choice. I clawed at him and found, more by accident and by pain than by intent, the knife at his waist. I pulled it free and shoved it into his side. Even as I drew back for another blow, I felt an odd thump and a shock of confusion that did not belong to me. A crossbow bolt protruded from the very center of Duzayan's chest, solid and wonderfully potent. Duzayan looked down at it, then at me. As he did, an arc of glittering silver touched his neck, and sent his ruined head rolling.

It was the most terrible, most marvelous thing I had ever seen—and I screamed in a bizarre, guttural mixture of shock and victory. Tanris shoved Duzayan's body over sideways and stood there, his upraised sword stained crimson.

"What did I tell you," he bit out, "about doing dangerous things on your own?"

A spasm made me clench my teeth.

"I didn't want you to kill him *for* me, I wanted a piece of him!"

It seemed to me that a head was a pretty substantial piece, and I was more than happy that he'd arrived to take it. I shivered uncontrollably.

"Crow?" He kicked the corpse aside and went down on one knee next to me. The sword clattered to the broken pavement, and then Girl appeared, too, crying as usual. I would be surprised if she *didn't* cry. My body continued to jerk and shudder with the remnants of Duzayan's spell.

"Egg—" I managed.

"To the Dark with that, what's he done to you? Where are you hurt?"

Everywhere hurt. Every *thing* hurt. To make matters worse, a low, persistent whining filled my ears and grated on my nerves. The wind of the Ancestors continued unabated, the three of us occupying a little pocket of air free of dust and debris. Thanks be to the gods of breathing and seeing.

Waving her hands helplessly, overcome with relief, Girl finally settled on kissing me, then stroking my face in a fruitless attempt to soothe me. A smear of dark blood stained her cheek. Mine or Duzayan's?

"M-m-magic," I croaked, unable to stop convulsing. "N-not-an-Eg-g-g."

Tanris gave me a distressed look. "Crow, look at me. Can you hear me? Are you all right?"

Yes, I could hear him, couldn't he hear me? And I certainly was not all right. I tried to sit up and only ended up curled on my side, awkwardly clutching my belly. "Help—help me up." The compulsion to go find Not-An-Egg was just as strong as the wizard's had been, and fueled, perhaps, by my fear for him.

"Will you lie still, you mutton head?"

I could not fight the weight of his hands. I found myself lying on my back, my head resting in Girl's lap. I could not see the stars overhead, which was slightly disconcerting, and the walls of the ruins were lit by a strange, pulsing reddish light. "We've got to move him," Tanris said, contrary to the whole "lie still" order. Tension came off him in waves. "It's getting worse."

"What—Wh-what is worse?"

Pale and taut, Girl pointed away to one side, and with an effort I turned my head. Duzayan's Gate throbbed with a sick scarlet glow. The center of it, darker than the darkest night, stretched and writhed as something pushed against it from the opposite side. As we watched, the fabric thinned and gave way. A man-like figure oozed through the rend, unfolding to a height of seven feet or more. A pair of horns protruded from its head above its brows, and a row of spikes sprouted down the creature's neck and spine and tail. The tail hovered for a moment, then lashed back and forth as it caught sight of the three of us. Golden eyes gleamed bright in its furred, snouted countenance, and a rumbling growl filled the air. There's no need to get into a lengthy description about its teeth. Suffice it to say that there were lots and they were large.

"Great shades..." Tanris whispered.

"Sh-sh-shoot it!" I squawked, wondering what he was doing just crouching there next to me, staring at disaster like a lunatic.

Tanris didn't have the crossbow. As it turned out, neither did Girl. She dove one way while Tanris, his bloody sword suddenly in his hand, leaped to his feet and ran straight at the demon, thereby confirming his lunacy. My head, which Girl had sweetly held in her lap, hit the pavement with a resounding thump and I was left to my own devices. Unfortunately, my devices were few. I had a knife—no, two! I still had Duzayan's. Imbued with magic, the thing burned my skin and I wanted badly to put it down, but I needed every advantage. I had no idea what I might be able to do against either demon or magical portal, but I was determined not to simply lie there on the ground—though in retrospect it's possible that I might have been assumed dead and thus ignored, which might have been a good thing, at least until the demons flooded through the Gate and trampled me to death. Stark fear played a large part in the movement I achieved. More or less propped on one elbow, I looked about for the dragon. The twitching and cramping eased a fraction, but refused to let me go.

"Egg!" I called, but if he made an answer I couldn't hear it. The demon's howls and Tanris's shouts rent the air, not to mention the increasingly maddening thrum the Gate produced. It occurred to me that it wouldn't be long until the neighbors arrived to investigate the strange goings on, and the Imperial Troops couldn't be long behind them. The Imperial Troops, however, wouldn't last long against a tide of demons. When it came to that, neither would we.

"*Crow!*" Tanris roared in that "Do something!" sort of voice. Hideous magenta light bathed him, and he slashed at the demon like a madman. The demon slashed right back, and not only did he have a spiked tail to flail, but he sported impressive claws on his ham-like hands.

I heard a *thump* and a buzz, and the demon jerked as a crossbow quarrel stabbed into the base of its thick neck. I wondered how Girl could see through her tears to aim so nicely. Tanris made good use of the distraction and directed a two-handed swipe at the demon's head with his sword. The sword didn't go all the way through, and the demon howled loud enough to make the walls shake, grabbing at Tanris as it fell. In the meantime, the surface of the Gate stretched and bulged as more demons pressed through. One, two—Faster than I could blink, four little ones popped through, shook themselves like dogs shedding water, and then launched an attack at Tanris's legs. Right behind them, the fabric of the Gate bulged again.

What could we do?

Crawling across the ground, I picked up the extinguished torch. Bracing it against the ground, I struggled to my feet. Another crossbow bolt zipped past me and I nearly fell over in an instinctive jerk to get out of the way. With a squeal, one of the little demons came rolling past me, tumbling head over heels. For a demon, it was sort of cute. It looked something like a hedgehog, but nearly as big as Not-An-Egg and with a wide, flat face. A large mouth bore an extreme overabundance of needle sharp teeth, which it was more than happy to apply to me. It moved with shocking speed.

I yelped and smacked at it with my torch-turned-cudgel, leaping out of its path. Well, that was my intention, but the demon was not only speedy, it was agile. Not like me in my current condition. Its teeth pierced my boot without any trouble and I immediately had a furious ten pound fur-ball attached to me. My attempts to pry it off shortly had me on the ground again, and the wretched thing wouldn't budge except to grind its jaws and further mutilate my boot and, in a few seconds, me. I had no choice but to beat it to a pulp. Even dead, it clung to my ankle.

A burst of air bowled another of the furry demons off course as it sped at me. It bounced off a piece of fallen masonry, squeaked, rerouted, and came at me again. I met it with a swipe of my cudgel, sending it flying into the shadows, only to find myself face to face with something else altogether. Five minutes, and already the Gate had produced an admirable assortment of fiendish figures. I did not want to know what it would cough up in an hour. First, though, I had to deal with the six-legged dog-looking thing with the tongue like a snake. It was not a pretty sight. If I'd had time to be frightened I might have tried to run. Weakened, trembling still with the affects of Duzayan's spell, and with a furry weight attacked to my leg, I wouldn't have gone far.

The dog thing leaped at me. Still lying on the ground, I braced the torch and caught the dog demon in the chest, hurling it over my head. I twisted around. So did it. It came at me with its crazy tongue and an inordinate amount of drool. The impact of the torch against its skull jarred all the way up my arm and rattled my teeth. Its claws raked my thigh as I stabbed it repeatedly with the knife. That, too, sent painful reverberations up my arm.

A squeak alerted me to another attack by a hedgehog demon, but as I spun to face it, a winged shape flapped past me and plowed into it. Not-An-Egg! I was relieved and terrified all over again. He was going to get hurt! And I could not help him. The dog thing wasn't finished yet and even though its flailing was weak, it dug at me. Licked me, even, with its ungainly tongue. The spittle stung, and I wiped my hand on my pants to be rid of it. As I dealt with the creature, the Ancestors gathered around me. Their familiar touch riffled clothing and hair, but it was not an unpleasant sensation. I felt, in fact, strangely safe. They created a space perhaps as wide as my outspread arms, and just beyond that circumference the wind blew with stunning fury, snatching up debris and flinging it away again. Two of the hedgehog demons catapulted themselves at me, stopped short, and disappeared.

"Egg…" I croaked uselessly. Caught up in a tiny, ferocious battle, he tumbled every which way with his prey, fur flying. For a truth, he looked to have the upper hand. I still wanted to go to him, but I found my feet taking me away. The whine of the Gate seemed a distant thing, cushioned by the wind and the voices of the Ancestors as they whispered to me, layers and layers of words tumbling past me. Through me. *Girl. What of Girl?*

I was aware of her much as I had been in the Ghost Walk, but even more clearly. Although I moved away, I turned my head to find her with my eyes. She stood atop a crumbling wall using her crossbow to beat off half a dozen leaping, snarling shadows. I needed to hurry.

Away to my left Tanris had his back to the wall. His sword in one hand and the ax in the other, he fought a losing battle. The blood drenching his face appeared a garish red in the light of the throbbing Gate. It was a terrible sight to behold, and I feared for him. I had, for a fact, never been so afraid in all my life, nor had so much responsibility placed upon my shoulders. I had never needed the love and guidance of the gods more than I did at this moment, and I knew in my heart I could not allow doubt or terror to cripple me.

A ululating cry jerked at my attention. A dozen figures poured over the lip of the crater, the odd light winking off raised weapons. Another score appeared on the right. Soldiers! Never had Imperial blue been more beautiful.

I turned as though in a dream, everything surreal, slow, liquid. A new menace came out of the Gate and rushed at me. It was big, very big. I staggered beneath the weight of it as it met the Ancestors, but I did not go down and it slid away, arms and legs waving, tail lashing. Golden light blossomed here and there around the broken walls of Duzayan's ruined mansion, turning the sickly glow of the Gate to sunset orange. Faces, human faces, appeared in my peripheral vision, and with them came the knowledge of shouting and the clash of weapons. The Imperial Troops were dying. Their bodies laid in the fringes of garish light and for the first time in my life I was alarmed for them. For the group and for the individuals themselves.

Surreal, yes...

Twice more the Ancestors moved me out of the path of demon attacks, bringing me at last to the back side of the Gate, which had by now grown to nearly twice my height. So close to it, even they could not completely protect me from the uncanny noise it made. It seared the eardrums and turned the belly.

"What must I do?" I asked, and somewhere behind me I heard my name shouted, echoing. Ignoring the call, I looked at the thing before me, feeling abysmally small and useless. I could not make out a single word the Ancestors said, but I recalled sitting in the sun, talking to old Jelal while he read the bones. He'd said my friends would be with me to shoulder the burden. While they strove to keep the creatures away from me, I must act or they would be crushed. Reaching out to touch the nearest part of the glimmering frame, I did not even realize I still had Duzayan's knife in my hand until the blade began to change. As though the metal were drawn to the magical doorway, it lengthened and bent toward it. I stared for a moment, then my heart contracted painfully in my chest and I tried to throw the thing from me. It would not leave my hand, which prompted the hundredth panic of the day. Bit by hard-won bit I loosed my fingers from their grip around the jeweled hilt, and it still stuck to my palm. From the perspective of a thief, it was a beautiful thing, well-crafted, decorated with valuable jewels, and utterly pleasing to the eye. This particular thief wanted nothing more than to get rid of it.

I shook my hand violently, making the pretty gems sparkle in the light of the Gate. With the wonderful hindsight induced by absolute terror, I remembered the knife had not left my hand when I'd desperately beat the dog thing and had, in fact, been right there in my palm when I killed it. It was strange and horrible and true—and I couldn't quite bend my brain around the concept. It was something I would have to save to ponder later, for I'd begun to slide even closer to the Gate as its magic pulled the blade. My first impulse—or my second, since we must count the unsuccessful hand shaking—was to use my free hand to grab it and pull it off, but what if that hand, too, stuck? I couldn't afford such a handicap. As it happened, I still held the torch in a white-knuckled grip.

From every side came the urgency to *do something!* to *hurry!* I had to get the knife off, and it was not a moment to wonder if the gods inspired me, or the Ancestors, or genius struck me. I bent to press the weapon against the stone floor, stepped on the transforming blade (hoping my boot didn't count as an actual part of me), and yanked my hand away. *My hand! My hand! What is a thief without both of his hands??*

One of the requirements for performing great deeds seems to be suffering tremendous pain. Another is the shedding of copious amounts of blood. I have an exceedingly strong aversion to both, and I would have liked nothing better than to abandon any and all prospect of being a hero, take back the skin and blood, return the pain, and hie to the nearest tavern for a nice tankard of ale, leaving the job to someone else. Well, not the nearest, perhaps, as the safety of the neighborhood was a bit precarious at the time. Alack and alas for me, everyone else had other plans, and they paid not the slightest attention to my ardent desire to be elsewhere. On my own, I had no idea how to deal with the Gate or the creatures streaming from it.

Tanris hollered at me to close the thing but didn't offer any ideas for how to go about it, too busy fighting. The demons wanted to kill me; the air was thick with their craving and being on the opposite side of the Gate didn't keep them from seeking me out and throwing themselves at me furiously. I felt every impact against the shield of the Ancestors, and with every one the sense of urgency grew. Time was running out, and I had no training for this sort of thing. How I had become the key to victory was anyone's guess.

The key!

I had to drop the torch to dig beneath my shirt for the bone disk I'd taken—no, been *given!*—at Hasiq. I looked at it with its etching of a portal and then at the Gate. The Ancestors had told me it made or allowed a passage. Did it not follow that it could do the reverse as well?

Close the Gate! Shut the door! Bind the passage!

Hurry! Hurry!

The Voices lifted around me in a frenzy of urgency. A flurry of images came with the words, too fast and too fragmented to be of any use.

"Help me!" I cried out, and perhaps my plea loosed whatever constraints held them. I felt their cool touch upon my skin, and then *inside* my skin. Tanris had said before that I had spoken strange things. I did so now, an audience to myself as my mouth moved and words came forth, edged in icy, glimmering green light. I stood a fraction of a world away from myself, and it was peculiar in the extreme. Lifting over my head the plain leather cord that held the amulet, I took it in both hands as I knelt between the pillars of shifting light. I laid the amulet on the ground between them, still speaking as I watched my blood flow into the carved marks, quickly filling them. I knew it was necessary but, as usual, I did not know all the whys and wherefores. Neither did I know it would cause even more excruciating pain than I already bore, else I would have politely declined and let someone else—say, Tanris, who is brave and stalwart—take over.

I do not know how the others around me perceived what happened next, and words are insufficient to explain my own observation. Time stilled. The cacophony around me retreated to a distance. The very air turned to ice. I could hardly draw breath. It hurt my heart to beat. It hurt to bleed...

But bleed I did, and not just my life blood, but the energy of my very essence oozed out of me, weaving through the fabric of the Gate to knit it closed in spite of the efforts of those on the other side determined to come through. I was the bandage for this terrible wound in a very real and very personal way. I lost parts of my Self, and felt the agony in every fiber of my being. The pain of it made every other hurt I'd ever suffered utterly insignificant. I do not know, once it had begun, if some exterior force might have stopped it. I could not. Or perhaps it is better to say that I *did* not.

I was aware of the world, of existence, in a way I had never known before and had not even realized was possible. It was infinite and beautiful and *intimate*. In those moments I knew exactly how I fit into the greater pattern, and how the pattern fit into me, all inexorably connected together and each minute element essential to the existence of the others. To my great grief, the purity of that knowledge did not remain indelibly etched into my brain and my heart. I have now only the memory of it, but it is strong and *I believe*.

The world from whence the creatures Duzayan summoned came was not meant to be a part of my world. That did not make it—or them—either good or bad, but simply different. They were merely the subject of a summoning they could not deny. Their existence in my world was the wrongness, and I felt a deep need to right it, no matter the cost. When at last the Gate closed I knew a moment of absolute nothingness. No breath, no sight, no sound. Nothing.

Then reality crashed into me.

The Gate simply ceased to exist. One moment it was throbbing and filling the air with the most abominable, most *wrong* sound imaginable, and in the next it disappeared as if it had never been. The creatures caught on this side howled and wailed in shock and fear. The men and women who battled them screamed back their own fear and many, many souls died. The smell of death and sulphur filled the air. Streamers of smoke from torches and fires hid the beautiful night sky.

Strange, unwelcome creatures...

Poor, unfortunate creatures...

All of this sound and scent and sight slammed into me like an avalanche, and then I fell.

— 37 —
Unexpected Visitor

Contrary to everyone's expectation—including mine—I did not die, nor was I allowed to drift in the sweet oblivion of unconsciousness. Duzayan and the chaos he'd loosed plagued my mind and the living tormented my body, hitting me, dragging me, and the gods alone knew what else.

"Crow, can you hear me?"

"Yes." Someone—Tanris—had asked me the same question only a moment ago. Did he think the answer would be different now? Could he not just let me die in peace? I had not the strength to move, nor the energy to devise another desperate attack on the enemy.

"Crow?"

"What?" I ventured to lick my lips. My tongue did not belong to me and the flavor on my lips was strange, cool—if one can call that a flavor—and green like grass; not at all the taste of ash and sulphur and death I expected. Confusion burbled up in me.

"I think he's waking up."

The speaker was an idiot. To wake one would have to sleep, and as marvelous as that might be, it just wasn't a practical thing to do in the middle of a battle with a crazy mage and creatures from another world. I just hadn't opened my eyes yet. Dreaded to, for a fact, though it was ridiculous to hope keeping them closed would prevent further mayhem or damage to my person. I wanted only to enjoy the sweet respite of quiet for another moment or two.

Wait, quiet?

The small effort of bracing myself to move immediately brought to attention every agonizing ache in me. Someone groaned horribly and it made my throat hurt, which enlightened me to the fact that the awful noise had come from myself. I could not do this any more. I had nothing left to give. An attempt to roll over onto my side and curl into a ball of misery—and perhaps give in to the temptation to cry like a baby—was arrested by a weight on my feet and a hand on my shoulder.

"Easy. Easy, now… You were pretty badly hurt."

Did I mention the idiocy of the speaker? Only Tanris had such a keen grasp of the obvious. Something wet and cold pressed against my face was the perfect solution for getting my eyes open and for sending me flying upward in a flurry of panic.

"Get it off! Get it off!" I shouted. I heard noises I couldn't identify, but Tanris spoke clearly and concisely.

"Stop it, you fool."

I stopped, firstly because he was holding me down and secondly because he looked absolutely frightful. He had a fantastic pair of cuts scribing his cheek and another slicing into his hairline, fierce bruises covering most of his face, a cut and swollen lip, and wildly bloodshot eyes.

"What happened to you?" I croaked, and he gave me one of his characteristic you're-out-of-your-mind looks.

"He's fine," he said to someone, and I turned my head—slowly and with great effort—to see Girl standing some feet away with a damp cloth in her hand and a frightened look on her face.

"Girl, you don't look so well." She didn't, though she looked considerably better than Tanris. In addition to the fear, she sported bloodshot eyes too, more than her usual pallor, and a wild expression. A startlingly black bruise marred one side of her face, and she wore one bandaged arm in a sling. "Are you all right?"

She gave me a curt nod, then hesitantly approached and perched on the edge of the bed to bathe my face. The sensation became much more pleasant now that I knew it was a damp cloth wielded by our very own Girl and not some disgusting thing licking me. It was very strange to find myself in a quiet, clean room—on a bed, no less—when the last thing I remembered was the flaming, clamorous ruins of Duzayan's mansion and all of those odd creatures cavorting about. But here were Tanris and Girl, looking a little worse for the wear but clearly having survived the encounter, and I, although aching in every part, still lived and breathed. All of us—

Tanris arrested my sudden upward movement again with a hand on my chest, and it hurt! Great and glorious stars, it hurt! "Where is he?" I rasped. How frustrating to have him push me down so easily and hold me still!

"Dead." Tanris's horrible face somehow managed to produce a very convincing glum expression. "He's dead, Crow."

"What?" I whispered, staring in utter disbelief. It wasn't true! Wouldn't I know somehow? I had no doubt in my mind that Not-An-Egg had flapped awkwardly to my rescue; he had not been some bizarre hallucination. A curious dizziness threatened to overwhelm me. "No. No, that can't be…"

"I very much doubt he's going to recover. Beheaded people usually don't, even wizards."

"People?" I stared. Who? What? "Not people, Egg!" I exclaimed, though the news of Duzayan's permanent death was certainly welcome. "Where's Egg?"

He just looked at me, a strange assortment of emotions muddling across his face. Girl tapped my cheek and pointed to the end of the bed, where I discovered the source of the weight on my feet. Thank the gods of dragons and good fortune and otherworldly creatures with bad aim! I had never felt so relieved in all of my life. Well, maybe two or three times, when the circumstances had been dire, but this was different. "Egg!"

Tanris winced. "Please tell me you're going to give him a proper name. Fang? Claw? Flametooth? *Egg* is just humiliating."

The little dragon lifted his head and creaked at me pitifully.

"Is he hurt? What happened to him? Come here," I coaxed, but reaching for him sent a million shooting pains up my left hand and arm—an appendage so heavily swathed it might have belonged to a mummy. Fortunately, my horizontal position made fainting less obvious. I did not entirely lose consciousness, but I did alarm Girl and Tanris. The latter scolded me severely, but helped prop me up with some pillows, then moved Not-An-Egg up next to me. He, too, sported bandages. Poor baby. With my good hand I rubbed the dragon's knobby little head while Girl carefully supported my injured arm on more pillows. It burned badly, but I was afraid to look at it, afraid to ask the extent of the damage, and so I tried to focus my attention on the dragon.

"He got torn up pretty badly by something with claws, and broke a bone in his wing," Tanris offered, sitting down in a chair next to the bed. A pillow beside it and a blanket draped carelessly over the arm indicated recent, lengthy occupation. My chair, in my room, in my apartment! The realization and acceptance brought a dizzying wave of relief.

"Girl fixed him up as best she could," Tanris went on. "I thought he was a goner, but you wouldn't let us leave him behind."

I did not remember that. "Of course not," I said indignantly. Not-An-Egg looked up at me and heaved a little sigh. His emotions wove a more complicated tapestry than usual: adoration, worry, pain, exhaustion... He had been through a great deal, and him just a baby. "Brave little thing," I murmured, scritching his chin.

"Girl and I are pretty much fine," Tanris said drily. "In case you wondered."

I looked from one to the other in no little confusion and they looked back reproachfully. "Of course you are."

He snorted.

"You're always fine, Tanris," I pointed out.

Abruptly, he got to his feet and stalked out of the room.

"What?" I called out after him, but he did not answer. In a sulk Tanris was difficult to dissuade from his path. Currently, I had no dissuasive powers available. So, "What?" I asked Girl.

She pressed her lips together into a thin, tight line, marched around the bed, and slugged me in my good shoulder, which jarred me considerably and woke in me a fairly intimate knowledge of my other injuries.

"Ow! Hey! What was that for?"

She did not answer, of course, but stomped out after Tanris.

The Ancestors reminded me of their presence, darting about the room in a flurry, then becoming still again. I had the distinct impression that they, too, were displeased.

I slept a great deal in the next few days, and spent most of my waking hours reading. Tanris was not the only one that could indulge in that sort of thing. Reading, however, could not fill all the time I spent convalescing. Whatever Duzayan had done to me had long-lasting effects that even the Priests of Ishram could not change, and evidently the magic of the Ancestors interfered in some way as well—an occasion that baffled the good brothers no little amount. I would have to recover in my own good time or not at all; a daunting prospect, particularly given the condition of my hand after ripping off the enchanted knife. It was strange, I suppose, but in spite of my career being so dependent upon two deft hands, I could not bring myself to look beneath the swath of bandages. Girl could tell me nothing, and Tanris would not. Neither would he tell where he went or how he spent his days. Conversation was minimal at best, and when I could not read any more, could not sleep any more, I thought. Copiously.

Duzayan, intentionally or not, had influenced my life tremendously. Because of him, everything changed completely and, I imagined, forever. The Ancestors kept a distance, but I knew they had not left me and never would. I was theirs and they were mine, and although I had come to understand that connection through dreams and through our strange interactions, it was a difficult thing to fully accept, particularly now that I'd returned to Marketh and hovered on the edge of my old life. I was eager— no *anxious*—to return to the way things had been, but the more I came to understand, the more I realized that would never happen. I could resume my career, hopefully, but I was different now in ways that might mean little to anyone else, but meant much to me.

Through those initial days of healing and musing, Girl patiently tended to my needs, and to Not-An-Egg's, and dealt with the cleaning and shopping and cooking. Who would suspect a deadly marksman beneath her quiet, docile façade? She had lost everything, and while she could have —should have—stayed with the good people of Uzuun, she had chosen instead to cast her lot with us. More and more I wondered why. It is true that my countenance is good to look upon and my manner more than a little charming. It is true, too, that while Tanris is not at all charming or good looking, he is steady and honest and noble. But we are both nearly old enough to be her father. Well... Tanris is easily old enough. If she did not already know how to read and write, a fact she had never disclosed in our months of traveling together, I would have to teach her. Perhaps she would become less of a mystery, though I had little doubt that she, being a woman, would continue to remain mysterious as only women can.

I also had a visitor to break the monotony. On that particular morning, I was reclining on the couch in the parlor, enjoying a breeze idling through the open windows and lazily contemplating the philosophies set forth in my latest literary study when there came a knock at the door. Girl appeared to answer the summons and I soon heard the door open and a quiet request voiced by a female. She spoke my name, and there the civilities ended.

The soft entreaty gave way to a shriek and thumping, and the next thing I knew a fight erupted in the entry. Curiosity prompted me to investigate, and I put some effort into levering myself up off the couch, wishing Tanris hadn't gone out.

"Don't you dare! You have no right! Let me in, you—"

The description applied to Girl was neither polite nor accurate, but it was handily brought to an end by some generous thumping. When I arrived on the scene, a distance of only about fifteen or twenty feet, I found Girl on the floor straddling our guest, whose disheveled gown amply revealed a fine set of legs. A fierce scar marked one ankle. She'd lost one slipper and stood—or it might be more accurate to say she laid—in danger of losing the battle in its opening moments.

"Tarsha." Casually, I propped a shoulder against the wall and folded my arms across my chest, protecting the injured one and adopting an air of lackadaisical interest. "I don't recall sending you an invitation. What are you doing here?"

"Get her off me!"

She struggled, but Girl had the situation well in hand in spite of her injury, and I couldn't help but admire her fortitude. And Tarsha's humiliation. She had not escaped the conflict at Duzayan's ruined house unscathed. In addition to the damage done to her leg, she had some nasty scars across one cheek. Between them, they spelled the end of her career as a dancer.

"Crow!"

"If you promise to behave yourself nicely—and keep your hands, feet, teeth and any other weapons to yourself, I'll ask her to let you up."

Tarsha hissed her frustration, then rolled her eyes. "As if I would assault you."

I snorted. "No, I suppose it's more your style to set me up so you can watch someone else assault me." I made a motion with my head to Girl. "Let her go, but why don't you get your crossbow?"

Girl peered at me inscrutably, then got to her feet and disappeared down the hall.

"That is completely unnecessary," Tarsha protested. Yanking her clothing straight, she got to her feet.

"So is your presence here."

Her chin lifted. She was such a proud thing, which I'd always found attractive. That, and the fact that she was utterly beautiful and graceful beyond measure. None of her attributes, however, compensated for the way she'd deceived me and broken my heart.

"I came to thank you," she sniffed.

"For what?" Such an easy thing to act the part of ignorance.

"For saving my life," she murmured, dropping her scornful, indignant attitude and folding her hands across her middle demurely.

"I hate to shatter your romantic illusion, but saving your life never even occurred to me." I watched her eyes widen and her lovely mouth form an "oh" of surprise. I then went on before she could ask the question they moved to shape. "Duzayan used your blood to power his spell for the Gate. You bled enough for him to open it, and if you'd died, I doubt it would have been so easy to close." Not that it was easy at all, but why should I share that with her?

Her face paled, and she looked away. Uncomfortable silence that grew between us, and I did nothing to relieve it. I could not begin to imagine what was going through her devious little mind, but she did not keep me in suspense for very long.

"I'm—I'm sorry, Crow," she murmured at last, remarkably subdued. "I treated you very poorly. I thought—I didn't know that you—" Head bent, she rubbed her fingers and fretted. "There is really nothing I can say that won't sound like an excuse. I'd like to make up for what I did to you." She gave me a tentatively hopeful look. Very appealing.

I was not swayed. Curious, yes, but not so much as to inquire about her thoughts on the matter. "You can't," I said bluntly, without a single trace of sympathy. "You completely destroyed something irreplaceable, Tarsha. What I really want is for you to go away. Far away. It shouldn't be very difficult for you to forget all about me; it's not like you actually cared to begin with."

Tears sprang to her lovely dark eyes and she took a step forward, reaching out as though to put a hand on my arm.

"Don't. If you touch me, you'll get a crossbow bolt through your back."

Startled, she looked over her shoulder where Girl stood with the loaded and cocked weapon held steadily in her hands and a grim, uncompromising look on her face. Too easily, I discerned the pain it cost her. The sacrifice touched me unexpectedly.

"Crow…" Tarsha whispered in patent disbelief.

"Don't let the door hit you on the way out," I said, nodding at it pointedly.

The pooling tears spilled over her cheeks. "Crow, please—"

Her persistence irritated me. Deliberately, I moved my head from side to side, stretching and crackling the joints. All this laying about had made me stiff. "Don't you have a husband to attend to?"

Taking her cue at last, Tarsha pressed one hand to her luscious mouth and fled.

Thank the god of fortuitous deliverances. I heaved a sigh of relief and straightened, turning to Girl. "What do you say to a nice cup of tea out in the sun?"

— 38 —
Who Would Have Thought?

It was after a long afternoon of sitting on the balcony drinking in the gentle warmth of the spring sun that I realized what I had done. Pain and exhaustion must share the blame for my dull wits, for my callousness. As a student of humans and all their vagaries, I should have known better. I wondered if my lack, my blindness, might have had anything to do with the relationship Tanris and I had previously shared. More food for thought was the fact that he had not, you might have noted, turned me in for the bounty he could no doubt have used, and it would have been easy to collect, given my state of poor health. I couldn't run down the hall, never mind scampering up to the rooftops and across the city.

Tanris didn't return to the apartment until after the evening meal, and while Girl cleaned up, Not-An-Egg and I had retired to the balcony. The dragon curled up on my lap and watched the sun setting with me, creaking softly. As I enjoyed the beauty of the view, it occurred to me that I had not thought of selling the apartment even once in the time since Duzayan's demise. The door to the parlor stood open, and I had no difficulty hearing the apartment's front door open and close, though Tanris himself moved lightly enough that his footsteps could often go undetected.

"Tanris." I glanced over my shoulder to watch for him. He appeared reluctantly in the doorway a few minutes later. "Come sit with me."

Surprise pricked him, but he took a seat in the other chair without a word. "You're mad at me."

"Aye," he grunted, lacing his fingers across his belly, posture stiff.

"Because of Aehana? I'm awfully sorry, I—"

"No." His jaw knotted. "You did it again, Crow. You knew bloody well I wanted to be there to destroy Duzayan, and you took him on by yourself."

Little fingers of wind ruffled my hair but did not touch Tanris. "I had to, he'd already started the spell. I knew you'd be there as soon as you could. I was counting on it."

"Were you? Or did you think you could just do it alone?" For once I didn't mind his skepticism. In fact, I found his familiar attitude wonderfully assuring.

"You are my fr—We've been through a lot together. You wouldn't have been in this mess if not for me. Well," I paused, reconsidering. "You wouldn't have been so badly off, anyway. Besides, I owed you."

He did not miss what I'd almost blurted. For a moment I thought he would drag it out of me, but he resisted the temptation. "For what?"

"Saving my life several times."

"Then you probably still owe me. A lot."

You may ask how I could resist asking him about the bounty on my head, and I would have to tell you that I do not know. The words leaped to the tip of my tongue, but I did not speak them. "Good to see your sense of humor's returned. Where have you been?" I asked.

His mouth twitched in a grimace. "No place you'd care about."

"If I didn't care, I wouldn't ask." I didn't look at him, but at the beauty stretched out before us, a city gilded by sun and the first twinkling of lights.

He shifted forward, elbows to knees, staring at the city for a space. "I've been… explaining things to my superiors."

"Any luck?"

"More or less." Another silence followed. Not-An-Egg shifted to rest his chin on the arm of the chair and watch him. He had become quite delicate about the process, having learned that I did not much like him piercing me with his wickedly sharp claws every time he moved. I rubbed his little head.

"Some of those demons avoided capture," Tanris finally said. I couldn't claim surprise. There had been quite a few of them, and I had no idea how long the Gate had remained open. "We ought to do something about that," he suggested, a note of caution in his voice.

"Us?" He took me by surprise although, knowing Tanris, I should have expected nothing less. "How?"

He shrugged. "Maybe you could use your magic to find them."

It wasn't *my* magic, but—could I? What a horrible development. I hadn't the slightest desire to hunt or battle the things, even if they weren't technically demons. And who would believe me if I told them such a thing? Did it really matter to anyone besides them and me?

Tanris tipped his head, looking at me at last. "Don't you think?"

Well, yes, I do think, thank you very much, just not about demon hunting. "Isn't the army looking for them?" I hedged.

"Yes."

Well, then! Need I say more? I thought not, but Tanris evidently did not agree. From the way he looked at me—and the prickly emotions he gave off —he seemed to be testing me. It made me want to fidget. I knew what he wanted from me because it was the same thing I'd been considering for hours. Days, even. And in spite of a growing conviction that I must, I did not want to get involved. At all.

"But the army doesn't have magic to help them," Tanris said reasonably, "and they weren't responsible for letting them loose."

"Neither were we." For a truth, it had not been our choice and we had not known until very late in the game what Duzayan planned to do. Still, a little voice that did not belong to the Ancestors whispered that I should have known better, tried harder, been quicker. I wished it would shut up.

"What happened?" I asked. "I don't remember much."

"No? You shouldn't sound so disappointed. It was not good."

Tanris, the captain of understatement.

"What kind of not good?"

"People dying. Blood all over the place. That Gate making the most awful noise I have ever heard in my life. Demons pouring out and no sign of stopping until you did whatever it was you did." He licked his lips, then drew his teeth over the lower one. "I thought you were dead. We couldn't just leave you there, so I picked you up. Tossed you over my shoulder. Girl grabbed your necklace—"

"Pendant." A necklace sounded far too feminine to suit me.

"Tarsha was there."

"I know." I stubbornly ignored the urge to look away. "You want to tell me how that happened?"

He made a rueful face. "I can only tell you what I've been able to decipher from Girl's acting. As I understand it, Tarsha cried so much Girl couldn't stand it any more. She tried to help her. Tarsha attacked her and escaped."

"Escaped our Girl?" I marveled.

Tanris shrugged. "These things happen. At any rate, we found Tarsha at the top of the crater. She was hurt, but still breathing, so we pulled her away and off to the side. I didn't see her when we left. Maybe someone found her and took care of her."

"She came to visit me the other day." I gritted my teeth, then forced myself to relax again. Not-An-Egg gave my cheek a tender little, fishy-smelling dragon kiss, then resumed watching me.

"She did?"

"Doesn't matter. I don't remember you carrying me off."

Tanris looked at me curiously for a moment, but chose not to ask any questions about my former love. He wasn't all bad. "You wouldn't. You were unconscious. We took you to one of the Ishram temples, but when they tried to heal you, you screamed and kept screaming. The priests were upset. Girl was upset. The other patients were upset. So we brought you here and did the best we could, which wasn't much," he said glumly.

The gods are sometimes strange and inscrutable, even to their most devoted adherents. Sitting on the balcony in the falling evening, I understood that Tanris actually cared about me as I had come to care about him—not as the quarry he'd chased for years, not as an elusive criminal, but as a friend. He had saved my life on several occasions in spite of danger to himself. He guarded me. Nursed me back to health. Gave me advice. Comforted me as best he could.

"How did Girl find me?" I whispered, confused and overwhelmed. Tanris, I knew, had gone to alert his superiors in the Emperor's Eagles.

"The dragon." The announcement came as another surprise, but the details belonged to Girl. "We could have stopped Duzayan in the beginning," he said morosely.

"No, we could not," I countered. "We had no way of knowing what he would do."

"But we knew what he *did* do, and it shouldn't have gone any further than that."

"Tanris," I sighed and gave the beautiful view a grimace it did not deserve. "What you did—It was noble and brave."

"And useless."

"Aehana didn't think so, and neither do I."

Hurt scraped at him.

"I'm sorry, Tanris," I murmured, a strange and unfamiliar knot in my throat. "I'm sorry she's gone, and I'm sorry I was so inconsiderate the other day. I shouldn't have said what I did."

He bent his head, breath quickening, body tensed, fist pressed tight to palm. "I appreciate that, Crow," he said roughly, eyes focused on the floor beneath him. "What you did—I haven't thanked you."

"I didn't do anything." Not unless one counted failing abysmally.

"You're the one that came up with the plan to get the antidote, and you were the one in the most danger. You're the one that got hurt doing it."

It was my turn to fall silent, wreathed in surprise.

"I don't think I've ever seen you do anything so selfless before. It—" He had to stop and rub his face. "It means a lot to me."

"It means a lot to me that you weren't planning to kill me in Hasiq jum'a Sahefal."

"I wouldn't have. That wouldn't have been fair. I've always enjoyed hating your guts. You and I—Well."

Now we were getting mawkish. "Well," I echoed. It was high time for a change of subject before one of us started crying or something equally embarrassing. "So we should help the army, eh?"

"I'd like that." Tanris looked up, sincerity writ all over his ruined features. The bruises looked quite horrendous. "You're sure?"

I avoided his eyes, rubbing Egg's head instead. "I think we must. Tidying up, as it were." I had truly lost my mind, but was that really any surprise?

"I'm glad you think so. I convinced the powers that be to give you a full pardon if you volunteered to, ah, serve."

I blinked. "You did what?"

"I told them the hunting would have to be on your terms, and that you are quite capable." He lifted a hand to rub his bristly scalp. "They won't let you do it completely on your own, of course, but since we did such a thorough job with Baron Duzayan they decided we should continue to work together."

If I had been in their illustrious positions I would likely have said the same thing, but that wasn't what astounded me. "You stood up for me?"

He gave a slow nod.

"Really?" I had never been at such a loss for words.

"I'm still not sure what possessed me."

"It must have been an illness of incredible strength. Would you like me to take you to see the healers?"

"I already did. They said there's no cure."

"Tanris…" I sniffled and dabbed at the corner of my eye. "I'm getting all teary-eyed."

"Oh, stop it," he said gruffly, and gave me a half-hearted swat. "Are you going to make me regret this?"

"Every day," I promised with a wide grin. "I expect this arrangement comes with a prohibition against further relocation of resources."

"Of course."

"Mmm." I nodded sagely, not making any silly promises we both knew I wouldn't keep. If things had gone his way, and it sounded as if they had, he should have been more cheerful. "So what are you not telling me?"

He held both hands out to his sides, disbelief all over him. "How do you do that? I hate when you do that."

"Then don't make me. What's wrong?"

"They think you're a wizard."

"That's ridiculous!" I nearly came up off my chair, but the weight of Not-An-Egg and the prick of his talons threatening my skin kept me down.

"Not really," he replied, folding his arms and leaning back again, calm and pragmatic. "When a magical door materializes, letting all kinds of nasty things through, it's only logical to suppose a wizard opened it and logical to suppose it would take a wizard to close it."

"What is logical about that?" I asked, knowing full well that I would have supposed the very same thing if I had been one of the witnesses rather than one of the participants. "It takes years of training to be a wizard! Secret rituals! Arcane spells! Magic artifacts!"

Tanris crinkled his brow. "As far as I can tell, you've covered three of the four."

"I have not!" I protested indignantly.

"Mm. What do you want to call that bit in the tunnel with the lights and the voices and the writing on the walls? That might have been a ritual for all we know. You keep saying things in a strange language, and you can't deny the odd and powerful results. Arcane spells, no? And how about that thing you wear around your neck?"

My hand went automatically to the pendant beneath my shirt.

"If you're not a wizard, what are you?" he pressed.

"A druid." My eyes widened and I clapped that same hand over my mouth. Had I just said that? "I didn't say that!"

"Don't be ridiculous. What's a druid if not a wizard?"

"Nat-natural," came out. I had no idea what I was talking about, but the concept hung just on the edge of my knowing. "Not like Duzayan."

"You are nothing like Duzayan, or you'd be dead now, too."

"That's comforting. You'd kill me?"

"For being like Duzayan? In a heartbeat," he said with devastating conviction.

My own heart stuttered in my chest. "I'll endeavor to remain as un-Duzayan-like as possible."

"I hope so," he said with vehemence. "You do have public opinion to contend with, and that includes whatever soldiers we might... borrow. Everyone knows trapping a wizard is no easy feat, so of course people wonder if an enemy wizard was involved in Duzayan's destruction." He hesitated.

"And?" I glared.

"And you have made quite a reputation for yourself over the years. I don't want this to go to your head, but you've developed some pretty impressive skills. If people wondered before..." His voice trailed off and he shrugged one shoulder.

Wasn't that just dandy? My career teetered on the verge of death. Maybe, though, enterprising clients would appreciate having a... wizard working for them, never mind how the very label made me feel distinctly light-headed and queasy. "Then I suppose," I managed in a remarkably calm tone, "I'll have to figure out a way to change public opinion."

"Not an easy task, especially with a dragon for a companion."

Toddling forward on the stilts of reconstructing my reputation, I abruptly found my memories speeding back to the fateful night in the ruins of Duzayan's mansion. "They saw him?"

"He was hard to miss. Maybe people mistook him for another demon, though."

"They aren't demons," I muttered, glowering at the remains of the sunset on the city. The golden roof of the palace caught the last rays, and its brilliance contrasted magnificently with the reflected orange of the scattered clouds. Away to the east, the sky darkened. Rather like my mood.

Tanris didn't argue with me, and I suspected that he had elected not to debate what was obvious to him and nearly everyone else in Marketh. Never mind they were wrong. Never mind that trying to explain the truth would only further condemn me.

"Well," I said, and made myself focus on all those things I'd been considering before Tanris's return. "That brings us rather directly to another subject. I need to go back to Hasiq."

"Where?" He was utterly, wonderfully blank.

"Hasiq jum'a Sahefal. Where we got the dragon."

"Why?"

"It is where Not-An-Egg belongs," I explained, and wondered why the idea of taking him back and leaving him with whichever of his parents had survived made me feel so… alone. I ought to feel endangered. I couldn't imagine the adult dragon would welcome me back with open arms, or wings, however you'd like to look at it. "And there is the library and the collection. Without Melly, what will become of all of it? It's dangerous."

"I shudder to think what will become of it in your hands," he said drily.

"Mine? No, I don't want it. Too much responsibility." The books might perhaps prove interesting, providing they weren't wizard's lesson books or spell books or the like, but the thought of all those enchanted things in the underground chamber and the way their magic affected me—No, I could live quite happily without any of those.

"Then what?"

"I don't know yet, Tanris."

He chewed on the inside of his cheek and studied me until I felt like something in the emperor's exotic animal park. "And you're—I don't want to say this wrong, but you're what? Worried about the dragon?"

I was quite aware how un-Crow-like such a thing was. "Yes. Do I look like a dragon to you?"

"Not a lot, no. Well maybe a little around the nose."

I regarded him with narrowed eyes, which did not much impress him. "And do I know anything about raising a dragon?"

"You're doing pretty well so far," Tanris pointed out, though he still managed a dubious expression.

I just rolled my eyes. "I like him, don't get me wrong." That was an admission worthy of note. I am not, you might have guessed, particularly fond of animals, except as meals and even then I am somewhat selective.

Not-An-Egg lifted his snout and *smiled* at me, I swear he did. Teeth and all. He is a cunning little creature and, being clever and canny myself, I could appreciate that sort of thing in another person. Or dragon. I cleared my throat. "But can you imagine me trying to feed him and—and teach him whatever dragons are supposed to know?"

"Yes." Tanris was, on occasion, prone to being evil in spite of his outwardly noble demeanor. He did not fool me. "All right, no," he surrendered. "But it would probably be funny to watch."

"Ha ha." It was good to know Tanris still had a sense of humor, odd or not. "I suspect he will grow, and soon he will not fit in my apartment."

"That might be a problem." He paused and pressed his lips together. Was he trying not to smile? "And the neighbors will probably notice."

"Yes, the neighbors…" I heaved a sigh. "So I need to take him back."

Tanris nodded. He did not, as I'd hoped he might, volunteer his services as my guide and traveling companion. Instead, he leaned back in his chair and stretched his legs out, lacing his fingers together over his belly as he took in the view. "You have any of that Taharri Red left?"

"Yes." He made no move to get up and neither did I. I found myself in an internal debate. He'd just lost his wife—should I ask for his help? Maybe it would be good for him. Keep him busy, as it were. And he'd just asked for *my* help! "Will you go with me?"

His head twisted and he met my eyes, surprise reflected bright in his own, and I waited to hear why. "You know the way," he said slowly. "And the weather should be good now. Probably pretty, even."

"Yes, but no one loads things like you do. I'd have to take a whole pack train."

His snort startled Not-An-Egg. "What about Girl?" he asked.

"Are you going to keep calling her that? Don't you think she ought to have a real name?"

My words earned another snort. "Teach her to write and maybe she'll tell us."

"Me? I'm supposed to teach her how to pick pockets."

"You will do no such thing."

Maybe not when he was looking. "I can't picture her remaining behind, can you?"

"No." She'd already refused a perfectly comfortable and reasonable position to follow us into danger. Perhaps she secretly liked it. "There's no accounting for other people's peculiarities. Besides, she's awfully handy with that crossbow and she makes a very good pot of stew. So you'll do it?"

"How long do we have before the dragon outgrows his box?"

"About five minutes." My sigh lifted the hair across my forehead, and Not-An-Egg looked at me again, stretching his nose up to sniff at my jaw. I pushed him and his fishy-smelling breath gently away. "He's going to get too big to hide. Sooner rather than later at the rate things are going."

"Then we'd best get to work hunting those demons."

I knew I wasn't a wizard when my scathing look didn't immediately turn Tanris to ashes, but rather produced a curious noise I realized was laughter.

Druid. I might come to like the sound of that…

— THE END —

Hello! I hope you've enjoyed reading As the Crow Flies as much as I enjoyed writing it. If you did, please consider taking a little extra time to leave a review, or a rating. Your recommendation means a lot!

Thank you!
~Robin

About The Author

Robin Lythgoe was born in Maryland, but spent several years in Oregon and did a short stint in upstate New York before moving to Utah. She married an artist, and together they have four wonderful children. Reading and writing have always been a part of her life, and she is particularly drawn to fantasy. Before she managed the art of the pen she dictated her first fiction—a tale about a rabbit—to a scribe (her sister). Her mother often headed up expeditions to the library, from which the entire party invariably returned laden with a stack of books guaranteed to make the arms longer. Robin read everything voraciously, and when she finished her stack, she'd start on her mother's'… and then her sisters'. Today she writes tales about wizards and magic, fantastical places and extraordinary journeys.

Connect with Robin online:
Website: http://www.robinlythgoe.com
Twitter: http://twitter.com/robinlythgoe
Facebook: https://www.facebook.com/RobinLythgoeAuthor

Made in the USA
San Bernardino, CA
06 August 2013